Between Friends

A Between the Raindrops Novel
Book 3

Susan Schussler

Cover art by Rocky Shore Media LLC
(Some Photos licensed through Shutter Stock)

ISBN: 978-0-9890333-4-3 (Paperback)
978-0-9890333-5-0 (e-book)

Library of Congress Control Number: 2016959072

Rocky Shore Media LLC, St. Paul, Minnesota

First Printing, December 2016

Contents

Chapter 1 1

Chapter 2 7

Chapter 3 15

Chapter 4 25

Chapter 5 33

Chapter 6 43

Chapter 7 55

Chapter 8 65

Chapter 9 81

Chapter 10 87

Chapter 11 103

Chapter 12 107

Chapter 13 117

Chapter 14 129

Chapter 15 139

Chapter 16 145

Chapter 17 155

Chapter 18 161

Chapter 19 165

Chapter 20 173

Chapter 21 181

Chapter 22 199

Chapter 23 203

Chapter 24 211

Chapter 25 217

Chapter 26 221

Chapter 27 229

Chapter 28 233

Chapter 29 237

Chapter 30 243

Chapter 31 251

Chapter 32 257

Chapter 33 267

Chapter 34 275

Chapter 35 285

Other Books 290

Acknowledgements 291

Baggage

Each year adds more weight to the load of luggage we carry on our path of life. Make sure your arms aren't burdened by someone else's baggage.
Write your own story.
Don't let others write it for you.

Megan

I hand the cashier my card and the hair on the back of my neck stands on end. I know what it means—he's here. I can sense it. As I scan the tables in the coffee shop, relief trickles through my limbs. I don't know what is wrong with me. Maybe it's my lack of caffeine. I take a relaxing breath to calm my insides and then I hear it.

"Hey, babe."

The sound pierces my spine and I freeze as a chill spreads across my skin. *Damn.* I haven't heard that familiar voice in almost four years, but it still burns in my mind. I know I should pretend I didn't hear him. I know I shouldn't turn around, but I can't stop my body. His bright blue eyes and that cocky half smile almost knock me to the floor. God, he looks good— better than I've ever seen him. His wavy honey hair, longer than I remember, shines with golden highlights. Our eyes meet and I'm completely gone.

My body would jump him right here in the coffee shop, if not for the little control my mind still possesses. My World Cultures professor stands three spots behind him in line. I struggle to put up my wall quickly and smile, but he knows me so well. Those eyes could always read me. It's like we're back in his Ford pickup in high school and no time has elapsed. I move down to the end of the counter to wait for my latte, trying to put as much physical distance between us as I can.

"We should catch up," he calls to me as he pays for his coffee.

My breath hitches and I know he heard it because he chuckles. Damn my professor for being here. "I have a few minutes right now," is all I can squeeze out as I try my hardest not to let my body win. *Limit our time together. Do it now and never again. In public—always keep it in public.* I grab my skinny latte off the counter hoping he will decline.

"I've got all the time in the world for you, Meg Billings," he says with that smile.

He pulls out a chair at a nearby table, spins it around and straddles it. He crosses his arms over the top of the chair's back and stares at me as I hang my purple jacket over the back of my seat.

"Your coffee is ready," I remind him and he lifts his chin in acknowledgment, like he always did. When he returns to the table, he pulls his sweatshirt off over the back of his head, in the sexy way that always meant "get ready, Meg," and turns his chair back around before sitting down. I know it is a mistake to be here without my friends for support. They are my backbone when it comes to Chase Maxwell. If my girls were here, they would tell him where to shove that beautiful face of his. I should just get up and walk out the door right now. Why does my body react to him? No one else does this to me. I'm always in control, except with him.

"Short hair suits you," he says, raising his chin again.

"What does that mean?"

"Relax, Meg. It's a compliment. I like it. It's feisty. You really need to learn how to take a compliment."

I am impressed with what comes out of my mouth next. "It's just you I have a hard time believing."

Then he looks at me with those blue eyes and says, "Don't hate me. I never meant to hurt you."

"But you did," I say. *I can do this:* I think for a second, until he reaches out and touches my hand. The goose bumps shoot up my arm. I can tell where he is looking and am grateful for the thick sweater I'm wearing. I quickly pull my hand back, tucking it away on my lap. Here we go again.

"You left me remember?" he says, his blue eyes penetrating mine.

"You gave me no choice." I don't want to rehash this again so I'm relieved when the text from Alli buzzes on my phone. It gives me an out. I can tell him I have to meet her. I'm sure he remembers how neurotic my roommate is about being on time. I set my phone on the table, readying my excuse—big mistake. Always good with his hands, he snatches it off the table and quickly punches in his number to send himself a text.

I stand up and slide my jacket back on. I hold my hand out for the phone. "I need to go," I say as convincingly as I can.

"No you don't," he replies, looking up at me. He's the only one who can see through my walls. How does he do that?

"I just want you to know I went through rehab. I'm clean."

I look at him skeptically.

"Have been for two and a half years," he claims. "I miss you, Meg. I gave up all my old friends after treatment. You weren't one of my drug buddies and no one knows me like you. I just want to talk. You've got my number, now. I have yours. Let's talk."

I nod and that cocky smile appears again. God, I hope I can handle this.

As I leave, I consider dropping my phone down the storm drain on the way to the bus stop, but I just can't. Part of me has wanted to run into him. I knew I would someday. I ran into his younger brother last summer. His dark hair so different from Chase's, but his eyes were the same and it threw me off. He carried a toddler in his tattoo-sleeved arms and the boy had Chase's eyes too. His brother hugged me like I was his long lost sister and we chatted on the sidewalk for an hour. He told me then that Chase had gotten into rehab, but didn't offer his number or a way to contact him and it took everything I had not to ask. I told myself then that being clean didn't matter, but when I see him now, I don't know what to think.

I finish my coffee waiting for the bus and toss my empty cup into the garbage can on the sidewalk. The February wind bites up my short ski jacket and I peer down the street hoping to spot my bus turning the corner. I see Chase jay-walking across and getting into a bright yellow sports car. It's not a make I recognize—too expensive. He must be selling drugs instead of using or maybe he's turned to pimping.

The bus comes before he pulls out of his parking spot so I don't get a closer look. The heat on the bus is stifling and such a change from outside that I unzip my jacket to get some balance.

My phone goes off in my pocket and I pray it isn't Chase. I need more time to recover. The text is from Peterson.

Are you coming to the game tonight?

I totally forgot about the game. Dylan Peterson and I have this standing date for the Gopher basketball games. His younger brother plays and his family has a block of six season tickets. His parents don't go that often and even when they do, Peterson always brings me. He calls me his lucky charm. Every game I've missed the team lost and every game I've gone to, they've won. I can't explain it. I think it's just a coincidence, but Peterson swears it's me. I don't mind. I like basketball and it's free. I reply: *What time are you picking me up?* He probably is placing a bet and wants to make sure my plans haven't changed.

Peterson: I'll be out front at 3:30.
Me: Why?
Peterson: I owe you dinner, remember?
Me: Yeah, I remember. You're supposed to cook it. Are you cooking?
Peterson: No time. We have a game tonight.
Me: At least your culinary skills won't kill me.
Peterson: That's what I said. See ya soon.

Peterson and I have been seeing each other off and on for a while now—mostly off. We met at a basketball game and that is really all we have in common. He's a big guy who played football in high school and lives in a frat house off campus. He's entertaining to hang with and kind of like one of my brothers, only bigger and not an asshole. We don't have a serious relationship and we both date other people, but during basketball season we pretty much only see each other. It's just an understanding we have, not that it would upset me if I caught him out with someone else. It wouldn't. And he doesn't have any claim on me, but dating someone else would complicate game night. It doesn't matter to me. I don't get serious with anyone anyway, not since Chase broke my heart.

Peterson picks me up and we meet up with four of his buddies at Keane's Pub for dinner. I get a burger and fries and of course, Peterson eats most of my fries. Why do guys always assume that a girl is too full to eat her fries? Give me enough time and I can finish them.

My mom used to say that my metabolism would slow down someday and all the food I eat would find its way to my thighs. It hasn't happened yet. I can still eat what I want and she didn't stick around long enough to say "I told you so," so it doesn't matter what she thought. Maybe I'll be one of those lucky chicks and not have to spend my life eating nothing but lettuce.

When we get to the game, Peterson plants a kiss on my lips before the first buzzer. The kiss is full of excitement and anticipation and part of his ritual. He's very superstitious and very predictable. We watch Minnesota annihilate Nebraska with a forty-six point spread and talk player statistics most of the game. Statistics is the reason I like the game. Statistics is my thing. I especially like basketball because of the sheer number of points scored in a game. The ratios are less subjective, more concrete.

Most guys don't know I have a gift with numbers. They hear I'm an education major and think I'm just some sweet little innocent who likes children. They don't know I can whip their butts at poker or black-jack because I count cards or that I know more about sports statistics than they do. I don't usually share that my second major is math and I've been offered a fellowship for my doctorate. It just intimidates guys. They would much rather think I'm some hot little blond teacher. They don't need to know. Dylan Peterson knows, but he doesn't want to share the knowledge with his friends. He would much rather keep me to himself and pick my brain during basketball season.

Peterson gives me a fist tap and then dips me back for our end of the game kiss, just like he always does. He rights me and squats down so I can climb onto his back. I slip into my jacket and jump on. He folds my legs around his waist and carries me out of the stands, showing no strain as we head up the stadium ramp. I know he can bench press three of me. He likes to brag about it to his buddies. When he gets us out into the cool night air, he drops me to the sidewalk and tucks me under his arm to keep me warm.

He really is sweet, like a giant teddy bear.

We head back to his place, where the usual Friday night party is in full swing. Games aren't usually on Fridays and I don't always see Dylan on non-game nights, so I've only made a couple of the house parties this year. A year ago, my roommates would have met me at the frat house, but now I'm on my own with Peterson. My closest friend, Alli Cole, is trying to maintain her grades until her acceptance letter for medical school comes. She's applied to four schools, but her first choice is right here at the University of Minnesota. I know she'll get into the U. Her father and mother are legacy med students and her grandmother teaches at the medical school. Alli could get in through nepotism alone, but the fact that her MCATS were pretty close to perfect doesn't hurt either. Alli doesn't come out anymore. Maybe she'll revive her social life after her acceptance letter comes.

My other besties have already found the loves of their lives and aren't motivated to go to a party with a bunch of drunks anymore. Jessica Flynn is practically married to her boyfriend Jeff—all she needs is the ring. They've been together forever, it seems. And Sarah Austin—snagged a famous Hollywood hottie on the internet a year ago and already has her ring—four karats according to the tabloids. She moved out to L.A. a month ago to start her new life. I'm left here, stuck in limbo, so broken I'm sure I'll never find someone to love.

Liam

Crap. Crap. Crap! What the fuck was I thinking? Her short blond hair sticks to my arm like dust on a black town car, and even though her sprite sized ass presses against my side, all I can think is—would it be better to pull my arm from under her head slowly or quickly? Either way she'll wake up, but if I do it quickly I could probably get my pants on and be halfway out the door before she realizes I'm leaving. But without a car, I would have to call for a ride or get one from the girl in the bed and that would make the quick exit pointless.

The girl is familiar. I've hooked up with her body several times over the last year. Tara Waters and I have an understanding. Even though we see each other at the clubs all the time, she knows I don't do relationships and doesn't hassle me about it. We hook up with other people, but if the barometric pressure is just right and we're both alone at the club at the end of the night with no other prospects—we let things happen. Neither of us look at it as more than a hookup. Tara may post a picture of us once in a while if we get really crazy, but she always okays it with me before posting. The right picture at the right time helps both our careers.

But, I hope to God there are no pictures online from last night. First, because I have no recollection of what happened, and second, which is the bigger problem—this is not the bedroom I normally wake up in. This is Tara's twin sister's room and Tina is the queen of social media.

I slowly edge my arm free and crawl off the bed, scanning the floor for my clothes as I stand. I spot my boxer briefs hanging off the bedside table next to Tina's phone and I grab them, quickly pulling them on before turning around. I seize my pants off the floor and slide those on as well.

"I finally understand what all the hype is about. There is no reason to sneak out." Tina sits up letting the sheet fall to her lap. Yep, they're identical, right down to their nipple rings.

I smile. At least I didn't piss her off last night. She's been trying to get me to sleep with her for over a year. She even dangled a threesome with her sister, hoping to get me to take the bait. I know most guys would have jumped at the opportunity to sleep with identical twins, but my experience has taught me that no matter how equitable a guy is about satisfying both parties—one girl always feels slighted in a threesome. In this case, it would have been Tina, because I like Tara better. I've vowed to never do one again and I won't.

Which brings me back to defusing my current problem. Tina and her phone. The tricky part about sleeping with a habitual poster is that anything you say or do can be held against you. Whether it's true or not, you don't want to piss them off because you will end up looking like a douchebag in the press. I usually avoid sleeping with girls addicted to posting. I pick up her pink rhinestone-blinged phone before plopping down next to her on the bed. I hand her the phone, kissing her cheek because playful comes off better than demanding, and say, "Show me the damage." At least I'll be able to reconstruct the night from her posts.

"I didn't post anything. That's not what last night was about."

I pause before speaking, because brooding works. It's better for a girl to think I'm contemplative and deep than to be offended by what I'm really thinking.

"Don't be mad. Take it as a compliment. Tara and I share everything, even guys. But when you wouldn't, we had to get creative." Her hand smooths across my chest. "She's out of town, and well, you know the rest."

I've somehow blacked out the rest. Her finger runs along the exposed edge of my boxer briefs, and I grab her hand, pulling it to my lips to stop her without offending her. It's better to flirt than to be smeared in the tabloids. *God, I hate games.*

"My sister's too sweet. If I had you first, I'd keep you for myself."

"So you're keeping the posts to yourself?" I ask. I'm not leaving anything to chance.

"Of course. Like I said, that's not what it was about. I just want to be in the lineup."

"Show me all the pictures from last night, then we're deleting them, and if we hook up in the future, we hook up. If we don't, we don't," I say. *We won't, but I'm not telling her that.*

She sighs, opens her phone to her photos and hands it to me. "I've only got a few."

I scroll through them, deleting each one after viewing it. The first six are at the club, one in the car, and the last one in the condo. The last one is a picture of me naked on the bed and I appear to be posing for the shot. *Delete.*

"Oh. You didn't have to send the last one to the recycling bin. It's not as if I would post it. It was just for me."

Her words remind me, and I delete everything in her recycling bin. "It's not that I don't trust you, Tina, but after last night, I don't." I stand up and toss the phone next to her on the bed. Then I find my phone and since I don't want to ask her for a ride back to Malibu, I shoot my roommate a text.

Me: Any chance you can pick me up from Tara's ASAP?
Nak: Sure. It's not as if I have a life.
Me: Thanks.

As I see it, Nak owes me. He was supposed to be my wingman last night. If he had been doing his job, I never would have ended up here. Maybe he can reconstruct my night for me on the drive home. Tina gets up and walks past me as I stuff my phone back into my pocket.

"You can shower if you want. I'm going to make us some breakfast. Any preference?" she says on her way to the kitchen. She's slipped on panties and a bra, but that's all she's wearing. I'm surprised she put anything on.

"Anything with protein," I say. Protein helps with hangovers and the longer I'm vertical, the more my head feels like a truck ran over it and then backed up and ran over it again. I'm not taking a shower. She probably has cameras staged in her bathroom. I find my shirt and slip it on before collapsing on the couch.

"Hung over?" Tina calls from the kitchen. "It doesn't surprise me. You were crazy last night. I've never seen you like that."

Crazy. That would explain why I woke up in Tina's bed. We eat breakfast with minimal talking because my head is pounding and talking hurts. Then, after breakfast, I rest on the couch until Nak's text notifies me of his arrival. "I'll see you at the club," I say, opening the door. I'm out of there and never going back.

I slouch in the passenger seat of Daniel Nackerson's car, not because I'm hiding from the paparazzi, but because the sun seems to be breaking through the L.A. smog today and it hurts my head almost as much as the noise blaring from the speakers. My hand swings over without a second thought, and eliminates the noise with a touch.

"Rough night?" Nak asks.

"You could say that."

"You didn't drink that much, not that I saw. What happened?"

"You tell me."

"You were crazy. By the way you were acting, I'd say probably Ecstasy or something in that genre."

"Damn. Now that you say it out loud, it makes sense. This is exactly what it feels like. I'm dehydrated from the alcohol, but yet surprisingly not as pissed off as I should be at that little bitch."

"I take it you didn't knowingly ingest it."

I glare at him. "Ya think? I've been clean for eleven months only to be derailed by a horny blond pixie."

"I thought Tara knew about your stent in rehab."

"She does. Except it was Tina at the club last night, not Tara. She probably didn't want to leave anything to chance."

"That explains a lot. I can't tell them apart unless they're standing next to each other."

"Apparently, I can't either," I say with a groan. "And, yes, their bodies *are* identical, right down to their nipple piercings, in case you were wondering."

"I don't understand you. You could have them both and you just walk away."

"I have had them both," I say closing my eyes and resting my head against the cool glass of the window.

"I mean at the same time. What is wrong with you?"

"I don't do threesomes and I don't sleep with sisters of friends. Not anymore. I thought Tara and I were friends and I didn't want to mess up what we had."

"It almost sounds like a relationship."

"Nope. I don't do relationships."

"No, Ever since Kelsey moved out, you just rotate through a string of hookups. You let a new one into the rotation once in a while and move someone else out, but it's as if you're in a relationship with thirty different women at the same time. You're a polygamist."

I laugh, still keeping my eyes closed. "They don't seem to mind."

"Or they don't tell you. Because what happens to a girl who wants more?"

"I move her out of the rotation. And it's not thirty. It's more like ten." I sit up and glare at him. "What about you? When was the last time you got laid? You've slept with exactly two women since you and Leslie broke up, with no repeats. That's two times in thirteen months. You're a good-looking guy. Do you not like sex?"

"I like sex just fine, thank you. What I don't like is screwing for the sake of screwing. If I want a workout, I can go to the gym. Girls who have brains…"

"You mean like Leslie?" I interrupt him with my taunt.

"Yes, like Leslie. Women who actually can think for themselves—ones who can hold an intelligent conversation with you and challenge you are worth waiting for, worth fighting to keep. If you get inside the mind of a woman like that, it brings sex to a whole other level."

"If I ever meet someone worthy of your memory of Leslie, I will try out your theory and get to know her before I get in her pants. Better yet, I could just invite Leslie into the rotation."

"She's too smart to get caught in your web. Besides, she's like a sister to Jonathan Williams, and I thought you didn't sleep with friends' sisters."

"You're right. Leslie's out." I have five basic rules when it comes to sleeping with women. Most of them are just common sense, like one, don't sleep with girls who live their lives in social media. You will always get burned in the press. The internet is forever. That one is a no-brainer.

Two, don't sleep with sisters of friends. This one I had to learn the hard way. Yes, I slept with a friend's sister. It was a douche move, but I was young and stupid, and now at the age of twenty-four, I've matured to the point that I can control my desires.

Three, only date blondes because brunettes are batshit crazy. I could talk for days about my experience with this. Trust me.

Four, no threesomes.

Five, don't sleep with the people you work with. This probably is the hardest rule to follow as an actor. Normally, that's what actors do, we sleep with our co-stars. We're trapped with them for long hours on set. Long, boring hours of waiting for nothing to happen. They may be the only people you see for days or weeks. It can be hard to avoid hooking up with them. And as an actor, if you get deep enough into your character's head, you may want to have sex with the co-star that your character is having sex with. I'm not immune to the perils of method acting. I've started love scenes on camera and finished them off backstage or in my dressing room.

Maybe I should say, don't bring your work home with you and only hook up with co-stars, no crew. On my show, a co-star may only be around for an episode or two, and honestly, my character sleeps with most of the women on the show so it is difficult to eliminate all of them and still make Ashton Post believable. The crew is a different story though. They stick with you season after season. Never break this rule with a member of the crew. I learned this one the hard way, too.

My phone buzzes plucking me out of my eerily philosophical thoughts.

I hate Ecstasy hangovers. It's my dad. I don't really want to answer it, but Jim never just calls to chat, so I'd better.

"Dad," I say because he thinks greetings are a waste of time. But how does someone answer a phone without a greeting?

"Have you talked to Seth lately? Blair Halbrook's daughter saw him at a house party, baked out of his mind and now your mother has it in her head that he's got a drug problem. Did you know about this?"

"I'm not my brother's keeper, Dad. I haven't talked to him in weeks."

"Well, connect with him and see what's going on. Your mother's not going to let it go until she has answers."

"I'll try."

"Do more than try, Liam. Your brother idolizes you." Maybe he did when he was twelve, but not at seventeen.

"Okay. I'll let you know."

The call ends and I glance at Nak, who gives me a sympathetic look.

"Trouble on the home front?"

"Yeah. Jim and Natalie want me to take Seth out for ice cream and find out what drugs he's doing, because, God knows, I'm the expert on drug addiction."

"They're never going to let that die, are they?"

"Probably not." I lean my head against the window again. I don't want to talk anymore.

I get where my mom is coming from. She's the crowned head in foundation fundraising, and most of her causes involve suicide prevention and rehab facilities. I'm sure it is embarrassing for her to have one son go through rehab and another who is well on his way to needing treatment. Yes, I know a little bit more than I let on about my brother's drug problem. The last time I talked to him he assured me he was only using socially and only on occasion. What kid doesn't do a little experimenting? But, if he was at a party with Blair Halbrook's daughter, he should have known better than to be using. Mrs. Halbrook donated a million dollars to one of Mom's charities after her son died of a drug overdose.

Seth and I aren't completely responsible for Mom's neurosis about addiction and suicide. She was obsessed long before we were born. Her father takes most of the blame for that. He committed suicide after his cocaine addiction and the burst of the housing bubble of the late '80s drained every penny he had. I never knew the man, but apparently Seth and I have inherited his addiction gene.

My problem started about a year ago when I got in a motorcycle accident. Some asshole used me for target practice with his car and I ended up thrown across two lanes on the 405. My leg shattered under the weight of my bike and the pain was unbearable. Opiates helped. My pain was real and the drugs were always prescription, but the funny thing about addiction is that it doesn't matter if what you crave is legal or not, it's still addiction. When I lost control of the pills, I checked myself into rehab.

If I had been able to disappear for a month without telling my parents where I was, I would have. Because now, in their eyes, I will forever be an addict on the edge of a relapse. It doesn't matter that I recognized the problem and worked to fix it on my own—my parents still act as if my coke-addicted grandfather and I spring from the same mold. My brother, on the other hand, still has the ability to avoid this parental judgement, and that's why I've been encouraging him to fix the problem without rehab. So far that hasn't happened and by the sounds of it, it won't.

Megan

I'm sitting in Peterson's kitchen and he's toasting me a bagel as I sip my coffee. I tuck my feet up on the stool's footrest to prevent them from sticking to the floor and hold the mug in my hand so I don't have to touch the disgusting surface in front of me. The room smells of beer and gym socks and the only thing keeping me planted is the promise of food. It's almost noon and I haven't had anything to eat.

"You and your brothers really need to hire someone to clean this place. Someone full-time to make it, you know, livable."

Peterson wets a paper towel and wipes the counter directly in front of me. He laughs as he tosses the now red-stained rag into the trash and then sets my buttered bagel's paper plate on the almost clean surface.

"Why would we want to erase all these memories?"

"I'm pretty sure your frat brothers don't remember any of this." I wave my hand around the room and shudder. Bottles of beer pile every surface. Some lay sideways with their half-dried contents spewed out preventing them from rolling off the counter. Used red plastic cups stack in towers like garbage cans weren't invented and the only place to go with them was up. Pizza boxes spill onto the floor and I wonder if a girl was using them as stepping stones so she wouldn't get stuck to the linoleum.

Dylan Peterson sits down on the stool next to me with a piece of cold pizza in his hand. I pray he got it out of the refrigerator, but I don't want to ask. I avoid looking at it. He is usually pretty hygienic, but I've seen guys eat food out of the garbage, so nothing would surprise me.

"Cleanup starts at one and you're welcome to stay and help." His eyes meet mine and I'm pretty sure he knows what I'm thinking. "I can take you home, but I can't be late for clean up or I get fined fifty bucks."

"That's fine. I've got plans this afternoon anyway."

I told my dad I would stop by the marina's office and review some of the accounts. He thinks the accountant is embezzling, but he can't find any proof. Even though it is not my favorite place, I don't want anyone stealing from my family's business. We finish up our food and head back to his room to change. His room is much cleaner than the rest of the house. He keeps the door locked during parties so it doesn't get trashed. He said he once walked in on two total strangers going at it wrapped only in his sheets. That's when he realized he needed to lock the door.

Peterson is lying on his bed watching me change out of his giant T-shirt into the clothes I was wearing last night when my phone goes off. It's not a ringtone I recognize, but my phone is so old that it sometimes changes a person's ringtone for no apparent reason, so it could be anyone. I'm frantically hooking together my bra, hoping I don't miss the call, when Peterson bends over the edge of the bed, plucks it off the floor, and answers it.

"Hello." He looks over to me and his eyes sweep my half naked body. "Yeah. She's right here, but you're going to have to hold on a second. She's getting dressed."

Oh my god. I'm going to kill him. It's probably my dad. I slip my jersey over my head and reach for the phone. I cover the mic with my hand and mouth, "Who is it?"

He shrugs and lies back on the bed as I glare at him.

"Hello," I say, praying it's one of my roommates. The voice on the other end is familiar, but not what I expect.

"I sent a couple of texts wondering if we could meet for lunch. You available?"

"Chase, I'm busy right now. Maybe some other time."

Peterson scoots to the end of the bed, pulls me onto his lap, and says, "Tell him to take a hike. You're seeing someone." His voice booms through the room and I'm sure his words are meant for Chase.

"I just want to reconnect, Meg. I'm not trying to mess up anything you've got going," says Chase with a hint of disappointment.

I'm pissed that Peterson has taken this moment to make his claim on me and just a little relieved that his claim may help me with the crumbling wall I use to keep Chase away. I stand up and pull on my tight jeans as I say, "I'll talk to you later. I've got to go." I end the call not waiting for his response and shove my phone in my back pocket before I snap my fly and zip.

"Who was that?" Peterson asks, acting innocent as if he's oblivious to what he just did, and then lies back on his pillows again.

"Just an old friend—no big deal." I scoop up my earrings off the night-stand and catch the confused expression on Peterson's face.

"We *are* seeing each other, right?" he asks with narrowed brown eyes.

"Yeah." I crawl across the bed and plant a kiss on his cheek. I hope he's not getting attached. I like him. I try to reassure him without defining our relationship any further. Maybe he's acting all Neanderthal because I was half naked when Chase called.

"I just never know what's going on in that head of yours," he says wrapping his big arm around me and pulling me down next to him. "Was that Chase the drug dealer or some new guy?"

I didn't even know he remembered Chase's name, let alone cared. "The drug dealer," I say. "He was just a user, not a dealer, though."

"Why is he calling you?"

"Are you jealous?"

"You sounded pissed. Is he harassing you? Because I'll pummel him if you want me to."

I wish I had someone to pummel him three and a half years ago. I smile at that thought and say, "Not today, but I'll keep it in mind."

"Just stay away from him, Megan, once an addict, always an addict."

"How do you know about him, anyway? Have I been having night terrors and talking in my sleep?"

"You've mentioned him. I do listen to you."

"Peterson, you act like you actually care about me."

He looks down with an expression I can't read and rolls off the bed. "Come on, I've gotta get you home." He holds his arm out to help me up and I take it. Then he yanks me into his arms and kisses me. It's unexpected and better than I'm used to with him. It's not that he's a bad kisser, but his kisses don't really spark anything in me.

The old rental house is quiet when Peterson drops me off. I shower and change clothes, slipping on a clean pair of skinny jeans and a sweater. I'm pulling on my boots and zipping them up when I hear someone come in the front door. It's my housemate Jessica and she's alone. Miracles do happen. Jeff is always with her. It seems like he lives here. *He does live here.*

"Where's your ball and chain?" I call to her as she passes my room.

"He's playing murder with the guys today." She stops in my doorway, her hands full of shopping bags.

"Murder?" I ask.

She laughs and drops her bags in the hall before joining me on my bed. "He's playing paintball with twenty guys at some farm near Forest Lake, so I went shopping. I can't shop with him, ever, and I needed a new dress for my dad's engagement party."

"Man games? You let him play with the other boys?"

"I know you think it's funny, but we're not always together."

"Yes you are. You just don't notice it because you always have each other."

"How was Peterson's party last night?"

"Same old, same old. Frat boys are pigs—a bunch of drunks pawing each other." I give Jessica a hard time about Jeff, but maybe I'm envious. Not of Jeff, but of their relationship. Jeff is actually our friend Sarah's brother and there was a time when I was attracted to him, but now that I know him, hmm…not so much. He is way too vanilla for me, but Jessica needs vanilla. She's seeks stability because her dad is a cheating whore, who is marrying for the third time. This one is the same age as Jessica's sister. Jessica needs a man to be loyal and responsible and predictable and boring. I need mystery or I'll end up being the cheating whore. I need to know a guy has a dark side, that he has options and still picks me. I don't do stable. Maybe that's the problem I have with Peterson—I can predict his every move.

"I think Peterson is getting attached."

She knows me well enough to know this is not a good thing.

"What makes you say that?"

"Chase called my cell and Peterson went all caveman on me." *Oh crap!* I shouldn't have said that. The second it left my mouth I knew I shouldn't have brought it up. I can see the horror on her face.

"What? How did he get your number?"

I explain what happened at the coffee shop with Chase, as she stares at me, her mouth hanging open in disbelief. I know all she can focus on is that Chase is contacting me, but I want her to reassure me that Peterson is just interested in my statistic skills or he just wants sex—anything but a relationship.

"We can go to the mall to get you a new number but you should check online. I bet they can change it without you even having to go in."

"I'm not changing my number. Chase is not the problem here. What do I do about Peterson?"

"Marry him. He's big enough to keep you away from Chase."

I roll my eyes. "I like him and don't want to give up what we have, but he basically told Chase I was taken and then he asked me whether we were seeing each other, but he implied exclusively. I don't do exclusive."

"Have you dated anyone else since basketball season started?"

"Not really, but it's not that I couldn't. It's just easier not to date anyone else."

"Then you're dating exclusively. Give it a chance—maybe it will be good."

She obviously doesn't understand my dilemma. I am glad I ran into

Chase. Maybe I can finally get closure with him. He and my mom are anomalies in my life that I have never been able to statistically reconcile. Even if I can't get closure with my mom, maybe I can with him. If I don't get some kind of answers before I leave for grad school this fall I never will.

"I told my dad I would help him with some accounting issues at the marina and I'd better get going."

"Do you want me to come with you? I could bring my laptop and work on my case studies. I have a ton of them to write up before my clinical on Monday."

Jessica is a nursing student and is always talking about some patient she took care of during her clinical class at the hospital. If she came with me, I would probably have to endure another detailed description about an accident victim. The last one's leg had been ripped open—exposing bones and tendons and after a week of healing—the still-gaping wound started oozing different colors of pus. And then my other roommate, Alli, joined in and they started talking bacteria. Oh my god, I had to leave the room to vomit. I can't handle body fluid discussions.

Even though Jessica seems to find humor in disgusting me with hospital horror stories, she really does care about her patients. She spent a week trying to figure out how the accident victim's family was going to get by on one income if he ended up losing his leg and had to spend eight months in rehab. She's not supposed to talk about patients, but she doesn't use names and I know she needs to vent, so I do my best not to vomit. She puts her heart into everything she does and I respect that.

She knows how much I hate the marina and that's why she volunteered her afternoon with me. It's not that she's a sadist. She would leave her laptop at home if I asked her to. She knows what going to the marina does to me. We've known each other since high school and she's been around to see most of my ugly secrets—most, but not all. Some secrets are just too dark to share.

"No, that's okay. I'll be fine," I answer with the best smile I can conjure. She looks at me as if she doesn't believe me.

"Honestly. I have a mission. I'll just focus on that and when I get home,

I'll binge-watch the entire second half of season three of *Impassioned*. I'll be fine. If anything can distract me from the marina, it's that incredibly hot Ashton Post."

Jessica smiles. "Call me if you need to talk."

"Okay." I nod, head downstairs and out the door. My buttercream yellow bug is waiting for me by the curb. It is such a contradiction to the way I feel most of the time. I climb in and crank up the music.

When I reach the drive to the marina, my heart begins to pound in my ears. It doesn't feel like the start of a headache, so it must just be anxiety. I park the car in front of the clubhouse. I'll have to walk through it to get to the office. The bell jingles over my head, when I open the door. I used to love the friendly tinkling. Now it's just annoying. I buy a water from the machine just inside the door and crack it open as I make my way to the office. No one is in the back. I expected my dad or one of my brothers, at the very least, to be somewhere nearby. In the summer, there's always an attendant, but maybe it is too early in the season for that.

I look to the corner with the window where my dollhouse used to stand. There's a big plant there now. My doll would have climbed it and gone skydiving if it had been there when I was six. I sit down in the worn, black leather chair and log onto the computer. The password is the same as when my mom did the books. I helped my dad with the accounting for a few months after she left us. He needed me and that's what family does.

I've been looking at the numbers for about thirty minutes and haven't spotted any obvious problems. I open another spreadsheet and start punching in formulas. The spreadsheet the accountant is using is too confusing. My mom never had the books set up like this. She preferred a simple layout, like I do.

I get my math skills from her side of the family. Her father helped reengineer parts of the space shuttle after the Discovery disaster, and my mother was in the top of her class in high school. She went to university and met my dad her sophomore year. He played football and she fell for his good looks. They didn't know each other long when she got pregnant with my brother Braden. They both dropped out of school, and my dad went to work for his dad, while my mom got a two-year accounting degree at the community college at night. I always thought it was such a waste for her to be stuck doing the books at the marina when she could have been anything she wanted, married anyone she wanted. I guess she did too. Don't get me wrong, Dad's a great guy, but he's very vanilla, very old-fashioned, and his and Mom's relationship never really sparked. I've vowed never to let what happened to her happen to me. That's why I am going for my doctorate, and if something derails me at least I will have my teaching certificate. I always have a backup. I don't want to end up like Mom.

I've got most of the numbers for the past six months transferred to my easier form before I hear the bell tinkle and my dad's voice boom from the front room. He's laughing about something my brother said as he enters the office. When he sees me, his smile dissipates.

"Sweetheart." Pain fills his eyes. "I didn't think you would be here yet."

"I am." I make eye contact with my brother Braden and his eyebrow furrows. I know it isn't me causing the pain—yet it is. I look just like her. The shape of my face, my long legs, and even my blue eyes are hers. And now that my blond hair is short, I'm a dead ringer. The look on my dad's face is one of the biggest reasons I hate the marina. I don't like to hurt him. He's been through enough. The look on my brother's face is the second reason I shouldn't be here. He still blames me for all that went down with Mom.

My dad walks over and places his hand on my shoulder. "Have you found anything?" His hand feels weighted as if he's too tired to support it himself. I understand because that is how I feel sitting in this room.

"Not yet, but your books are a mess. I'm going to set up a new system just to be able to see where the money is going."

"The boys and I are going to grab an early dinner downtown. Do you want to come? It's been a long time since the whole family ate together."

"Dad, there's a lot to look over here and I have plans tonight." I don't tell him my plans are with a hot fictional character found only in the reruns of my favorite cable drama. I don't want to ruin his night.

"Maybe next time," he adds.

In come Tyler and Wes. They both freeze when they see me. I know what they're seeing. They see a young version of Mom sitting at the desk she always sat in. I should have left my hair long. It wasn't so obvious when my hair was long.

I smile at my brothers and they just stare. "Would you mind if I save everything to a flash drive and take it back to my place to work on it?" I ask. "My computer is faster and it will take less time."

"Anything you want, sweetheart." He's looking down as he speaks, not at me. Then he looks at my brothers and they start filing out of the room. They don't even say goodbye. *What the hell?* Didn't their mother teach them any manners? I don't care anymore.

It takes me about forty-five minutes to upload the information I need. After stuffing my USB drive back in my bag, I look around the room, wondering what has changed in the last four years since my mom left. The plant in the corner is new, but everything else looks the same. I drive home, my head clouded with thoughts of my mom.

She once told me she didn't really love my dad when they got married. She was still hung up on an old boyfriend who would probably always have her heart. She said that though she found Dad attractive, the chemistry wasn't there. They made the best of the circumstances they were thrust into and she learned to love him. I understand why she told me. She didn't want me to make the same mistake she did. She knew Chase had captured my heart and was encouraging me to get him help. I think about her words too often. They are embedded in my brain and I wish she had never told me. It's probably the reason I'm still fixated on Chase.

By the time I get home, I'm completely wiped. All I want to do is change into my favorite comfy pajamas and sink into my *Impassioned* binge. The second-half of the season was just released and I can't wait to watch it. I'm not hungry enough for a meal, but I will probably want a snack once my brain relaxes. I head to the kitchen to fill my oversized glass with ice water and find some food to stuff into my body.

Jessica is heating dinner in the microwave. She must have just gotten home.

"Are you doing all right?"

"Yeah. I'm fine. I've got a date with a struggling actor."

"Seriously, I don't get the appeal of that show."

I stare at her in disbelief, and she adds, "Okay, the Ashton Post character is hot, but he sleeps with every girl on the show."

"You know me—I'm not one of those crazy fangirls. He's just a good distraction and nice to look at." *And we may have a few children together in one of my recurring dreams.* "He's just a misunderstood bad boy. Deep down, he's trying to survive life in the cruel world of Hollywood. And, in about five minutes, I'm going to find out if he died in the motorcycle crash in the mid-season finale. I know he survived though because they would never kill him off. You are welcome to join me, but there will be no talking if you do."

"I'm not a fan."

"You're dead to me," I say.

She laughs and pulls her plate from the microwave.

I normally don't rant, but this is *Impassioned*. It's my one dirty little pleasure, and after the day I had, I deserve some entertainment. I just found the show a few months ago and it's already my all-time favorite. I finish rummaging through my cupboard, plucking a box of cereal from the shelf before filling my glass with ice water and rushing back upstairs to my room.

Chapter 4

Liam

It's taken me a week to finally get Seth to respond to a text. He knows why I'm contacting him, which doesn't surprise me. Dad probably said something to him. The kid is still in high school and lives at home. He has to run into Mom and Dad once in a while. Still knowing my motivation, he's agreed to meet me for lunch, as long as I'm paying.

I'm sitting at the restaurant where I used to take him when he was thirteen. I was in college, completely disappointing my parents by pursuing a degree in the arts. *I should follow in my father's footsteps and go to law school, right?* My parents thought it was important for me not to abandon my little brother while I was in school. I remember thinking at the time that I wasn't his parent and I definitely wasn't the one who let the nannies raise him. Talk about abandonment. My parents are a little hypocritical when it comes to my brother and me. And maybe their lack of parenting is the reason I feel responsible for Seth. He needs to know he's not alone in the world and someone actually pays attention to what he does.

I know what happens at the prep school he attends, because I went there. I know it is chock full of drug pushers who are exactly what the students' parents pay high priced tuition to avoid. Hell, the drug pushers' parents pay the same tuition. The drugs may be designer and cost more than the ones at other schools, but they do the same job—provide an escape from whatever problems life brings.

Seth is about thirty minutes late before I text him and to his credit, he responds immediately.

> Seth: *Having car trouble. Caught a ride. Hope you're not on your bike.*
> Me: *Got my car.*
> Seth: *See you in 5.*

Interpretation: he needs a ride home and doesn't want to ride on the back of my motorcycle. I have to wonder what kind of trouble a not even two-year-old Mercedes has. I don't get to ponder this long because the server is back for the fourth time.

"I don't think she's coming. I could take my break and sit with you while you eat."

She's cute, but brunette and probably barely legal. She looks young.

"My brother will be here. He just sent a text."

With this news her eyes peruse my body. I've seen her expression a thousand times. The next words out of her mouth will be telling me she gets off soon and blah blah blah…if I'm interested…blah blah blah…we could just hang out and chill. Meaning she wants me to get her off. I scratch the back of my neck and wait.

"I get off at two. We could grab some coffee somewhere and chill?" She bats her big brown eyes at me.

I wonder if she watches my show and really wants to sleep with Ashton Post. I smile and say, "I'd love to, but my brother and I are going to be busy all day."

"Shit, Liam." Seth slides into the booth across from me. "I thought it was only going to be lunch."

"Let me know if you change your mind," she says with a smug smile, before asking Seth for his drink order.

"You look like hell," I say after the server leaves. He looks like he's lost about ten pounds.

"Great to see you too," he practically growls as he rolls his eyes.

He picks up the menu and opens it.

"I'm starved. My car disappeared and I spent all morning looking for it."

He holds the menu up in front of his face and I can't read his expression. *Is he joking?*

"Someone stole your car?"

"Nah, just can't find it."

"You lost your car? What do you mean, you lost your car? Mom and Dad are going to kill you."

"That's why they are never going to find out. You're going to help me find it. I have it narrowed down to maybe five locations. All you have to do is drive me around a little bit and problem solved." He shrugs as if he lost his tennis racket. "You're still buying, right? I'm flat broke. I can't wait for my birthday. Is there any way you can spot me some cash until then?"

Really? "Have you forgotten about the thousand dollars you borrowed from me last month? Get a job. I'm not supporting your drug habit anymore." *When did I grow up?* Somehow in the last six years I've become my parents.

"Oh come on, Liam. I don't have a drug habit. It's just social. You know how it is."

"Yep, I do. And here's my advice. If you are so baked you don't know where you parked your car then it is no longer social. Quit cold turkey or you are going to find your ass in treatment. Blair Halbrook's daughter ratted you out to Mom and Dad, and they don't care whether you classify it as social or not."

The server comes back for our order and as soon as she records it, she asks, "Are you really brothers, because you don't look anything alike, except for the shoes."

I look down at our feet and laugh at the coincidence, because we are wearing the same brand and model of shoe. I guess we have similar taste in clothes. She's right, besides the shoes we don't look anything alike. Seth has my dad's dark hair and my mom's fair skin, and I have my mom's blond hair and my dad's tanned skin. My eyes are brown and his are blue. It's a pretty mixed-up gene pool. I nod and give her my order. Seth follows.

"So are you doing meth?" I ask, examining his face.

"Quit checking out my teeth. I'm not doing meth. You act as if you've never experimented. You're the addict. Stop with the judging. I get enough of that at the house."

"So do you think you could give up whatever it is? At least until you leave for school, because you know what Mom's thinking. She'll have you on suicide watch next and then Dad will step in and you'll be peeing in a cup for him every Sunday morning."

He laughs, shaking his head, but he knows I'm right.

"Did he ever drug test you?" Seth asks, slouching in his chair.

"Nope. But I wasn't as stupid as you," I say. "You're living in their house, burning through money like it is lemonade. What are Mom and Dad supposed to think? You better start being smarter."

"Screw you." He takes a sip of his Coke and looks out the window.

I'm waiting for his comeback to tell me what a poor example I've been, how I abandoned him when I left for college, and even now as I fight to find a path in Hollywood, I never make time for him. I don't make time for him. I know I should because Mom and Dad don't pay attention to him, just like they didn't pay attention to me, except when I screwed up.

"You know, you're Mom and Dad's favorite, right? You can do no wrong in their eyes. Can't you talk to them and tell them it's just a phase or something? They listen to you."

"Are you kidding me? They don't listen to me. Everything I do is wrong. I open my mouth and I'm wrong before I even speak. Shit, Seth. Dad's got a list a mile long of my mistakes. You should be able to float by unnoticed." Oops. I can tell by his expression it was the wrong thing to say.

"Maybe I'd care if they cared. Maybe I wouldn't need the drugs."

"There you go. The first step is admitting you need the drugs. Now that you realize you have a problem we can work on resolving it."

"Are you therapisting me?" He looks at me with an appalled expression, his jaw hardening. "I don't need your help."

"So you found your car?" I ask, because who the hell loses their car? I look him directly in the eyes. "I know what it's like to have that empty feeling. The one only a high can fill. I know what it's like to have cravings. You can talk to me."

"You're an addict. That doesn't make me one."

"Why don't you come out to Malibu and hang out over the weekend… to get away from Mom and Dad?" Maybe it would be a way to break the drug cycle with his friends and get me merit points with my parents. It's been a while since we've spent time together.

"All right." He agrees too quickly, and I'm not sure what to make of his concession.

After lunch, Seth and I drive around looking for his car. We search parking lot after parking lot and street block after street block outside clubs. Which tells me my little brother has a worthy fake ID. We even check the impound lots. We end up having to stop at a convenience store to replace the battery in his key fob. We use it so much, trying to magically light an invisible car.

"If you didn't have your key fob, I'd bet you left it in some club's valet."

Seth's head slams against the back of his seat. "Valet." His head bangs two more times. "I left it at a valet. I didn't have any money to pick it up. Kian was supposed to pay for it but he disappeared." He starts digging through his wallet. "I should have the ticket. I couldn't get it out when we left the club so I caught a ride with the rest of the group. How did I forget that?"

"Why do you have your keys?" I ask, because the valet should have his keys.

"Some girl gave me a ride. And this is my spare set. I thought I lost the keys."

"You know losing your car is not normal. It is a sign you have a real problem."

"My car isn't lost anymore. We just have to pick it up." He hands me the ticket with the name of the club on it. "I don't have any money, can you help me?"

"You owe me big time, little brother."

"I know," he admits. Then he completely changes the subject. "How hard was it to break it to Mom and Dad that you weren't going back to school after you got the job offer on *Impassioned*?"

"It was awful." I smile because we are actually talking about something other than the drugs or his car. "My first contract wasn't much more than scale and frankly that is about as much as my trust was paying me to go to school. School is a hell of a lot easier than acting."

"Not as much fun though, right?"

"No, not as much fun. What are you doing in the fall? You got a school picked out?"

"No. My grades suck. I could always go to tech and get some generals out of the way, but Dad basically told me that's not a choice. I don't know what I want to do with the rest of my life, but God forbid, I go to tech and embarrass Mom and Dad. I think my grades are too far gone to go anywhere else. Maybe I should become an actor. Do you think you could get me a job on your show?" His voice lightens as if it is a solution to all his problems.

"Not the kind of job you want, but I could try. You'd have to audition on your own and join the union. I didn't think you liked theater."

"I don't. I just don't know what to do."

This is the first real conversation I've had with him in over a year. "We can brainstorm it over the weekend. You don't have to go to school. You just won't get as much from the trust every month. The money still stays there. You'll eventually get it."

He looks at me as if less money isn't an option. "It's my money. Why should I have to wait?" he asks.

"It's Mom and Dad's money. Not everyone has a trust waiting for them when they turn eighteen."

"All my friends do. Why does Dad have to complicate everything?"

"He thinks he's doing what he can to make us successful. Otherwise, you would never get a job. Think of it as a safety net not a paycheck."

"I've heard that speech before." He looks out the window and I know I need to change the subject before he disengages.

"Are you seeing anyone?" I ask.

"No. There are a couple of girls I hook up with once in a while, but nothing more. You?"

"Same," I say. "Nothing worth noting."

He nods in understanding. And girls might be the one subject we connect on. There is no reason to move beyond the hookup stage. After all, we are our parents' children. We pull up to the club and I park my car on the street. I don't have any cash and I don't trust Seth with my credit card. It takes a few minutes before we find someone who can help us with valet parking. It's three in the afternoon and valet parking doesn't start until seven or eight. I pay the guy an extra twenty bucks to get Seth's car, which brings the cost to over a hundred. It's almost as much as an impound lot. When the car pulls up, I remind Seth that he's spending the weekend at my place and he nods before getting into his car. I hope he shows up.

Megan

Two weeks have passed since I ran into Chase at the coffee shop. I tried to avoid him at first, even though part of me needed to see him to know if the chemistry is still there with us. I know who he was when I left him, but that doesn't mean he's the same person now. I'm not the same. That's why I gave into his texting barrage. I told him I'm seeing someone, hoping to discourage him until I know if I could deal with getting back together. I agreed to go snowboarding with him as friends. He knows how much I like to board and I'm sure that is why he pushed for it. Boarding was something he and I used to do together in high school and he got me to admit that I hadn't been boarding all season. The weather was really mild this year and once it got cold enough for snow to stick, basketball season hit full swing.

So here I stand looking up at a black diamond hill. The white surface of the slope glistens in the sunlight. Colorful ants breeze down crisscrossing in front of each other in a rhythmic dance.

"There is no way in hell I'm going down that. I can't even see the top."

"Come on, Meg. Live a little. I promise I won't let you die."

He can't promise that.

"The green ant in the middle looks dead. It hasn't moved for like five minutes. Let's find another hill."

He grabs my hand and starts to drag me towards the chairlift. "It doesn't look as big from the top. We used to ride this hill all the time."

"That was some other chick. I've never been down that hill before." I swear they redid all the runs since I was here last. Nothing looks familiar.

"It was you," he whispers conspiratorially in my ear. "You just never rode it sober before. I got in your pants behind one of the trees near the top. Remember it now?" He smiles that cocky half smile I can't resist.

I'm surprised he remembers. I totally forgot. Maybe I was trying to suppress it. I must have drunk a lot more then. I look to my feet because I can't meet his eyes. Damn him. I wish I could control how he still makes me feel.

"Well, that will never happen again," I say as I pull my hand away from his. "If I do go up this thing with you, we are not going anywhere near the tree line."

"We'll see," he mumbles under his breath as he waits for me to jump on the lift.

"No. I can't be that for you anymore. I've moved on."

"So you've got a boyfriend? Why are you here with me?" He jumps up next to me and there's his smirk again.

"We're just friends. It doesn't matter." I can't tell him it's a trial run to see if we still have chemistry or he will take complete advantage of me.

"So tell me about this other guy you're stringing along?"

"You and I are just friends. The other guys in my life are none of your business."

"Guys huh? I bet that guy you were dressing in front of doesn't know about the others. How many?"

"Shut up. I'm not going out with you."

"Yet, here you are."

"As friends."

He smiles and places his hand on my shoulder. "Don't be nervous, Meg." His blue eyes burrow into mine.

"You don't intimidate me." I can't believe I'm letting him get me so flustered. What is wrong with me?

"Not me, the hill. I've been on this hill sober. It's not so big—me on the other hand—huge." He holds his hands two feet apart. "Well, you know."

What a smart-ass. I should never have agreed to go snowboarding with him. He is so much better than I am at it and it allows him to be cocky. He grabs my hand again as we dismount the lift and I don't pull my hand away this time. He knows where I stand, right? *Oh god, I'm in so much trouble.*

The run exhilarates every part of me. Even my fingertips are tingling when Chase grabs me from behind and yanks me down on top of him in the snow. He knows me well enough to remember I'm most vulnerable when my blood is pumping. But I know him too. His next move is to pull me flush against him and start kissing the back of my neck. Part of me welcomes his touch. My body misses him. It's been so long since I've felt anything. The other part of me wants to elbow him in the balls and smash a snowball into his face for all the crap he put me through. I'm waiting. *Where are his lips?* Why isn't he kissing my neck? I turn my head to meet his eyes. He's laughing at me. Definitely snowball time. I find great satisfaction as my handful of snow crashes into his face. He surprises me by just brushing the snow off and not retaliating.

We drop our boards at the stand and head into the chalet for a snack. I laugh when clumps of snow roll into Chase's collar as he pulls off his beanie. I got him good. We grab some nachos and a couple of lemonades and bring them up to the register. I'm reaching in my pocket for my cash when Chase hands a twenty to the cashier. I'm so not used to him paying for anything. When we dated in high school, he always made an excuse not to pay, but today he offered to pay for my lift ticket. I didn't let him, though. I want clear lines drawn so he won't think it's a date. I let the snack slide. It doesn't make me feel obligated at all.

We find a table overlooking the hill we just ran and sit down across from each other. We're halfway through the nachos when a couple of Peterson's frat brothers plant themselves at the long cafeteria-style table with us.

They eye Chase and me suspiciously and Scott says, "Megan? Peterson didn't say anything about you joining us at the slopes today."

"Is he here?" I try to hide my concern. He and I don't always check in with each other except on game night. If he is here I don't want him and Chase to get into a fight over me. Chase wouldn't physically start a fight, but his smart mouth may cause Peterson to go off.

"Nope. He has an economics paper to write by tomorrow." Nash holds a hand out to Chase and says, "Hi. I'm Nash and this is Scott." He nods toward Scott.

Chase looks at me. After years of being together, I hope he knows how to read my expressions. I probably should just be happy I got caught. It will give me an easy out with Peterson. He won't want his buddies harassing him about me cheating if he really is wanting more than basketball night. But part of me doesn't want to end things with him and I'm pretty sure my expression tells Chase that.

"I'm Wes, Meg's brother." Chase meets their hands and the scowl on Scott's brow relaxes. Chase and my brother Wes were friends at one time, not good friends, but friends. That's how we met. Chase meets my eyes with his smug grin.

"I didn't know Megan had any brothers," says Scott.

"I'm not surprised. She thinks we're asshats. I'm the least ass of the three."

The guys all laugh. Scott looks at me and says, "You should hit the hills with us. Candice and Caitlyn are in the bathroom. It will be a riot."

I wonder how long they've been here. I hope none of them saw Chase holding my hand. I start to say no when Chase says, "Sure I'd love to get to know Meg's friends a bit." *What an asshat.*

Scott pulls out a fifth of Southern Comfort and starts to pour it into his drink cup. He passes it to Nash who dumps some in his cup and then passes the bottle to Chase. Chase takes my cup and fills the cup to the brim. Then he passes it back to Scott who stuffs it into his jacket. I'm floored by the fact that he skipped his own cup and ask, "What about you?"

"Sis, you know I don't drink anymore—not since rehab."

I give him a dirty look and don't say anymore. As I take a sip of my lemonade, almost gagging, the guys' girlfriends join us.

"Hey, Megan," one of them says. They're interchangeable so it doesn't matter which one.

I can see on their faces that they are wondering who the blond guy seated across from me is. I smile at Chase and say, "This is my brother, Wes."

They greet him like we're best friends. They are both so fake, the epitome of the girls in my dance troupe growing up and the reason I quit dance.

"So…Wes, do you go to the U, somewhere else, or have you graduated already?" asks Candice. She's probably looking for her next victim. Her and Scott's relationship has run its course.

"No. I never went to college," Chase says. "I work at our family's marina on the St. Croix with my dad and brothers." It's not too big of a stretch for Chase to carry out a conversation about the marina. He worked there two summers. He knows the business well enough to make it believable.

"Megan, you never said your family owns a marina," Scott says, holding his cup up for his girlfriend to drink.

"You never asked."

"Do you have a boat? You've got to take us out on the river this summer," he adds.

"Yeah. We've got a fifty-one-foot houseboat and a couple of speedboats. We'll have a great time," says Chase as I glare at him, shaking my head.

"Did you live on the boat growing up?" asks Nash.

I smile and say, "No. It's not really for living on. It's more of a destination just for recreation and business entertaining. Most people call it a yacht and I doubt my father would allow me to take a bunch of frat boys for a cruise on it. The speedboats are fair game, though."

"Does Peterson know you own a marina?" asks Scott.

I shrug. "I don't own a marina—my family does. I hate the marina."

Chase looks at me confused. I guess that is new to him. I used to love the marina when I was younger. Now, I'd rather be just about anywhere else.

We talk a little bit more about the marina and then as they start to finish their drinks, they stand up and push off the bench. I think I may need to take the edge off in order to pull off this ruse. I down the sweet turpentine in my cup and join them. Outside, Chase doesn't grab my hand, but instead wraps an arm around my shoulder and I wonder what kind of incestuous relationship the others must think we have. I would never let one of my brothers put his arm around me like this. I know this web of lies is going to fall apart at some point and it worries me that I care. It's not like I'm cheating on Peterson. Chase is a friend. I just don't want to hurt Peterson. Even though the spark between us isn't great, he's a good guy.

I'm a better snowboarder when my inhibitions have been lowered. The alcohol is helping or maybe I just think I'm better. The black diamond hill doesn't seem so intimidating anymore. We've been down it about four more times since our snack. We hit the chair lift for another run and as we ascend I ask Chase why he stopped drinking when he gave up the drugs. The chair lift is our only chance to talk without others hearing us.

"I just don't like the feeling of losing control. I think I killed enough brain cells for a lifetime, don't you?"

I smile and nod. "Do you still crave the drugs?" I knew the alcohol would be easier for him to give up than the drugs.

"Sure. I still crave them. Smoking was even harder than the pills, more addictive. I still crave the cigarettes, but I'm not going to poison this temple ever again," he says passing his hand in front of his face.

"You gave up smoking too. Wow. How did you finally get help?" I had heard the story from his brother last summer, but I want to hear it in his words.

"I took too many pills one day and my parents had me committed. By the time the hospital let me out, I was three days into sobriety. I figured, 'why the hell not?' It was the longest I had been sober since junior year in high school. I went to rehab and after three months, they kicked me out. Then, I moved into a halfway house for people struggling with addiction. My parents paid for my room and board for almost a year. It was cheaper than paying for another stint in rehab. It was a hellhole, but it worked."

His brother had shared way more details, but I understood why he didn't want to talk about what really happened. We reach the top of the hill and head back down with the rest of the group in front of us. Toward the bottom, Chase starts circling me. He's going to make me trip. I'm going to fall on my face in front of everyone. I can see them all starting to gather at the bottom. Why doesn't he just meet the group at the bottom like he did last run and let me make it down in my own time?

"Let's get out of here and go somewhere we can talk," Chase yells as he crosses my path.

"Okay," I yell back. I'm tired of our little charade.

We reach the bottom with the rest and Chase announces, "We're heading out. I have to be to work early at the marina." He lies so smoothly that no one questions it. It is one of his many talents. He usually used it against me when we were dating. I never knew when to trust him.

"It was great to meet you, Wes," says Candice, shaking his hand and then giving him a hug. "I hope we get to see you again."

"You should come to the party on Friday at the frat house," adds Caitlyn.

"Maybe I will." Chase winks at Candice.

"I'll bring all my brothers," I say, turning away from the group as I roll my eyes at Chase and head toward the parking lot. There is no way in hell he is going anywhere near Peterson's party. We make it back to the lot before I realize I drank too much to drive home. I stop by the Beetle and pull my board bag out. Chase sets his board against my car and holds the bag as I stuff my board into it.

"Why don't we leave your car here and come back for it later? I don't think you should drive right now."

"You did that on purpose," I say as I stuff my gear into the back and pull my purse out from under the seat. I slam the door shut. "Where's your car?"

He points to the yellow car I'd seen at the coffee shop and says, "We can go to my house so we can talk and I'll drive you back in a couple of hours."

"In your dreams, gaper." There is no way I'm going to let him take me back to his place when I'm buzzed or *ever*. Besides, he probably still lives in his parents' basement. "Let's go to a restaurant and you can buy me dinner."

"Oh? Like a date? How incestuous, Sis," he says with a laugh.

"Shut it, now you're creeping me out."

He deactivates the car's alarm, opens the trunk, and stuffs his board into it—somehow feeding it into the area behind the bucket seats. He closes the trunk and gets into the driver's seat. "Come on," he says as he closes his door.

I open the passenger door and climb in. I want to find out more about what happened to him, but there is no way in hell I am going anywhere with him that isn't public.

The sweet peppery smell fills my nose as the hostess greets us. I didn't realize I was so hungry. Chase's hand slides down my back and parks right above my snow pants as we're guided to a secluded table toward the back. It feels so natural that I'm not going to pull away. We're seated at a small table and Chase sits across from me. I had slipped out of my coat and left it in the car. I am still warm in my boarding pants over my leggings, but I am not stripping off my pants in front of Chase.

We order quickly and make small talk until I finally ask, "So what do you do now? You're clean, but you're not going to school. Do you have a job?"

A loud guttural laugh escapes his chest. "No. I work for myself."

"Oh, instead of using, you're selling, huh?" I say it jokingly, but it would explain the car.

He laughs again. "So little confidence in me, Meg?"

"Explain your car then. Where did you get it?"

"I bought it used, paid cash."

"So you *are* dealing?"

"A friend and I wrote an app. It took off and we sold it. I'm completely clean. The Ferrari was my first purchase. It's a great app."

"What kind of app? Some porn game, I suppose?"

"You know me so well." He grins as if he is hiding a secret. I raise my eyebrows and he says, "Actually it was Mad Moronic Monkeys. Have you heard of it?" He knows I have. It's everywhere. Peterson has a T-shirt with two Mad Moronic Monkeys fighting that says, "Ever have one of those days?" A monkey with a missing arm is hurling through the air while a second monkey stands in the background holding the detached limb.

"No, you didn't."

"I'll bet you ten bucks."

"Prove it, liar."

"If I prove it, you owe me a kiss and not just a peck on the cheek—tongue and spit and all. We could go all *Game of Thrones* if you want, but all I'm asking for is a kiss."

"I'm not going to kiss you, but prove it anyway." I smile at him knowing there is no way that he wrote that app. I have the app on my phone and I would have known if his name was attached.

He takes out his phone and flashes me the app. He holds it up as he advances the screen to the credits. "That's me." His cocky smile overtakes his face.

His name is plastered throughout the credits. His and one other are practically the only names listed. I take out my phone, thinking maybe he had a fake one made to impress chicks—nope, mine says the same as his. I guess I've never looked at the credits before.

"You're a fan. Who knew?" He puts his phone away and his blue eyes meet mine.

"Wilson is your friend, I take it. How did you meet him?"

"He and I shared a room at the halfway house. He's a genius when it comes to coding. I can code, but he can map it all out with lightning speed. I came up with the idea and did the graphics. We developed it when we lived together."

This is what he wanted to tell me. He wants me to know he is successful. "I'm so happy for you. That's amazing," I say, and I mean it.

He's come so far from high school. I remember our last kiss. It wasn't anything special, but the look on his face when I told him I was leaving gave me strength—so cocky, like he didn't believe me. I looked into his glassy eyes with his pupils so dilated I could hardly tell his eyes were blue and I knew he would never give up the drugs. I wasn't worth that kind of sacrifice. My entire last two years of high school were consumed by me making excuses for him to my friends, my family, and his family. I was a total enabler. I wasn't going to be one anymore. I told myself never again would I let him be a part of my life, but here I am, trying to recapture the chemistry. I'd like to believe he's changed. Am I being stupid letting him back in my life? I know what my friends would say.

Run! Quick. Run away!

Megan

Last night, Chase dropped me off at my car after we ate, and didn't even try to kiss me. He'd told me what he wanted, and I thought that would be the end of our encounters. We said our goodbyes and didn't make any more plans to talk or see each other. I felt relieved on the drive home, happy he's been able to turn his life around, and that I finally had closure with him. I don't hate him. My body obviously still desires him. I don't want to desire him and that's why when I get home from class and I see his car parked outside the rental house, I'm pissed.

Pissed at him for stalking me.

Pissed at me for getting into the situation where he could.

And pissed he's sitting on the front step, out in the open, where any one of my roommates can spot him.

"Did anyone see you?" I ask leading him inside.

"No." He follows me upstairs to my room.

I don't speak again until I close my bedroom door. Alli may already be home and I don't want her to know Chase and I are in contact with each other, and I definitely don't want her to know I went snowboarding with him. His visit isn't going to help me, which isn't new. He drags chaos wherever he goes.

"Why are you here?" I don't ask how he found me. He probably followed me home last night.

He ignores my question, sits in my desk chair, and spins around to face my bed. "So this is where it all happens. I never pictured you with some frat boy. In high school, you never gave the dumbass jocks the time of day. You're smarter than that."

"Well I've changed. Four years is a long time."

"Were you here or at the frat house when he was watching you dress?"

"Why are you here, Chase?" I ask again just in case he thought I was talking to an invisible person the first time. I ready myself for a lengthy story as to why he had to find me. He always had a story when we dated. Usually, it was a lie.

He reaches into his pockets and pulls out my ski gloves. I must have left them in his car. I didn't even miss them because I only wear them on the slopes.

"Thanks." I toss them on my desk and add, "I appreciate you dropping them off, but I don't have time to chat. I have a paper due on Monday and my weekend is pretty booked."

"Okay. I'll see you around, then." He gets up and starts walking toward the door.

I quickly step in front of him. I need to check the hall and make sure Alli is in her room. "I don't want anyone to know you're here. I'll check the hall and if it's clear then you can go."

"Wouldn't want the frat boy to find out," he says with a grin and I don't correct him. Sure, I don't want Peterson to know about him, but the bigger problem is my roommates.

I check the hallway and it's clear. I can hear music playing from Alli's room and she wouldn't leave it playing if she wasn't in there. "I'm glad you understand. Thanks again for bringing me my gloves."

He smiles over his shoulder at me before closing the door. Part of me hates him for showing up in my life again and the other part likes him. If he hadn't abandoned me four years ago maybe we would still be together. It was him who gave up on me, not the other way around. I know in his mind it was me and in reality, I'm the one who made the cut. I couldn't get him to give up the drugs and he was dragging me down with him. But, he gave up on me by cheating and continuing to use.

I wonder if it is too little too late for us? I don't know how we could be together at this point. My roommates would kill me. And, I still have to worry about Peterson. Would it look too obvious to end it with him right now or should I wait out basketball season? I don't want to hurt him and the longer I string him on, the more he'll get hurt. I don't want to be the user, the one who stays in a loveless relationship because a few benefits outweigh the mediocrity. I don't want to be like my mom.

Dylan wants me to come to the party at his house tonight. It won't be the right time to talk to him though—not with all the noise and drunks. I tried to make an excuse not to go because each time I spend the night with him, he seems just a little more attached.

I told him I have to finish my paper on equidistribution in chaotic dynamical systems, but I think he stopped listening when I said equidistribution. I really do have to finish the paper by Monday. Maybe I can get Alli to come to the party with me and I can make an excuse to leave with her. If I don't stay the night, it would help me to start to separate and make it easier when I break it off. *Who am I kidding?* Alli would never go. I think I'll just wait out basketball season.

I've taken out my laptop, and have been working on my paper for about an hour when Alli pops her head in my door.

"Jessica is picking up some food from The Palace. Do you want anything?" Her phone is perched on her shoulder and she's gathering her long red hair at the back of her neck.

"No, I'm not that hungry. I had a late lunch."

She relays her order to Jessica, ends her call, and turns to me with her hands on her hips. "And, I heard you ran into Chase."

"Yep." I look back down at my laptop. I'm not going to see him again, so I don't feel the need to explain myself.

"So?"

I can feel her furious eyes burning into the side of my head. I glance up to meet her glare. "I ran into him, so what? I'm not going to see him again," I repeat out loud as I look down at my screen. "I have to get at least two more pages written before I leave for the party tonight. It's due Monday and there's a game on Sunday. I really need to get this done."

"He has your number?"

"That doesn't mean anything," I tell her, though she knows the truth.

"Was that him in your room earlier?"

I shake my head without looking up. If I admit it, my roommates will never let it die.

"Whatever."

"Do you want to come to Peterson's party with me?"

"Why, so you can distance yourself from him and get back with Chase? No way. Peterson's a nice guy. He's good for you."

Jessica must have let her in on my latest issues with Dylan. *No one in this house can keep their mouths shut.* I start back on my paper without responding to her comment and she stands in my doorway for almost a minute, waiting, before heading to her room. *Am I distancing myself from Peterson because I subconsciously want Chase back?*

By nine o'clock I've finished my paper, except the citations. I've showered and thrown a sweater and a skirt on. I figure I may as well show off my legs as long as I'm not going to be breaking up with Dylan tonight.

Alli is in her room talking on the phone, probably with someone in her study group or the teaching assistant that's been taking her out for coffee. Jessica and Jeff are sitting on the couch watching a movie in the living room as I come down the stairs.

"Say hi to Peterson for us." Jessica smiles. I'm sure she's sincere, but it feels like a taunt.

"I'm coming home tonight so take it to your room before getting naked." I say.

"Thanks for the warning," Jeff hollers as he pulls Jessica onto his lap.

I'm glad I'm leaving.

Parking is scarce outside the packed party, but I manage to squeeze my car onto the grass next to Peterson's car in the alley. The thumping of the music vibrates the floor and kicks up my mood when I enter the kitchen. Dylan is talking to Scott who is manning the cups next to the keg. Scott likes to be in charge of cup sales, because it allows him to meet each and every girl who comes to the party. Scott hands Peterson a cup and he fills it before handing it to me.

Scott looks me up and down and Peterson glares at him, but it doesn't stop his gawking. Dylan wraps his arm around me and pulls me out of the kitchen.

"I like your skirt," he says in my ear as we maneuver our way through the crowd.

"No, you don't. You like my legs."

"I can't argue with that." He slaps my behind playfully and it makes me laugh.

Miller grabs my shoulder as we walk into the room and says, "Nice skirt, Billings."

I roll my eyes. They're acting like I've never worn a skirt before. Peterson punches Miller's shoulder agreeably and then places him in a choke hold. Maybe I should have worn jeans. They joke around for a few minutes while I start up a conversation with Scott's girlfriend, Candice. She's so superficial that I'm not sure I can stand talking to her very long.

"Is your hot brother coming tonight?" She sits on the back of the couch and fluffs her straight bottle blond hair. I shouldn't criticize. I color my hair, too. But at least my hair is the color it used to be when I was little. Her color doesn't even exist in nature.

"No. He's got a date, some stripper I think." There's no need to encourage her. "He's never had very good taste in women. One time he slept with his best friend's girlfriend." True story, Chase not Wes.

"Oh. That's too bad. I thought he was kind of cute," she says.

"So does he."

Makayla Andre wraps her arm around my shoulder and I breathe a sigh of relief. Finally, a woman who can hold an intelligent conversation has arrived.

"So, basketball season is ending. Are you still going to show up for the frat parties?" she asks with a sarcastic smile. She and I have talked about my relationship with Dylan. She knows it centers on the games we attend together. I look over to Dylan and he's laughing as Miller relays a story. His eyes meet mine and I smile at him before answering Makayla.

"Of course," I say, but it isn't true. I nudge her and she figures out that I can't talk about it in front of Candice. "Are you seeing anyone? I haven't seen you for a while."

"No. Miller and I have a tech elective together. He reminded me about the party."

"But you're not here with him, are you?" asks Candice, standing up and straightening her skirt.

Makayla shakes her head and says, "No. We're just buds." Then she looks at me for an explanation of Candice's question.

"I'm going to find Scott. It's someone else's turn to man the keg," announces Candice before whisking off in the direction of the keg.

"Scared I'm going to sink my teeth into Scott, I guess. As if I would touch him without latex gloves on," Makayla says once we're alone.

"She's just possessive of all the guys who live here. She and Scott aren't going to last much longer. Besides, she knows she can't compete with your gorgeous skin and silky black hair." Makayla is stunning. "I'm sure Candice is just jealous." I lean back against the couch. The boots I have on are one of the most comfortable pairs I own, and yet still aren't meant to be worn longer than an hour or two. There is no way that I am walking around barefoot on this floor though, so I am going to have to endure my wardrobe choice. "Is your brother dating my roommate Alli or are they really just going out for coffee?"

"What...my brother's dating someone?"

"Neil gets coffee with Alli almost every day. He was her teaching assistant in Organic Chemistry last semester. I just can't figure out if they're dating or not."

"Good luck with that one. He never tells me anything."

I laugh because she seems so different from her brother. He is very reserved and she is not. It is hard to imagine they come from the same gene pool. We talk about what we will be doing this summer after graduation and I spill the news about the two fellowships I have been offered. She's doing a paid internship in hopes that it will lead to her ideal engineering job. The internship is in Texas and it brings on a discussion about moving away from our families.

"I can't wait to move," I tell her. It's the absolute truth. "My family hates me."

"What about your parents? Won't you miss them? I'm pretty sure I'm going to have to call mine a couple of times a day, just because they won't be able to check up on me unexpectedly."

Her comment makes me think of Alli whose parents are crazy overprotective. Maybe that's why she gets along with Makayla's brother. They can relate to each other's insane parentage. "Mine don't even know I'm still living in the Cities. Moving won't change anything."

She chuckles not quite believing me, but I give her a sincere glance and her expression changes to sympathy.

"I'm okay with not having a close family, honestly." Just as the words escape my mouth I feel the hair on the back of my neck prickle. It can't be. I'm afraid to look. Makayla must be able to read the fear on my face because her eyes are wide. Then his lips touch my cheek and his arm wraps around my shoulder. The bottom of my stomach drops as he reaches a hand out to introduce himself to my friend.

"Hi. I'm Wes, Meg's brother."

My head begins to shake uncontrollably. "No. No. You can't be here. You have to leave. Right now. You have to leave."

"Excuse us for a second," he says to Makayla. He braces my shoulders in his hands and whispers into my ear, "It will be fine. I've got this." He's got a plan—I can hear it in the tone of his voice. He always has a plan. I don't know if it will be good for me or not, though.

I close my eyes trying to gain strength and when I open them, Peterson is glaring at me over Chase's shoulder. Years ago, I decided never to get into a self-sabotaging situation ever again. But as I open my mouth, I know that is exactly what I am about to do. There is no escaping this without blood if

I don't. I step back away from Chase and plaster a smile to my face. I glance up at Peterson and he looks as if he is ready to punch the blonde standing in my personal space.

"Dylan, this is my brother, Wes. Wes this is my boyfriend, Dylan."

Peterson's jaw softens at my label and I know I've averted a fight. When Chase turns to shake Dylan's hand, his eyes bulge out of his head and I have to fight back the laughter in my throat.

"Meg didn't tell me you were an entire football team," Chase says extending his hand. He leans into me and adds, "Seriously, you should have told me, Sis."

I don't feel sorry for him. He brought this on himself by showing up here. He's lucky I didn't tell Peterson who he really is.

"Scott says you and Megan went boarding on Tuesday. Maybe we all could hit the slopes sometime before the runs close for the season. Is Monday good for you?"

I take a breath and my heart rate starts to come back down. I look over to Makayla. She's smiling and shaking her head as if she doesn't believe any of it.

"Come on, Wes. Let's get you a cup, and you can fill in all the holes in what Megan has told me about her family."

As Chase follows Peterson to the kitchen, Makayla sidles up next to me.

"So who is the hot preppie? He's not your brother. He was completely undressing your backside as he approached you. Unless that's why you hate your family? You can tell me. I won't judge."

"I may as well just leave now and wait for this whole situation to implode." I roll my head back with exasperation.

"Are you dating them both?"

"No. Chase is my ex. We dated for three years in high school. I ran into him recently, but I'm not dating him."

"Well he definitely wants you."

I swallow hard, not wanting to accept her words.

"You're not afraid to leave the two of them together?"

"I'm terrified. Chase is a really good liar though." I position my body so

I can see them through the kitchen door. Peterson is laughing and patting Chase on the back as if they are best buddies. "This is going to end what Dylan and I have. I don't like lying to him."

"Wasn't it going to end at the end of basketball season anyway?"

"Yes, but on my terms, not Chase's. I still wanted to be friends."

"You seriously believe that's possible? Friends with exes doesn't ever work."

"We'll maybe I'd throw some benefits in once in a while."

"That just makes it worse, Megan. Someone always wants more."

"But it's usually the woman and that's not me. I'm fine with casual. It's easier. Relationships get too complicated when more is expected." Who was I trying to fool? Peterson already wanted more. That was the whole problem. I tilt my head toward the kitchen. "Let's go get our cups filled. I can't let them be together too long. Will you help me? I need to talk to Dylan alone."

"Sure, I'll distract him. I don't care what his name is." Makayla smiles and follows me into the kitchen.

Of course, Candice has found Chase. She's sitting on the counter right next to where he's standing and is practically hanging on him, right in front of Scott.

"Megan, your brother showed up after all. And he's not dating a stripper," states Candice in her "you're so stupid" voice.

"She wasn't a stripper," Chase adds. "She danced ballet as one of the Sugar Plum Fairies in the Nutcracker. She was really flexible, but I'm no longer seeing her. Dylan, has Meg ever showed you her dance moves? She took dance for years. Her troupe even won state one year."

Dylan looks at me as if I've been keeping pertinent information from him. "Nope. She never mentioned she was a dancer." His face scowls and I'm not sure what he is thinking, but he seems mad.

I slip my hand into his and whisper in his ear. "Can I talk to you in private?"

He nods, his jaw tense. He follows me out of the room, and Chase calls, "Don't do anything I wouldn't do, Sis."

Dylan's hand balls into a fist as we head up the stairs. He drops my hand, before reaching for the key in his pocket and opening his door. I squeeze through the doorway first and sit against the headboard on his bed, pulling my legs up and wrapping my arms around them. He closes the door and locks it, but doesn't come any closer to me. He leans against the door with his arms crossed over his chest. *He knows.*

"So what do you need to tell me in private?"

"Would you come sit on the bed?"

"I don't know if I want to, Meg."

"Don't call me that."

"Sorry. Only your *brother* can call you that?"

"He's not my brother." I watch his face, looking for relief that I'm telling the truth, but he's still fuming.

"You don't think I know that?" He combs his fingers through his dark hair and glares at me. "You bitch and moan every time one of the guys makes a blonde joke at your expense, but you look at me and think I'm some dumb jock or I've taken too many concussions on the football field. No guy would ask about his sister's dance moves and I recognized his voice from the phone call last weekend. I'm not stupid. "

"I know you're not stupid. I didn't invite him here." I take a deep breath, in through my nose and out through my mouth. I can't defend this.

"Candice did. But you went snowboarding with him." He moves to sit down on the bed and it dips, almost tipping me over. "Are you sleeping with him?"

"No. You are the only one I'm sleeping with."

"How does he know so much about your family? You've barely told me you have brothers. I just learned from Candice your family owns a marina on the St. Croix River. You never tell me anything personal and he knows your family intimately."

"We dated for three years."

"Well, we've dated for over a year and I've never met any of your family."

"We haven't dated that long."

"We have. We started the second home game last season. It's the end of our second season. You're the math expert, you tell me how long we've been dating."

"We were off all of last summer." I try to clarify, but it's not enough. "I was in high school and living at home when I dated him. We went to prom. I don't think my parents would have let me go if they hadn't met him. I have my own place now. You don't want to meet my family."

"Or is it that you don't want them to meet me?"

"That's not it." It's not that I'm embarrassed of him. He and my dad would easily bond over football, but I haven't told him about my mom and that's the hard part.

"Is it too big of a commitment for you? I've tried to be patient." His voice softens. "I knew you'd been burned before and I kept waiting for you to let me in. Is it ever going to happen? Because I don't know how much longer I can wait."

I lean back and stare at the ceiling. I'm silent. I don't know the answer to his question. The room is quiet for a long minute.

"Why the hell would you agree to go snowboarding with him? He's obviously the one who messed you up. Why let him back into your life? Are you ever going to be able to move forward?"

I feel my eyes well up. I don't cry, but I've been feeling sorry for myself lately and this is just the icing on the cake. "I don't know if I can have a normal relationship," I admit.

He gets off the bed. "I'm going to kill that little weasel."

"Please don't. He's not worth it."

He leaves anyway, so I take out my phone and shoot Chase a text.
Me: DYLAN IS COMING TO KILL YOU.

Within minutes of sending the text, I hear shouting escalate from downstairs and I can't deal with it. I head downstairs. Without looking toward the commotion, I find my jacket in the corner heaped with all the other coats, and slip out the front door. I don't want to hear their discussion about me and I don't want to watch Chase get bloodied. I'll text Makayla later and she'll tell me anything relevant. I start my car and crank up the music, collecting my thoughts. Why does Chase keep messing with my life? Is he the one I'm supposed to end up with?

I carefully back my car into the alley and head to the rental. I just want to go to bed. I don't know what is wrong with me. When I reach the house, there is, of course, nowhere to park. I find a spot a block and a half down and trudge my way down the slush-covered sidewalk to the front door. Jeff and Jessica are nowhere to be found. They must have taken it to their room like I suggested.

I lock my bedroom door behind me and unzip my boots before taking off my jacket. What did I do to deserve the life I've been dealt? I wish I knew so I could change it. I collapse on my bed, slipping my boots off as I sink into my pillow, exhausted. That's when the texts pour in.

Makayla: Holy crap. Are you Okay? I guess you told Dylan.
Peterson: Where'd you go?
Chase: Thanks for the warning. It could have been ugly. But don't worry about me. I'm quick, Sis.
Chase: Does he greet all your family members with his fists or did Wes do something to piss him off?
Chase: Why are you keeping the giant from your family?

I wish he would stop texting. I'm not going to answer him. He's such an ass.

Peterson: Did you leave with him?

I don't feel like getting into this right now. I silence my phone and go to bed.

Megan

I feel hung over as if I drank much more than one beer last night. My head is heavy. I'm not sure if it is the burdening thoughts about how to fix what happened last night or if I'm worried about what I might do being free of Peterson. I can't think about it. I throw on a sweatshirt and a pair of jeans before heading downstairs. I can smell the coffee as I round the corner into the kitchen. Jeff is sitting at the table reading the BBC News app on his phone as Jessica sits next to him peeling back the skin of a grapefruit. They're like an old married couple. They let me fill my mug and take a few sips of coffee before asking me why I came home early.

"I told you I was coming home." I try to smile, but I know it's not very convincing.

"Did you break it off with Peterson?" Jessica asks, looking up from her grapefruit.

"No. Not officially, but we had a fight." I can't mention Chase. Jessica would blame me for letting him back in my life. She wouldn't understand why I would allow it. *Hell, I don't understand it myself.*

"Don't do it, Megan. Don't let Chase mess up the good in your life."

I nod as I take another sip of coffee. I know she's right, but I'm not going to let her know just how involved Chase was in causing the problem last night. The truth is that I don't see myself being with Peterson five years from now. I can't change how I feel about him. We never had the spark Chase and I had. *I'm so screwed.*

"Are you going to the game tomorrow?" asks Jessica, probably trying to gauge how big of a fight we had.

"I'm not sure. I'll have to figure that out." I sit down at the table across from Jeff and slide my phone from the back pocket of my pants. When the screen lights up, I see five more messages. Four are from Chase and one is from Makayla. Peterson didn't send me anymore. I click on Makayla's. I'm not going to check Chase's.

Makayla: Dylan is pissed and drinking his aggression. Hope you know what you're doing. Let me know if you want an update.

I type out a response to her text from last night just to feel out Peterson's mood.

Me: What happened after I left?
Makayla: I don't want to tell you.
Me: That bad? Did he hit someone?
Makayla: Kind of.
Me: Just tell me.
Makayla: After you left, he and Scott got out the beer bong and got stupid.
Me: How stupid?
Makayla: I left the party when Dylan carried the sophomore who had been making out with him up to his room.
Me: Thanks for the info.

I have nothing else to say. I shake my head in disbelief, stuffing my phone back into my pocket. I'm numb. I sit in silence sipping my coffee. I can feel Jessica's eyes on me, but I can't even look across the table at her and Jeff. I will never have what they have.

I hate men.

The rest of the weekend crawls by as I finish my paper and get all the data from the marina's books transferred to the simpler spreadsheet. There are some mistakes in the books, but nothing that screams embezzlement. By Sunday morning, I've run out of ways to avoid my roommates. I think about going to the campus fitness center, but I don't want to run into anyone from the party there either.

Peterson has just sent me a text and it makes me want to punch him in the balls. I realized now the walls I erected to protect me were a lie. I thought our casual relationship kept me from getting hurt. I believed it wouldn't bother me if we saw other people, but I was wrong. Even though our chemistry wasn't great, I still cared about him.

Peterson: Are you coming to the game, lucky charm?
Me: Why don't you bring the sophomore you fucked? Maybe she
*   can be your new lucky charm.*

Does he think I wouldn't find out? I can't believe he's acting as if nothing happened. I know he never would have brought that girl to his bed if I had responded to his text, but I refuse to take the blame for his actions. Several minutes pass before his next text comes.

Peterson: We need to talk. I'm coming over.

Screw him. I don't want to see Dylan. All I can think about is him taking that girl to bed. He acted as if I was the one holding back and then he does that. I know it's my issue. I tried to tell myself I wasn't getting attached. Everyone I care about leaves me. It's just easier not to care.

My issue.

I grab my coat and purse, and head out the door. My car is still a block and a half away because I didn't leave the house at all yesterday. When I finally reach it, I get in quickly knowing Peterson could be coming around the corner at any moment. I take off as soon as my seatbelt clicks. I don't know where I am going, but I can't be at the house when he arrives.

I have to get away from campus. There were too many people at that party and I don't want to run into any of them. I just drive. When I drive past the marina, I realize where my subconscious mind has taken me. The riverfront park just above the City of Stillwater's lift bridge is barricaded by a road closed sign. It seems early for the road along the river to be closed. The St. Croix River floods every year, but right now, the water laps well below the levy walls.

I park my car in the public lot and walk past the road barrier to the sidewalk running parallel to the river. I find a bench about half a block down and stare out over the dark water. The water rushes unencumbered by anyone else's agenda on its path to join the Mississippi. It's calming and disturbing all at the same time.

I wonder if the river called to my mom like it does to me. Was she drawn to it? Or am I drawn to it because of her? Watching the water churn, I can't help but think about how different my life would be if she had just stayed. She was always the one I confided in. Sure, I had friends, but I never really relied on them for advice until she was gone. What advice would she give me about Peterson? Would she tell me men are pigs and he's the best I can hope for? Or, would she tell me to cut what strings I have left with him? What would she tell me to do about Chase? I imagine she would have a lot to say about him.

Since it's early March and the ice has already cleared most of the river, I am sure my family is working hard to get the docks in at the marina. I'm relieved to no longer be a part of that madness. If I learned anything from my mother, it's that I will be much happier doing what *I* want. This time next year, I will be immersed in my studies thousands of miles away from here. I wonder if I will miss the river.

I can't even think straight today. I didn't expect Peterson to bring another girl to his bed. I wouldn't have predicted it and I wouldn't have predicted it would trouble me so much. I always knew it would end. I just thought it would be me ending our relationship. That must be why I'm so messed up.

The wind picks up and the cool air stings my cheeks. I should probably go. I just don't know where to go. My phone buzzes and I check it because that is who I am. It's a text from Alli.

Alli: Peterson is here and says he won't leave until he talks to you.
Me: Tell him to go fuck himself.
Me: Better yet, tell him to go fuck the sophomore from Friday night.
Alli: Are you breaking up with him because of Chase?

I'm not going to respond to that.

My phone goes off again just as I'm stuffing it in my pocket and this time it's Chase.

Chase: Why haven't you answered my texts? Is it something I did?

There's a smiley face emoji at the end. He knows exactly why I'm not answering his texts and he's trying to be cute. I walk back to my car before my phone learns a few new swear words.

Since I am not ready to face Dylan, I pull into the marina on my way out of town. I figure I should show my dad what I've found, even if it doesn't show signs of embezzlement. I know he will be here even on a Sunday afternoon. The only reason I can come home from school for the summer is because no one is ever at the house once the ice is off the river.

The bell tinkles above my head as I open the door and I can hear laughter coming from the lounge area outside the back office. As I walk in, I see my real brother Wes sitting in one of the wheeled desk chairs. It's pulled up next to the leather sofa where my younger brother Tyler lies sprawled. Standing next to them is a dark-haired woman. She's too old for either of them, maybe in her late forties or early fifties. Her tan, almost leathery skin, indicates that she doesn't use sunscreen and probably has a boat in the marina. Her face is kind and her eyes are the warmest honey color. When she sees me, her expression brightens.

"Oh, Megan, you're even prettier than your father said," croons the woman as she approaches me and pulls me into a hug. She smells of sunshine and fresh air, but I've never seen her before in my life and yet she knows my name. The fact I haven't showered today makes me wonder what my dad thinks of me. I'm not sure if I should take her comment as a compliment or an insult. She pulls back, sensing my stiffness, and adds, "I'm Joann." She says it as if her name has meaning to me.

I look to Wes and he clarifies. "Dad's girlfriend Joann."

I didn't even know Dad was dating. I'm glad he can get past what Mom did, that he has found a way to move forward. *Am I the only one still utterly destroyed by Mom's abandonment?* Maybe I'm the only one who deserves to be destroyed.

I smile and say, "It's nice to finally meet you." I have no idea how long they've been seeing each other but I figure if Dad has told her about me, then it must be a while.

"We're planning to head over to the Freight House for lunch. Please tell me you'll join us. I would love to get to know you better." Her hands are posed in front of her and she looks like she wants to hug me again.

"Are you going?" I ask Wes and Tyler.

"Nah, Braden had to run to Minneapolis for some stupid part that sheared off and as soon as he gets back, we're back to work. We're already three hours behind and it's supposed to snow tomorrow. You go," says Wes.

"For Christ's sakes, Megan. They've been dating for years and you're meeting her for the first time today?" Tyler spouts off before placing his arms up over his face as if he's blocking out my reply.

Years? How come I didn't know this? I look to Wes and one corner of his lips turns up confirming what Tyler said.

I'm an awful daughter. Why wasn't this woman at our family gatherings? When was the last time we had a family gathering? I went to Peterson's parents' house this past Christmas. The rest of my family must have gotten together without me.

The whole getting together for holidays has been all messed up since Mom left. She was always the one to host the gatherings. The first Thanksgiving after she was gone, I tried to cook a big meal with turkey and mashed potatoes, but it turned out awful. The meat was dry and the lumpy mashed potatoes stuck together like oatmeal. My brothers criticized the meal so much I vowed to never cook for them again. It wasn't as if they offered me any help in the kitchen. After that thanksgiving, I always found somewhere else to go. I have friends with normal families. It wasn't hard.

"I'm not very hungry, but I'll go. It would be great to get to know you," I agree with a smile. I guess it's time I re-engage with my family. I'm going to be leaving at the end of summer and who knows where I will end up in the next ten years. I may never get another chance.

The conversation at the restaurant is uncomfortable with Joann asking me a million questions about my life. I don't know what it is about her, maybe her straightforward, matter-of-fact attitude, but she reminds me of my mom. And even though I'm apprehensive about answering the questions, I feel an instant closeness to her.

"Your dad is always bragging about how smart you are—way too smart to be stuck working at the marina. Have you chosen where you're going this fall?"

"UCLA has offered the best package for me. I think I am set on there. It's a free ride plus a stipend. They have a great program and I have a good friend out in Los Angeles."

"That sounds wonderful. Do you know where you'll be living?"

"I don't have everything finalized, but there's a service that is helping me get connected with a roommate, so hopefully I should get it figured out before I get there."

"Megan's never had trouble making friends. She gets along with everyone," my dad says. "She's just like her mother in that way."

There it was, the first reference to Mom. I shouldn't complain. I've already compared Joann to her. I wonder how much Joann knows about what went down with my mother. I smile to hide my cringe at being compared to Mom. I think Joann senses my discomfort because she changes the subject.

"Are you dating anyone?" she asks.

"No. We just broke up. He cheated," I say. I don't want to tell them it was two nights ago.

My dad's face turns contemplative and I can't tell what he's thinking until he asks, "Was that the guy you've been dating off and on for a couple of years? Dylan, was it?"

I'm surprised he has paid attention to my love life.

"I bet there are tons of guys just waiting for the opportunity to ask you out," Joann says interrupting my answer.

"Actually, I ran into an ex and I may give him a second chance."

My dad's brow furrows and his jaw tightens. "Not Chase." It's not a question. "He cheated on you too. What makes you think he will respect you this time around?"

I'm confused. I never told him about my problems with Chase.

"Did Mom tell you about him cheating or how did you know?"

"No one had to tell me. Sure he walked the walk and talked the talk, but I could see right through him. His preppy *yes sir* attitude didn't fool me. Have you forgotten how conniving he was? He always had the answer a father wanted to hear, but I could tell it was all for show. I knew guys like him growing up, sweetheart. You can't trust them. You're not thinking about giving Chase another chance, are you?"

"No, Dad. It's a different guy." I wonder if he can tell I'm feeding him the answer he wants to hear. *I'm as bad as Chase.* The anger quiets on his face and I think I've convinced him. I better change the subject again. "How did you and Joann meet?"

"Well, Joann's brother died and since he didn't have any children, he left his boat to her. He kept the boat on Lake Pepin, but she didn't want to travel that far to use it and she moved it to our marina. She used to come in and drink coffee with me in the morning. One day, she asked me out and we've been together ever since."

"How long ago was that?" *Please don't let it be four years ago.* I don't want to blame my dad for all that went down with Mom.

Joann looks to my dad with a smile ghosting on her face. She knows what I'm thinking. "My brother passed just over three years ago. Colton and I started dating six months after that. I wasn't around when the whole fiasco with your mother happened."

Her words calm my fears and she obviously knows Mom's story.

"I would like to think your mother and I would have been friends if we had the opportunity. Just like I hope you and I can be friends."

"I'd like that too," I say.

I miss my mom and the connection we had. I used to be able to tell her anything and she offered real advice, not the carefully worded statements most parents give. She took me to the doctor and got me on the pill when I told her I was thinking about having sex with Chase. She knew how getting pregnant affected her options and she knew no matter what she wanted me to do, we lived in the real world.

When I suspected Chase had cheated on me the first time, she told me to take a two-week break from him to give me time to evaluate our bond without his influence, and to make a list of pros and cons for our relationship before talking to him about it. She also told me I needed to allow him to explain, even if I didn't want to hear his explanation. Chase and I had been going out for over a year and I was so in love with him at that point he could have given me any excuse and I would have believed him. Even with my list, he convinced me he was just flirting with the girl and the person who saw him was completely mistaken. My mom's point wasn't to break us up, but for me to look at the situation objectively, and I ended up pulling my list out several more times before I ended it with him. If I still had the list, last night's exploit would have made the con side just a little longer.

My dad, Joann, and I talk for another three hours in the restaurant. It feels good and is the longest time I've spent with my dad in years. I guess my mom isn't the only one I miss.

By the time I got back to the house that night, Peterson had left and my housemates were in their rooms. I didn't go talk to them about what Dylan said in my absence. I figured he probably brought up the fact I'd gone snowboarding with Chase, and then he'd showed up at the frat party. It made me look even worse because I tried to cover it up by saying he was my brother. I didn't want to see the judgement in their eyes.

"Are you all right?" Jessica asks as I enter the kitchen to fill my travel mug before class. I wonder what she thinks she knows.

"Yep," I lie, before turning to see her face. I take a sip of my coffee and she gives me a sympathetic smile.

"Peterson told us what happened at the party."

"Did he mention that he screwed some sophomore after I left?"

Her expression morphs from frustration to disgust as she shakes her head. "He didn't mention that."

"Scott's girlfriend invited Chase to the party. She slipped him her phone number when we were boarding. I didn't even know he would be there."

"Don't get back with Chase, Megan. He just messes you up. He's never been good for you," she says as if it's her last plea. She knows I will tune out her words eventually so she gets right to the point. My mind goes to the empty drug bag I found in my purse four years ago. Chase hurt me, more than my friends know. I can still feel the semi-rigid plastic sliding between my fingers. I can still smell the acrid aroma of the contents it once housed.

Imagine how much they would hate him if they knew everything he did. I do my best to push the memory back into the dark corners of my mind.

"I'm not." I know that's what she wants to hear. I'm still mad at him for showing up at the party, but I can't dismiss the chemistry we have, either. He is like slipping into an old pair of comfortable jeans that fit your butt perfectly.

I head to class without another word. It's late afternoon before I talk to her again. I've been worried all day I would run into Peterson. I know it would take effort on his part, but he does know my schedule and I wouldn't put it past him to ambush me outside of class.

Luckily, I don't see him. I'm not ready to talk to him.

I've just collapsed on my bed after class, content with sneaking a quick nap in before taking out my homework, when Jessica calls up the stairs that our friend Sarah is on the phone. I miss Sarah. It's been months since she moved out to Los Angeles to live with her fiancé and we hardly ever talk anymore. While Jessica is all hearts and flowers, putting her emotions out for everyone to see, and Alli is the opposite with her cold, logical view, Sarah is the middle ground. She uses both her heart and her head. I rush downstairs to join the conversation. Sarah's offered to fly all of us out to the West Coast for the weekend on her fiancé's dime. I bite on it immediately. I'd even pay my own way just to escape from this place. I wish we were leaving today.

Megan

I can't believe the size of Sarah's house—quadruple-patty, McMansion-sized. Okay, it's not really her house. It belongs to her fiancé's parents, but I read somewhere he made thirty-nine million dollars last year, which is a decent income even for a mega-movie star. Money is not keeping them from buying a house.

We eat at the house, and head to a ginormous club. It's crazy. There must be a hundred people standing outside to get in and we just walk right up to the front—while the crowd cheers, as if they are happy we're going ahead of them. It's such a weird culture. We had to pull out our IDs, but they didn't even look at them. I guess clubbing with a movie star has its perks.

Inside the club, we get whisked away to the VIP area upstairs. As we climb the open staircase, I gaze across the vast building and count eight dance platforms raised above the actual dance floors. Giant Jumbotrons on the wall capture dancers as they gyrate on the small stages. Lasers flash in all directions to the beat. I'm on sensory overload. The music is a loud, eclectic mix of familiar and amazingly fresh sounds. As we're seated, I see the section is sprinkled with young Hollywood faces. I may not know the names attached to the faces, but I definitely have seen some of them before.

After some drama with Jonathan's ex-girlfriend, Mia Thompson, who *is* so gorgeous up close that I can see why Sarah sees her as her mortal enemy, we're inundated by famous people. When Jake Gorboni plops his Adonis mass between Alli and Jessica, I think someone has slipped something into my drink. *Seriously?* Jake fricking "Gorgeous-body" Gorboni? Sarah started dating Jon last summer so I've had time to get used to him being around. Though we rarely saw him, the concept of him infiltrated our conversations all the time, He almost seems normal. But Gorboni just walking off the big screen and wrapping his arms around my friends, that's a drug induced-hallucination.

Then, within minutes of Gorboni's arrival, I see him.

The bad boy of my dreams, Ashton Post from *Impassioned.*

He saunters toward us as if he owns the club, his looks alone accounting for the arrogance about him. The rugged bone structure of his face accented by the scruff of a day-old beard makes me imagine the roughness scratching my neck as he kisses me. My eyes travel down his body and I can practically feel the silkiness of the silver gray fabric of his button-down shirt as it clings to his sculpted muscles. His tousled blond hair looks as if he just stepped off a runway, each strand placed to look sexy as hell. How many times have I woken up sweaty and flushed in the middle of the night after dreaming about him? He and a dark-haired guy sit down in the chairs at our table, and as Sarah introduces everyone, I swear he winks at me. I'm probably imagining it—a trick of the lighting or maybe the alcohol in my drink is stronger than I thought. He must know Jonathan pretty well because he calls him Will, and only those in his closest circle of friends use that nickname. His last name is Williams and his friends call him Will. It's not hard to follow.

Liam Nordstrom, the guy who brings my fantasy to life, sits across the table from me. I need to separate the character he plays from the man—the gorgeous man—who is burning me with his dark mysterious eyes. His ominous persona says *be careful, I'll hurt you,* but still it's hard to look away. Sarah's mentioned Jon's friend Liam before, but I never imagined he was my midnight fantasy. All of a sudden, Gorboni's lips are touching my cheek, pulling me out of my daydream.

Nordstrom makes a comment about nice Midwestern girls needing to stay away from Gorboni's lips and it makes me laugh thinking he's one to talk. Maybe I'm projecting his character a bit because I don't know him, but I can't help my mouth runs off at his comment.

"You know, we actually have brains and can make decisions for ourselves. We're the whole package, not the mindless plastic chicks you're used to."

He looks at me without smiling as if he's sizing me up. I just made an impression on him. I can see it in his brooding eyes, though I'm not sure if it's positive or negative. I don't want his eyes to burn me so I look away. Leslie, who is Jonathan's assistant, asks me to squish in so the other guy who came over with Nordstrom from the bar can squeeze in next to us on the couch. He's her ex-boyfriend, but he looks like he's forgotten the "ex" part. He kisses her on the lips and I no longer feel comfortable using her to escape Nordstrom's ominous glare.

I avoid looking back at him as the guys banter around me about who's a player and who's not. I'm starting to feel more comfortable until a set of twin blond pixies surround my fantasy man. One places her hands over his eyes and the next thing I know she's making out with him. Who was I kidding, thinking he was even giving me a second look? Identical twins? He is probably going to take them both home for the night. That's what his TV character would do. Actually his TV character would find a private room at the club to use—one with a bar at his exact hip height, no doubt. *Is it bad I want to join them?*

The kiss lasts way too long and I can tell it isn't the first time her lips have been on his. She's much too comfortable with his body. I wonder if they are his girlfriends or if it was just a hookup, or maybe serial hookups. Maybe he only sleeps with identical twins.

The pixy chicks don't seem to be leaving and I can't watch any longer, so I focus my attention back to the rest of the group. Gorboni drones on about the filming of his last movie. He's one of those guys who you drool over until he opens his mouth and talks. Then the drooling stops and he becomes a beautiful piece of art that you appreciate, but no longer want to buy. Apparently, his stunt double broke his arm during filming and Jake ended up finishing the scene that day without him. He had to roll down a thirty-foot embankment full of brush into a ravine and come up standing. He did it in one take, but it cost him. He shows us a scar that a sharp branch gave him and acts like someone should give him a medal because it was his blood on the film, not makeup. He sounds kind of like he doesn't deserve a man card the way he tells the story and I can't help but roll my eyes.

Just then I glance up at Nordstrom and he's staring at me, the two sisters still talking at his side. He shakes his head as if dismissing them, and they walk off into the club.

"Hey blond chick with the brain, I need some air. Will you walk with me?" he says and my heart stops. He's talking to me. Oh god, he's talking to me.

"Her name is Megan," says Jon.

I don't care what he calls me. My fantasy guy can call me anything he wants. I'm just stunned he's noticed me.

"Sorry. Megan, would you come with me to get some air? I need someone to buffer," Nordstrom asks.

I agree and the next thing I know he's grabbing my hand, saying, "I may have to kiss you, just to throw off the wolves. Is that okay?"

"Yeah…whatever." I look over to Sarah hoping she can confirm this is really happening. She just smiles. I'm pretty sure I've fallen asleep at the club and in my dream we're going to end up in a private room with a just-the-right-height-bar. My stomach drops at the thought. He interlaces his fingers with mine and I have to rethink the dream theory. He's never held my hand before in my dreams. He's held other parts of my body, but not my hand. I look around and we're not heading for a private room either, just the patio. *He really does want air.*

I always thought Sarah was being paranoid when she said people watch her every move when she's out with Jon, but she's not. I feel the eyes of every woman in the club on me right now, as if I'm on a red carpet and everyone is dying to know my name.

Two girls at the table next to the bench where we just sat down, raise their cell phones and take pictures, not bothering to turn off their flashes. How rude. I know he's famous and all, but would it hurt them to at least try to be discreet. Liam's arm is around me so I guess that makes me important somehow. This is the weirdest feeling and he doesn't even seem to notice.

"So what do you do when you're not in class?" he asks as his deep brown eyes pour into mine.

How does he know I'm a student? Is he a mind reader? I can't even think. *Breathe. In through my nose, out through my mouth.* How am I supposed to answer? "What do you do when you're not working?" I counter. Does he feel the spark I'm feeling? Or am I really just attracted to the character he plays?

"I asked you first."

Oh my god, he's hot. He looks so serious, but he has this sparkle in his eye that says don't believe a word I say—definition of hot. "I snowboard in the winter and hang out at the beach in the summer. What about you?"

"What color is your bikini?" He completely ignores my question. His smile is so damn cute. It's hot and dirty, like he can see right through my clothes.

"Why?"

"I'm just putting a mental picture together."

"What if I don't wear a bikini?"

"All the better. Swims naked. Hot." His eyebrows raise and lower, and his eyes glaze over as if he's deep in thought.

I smile at him, shaking my head and he taps his head gently against mine. He knows exactly how to play me.

"So?" I ask.

"What do I do?"

I nod.

"I club. I sleep. I hit the beach. I work on trying to further my acting career."

"You mean you work out?" I say trying to make him laugh.

"Yeah. I'll show you my favorite workout. Let's go," he says with his adorable smirk.

"You don't scare me. I'm in."

"I thought you were a nice Midwestern chick with a brain."

"Obviously, your bark is worse than your bite," I say trying to goad him. I'm starting to feel more like myself until he leans in and runs his tongue lightly over my lower lip. His hot breath smells of peppermint and lime. It's so enticing, I open my mouth to suck it in, and then his lips are on mine, pressing and claiming. *Whoa.* His tongue pushes inside pulsing electricity to the tips of my breasts. My hand brushes the scruff of his sexy, day-old beard, and he groans. Cupping the back of my neck, he pulls me in deeper. The kiss is effervescent. There is no other way to describe it. I've never been kissed like this, my whole body bubbles to attention. He sucks my lower lip into his mouth and bites down before pulling back slowly with a devious expression. That's when I feel it—my bra pops apart. The bastard unfastened it when I was distracted. I didn't even feel his hand under my shirt.

"You've got some talent, I have to admit," I say trying my hardest to glare at him without breaking a smile. He obviously knows how to kiss. "But if you were truly talented, you could put it back together, without me knowing it." He's an incredible actor to make me believe it was real. My whole body believed it. My mind reminds me I'm just a buffer to keep the girls away. *Stupid mind.*

"Where's the fun there?" he says with a very somber expression. He shrugs. "I'll try." He leans in and crushes his hot lips to mine again, all soft and firm at the same time. Then he's laughing and pulling back. *What the hell?* I want to make out in the middle of the club. I don't care that it's just for show.

"I can't do it," he admits, still laughing. "If I put my hand under your shirt again, it's not going to be in the back." His serious face lights with humor

"Fair enough. I can fix it later." He can ponder that while we sit here. As long as I don't move too much, it will stay in place for a while.

"So what are you going to be when you grow up?" he asks.

"I'm getting a degree in secondary education." There is no need for me to go into details about my double major in math. It just turns guys off. I don't need to tell a guy I may never see again I have a gift with numbers, and education is only my fallback.

He studies my face for a moment. "You're serious?"

"Yes. I did my student teaching last semester." I smile at him shaking my head as I wonder what he's thinking.

"Oh god, that's hot." He stares at me with his mouth slightly open. "I can picture you with your short skirt and low-cut white blouse sitting on top of your desk—all badass taunting your students like Cameron Diaz in that teacher movie."

I push my shoulder into his and nudge him off the bench. He catches himself before he falls and I move back over to give him room to sit down. We're both laughing. "Is everything a visual for you?"

"Yeah. Little movies play twenty-four seven. That's just how I see the world. Your students won't have a chance."

"My students could be twelve."

"And you'll satisfy their every wet dream."

"Eww. Don't talk like that."

"So I finally said something that shocks you?"

"Or disgusts me."

"Good. I like getting a reaction. What's the worst thing you've ever done?"

"I'm not telling you that."

"I'll tell you mine."

"Okay, you first."

"When I was sixteen, my parents took a trip to Milan and left me and my little brother home with the nanny."

"How old was your brother?"

"Ten. The nanny lived with us. It didn't bother me that we were left with her. She was foreign and wanted to stay in the US, pretty easy to manipulate."

I look at him with what I hope is a "shame on you" look and he just shakes it off.

"I had this huge party—three hundred people or so—hard liquor and beer everywhere. People were jumping off the roof into the pool. Someone smashed a second-floor window. We couldn't find the dog for a week. I'm still finding out about junk that happened that weekend. Anyway, being the responsible sixteen-year-old host, I got totally shit-faced and woke up in my parents' bed with the nanny."

"Eww."

"She was hot and only nineteen. It wasn't some sick cougar crap. I did it to keep her quiet. She didn't want to be deported and my parents would have made that happen if they found out. She helped me get everything cleaned up, got the window fixed, and never mentioned it to my parents."

"So you never got caught?"

"Well? Ten-year-old Seth documented the entire party with his phone. He even had pictures of the nanny and me in my parents' bed. I smashed his phone, but he had already saved it somewhere. He's been extorting money from me for almost eight years."

"I guess you wouldn't want that to hit the internet."

"It doesn't matter at this point. It can't ruin my reputation. Do you seriously not know my reputation? You know I'm on TV, right?" He holds out his hand and I take it. "Hi. I'm Ashton Post from *Impassioned*." His voice changes into the sultry baritone of his character and my panties drop to the floor.

"I've seen your show," I say, trying not to melt into a puddle because he looks and sounds just like Ashton Post. He *is* Ashton Post. I know Post's reputation, but I don't really know much about Liam Nordstrom's. By the way he's acted so far tonight, I imagine it is pretty bad. He's made out with two different girls in the last hour, including me, and the eyes of every girl we passed on the way to the patio tracked him like the sky camera on a basketball.

"I don't read the tabloids so I don't know your reputation. Let me get this straight, though. You keep paying your brother just so your parents don't find out? I can't believe your neighbors never blabbed or the police weren't called. How can that be? In Minnesota, the neighbors would be all over it."

"I'm just lucky that way. I usually scrape by." He smiles looking innocent. "What's the worst thing you've ever done?" He pushes his chin up, nodding to encourage me to spill my guts.

"Wait. Was Jonathan at that party?"

"Yep. A lot of people were at that party."

"So you're protecting everyone else too. What you did wasn't really that bad then."

"I slept with the nanny so she wouldn't tell my parents about the party. It was calculated, planned—it didn't just happen. I seduced her." His brow furrows like he can't believe I'm so dense.

"But she was the nanny. She was older and she was in charge."

"At sixteen, I was more experienced than she was. I took her virginity, and she was never in charge. She never had a chance."

"Okay. That's pretty bad, but I'm still not telling you my worst."

He turns to face me, straddling the bench and caging me with his legs as he gives me a death glare. "I just told you my deepest, darkest secret and, now you won't share yours."

"It's hardly a deep, dark secret, if three hundred people were at the party. You just managed to keep it from your parents."

He reaches up and fiddles with my dangling earring. He looks like he wants to kiss me again. "I like you, Meg."

"Don't call me that." I wrinkle my nose. Chase is the only person I have ever allowed to call me that. I told him I didn't like it, but he called me it anyway.

"It fits you. You're honest and say it how you see it."

"Whatever," I mutter under my breath. "It's tolerable."

His lips fall into a hard, straight line and he looks at me, waiting. I know what he's waiting for and I better give him something. "I don't know if this is the worst, but it made me feel guilty, and it's the only one I can think of right now." I am not telling him my worst.

A smile almost breaks on his mysterious face.

"Once, I organized an intervention on a guy I had been dating. I got his parents, his grandparents, and even his priest involved."

"You really are a good girl, aren't you? But you're trapped in that hot, tight little body."

Did he just say that? I know the skirt I borrowed from Sarah is a little short on me, but compared to the rest of the anorexic girls in this place, I look like an overweight nun. *Do I look like a nun?* I glance down at myself. No, my cleavage is showing. I look hot. *What the hell?* "Shut up." I slap his shoulder.

"What's so bad about an intervention?"

"I told everyone about his pill problem. I had been dating him for three years and had watched him spiral to what I thought was rock bottom. His parents didn't have a clue he was doing drugs. They just thought he was a slacker, but I saw how he'd changed. I couldn't get him to go to treatment by myself. He trusted me with all his secrets and I betrayed him."

"Let me guess…he went to rehab, he got help and you lived happily-ever-after?"

"No." I glare, and he raises an eyebrow. "He refused to go. He continued to use and I broke up with him. It was one of the hardest things I've ever done."

"Would you do it again?"

"I don't know. He eventually hit his rock bottom after the break up. The police found him unconscious in his car with vomit everywhere. His parents had him committed under the pretense he was trying to kill himself and he may have been. He was locked up for three days in a psych ward and they convinced him to get treatment. It was his only option. It was that or go to jail for possession."

"So why do *you* feel guilty?"

"I have to believe he never would have gotten that bad if I hadn't left him. I kept him balanced. He could have died and it would have been my fault."

"No. I don't believe that."

"He sent me a text telling me there was nothing left for him. I ignored it. I didn't even respond. I changed my number."

He looks at me his brown eyes calculating my words. "Did he come find you when he got out?"

I shake my head. "No. I let him go. I moved on. I'm just a cold-hearted bitch. I couldn't deal with it anymore." I wish I could tell what Liam is thinking. His expression is so vacant. He probably thinks I'm a prissy chick who can't deal with someone doing drugs. But that's not it at all.

"I went to rehab last year," he says as he studies my face.

"I was in a motorcycle accident and got hooked on prescription pain pills. It started to affect my sleep and work. I couldn't see the problem. I thought I could handle it—they were prescription drugs, not something I bought on the street corner. The doctor kept refilling it and I didn't think they could hurt me. But I was in a haze. Life happened around me and I didn't care. Jon's the one who convinced me I needed to break the cycle. I waited for production to end for the season, and checked myself in. Rehab was rehab, but I'm off the drugs." He picks his drink up off the bench and takes a long draw, never taking his dark eyes off mine.

"For being so dark and mysterious you sure are a sharer."

"Do you have a boyfriend, Meg?"

"Single," I answer without another thought.

He curses under his breath, as if that wasn't the answer he wanted. "You're easy to talk to." For a second, he looks like he wants to say more, then he glances around and asks, "Do you want to dance?"

Are we still at the club? I feel like we're in our own private room. This must be how celebrities cope. They filter everyone else out. The girls with the cell phones are still watching us. If I dance with him everyone will be watching and I'll totally embarrass myself. I want to say no, but I can't.

"Sure."

He grabs my hand and pulls me off the bench. I stand and realize my bra is still unhooked. Planting my feet my arm stretches out before me and I yank it back, pulling him with it.

"What?"

"My bra!"

"Come." He drags me to the patio wall, near the door, and wraps his arms around me. As he assaults my mouth with his tongue, his hands slide under my shirt. Before I realize it, my bra is fastened and his hands are on my breasts. I pull back, breaking the kiss, and I look down to where his thumbs have found my nipples. I can't believe he is doing this in the middle of a club, and I'm letting him. I grab his arms and squeeze them.

"What?" He pulls his hands out from under my shirt and tucks them in his pants pockets. "I warned you," he says with his dark, husky voice and a mischievous look. If he wasn't so damn hot, I would have broken his thumbs. He grabs my hand and nods toward one of the dance floors.

I follow closely. It's packed. I don't have to worry about anyone seeing me dance. I can't even see my own feet. His hands slide to my lower back and I attach my hands to his shoulders as the grinding starts. The techno beat pounds in every cell of my body. Within one song, we've moved across the dance floor and he's pulling me up on the stage. *What the hell?*

Then his feet start to move and he yanks me flush against his body. He whispers in my ear, "Just relax and have fun."

He spins me around in some crazy dance move. *Oh my, he can really dance.* He pulls me in with my back to his…um…front. His arm hugs across my stomach and his hips start to swing. I can follow this. I didn't take eight years of dance for nothing, though that was a long time ago. My arms shoot up and wrap around his neck.

"See you're a natural," he says. "I'm going to fling you. You ready?"

I am so not ready, but I nod anyway, and then I'm flying across the stage, spinning. As I start to feel out of control our arms go taut and he yanks me back. It's swing mixed with hip hop to a techno beat and it just flows between us effortlessly. We are amazing together. Two girls climb onto the small round dance floor with us. Liam drops my hand and turns his attention to them for just a moment. I turn my back and feign I'm pouting with my lip out, but my hips are still moving. He comes to me, grabs my hips and pulls me flush against him again. I thought Chase held the reins to my body, but I was wrong. With just a touch, my body knows just what to do, how to move. It's as if Liam completes a circuit with me and parts of my body fire that I didn't know existed.

The other two girls dance around us as he kisses my neck and his fingers run down my sides. His lips graze my ear and he says, "Don't be too obvious, but look at the screen. You're on camera."

"No," I tell him. And I don't look. I can't even believe I'm doing this and if I look I'll probably freeze up. We buzz through three more songs. He is an incredible dancer. I've never known a guy who could actually dance. Our bodies are in perfect synch. He spins me one last time and then he just jumps off the stage. Of course, he lands perfectly on his feet. Security clears a hole around him and he stands with his arms out for me.

I can't believe I'm doing this. He motions with his fingers for me to jump and I jump. I'm flying through the air and I think I've changed my mind. I just want to climb down now. I want out of this, but I'm already committed.

Liam's arms pluck me out of the air and he plants a kiss on my forehead as his arms wrap around my back. *Oh my god.* That was the wildest thing I have ever done. My heart is racing. I feel so alive.

"Can we do that again?" I ask, as I try to catch my breath. He looks surprised by my question.

"I don't want to be too exposed. I usually limit myself to once every two months and tonight was the night."

"So that was legal?"

He nods. "I get paid to show up here. And If I dance on stage, I make more."

"You are such a prostitute. You know that, right? I thought we were going to get kicked out for climbing on the stage."

"The cameras caught you jumping into my arms. I deserve to make double for our spectacular show." The corner of his lip turns up and he glances back up at the dancers on the stage.

"I was so scared you were going to drop me. I didn't hurt you, did I?" I'm used to Peterson carrying me around, but he's got eighty pounds on Nordstrom.

He grabs my hand and places it on his bicep. "Feel this." He flexes and I squeeze. "I could have caught you with one arm."

Wow, his arms definitely could support me and there goes the tingling in my core. "All right, you're buff," I say. "Can we hit the ladies' room?" I'm sure my makeup is sliding down my face and I need to check my bra.

"I didn't know you were into public bathroom sex. I thought you were a good girl from the Midwest. But okay, whatever you want."

"Shut it." He always has a comeback, doesn't he?

He leads me past the guard at the bottom of the stairs to the VIP section. Hand in hand, we ascend. I can see my friends sitting at the large table as we climb, but no one looks our way. I wonder if they saw us dancing on one of the big screens. I still can't believe I did that. As we near the restrooms, I start to worry he wasn't joking about the bathroom sex. Though, I don't know if I would say no. He stops in the hall outside the ladies' room, his body caging me against the wall.

"How long are you going to be in L.A., Meg?" he asks, pushing my hair behind my ear and smoothing my sweat curls. *Yuck. But the gesture is sweet.*

"Just the weekend."

"That's too bad," he breathes an inch from my lips. He crushes his body against mine before his lips follow. The kiss burns with hunger as his tongue completes an inspection of my mouth. He breaks away and straightens my shirt, looking around. I didn't realize his hands were roaming again.

"What was that for?" I ask. I hope he's not really expecting bathroom sex. It sounds hot in theory but I'm pretty sure the reality would be gross.

"I just want you to consider the possibilities while you're in there."

"Oh, I will," I say as I slide through the door opening.

I head for the stall right away to make sure my lady parts are in the right place after my wardrobe malfunction and everything seems to be in the correct position. When I find my way to the sinks, to wash my hands, the bimbo next to me is sizing me up. *What is her problem?* The look she gives me is disturbing. She is either going to mug me right here in the bathroom or ask me out. I do my best to ignore her and walk to the mirror to check my makeup. I wipe my damp hands in my hair. I'm so sweaty that it can't hurt and I don't see any towels.

My hair is a mess, and I bend over to try to fix it. When I stand back up the chick from the sink is standing next to me again. I fold my arms in front of me and with my coldest glare, I ask, "Can I help you?"

"So you're Nordstrom's blonde flavor of the week?" She says it like she was last week's flavor.

"The night," I say. "Just the night. A week is too big of a commitment for me."

"I haven't seen you around. Are you new to L.A.?"

"Nope. Just visiting." I take out my gloss and run the tip across my lower lip. My answer must be what she wants to hear because she smiles and her attitude toward me seems to change.

Her friend joins us and pulls a small plastic bag from her clutch. "I've got the latest and greatest in designer sweets." She places one of the fuchsia-colored capsules under her tongue and adds, "They're a cross between molly and purple fizzles. You want one? My treat." She hands one to last week's flavor and holds one out to me. I have no idea what a purple fizzle is.

"No. I'm good," I say, rubbing my lips together and stashing my gloss in the tiny bag slung across my left hip. I feel sorry for them—so eager to fit in they can't just be themselves.

"She won't need it, Chelsea. She's going home with Nordstrom."

The girl nods.

I'm pretty sure I won't be going home with him, but it's intriguing to think I wouldn't need to be high to enjoy myself. If his dancing is any indication, he's got to be pretty good in bed. My phone buzzes in my purse and I take it out to check it. It's a text from Sarah.

> Sarah: *Jon just called for the car. We're leaving in a few minutes and*
> *you're coming with us. Drag Liam along too. We're his ride.*
> Me: *Be right there.*

My phone is still in my hand when I find Liam. "Sarah says they're getting ready to leave and we're your ride," I tell him, holding my phone out to show him the text.

"Hmm. I guess Nak is finally making the move to get back together with Leslie. He's my roommate and my ride. He wouldn't have left with anyone but her."

He snatches my phone and starts typing on it. What is it with guys helping themselves to my phone? He poses next to me and snaps a picture. Now he's typing again.

I smile and hold my hand out. "I hope you didn't send that to your mother, because I'll tell her what you did with the nanny."

"You'd do that?"

"In a heartbeat."

"You *are* a cold-hearted bitch. I like it."

He snakes both arms around my waist and pulls me in. His fingers curl under the edge of my shirt, as he stands unreadable in front of me. He doesn't seem to understand the concept of personal space, or maybe I *am* a nun. I bet he's used to women submitting to his every desire. He has all the moves to turn them to mush. I wish I could tell what he is thinking. His dark brown eyes search my face.

"I've had a really good time with you tonight. Can I have one last kiss before we go back?"

I nod. I'm sad our time together is ending. If he wanted me to go home with him, he wouldn't ask for a last kiss. His lips brush mine and I'm sucked back in. They're soft, but commanding. His tongue grazes just inside my lips and goes no further. My whole body tingles. It is the most sensual kiss I have ever experienced.

I fight to keep my thoughts coherent. If I break it off first, I'm still in charge. I don't want to, but I pull back just as he pushes forward. "We should get back," I say against his lips.

He cocks his head slightly, like he can't believe I just broke off the kiss, and looks out into the club. I take off toward the table before he can kiss me again, his hand finds the small of my back, and he tucks a finger under the waistband of my skirt. He's right beside me as we reach the table, but something is different. The familiarity he showed me minutes ago is gone.

Liam

I'm so screwed. I admit it. Megan intrigues me. She's different than what I expected. She's one of Sarah's best friends and I thought she would be more like Jonathan's fiancé, smart, but sweet, and a little naïve. Meg's fierce, though, and not in a street cred sort of way, but in an *I can read every thought in your head because I am so smart and I will always be ten steps ahead of you—so don't even try to hide behind your brooding persona. It won't work with me.* Yeah, that's definitely the vibe I get from her.

If I'm being honest, I just needed a blonde to buffer for me. It's the first time I've seen Tara and Tina since the night Tina drugged me and I needed to get away from the evil twins. I'm not about to forget anytime soon how they used me. But, leaving the safety of the VIP area and joining the masses downstairs without a girl on my arm is never a good idea. Yeah, she's beautiful. Her long legs and hauntingly gorgeous blue eyes drew me to her and she was just sitting there—the only blonde in the group besides Leslie, and it looked as if my roommate had already reclaimed his ex. I'd be lying if I said her comment about not being some plastic chick didn't catch my attention. She's got this antagonistic playfulness that is so hot and from the second she opened her mouth, I knew she was trouble.

Normally, this wouldn't be a problem. I'd just hook up with her and get her out of my system, but I can't do that with this girl. First, she's probably too smart for me, and second, she's off limits. A couple of weeks ago Jon, Sarah, and I were talking over drinks about their upcoming wedding. Sarah had just finished telling me about her bridesmaids. It's not the first time she'd talked about her friends. She's very close to them and pretty much trusts them with all her secrets. Suddenly, Jon got really serious. "Sarah's friends are like sisters to her. That makes them like sisters to me, too. No sleeping with them. Just so you know, I'm talking to all the groomsmen, not just you."

At the time I thought, wow, that's blunt and a bit unforgiving, like my parents. It's not as if I'm our buddy Nick. I don't sleep with every girl I meet, not even every blonde. But the look on Jonathan's face when I asked her to buffer for me, reminded me quickly that she's a protected class, not to be messed with. He nonverbally told me with just the tone of his voice to keep it PG, or better yet G, and I planned to do just that. But, she kept taunting me, challenging me, as if she wasn't scared of me at all. That's when I slipped. I wanted to prove to her that maybe she *should* be more careful with guys like me. So I leaned in for a quick kiss just to exert my dominance and she met me with the same fierceness I had seen in her taunting. And when her tongue slipped into my mouth, it sent an unexpected shock right to my dick.

PG, PG, I chanted in my head, even as I kissed her the second time, cupping her perfectly rounded breasts, and thumbing the tips to stones. I couldn't help myself. When she grabbed my hands and stopped me, I wanted her even more. What is wrong with me? I'm so used to girls just giving me whatever I want that when one challenges me, it turns me on. *It's got to stop.*

And I tried to stop it. I brought her out on the dance floor hoping she had no rhythm. Okay. I may have chosen the one dance area whose monitors can't be seen from the VIP area, because I didn't want Jon to see us, but I wasn't trying to be deceitful, just cautious.

Nothing turns me off more than a girl who has no ability to dance. You can tell a lot about how a girl is in bed by the way she dances. If a girl just stands there barely moving while I dance around her that's how she'll be in bed. If she flails wildly with no direction, that's how she'll be in bed. But Meg? She blew me away with her ability to match my moves and anticipate what was going to happen next. And when I brought her up on stage, she didn't even care that she was on camera. The dance was for me, not the audience. Now I can't stop thinking about being inside her and that can't happen. She's like Jon's sister for God's sake.

I'm pretty sure I'll be camping out at Jon's tonight, now that Nak's abandoned me at the club. Nobody is going to want to drive all the way out to Malibu to bring me home. I could take a cab, but I hate cabs and cab fare to Malibu is ridiculous. Maybe I can sleep at Jake's, but it would make more sense just to stay at Jon's. I stay there all the time. I even keep a toothbrush there. The only problem is, Meg is staying at Jon's. Which means I'm going to need to work harder to stay away from her, even if I don't want to abstain.

When we finally get past the paparazzi on the sidewalk and load into the back of the oversized SUV, the girls are at each other's throats. I've never seen Sarah mad before and I don't think I ever want to see her mad at me. She starts ripping into the redheaded chick about the kiss she and Jake posed for on the sidewalk. The paps blocked our exit on our way out. One of the bouncers had mentioned they were shorthanded tonight so it didn't surprise me when the paparazzi overtook our exit. The guys with the cameras were all jacked up because Jonathan rarely comes out to the clubs and they all wanted to be the first to document it. All the camera guys want is something they can sell and in all honesty, I was getting ready to strip naked if it would satisfy them enough to let us through to the car. Fortunately, Jake dipped Red back in an impressively intense lip lock to get the vultures to open our path and they did.

That was what Sarah was upset about. We all knew the pap shots would be online within the hour, but I didn't understand why that was a problem until Meg explained it to me.

"Alli's parents are crazy overprotective. If they find out about the pictures online they will go into lockdown mode."

I give her a questioning look.

"I'm serious. She will probably have to move home or something. The girl had a ten-thirty curfew on weekends in high school. If they were my parents, I would have made a sex tape at sixteen just to piss them off."

Her explanation doesn't help my predicament. Now all I can think about is making a sex tape with her.

"You're thinking about the sex tape, aren't you?" she whispers in my ear.

I laugh because she obviously read my mind. "It would be good," I say with a cough to cover my words. I want to tell her exactly what the video would include but I need to keep it PG, especially in front of Jon. *PG* I join into the conversation discussing the photos hitting the internet. Red is not only worried about her parents seeing the pictures but also concerned about how the shots could affect her after she finishes her degree and becomes a doctor. She seems to think kissing a movie star on the sidewalk outside a club may come off as less than professional. I suggest that she becomes a plastic surgeon because the pictures could help her credibility that way.

Gorboni can't understand why Red is embarrassed to have the pictures go public and shakes his head in disbelief. I don't blame him. I've never dated anyone who was ashamed to be seen with me. I wonder what Meg's thoughts are about pictures of us. It's strange to me she didn't take a selfie of us together. That is the first thing most girls do, but she didn't even ask for one. If I hadn't taken the shot outside the bathroom and texted it to myself I wouldn't even have one of her.

With Jon distracted giving instructions to the driver about going back to his place, just as I predicted, I pull out my phone and take a picture of her.

"You've got a great smile. You should show it off," I tell her and it's true. Her lips are perfect, not the too big, artificially plumped ones that girls try to convince the world are beautiful, but in reality just look like a blowup doll's. Meg's lips fit her face perfectly and her blue eyes sparkle with brilliance. She can tell stories with just her eyes. I stroke the back of her neck with my thumb and she shivers. I hope no one notices our subtle touches. I can't help that I'm drawn to her.

When we get to the house, I feel a bit more relaxed sitting around the pool. I find I like talking to Meg and even when I can't touch her, she still intrigues me. *Such a foreign concept.*

Chapter 10

Megan

I can't believe Alli and I are playing strip poker with Liam Nordstrom and Jake Gorboni. This is crazy. I'm good at poker and they don't stand a chance. My brothers taught me how to play at the age of four and I've been beating them ever since because I count cards.

Here we sit in our swimsuits, under a wood and fabric pergola—the dark illuminated only by the glow from the pool. At least Alli and I have suits—Nordstrom and Gorboni are in their underwear. It's going to be a quick game. I almost feel bad for them. Jake just dealt our first hand and I somehow pulled off a full house without any pickups.

"Explain it again, the order of the cards. Two pair isn't as good as a straight, right? And does a straight have to be in the same suit?" I ask trying to make them believe I don't know how to play.

"Come sit on my lap and I'll talk you through it. We can work as a team," says Liam.

"No. I want to do this myself." He's warming up again since Jon and Sarah went to bed. He hasn't kissed me once since we got back to the table at the club and he's barely touched me, except for during the game of chicken in the pool. Now his feet are entwined with mine under the table and his dark brown eyes are burning holes in my skimpy swimsuit.

Liam explains how the cards play out and I ask another stupid question just for fun. Alli rolls her eyes at my question. She and I have been in this position a few times before. I know she will drop out early and even if she loses, she probably won't give up all her clothes.

Liam reaches for his button-down shirt and slips it over his shoulders. I can tell he has nothing or he wouldn't be trying to load on the layers.

"Uh uh. We play with what we start with. You can't add clothes as you go," I say.

"Then you take your top off and we'll be even. Otherwise, I'm going to start with just as many as you," Liam says without a hint of humor. He definitely has nothing in his hand.

"Fine."

We worked out a system where each player gets three dollars to bet. After the dollars are spent the player either has to fold or call. The winner of the hand gets to pick the person who loses an item of clothing and wins the item. After the hand, everyone gets their money back for the next round.

"Do you want any?" Jake asks.

I shake my head and say, "I pass. Is that the right term?" I look up and meet Alli's eyes. She looks away. It's just a show.

"Give me two," Liam says, laying two cards on the table and picking up the cards Jake passes him.

"I'll take three," Alli declares and Jake hands them to her.

"And two for the dealer," says Jake. He looks up from his hand. "Megan?"

"One dollar," I say and lay a bill in front of me.

"I'm in, and I raise a second." Liam lays two bills in front of him.

"I've got nothing." Alli lays her cards on the table face down.

I hope she realizes she can still lose her clothes even if she folds. The only way to win at this is to take major risks and win as many hands as possible.

"I see your two and raise one." Jake lays three bills on the table. "A pair of kings." He lays his cards face up. "You're up, blondie." He looks over to me.

I place my bills, lay my cards on the table and glance at Liam. "Show me what you got."

"You've got to be kidding." Liam sees my cards and slaps his two pair down, shaking his head.

"Beginner's luck," I say, and it really was luck. I can tell he's disappointed I won't be the one losing my top. I hold my hand out and he shrugs out of his shirt. Glaring, he hands me the shirt and I slip my arms into the silvery gray sleeves. It is almost silky and it smells clean, like expensive cologne— just like him. I hold the collar next to my nose and take a deep breath, staring into his eyes. Liam smiles.

Four hands later, Liam and Alli are both out and are each wearing a blanket. I've lost my top, but I still have my suit bottoms and Liam's shirt. Jake hasn't lost anything. I'm sitting on Liam's lap and Alli is on Jake's.

This game has been more about luck than poker skill. The setup is totally messed up. I have nothing, not a single face card—eight high. I know the cards that have been played and what cards Jake most likely holds. I flash Liam my cards, and he whispers, "Let's go to bed." I thought he would at least wait until I lost my bottoms so he could sneak a peek. The fact he doesn't could be taken two ways—either he doesn't want to see or he doesn't want Jake to see. I hope it's the latter.

"I'm out." I lay my cards down and rise out of the chair. Liam follows.

"Hey you owe me something," says Jake holding out his hand.

Liam slaps his hand and says, "We're going to bed." He bends down, scoops up his boxer briefs and slips them on, without a hint of modesty, as I watch. Holy hell he is gorgeous. Then, he wraps his arms around me from behind and envelops me in the blanket he's wearing. I'm flush against his almost naked body and my body lights with energy.

"Goodnight," I say making eye contact with Alli.

She smiles, raising her eyebrows. I know she'll be okay. She comes off as this organized, type A, neurotic, pre-med-student, but that's not the real Alli. She's had her share of hookups. Not that often, but more than I would expect if I didn't know her. She doesn't do relationships because she doesn't make time for them, so what's a girl to do? I think it's her way of rebelling against her parents. They are completely overbearing. Her dad is a brain surgeon and her mom is a psychiatrist—both mind doctors. I don't even think she wants to be a doctor anymore. Alli is a really good student and with her parents' connections, she's sure to be accepted into the U of M's medical school. I think she's going just to please her parents, though. Her rebellious streak is why we get along. You never know what to expect from her.

Liam leads me inside the house and I grab my weekend bag off the floor by the door where it landed when we got here. I had fished my suit out of it earlier so I have to zip it before I run to the bathroom. I wash up the best I can, brush my teeth and throw on a tank with pajama shorts. When I come out, Liam is leaning against the back of the couch with his hands full of blankets waiting for me.

"I know where we can sleep. I crash here all the time," he says. Then he leads me upstairs to the music room. Guitars line one wall and there's a huge, C-shaped mustard-colored couch with a round ottoman that fits into the center. He pushes the ottoman into place and the couch now resembles a big curved bed.

I set my bag down and ask, "So you bring girls to Jon and Sarah's all the time?"

He chuckles and starts to spread a blanket onto the couch. "I wouldn't do that to them," he mutters. His expression turns serious and hard to read.

He stands in his underwear, tossing pillows onto the couch. I don't know what to expect. He's quiet and contemplative after my comment. Maybe it was too close to reality for him. He plops a couple more blankets down and runs his fingers through his hair. He looks frustrated. I jump onto the middle of the couch and spread out.

"So where are *you* sleeping?" I ask.

A smile ghosts on his face as his dark eyes penetrate mine. I return my most innocent expression and pat the blankets invitingly. He kneels next to me and stops, leaning back on his heels. His lips twitch and his brows knit.

"I need to tell you something."

"Talk," I say. He's obviously changed his mind. Was it my pajamas or my comment?

"I promised Jon I wouldn't hook up with you."

"What?"

"Jon doesn't want any of his groomsmen hooking up with the bridesmaids."

"Why does he care?"

"He doesn't want anything ruining his wedding day. He thinks I'll piss you off and it will be awkward."

"Maybe you'll piss me off by not hooking up with me. Ever think of that?" I smile, throwing my hands over my head. My posture is open and inviting and I can feel his eyes roam down my body.

He groans and looks at me longingly. "As much as I want to be with you, I can't." He sits on the edge of the bed and then turns to me.

"I don't understand why you let Jon control your sex life."

He raises his eyebrow at that. "He doesn't control me," he says with a chuckle. "We've been friends a long time and I promised him I wouldn't. I don't want to betray his trust."

We are adults. I don't get it. "We could just cuddle," I say moving over to give him room to join me on the bed.

He lies next to me, all shirtless and magnificent, and I can tell by the enormous bulge in his boxer briefs he doesn't want to just cuddle. I can't help that my finger circles his nipple causing his face to wrinkle and a soft cuss word to grunt from his throat. He looks toward the door, then back to me.

"My father's a lawyer," he says, and I have no idea what he's thinking. "If I've learned anything from him, it's that there are always ways around the law. If we utilize my mad skills and use a politician's definition of cuddling…"

"And not the high school health class definition?"

"Exactly." He climbs on top of me, straddling my hips, unbelievably gorgeous. "There are always loopholes." He leans down and presses his lips into mine—not too wet, but hungry, very hungry. Then he sits back up, pulling me with him. Both his hands caress my sides and skim up my body, dragging my tank over my head. He tosses it over his shoulder like a backward shot from the free throw line. Then, he pushes me flat on the bed and his lips are on me again, my breasts painful with want. He smells so amazing. I've never met a guy who smelled so tantalizing. I literally want to lick him.

I don't care that I just met him. I don't care what Jonathan says. I want him. The chemistry is overpowering. I've never wanted to be with a man more. I trail my hands down the hard striations of his abdomen and brush my thumbs under his boxer briefs, following the natural V indent of his muscles. I could go off just touching him, not even taking into account what his tongue is doing to my breast at this very moment. *This is crazy.* He notices my touch and halts his assault, pinning my arms to my sides on the bed.

"You're first. Those stay on," he says. "I can't cross the line with you."

I want to scream at him to cross the line. I want to cross the line more than anything I've ever wanted in my life. Then his lips are back on me and I've completely forgotten my own name. He releases my wrists, and then smooths a hand down my body. His fingers tease under the edge of my panties and the anticipation of his touch is unbearable.

An hour or so later, I'm cradled in his arms pressed firmly against his hot, shirtless body as my hand trails across his magnificent pecs. I have been utterly and completely satisfied, but I'm definitely still hungering for the one act taken off the table.

We're chatting under a shared blanket and he's telling me about his last meaningful relationship. He had dated a makeup artist he worked with. Then one day, he woke up and realized she had moved in with him. After several months of living together, she told him she was going back to her husband.

"I didn't even know she was married. She was twenty-four. Who gets married that young?" He laughs and adds, "Besides Jon and Sarah. We'd been dating for six months."

"So what did you say when she told you she was married?"

"What could I say? She moved out and got a new job. I've seen her a few times, but she's still with him."

"How long ago did she move out?"

"Nine months."

"So you haven't dated anyone in nine months. No wonder you're all hands."

"I'll show you all hands," he says as his fingers skim across my stomach. "I didn't say I haven't dated since she left." He rolls me on top of him. "Technically, I don't date and I don't do relationships. Kelsey's was the longest I've ever had, the only real relationship since high school, and it just happened. Lately, I just go out with friends and then hook up with someone I know. I wouldn't call it dating. Honestly, I don't even know how to date. You're the first person I've wanted who I didn't hook up with."

"You're quite the sharer, Nordstrom. You don't even know me and you've told me half your life's story."

"I know more about you than you think," he says.

"You do not. The only thing you know is I organized an unsuccessful intervention on an old boyfriend. I can barely get a word in with all your jabbering." I slug him in the shoulder and his smirk grows.

"If I can tell you something significant about you then you have to run downstairs and make me a sandwich." He pauses. "Without getting dressed. If I can't, I will run down to the kitchen and make you whatever you want, without clothes."

"How is that a win for me?"

He leans down and kisses me. I think he does it to shut me up.

He pulls back and says, "If you have other desires besides food, just tell me. I can accommodate."

"What I really want would break up your bromance with Jonathan. So…" I pause to think, and he smiles at my words. "Okay, I've got it. If you know anything about me, I will make you a sandwich in my birthday suit, but if you don't and I'm the one who decides what is significant, then you have to give me a backrub for a full fifteen minutes."

"I don't lose either way."

"Only a backrub, nothing else. So share what you know."

"I know purple is your favorite color."

"I never said that." How the hell does he know that? I scowl at him.

"It is though, isn't it?"

"How did you know that?"

"The bra you wore tonight is purple, your panties too. You're on a trip and you only brought underwear you like. You wanted to feel sexy at the club because you might run into…me, so you wore your favorite."

"That was just a lucky guess."

"Okay. I know you have three brothers—two older and one younger. I know your education degree is your fall back in case you decide not to get your doctorate in math, and one of the schools you are looking at is UCLA. I also know you were playing me in the card game."

I think my jaw is on the floor. I stare into his dark eyes, trying to read him. How could he possibly know that? And why did he act so surprised when I said I was an education major? What a devious liar.

"I've spent a lot of time at Jon and Sarah's lately. I was warned never to play poker with you. Sarah talks about you and your housemates all the time. I know things that would make you cringe."

"I don't want to know what you know. So don't tell me." I'll be much happier not knowing what cringe worthy crap he's heard about me. "Stupid Sarah! Now I have to make you a naked sandwich." I get up and start walking toward the door, dragging a blanket from our bed with me.

"Naked," he says grabbing the blanket and yanking it out of my hands.

"Completely?" I ask, pushing my lower lip out, and he takes pity on me.

"You can leave your purple panties on. I'm not going to make you strip, though I should."

"What if I run into Jon and he asks me why I'm walking around his house naked. I'll have to tell him the truth because I don't lie. And what will he say when I tell him one of his groomsmen has defiled me. Okay, not defiled. Everything but defiled."

"Not everything. Not even close." He pauses. "We can work up to everything after we eat." He hands me the blanket and his expression turns serious. "Don't tell Jon. He doesn't ask for much from his friends and I don't want to disappoint him. He thinks I'm a better person than I actually am."

Liam sounds so sad, like he wishes he could live up to Jon's expectations of him. Now I feel bad, like I forced him into something he didn't want to do. He is a guy, though, and I don't think guys ever do anything they don't want to do.

"I won't," I say wrapping the blanket around me. "What kind of sandwich do you want?"

"I don't know what they have. I'll come with you."

We quietly make our way down the stairs. There are no lights on in the house at all. It's creepy walking around someone else's house in the dark, like I'm breaking in or something. I hear a whirring noise and look over my shoulder to see a giant green monster bursting through the wall, his eyes stalking us with an eerie green glow. The scream that escapes my mouth is quickly muffled by Liam's hand.

"Shhh," he whispers in my ear." He eyes me and slowly pulls his hand away.

"What is that?" I ask as calmly as I can. My heart is pounding so loud, I'm sure Liam can hear it.

"It's Pedro. He's from an old movie set."

He guides me closer to it. I hadn't seen it before on the wall. It seems to come to life in the dark and it's following us with its eyes. With Liam by my side I reach out to touch its rubbery skin and I take a deep breath. It's fake. The noise was the motors on its moving eyes. I nuzzle into Liam's arms with relief and he laughs without making noise.

Once we are in the kitchen, Liam flicks on the light and I head for the fridge. He finds a loaf of bread in the cupboard and sets it on the granite counter. I pull out the lunch meat and a couple of packages of different cheeses.

"That turkey will work and the fontina."

"The what?"

"That white cheese."

I look through the packages and find the one labeled "fontina."

"And mustard." He raises his eyebrows and pulls my blanket together in the front. I didn't even notice that it was hanging open. "I'm going to grab our clothes. If you can find some kale or spinach, that would be great too," he says, as he heads out into the courtyard.

I know he's covering up the evidence of our nakedness. I don't see any lights on out there and wonder what happened to Alli. She's not in the house and she's not by the pool. Sarah said she would kill anyone who left the property and I know she meant it, so they must have headed to the main house. I finish assembling his food and fill a tall glass with water from the fridge.

When he returns, we head back upstairs and he sits cross-legged to eat on the makeshift bed. I down about half of the water and pass it to him. He takes a sip and hands it back. "Tell me about yourself, Meg." He bites his sandwich and grins.

"It sounds like Sarah already told you my life's story."

"Uh uh." He swallows his food and adds, "What makes you tic? What makes you get up in the morning?" He takes another bite waiting for me to answer.

"The sun," I answer putting on a serious expression. Why does he want to know me? It's not like we're going to see each other again—maybe at Sarah's wedding, but I don't see us dating. He's a freaking Hollywood star—why does he care what motivates me? Maybe he's studying me for an upcoming role.

His eyebrows furrow and he says, "I want to know you. You intrigue me."

"I'm flattered." I smile at him. "I don't know what to tell you." He breaks a piece off his sandwich and holds it in front of my lips. I open my mouth and he stuffs it in. His fingers linger in my mouth and I caress them with my tongue, sucking them in deeper until he groans.

"You're killing me." He pulls them out, shaking his head.

"Tell me about your family," he says, before taking another bite of sandwich.

"My dad manages a marina with about three hundred slips. He owns it with my grandfather, and my three brothers work there. I hate the marina."

"Why do you hate the marina?"

"A million reasons," I answer.

"Like?"

"It consumes. It takes and takes and takes." I don't want to scare him. I'm not some psycho-bitch. "During the spring and fall, the entire family works to get other people's boats in and out of the water. In the summer, they manage the boaters and sell slips. They have to keep the boats gassed and maintained. In the winter, they do more maintenance and major repairs. It consumes every waking moment of their lives. My family lives and breathes the marina."

"Why don't you want to be a part of your heritage? You could work in management or sales. It would have to pay better than a teacher's salary."

I chuckle. "I don't think I could work with my brothers—they're assholes," I say, lying down and pulling the blanket over me. It's only part of the reason, but he doesn't need to know the gory details about my family.

"What happened to your mother?" he says, standing up and stashing the dishes from the meal on the floor. He lies down next to me and tucks his arm behind my head.

My breath hitches. "It's not something I ever talk about." Why would he ask that? It's like he can read my mind and knows what makes me the most vulnerable. At least Sarah didn't tell him the specifics about my mother's death.

"Sometimes it's cathartic to talk."

"Not about her."

"My parents were too preoccupied with work and their social lives to be good parents, but at least I always knew if I needed them I could reach them on their cells. Was she a bad mom?"

"No, she wasn't a bad mom. She was like a best friend."

"It must have been hard to lose her. Did it happen at the marina? Is that why you hate it there?" He turns to face me and weaves his fingers through my hair. He's gentle and it feels *so* good. I'm on my back, staring up at the ceiling and he's swaying in and out of my view with a thoughtful expression. No guy has ever really asked me about my mom. His dark eyes penetrate mine. He is so damn intense. I know he won't give it up until I tell him.

"She drowned at the marina." I don't know why I'm confessing this to him.

We're both silent for too long before he asks, "Was it an accident?"

I shrug. "The police didn't think so. It's late," I say closing my eyes. I hope he'll let it go.

"I'm sorry about your mom." I feel his lips feather light on my cheek and then he whispers, "Thanks for the naked sandwich."

I awake to the odd feeling of being watched and when I open my eyes Nordstrom's mysterious brooding face is staring down at me. I hope there's no drool running down my cheek. I stretch out and he's still staring at me. I feel like I just got to sleep. I didn't even get any dream time and I'm pretty sure the dreams would have been unforgettable.

"What?" I ask, and his eyes brighten.

"I had a good time last night."

"I'm sure you did," I say, and he laughs.

He cups his hand behind my neck, leans in and crushes his lips to mine. It's full and sensual like the kiss at the club. He takes his time and my body fills with warmth and desire. I know it's temporary and I savor it.

He breaks the kiss and says, "We should get dressed."

I nod, not wanting to close this chapter with my fantasy guy. I sit up, pulling the blanket around me. As I scoot off the couch-bed and start digging through my bag for some clothes, I'm overwhelmed with sadness. Maybe even devastated. Last night, I shared more with Liam Nordstrom than I have shared with any guy since Chase and he accepted me. Famous TV star not only helped me forget about all the baggage I carry, he acted as if he was really interested in getting to know me and it was refreshing.

We're both fully dressed by the time the knocking on our door starts. It's Leslie, and Liam opens the door.

"So you're back with Nak?" Liam asks, though it is more of a statement.

"I'm crazy. I know," says Leslie.

"It's about fricking time. You never should have broken up with him."

"Why does everybody keep saying that? I didn't break up with him. It was mutual. And since when do you frickin' curb your language?"

She leans in the door to spy me. I was trying to stay out of view, but she must have seen me move.

"Good morning." I wave as I watch Liam, reading his reaction to Leslie seeing us together. He stiffens a bit.

"The girl needed a place to sleep. I just offered to share."

"I'm sure you did." Leslie looks me over and then asks, "Did you sleep okay?"

"Yes. He was a perfect gentleman." I look over at Liam and he nods in agreement, but his eyes are laughing.

"Whatever. Jon is making breakfast," she says. Liam smiles at her and the scowl on her face softens. "All right, I won't say anything."

"Thanks, Mom." He kisses her cheek.

She smiles at me and pushes Liam's shoulder away. "Do you know where Jake-the-magnificent or Red slept?" Her tone indicates that Jake is far from magnificent.

"No idea," I say.

"Will you help me find them? Sarah doesn't want to miss the fitting and the car is going to be here at ten-thirty."

"Give us a minute. We'll be right down," says Liam.

I had completely forgotten about the bridesmaids' dress fitting. It's the reason Sarah had us come out for the weekend. I look over at Liam. He's shirtless. And beautiful. And contemplative.

When Leslie leaves, he says, "Help me with these blankets?"

We fold the blankets from our bed. It is such a weird thing to do with a guy. They usually just leave them in a heap. Most guys don't give a damn about leaving a mess. He must care about what Sarah thinks of him and that is a maturity I'm not used to. I set the last blanket on the top of the pile and look up to him standing in my personal space.

He scrunches his face on one side and says, "I wanted to say goodbye before we're in front of everyone."

"It's okay, Nordstrom." I smile at his vulnerable expression. "I knew what this was. I don't expect anything."

A look of relief flashes across his face and he places his hands on my hips. "I like you, Meg. I wish things were different."

His eyes are all dark and ominous, again. I don't know what he means by different—if I lived in L.A.? If I wasn't friends with Sarah? If Jon wasn't so freaking controlling? I doubt that anything would make a difference. I stretch to reach his lips and silence him with a kiss.

His hands find my ass and pull me to him. The kiss feels forlorn and definitely final. I hate goodbye. I push back. "I had a good time too. Maybe we can hook up at the wedding." I smile and wink at him.

"Definitely." He cups my face in his hands and kisses my forehead. I can feel him separating from me and I know that is just the way life works for me. Whatever I want or love leaves and whatever is toxic I can't get rid of.

He follows me out of the room and I sense his eyes scorching my backside. It makes me smile. We meet Jessica and Leslie in the living room and they haven't been able to find Jake Gorgeous-body or Alli. *Who knows where they ended up?* Jessica said, she and Leslie checked the main house completely and they weren't there. I hope they didn't leave. Sarah will kill them. We pass through the kitchen on our way to the courtyard and Jon is beating eggs in a glass bowl with a whisk. The nonverbal exchange between him and Liam is almost comical. It would be funny if I didn't know it was about me. I head out into the courtyard to avoid Jon. I get that he doesn't want the wedding messed up, but we're adults.

I look around and it's obvious there was a party here last night. It's nothing like the frat house, but there are empty beer bottles huddled on the bar. One dollar bills pile on the table under the veranda, just where we left them last night. I don't see the blankets, though, so I think I know where Alli and Jake are. I knock loudly on the pool house door and announce, "Alli, we've got to get to the dress fitting." I hear cussing and movement and there is no way I am opening the door. I find Alli's swimsuit on the ground next to the table and toss it next to the pool house door. Jakes clothes are on the back of a chair, but he's going to have to figure that one out without my aid. I help Leslie and Jessica pick up most of the bottles and toss them into the recycling…before Alli and Jake emerge into the courtyard. Leslie assures us she will finish cleaning up if we go get ready for the fitting.

Liam

I'm sitting in the courtyard with Jonathan, Jake, Sarah, Jessica, and Leslie. Jon's made omelets with peppers and melted cheese, and I've just taken my first bite when Meg and Alli walk out of the house to join us. I've made a space for Meg next to me. I even secured a chair for her to keep her close, which she sits in. While Alli sits on Jakes lap, Meg and I barely acknowledge each other for Jon's sake, and I appreciate she is mature enough to understand the situation with him.

After breakfast, as the girls file out of the courtyard to catch their ride to the dress fitting, I can't help staring at Megan's perfect ass. It's beautiful. I can still feel it in my hands as I pulled her against me last night. It took the willpower of a saint not to fuck her senseless. *Am I fifteen again?* I'm hard just thinking about it. Most girls don't affect me like this, but she's not like most girls. It's as if she could take me or leave me. She pulled away from kisses, not just once, but a couple of times, and didn't seem at all excited I put my number in her phone. Most chicks would have squealed like a little girl at the mere thought of getting my number.

Damn. As I shift in my seat to give my boys more room, I look up to see Jonathan glaring at me—a scowl forming on his face.

"Should I be worried about you and her at the wedding? Because

I'm not getting a good feeling about last night and you don't have the best reputation with sisters." Jon raises an eyebrow before taking the last bite of his omelet.

"No. We're good." I try my innocent look, but it just makes him scowl more. "I said I wouldn't and I didn't. I'm as trustworthy as a damn Boy Scout, what more can I say?" Though, if he knew what I did do, I'm pretty sure he would punch me and I'd have to let him because I deserve it. The girl is seriously attractive. Her blond hair and sexy blue eyes definitely fit into my brand of beautiful, but she also has this wit about her that kept me guessing about what was going on in her mind. It was hard to get a rise out of her, but when I did, she always had a spot-on comeback. *And her long legs.* What I wouldn't do to have those gorgeous things wrapped around me. I shift again and Gorboni speaks up.

"Well, I'm not. It's always the quiet ones who turn out to be the screamers. Am I right?" He picks up the pitcher off the table and fills his glass half full with orange juice. "I'm telling you, she made my top ten of loudest lays."

I look to Jon. He's pinching his lower lip between two fingers and shaking his head. We hang out with Jake because he keeps the world exciting. He's not afraid to do crazy shit and he usually makes us laugh, but what Gorboni doesn't realize is that Jon thinks of last night's screamer as a sister and you don't sex talk about a guy's sister. Ever.

"So what are we killing today, zombies or hookers?" I ask to break the tension. I'm running on about two hours of sleep. I'm going to need some downtime before we work off last night's drinks in the weight room and video games will give me a chance to rest my body at least.

"Aliens." Jon gets up and starts gathering up the plates and glasses, placing them on a tray to carry them.

I stand, grab the rest of the dishes, and follow him into the house. As we near the door, I pull Jake aside and whisper, "Sarah's friends are untouchable. The less you talk about last night the better." If he actually heeds my words, it will help me too. The less Jon knows about what happened between Meg and me, the better.

Gorboni silently nods in understanding, and moves around Jon to open the door for us as his hands are empty. We spend the next two hours defending our home planet from aliens and no one brings up last night or the girls. Normally, we would be hearing a recap of Gorboni's hookup, and I am thankful he's able to keep his mouth shut today.

When we move to the weight room, Jonathan opens up about his upcoming wedding. Non-disclosure agreements have already been sent to potential guests, which when they are signed, will allow the individual to receive an invitation with the event information on it. Once the invitation is received, a second NDA must be signed in order to RSVP for the wedding. Then, when the guests mount the private jet to the destination from either Los Angeles or Minneapolis, all electronic devices must be surrendered to keep pictures or stories from leaking to the press. I know the non-disclosure agreements will be solid because Dad's firm wrote them and someone would have to be crazy to violate the contract. Jon, Jake, and I have all been to these types of events where you have to give up your phone upon entrance. It's like valet parking—they give you a ticket and you get it back when you leave. I like these kinds of events. It's freeing when you don't have to worry about someone videoing you doing something stupid. A week on a tropical island without cameras with Meg will be incredible. Damn, I'm thinking about Meg again. And all the dirty little secrets we could share with each other that cameras couldn't document.

She's like Jon's sister. I can't forget that. I've made the mistake before and it still haunts me. Not that Ellie's brother and I were ever close, but he is part of my group of friends from high school I still keep in touch with and he will be at Jon's wedding. What a mess.

Ellie and I were better friends than her brother and I ever were. I knew she was attracted to me for a long time. She'd followed me around like a lovesick puppy since we were sixteen. It made sense she hung out with her twin brother and his friends. But, when she and I were alone, she made it clear she wanted me. In my mind, she wanted sex. In her mind, she wanted a relationship. We ended up in a secret relationship. When it didn't work out, it wrecked my bond with her brother, and I won't let that happen with

Jonathan.

I look up from the stationary bike I'm pedaling to see Jon spotting Jake on the bench press. It makes me wonder what kind of guy Meg dates. Is it some monster body builder like Jake, someone more like Jon and me—hard and fit, but still flexible—or some skinny prep with glasses and a doctorate? I can't see her with a hipster. Although, she's got a sharp mind and hipsters do a lot of deep thinking. I want to get to know her better. Maybe she could help me figure out what to do with Seth. Besides, Jon didn't say I couldn't call her. He just said don't sleep with her.

Chapter 12

Megan

The rest of the weekend buzzes by in a blur. My only regret is I didn't get any more Liam-time. I don't know if I will ever hear from him again. I'm pretty sure the number he typed into my phone is his, so maybe I will, and he *will be* at Sarah's wedding. It doesn't matter. I enjoyed the time we had together. It was what it was and I refuse to slut-shame myself for it. I'd do it again in a heartbeat.

I don't share the night's adventures with my friends, though. They don't need to know everything. They figure something happened between Liam and me, but I don't tell them about dancing at the club, the naked sandwich, or sharing my dark secret about my mom with him. The last one would probably blow them away. And, yeah, maybe I didn't share everything, but just to talk about my mom's death at all is a big step for me.

Alli was too wrapped up in her own experience with Jake "Gorgeous-body" that she couldn't listen to anything I said, anyway. Honestly, sometimes I wish she could keep her sexcapades to herself—just don't want to know the details. The entire flight back was a recap of her night. After all her hyping of the experience she admitted it wasn't the best sex of her life.

I have to confess my night with Liam, even though we didn't technically seal the deal, *was* the most sexually-charged experience, I've ever had, and it will be the one I measure every other guy against. Every touch of his hand, every caress of his lips, blew any other man into the stone ages. Even though I had already fallen for his TV character, I know I would still be enamored by him. Sure, they look like each other, but he and Ashton Post are not that alike. Liam is playful in and out of bed and an incredible dancer. He's open about his personal life and is far less brooding than his character. Face it, he's sexier than his character. I know it was just a one-night stand for him, but I hope he didn't ruin me—set the bar so high no attainable guy can compare.

All of us at the house have been on edge since we returned home from our weekend in Hollywood. Alli's parents reamed her out for hours in the living room about being held to a higher standard of expectation as a med student. They had to be stalking Sarah online in order to have even seen the pictures. They spent most of Sunday evening trying to force Alli to pack up her belongings and move home with them because she was "ruining her career with her irresponsible lips," and, if she didn't make some major changes to rectify what she'd done, they wouldn't be paying for her schooling. Apparently, med students can be dropped from their program for unprofessional conduct.

It probably didn't help when I jokingly said, "I guess we shouldn't tell them about the sex tape." I was just trying to show the situation with the kiss pictures could always be worse. The death glare Alli's mother gave me could have killed a village of small children, but I've grown immune to it over the six years Alli and I have been friends.

It was ridiculous such innocent images on a tabloid could be devastating to Alli's career. Sure, Gorboni had dipped her back in full lip lock and pulled Alli's leg up around his hip, but she still had all her clothes on and his hands weren't under her shirt or anything. Sarah said the pictures would be news for a week at the most, and then they would fade into oblivion. Besides, Alli's name wasn't attached to them so I didn't understand what all the fuss was about.

Two days have passed since my comment about the sex tape. And, just as I thought all had been forgiven, Jessica peeks her head into my room with the meanest expression I've ever seen on her face. *What is her problem?*

"Megan, there's a delivery at the door for you."

"Sorry. I didn't hear the doorbell." I can't help that I didn't hear the bell. If she answered the door, why couldn't she just take the package?

I head downstairs as she mumbles under her breath, entering her room. When I reach the heavy wooden door and pull it open, I figure out why she is so mad. It's not a delivery guy. It's Chase. He smiles and hands me a small box with a giant red bow. I hold the door open and motion for him to come in. Why didn't she just tell me it was Chase?

"I don't think Jessica was too excited to see me. I was relieved when you opened the door. She said something about coming back with her crossbow."

"She has a crossbow," I say with a laugh. I close the door and motion toward the stairs, because I don't want to flaunt his presence and I don't need anyone hearing our conversation.

"So you live with Jessica? Why does she want to kill me? She was always my favorite of your friends."

"You just liked her big tits."

He smiles because he knows I'm right. "So you still hang with your friends from high school?"

"Alli lives here too. And you have to leave before she gets home from class. I don't need any more death glares from my roommates." We round the corner of the hall and Jessica's door is closed.

"I forgot about Alli until this past weekend," he says as we enter my room. He scans the room, and adds, "Those were interesting pictures online this week of her kissing that movie star. She looks like she's loosened up a bit since high school."

"You saw those?"

"It was all over social media. Of course, I saw them. I keep up on what's now."

I shake my head. I don't even know this new socially-aware, gift-bearing Chase. "So what's this?" I hold up the package with the red bow.

"Open it." He closes the door and then sets his backpack against it.

I sit on the bed and tear off the wrapping. It's a phone—a really expensive phone.

"That's sweet. What's the occasion?" I say, and Chase plops down on my bed next to me.

"I can't let you walk around with the antique in your purse. It must be *at least* four years old. People are talking. It's bad for my reputation to be seen with you." He smiles. "Besides, when you didn't answer my texts, I figured yours was broken. It is, isn't it?" He stares into my eyes, searching them.

It would be so easy to slip him back into my life. I know those eyes, that body. It would be effortless. All I would have to do is lean in and his lips would cover mine. I can almost feel them.

His fingers graze my cheek and curl around the nape of my neck as his eyes paralyze me. I'm a deer in headlights and I have two choices: I can run as fast as I can to get out of the road or get hit by the speeding semi-tractor trailer. Before this past weekend, I know I would have chosen the truck, but now that I've experienced such intensity with someone other than Chase, I can see it is possible. He is not the only one to light that kind of fire in me. I have choices.

I slowly stand up and as his hand slides down my arm, I say, "I appreciate the phone, but if there are strings attached, I don't want it."

"No strings here. I just thought you deserved some luxury." He stands up, shaking his head, with eyebrows raised as if to say, *well, I tried.* He grabs the canvas and leather backpack he had staged near the door and sets it on the bed as he says, "Give me your old phone and I'll transfer your data and number."

"You can do that?" I don't know why I question him. He was always good with computers. I hand over my phone.

"I've got mad skills, Meg."

I chuckle because those are the same words Liam said about his bedroom skills.

"What's so funny," he asks. "Do you doubt my skills?"

"No." I shake my head trying to erase Liam's bedroom skills from my mind and clear the smirk from my face. But I can't stop the giggle in my throat.

As I'm wrestling to regain focus, he pulls a sleek silver laptop from his bag. It looks space-age and expensive—definitely not the kind found on the shelves of the average electronics store. He sits down at my desk and boots it up. He plugs my phone into a port I have never seen before and starts to type. As his fingers fly over the keyboard, I see my documents, music, and contact folders appear on his screen. He clicks into my contacts and I'm about to start bitching when he says, "Naked sandwich? Is this that Hollywood guy?"

I nod, blown away by the fact he seems to know about Liam. I didn't think there were any pictures in the tabloids of us except getting into the car. The contact picture Liam took on my phone was clear but the ones of me outside the club could have been any blonde.

"Please tell me you weren't the meat. The thought of you between two guys…I could probably live with you being the bread, but the meat? That's just gross."

"Shut up. Get out of my personal stuff."

"Seriously, I knew you would be more developed in the sex department. I mean, it's been four years. It's bound to happen. But naked sandwiches? That's advanced shit and a bit slutty, I'd say."

"I didn't do a naked sandwich with anybody and *you're* calling *me* slutty? You know…just forget it. I don't want your stupid phone." *What a jerk.* I was a virgin when I met him, and I can count the number of guys I've been with on one hand. He couldn't even count the number of girls he cheated on me with on one hand.

"I'm just messing with you, Meg. You deserve a decent phone. Take it. I'm practically done."

I reach for my old phone just as he pulls the cord off it. "I'm pretty sure all you really needed to do was take the card out of my old phone and put it in the new one."

"Really? I guess that would work too," he says, trying to look innocent.

I think it's an act, but he's too good of a liar for me to tell for sure. He shoves his computer back in his backpack and turns to me licking his lips. "Let me show you some of the features on this phone." He slips his arm around me so we can both view the screen. Then he taps the display.

"This app allows you to record conversations. It's one of my favorites."

I glance, a scowl evident on my face. "What would I use it for?" I ask.

"You're a student. You can record lectures. What did you think I meant? I'm legitimate. I don't blackmail people anymore," he says with a chuckle. "You never know when you may need to record a conversation, though. And, if you press this button, you can record phone conversations."

"I don't think I will use that app except for class. What else does the phone have?"

"Here's your music. The app you were using filtered out all the musical dimension. This one allows you to hear every aspect the artists infused into their work."

Who is this guy? And how did he get so knowledgeable? He shows me how to work the app, which saves me months of figuring it out on my own. He introduces me to a couple of new apps I've never seen before as well and my brain is starting to turn to goo. I probably won't remember much more. "I need to take a break. Do you want something to eat?" I skipped lunch and I'm starting to get hungry.

"How about a naked sandwich? One of your housemates could be the other bread. Jessica maybe?"

Is he ever going to let it go? "I'm not getting naked with you."

"I'll watch. I don't have to be naked. Two breads are better than no bread at all." He leans back on my bed like he'll wait or maybe he's picturing it in his head. I get up and walk to the door, turning back to him. "Do you want food or not?"

He sits up. "Yeah. Let's go out. Do you seriously live with your high school friends? Who does that? You're supposed to move on and leave childish things behind after you graduate."

"I left you behind. I like my other high school friends." It is getting easier and easier to resist him.

"Ouch," he says, as he meets me by the bedroom door and hands me my new phone.

By the time we get to the café restaurant just a few blocks from the house, it feels like old times between us—early old times—when he still seemed to worship me and not use me. He motions for me to choose my seat before he chooses his and tells me he will be paying—little pockets of respect I never saw near the end. We talk about his family, his parent's divorce—which I didn't know about, his brother and sister, and how he was the only one still speaking to his dad.

"Who would have thought that Dad and I would ever get along? When Ashley quit college to become a glassblower, he completely disowned her. She's doing all right though. She's never asked him for money. She's asked *me*, but not him, and I'm happy to help her. Why not help family? There are plenty of strangers taking more than their share."

"You are not the same person I dated in high school. The old Chase would have told his sister to go to hell."

"That's not true. If I had the money back then, I would have helped her and Tegan. Though my brother seems bent on making his way without anyone else's help."

"What happened with your parents?"

"My drug problem drove them apart. They argued about it all the time. Then Mom cheated and that pretty much sealed the deal."

"Sorry. I always liked your parents."

"It happens. You have to move forward and not dwell on the past. That's something I learned in treatment. If I hung onto all the crap I was responsible for, I would drown myself."

Wow. The elephant in the room just tripled in size and is now sitting on my chest. He has to know about my mother. Both his parents were at her funeral. Maybe he was so out of it back then he doesn't remember. I'd changed my phone number—tired of his rambling texts and all hour of the night calls pleading for me not to leave him. He knew what he needed to do to get me to stay, but he couldn't give up the drugs. I sit in silence unsure if I can face where this conversation is heading, unsure if I can breathe.

"So how did your friend Sarah meet the infamous bad boy Jonathan Williams? He doesn't seem her type."

"What you really mean is, why is *she* dating *my* type."

He laughs. "Yeah, why is she dating your type while you date frat boys?"

"Williams seems like a nice guy. He's nothing like the tabloids make him out to be. They're wrong. Imagine that." I pause, trying to curb my bitterness. "They met through friends and I was skeptical at first, but I think they are really good for each other." I'm not telling him they met online and I'm not going to talk about Sarah's personal life with him.

"You were skeptical because they started with a long distance relationship and you don't believe in those."

"How do you know what I believe?" He's right, but how does he know?

"When my sister left for college, you spent hours trying to convince her she should break up with her high school sweetheart. You said long distance relationships never work and you were right. They broke up before Thanksgiving her freshman year."

"I didn't remember that."

"I remember a lot about you, Meg."

He obviously doesn't recall our last year together. But, I know he's trying to make a better impression this time around.

"So what's up with you and naked sandwich guy? You don't believe in long distance relationships, but you got his number, so it has to be more than a one-night stand."

That thought brings a smile to my face. Why did he give me his number if it was just a one-night non-hookup?

"Are you going to see him again?"

I shrug unable to erase the smile from my face. I know, I'll see him at the wedding and I've already made plans in my head about the trip. I've thought about Nordstrom every couple of minutes since I left Los Angeles. I've tried to take our night for what it was. But no more midnight fantasy of Ashton Post, now Liam stars in my all the time fantasy. Luckily, I can still separate fantasy from reality.

"Because I think you and I are great together. We always have been. We still have that spark between us. I can feel it and I know you can too. You can't deny it."

"You can't deny he's hot." I have to say something, my imagination still picturing the wedding week in high definition.

The server takes our order and brings our drinks before he speaks again.

"I don't like him. I looked him up online. He's got a bad reputation. Honestly, Google the guy. You'll see. He only dates blondes, for God's sake. He probably has all kinds of twisted Hollywood fetishes."

"Really?" I laugh. "You think his reputation will be worse in my mind than yours because of what tabloids say? You don't know me well if you think I will listen to the tabloids. I have experienced your reputation firsthand. Do you remember when you told me you were going to visit your grandparents for the weekend and you ended up spending it with Anita Harris? *Your* reputation sucks."

"That was the old me. I wouldn't do that again. I've seen what's out there and I know what I want now."

"Well, forgive me for not trusting you. We have history, both good and bad."

"You have to let the bad crap go. You can't hang on to it. It will eat you up inside."

"Or protect me."

I had forgotten about Anita Harris or at least I had pushed that specific betrayal far enough down that I hadn't thought about it for years. It was Anita's best friend who told me about it. I questioned her motivation, so gleeful and willing to share. She had pictures, proof of Chase's cheating. It was the first proof I had. I almost resented the girl, with her innocent freckled face, more than Anita. I don't even remember her name now. It was Chase's fault more than Anita's anyway. He was the one I was in the relationship with. He's the one who lied to me and then begged me to forgive him. I was stupid back then.

"Give me a chance to prove it to you. Let me take you on an official date on Friday. I'll show you how I've changed." His cunning blues stare me down.

"I'll think about it," I say, breaking eye contact.

During the meal, he brought up Liam three more times, trying to convince me the guy was a poser. He didn't ask me once what happened at Peterson's party and I was puzzled, until I figured out he must have talked to Candice.

"Why don't you take Candice out on Friday?" I say. The server had just collected our plates and dropped off the bill. His lips purse with a slight smile like they always did when I caught him doing something he wasn't supposed to be doing.

"That's what I love about you, Meg. You always see right through the bullshit. I could never get away with anything. Somehow you always knew."

"Call it intuition."

"Yes, I have talked to her."

By talking, he most likely means her lips were wrapped around his dick and yet he's still trying to get back together with me. I give him a skeptical look.

"She told me what happened at the party after I left. Sorry I messed up what you had with the giant, but his blatant douchebaggery tells me it wasn't serious between the two of you."

He knows everything that happened that night. No wonder he's upped his game.

Megan

I'm packing up my tablet and notes at the back of the small lecture hall when a text comes in on my new phone. The message flashes briefly at the top of the screen and I spot the words "naked sandwich." *Enough about the naked sandwich already.* I had labeled Liam's contact that just as a fun reminder of our night. As I click on the message, all ready to rip Chase a new orifice, I gasp because the picture of Liam and me at the club lights in the text thread.

Liam: Want a Naked Sandwich, Meg?

I literally laugh out loud and five people at the front of the room waiting to ask the teaching assistant questions turn to stare at me. I can't believe he's texting me. I was starting to feel the night with him was a hallucination. I zip my backpack and throw it over my shoulder as I head to the door with my phone in my hand and my stomach in my throat. I never thought I would hear from him.

Me: That depends. Will you be making it?
Liam: As long as we're naked, does it matter?

I smile at the thought.

"Billings, are you going to the study session at three o'clock?" The fingers of some guy from my class lock around my arm, stopping my forward momentum. I try to tear my attention away from my phone to answer him, but it's hard. I meet his gaze and realize I've tutored him before in the math lab. I only work there a few hours a week, but I remember helping him before the last exam.

"Yeah, I'll be there," I say, and he lets go of my arm.

"Good, because I'm completely lost and the TA just keeps repeating what he's already said. He thinks if he says it again louder, I'll understand somehow. I need you to simplify it or at least explain it better."

"I'll do my best." I look back at my phone.

"Great. I'll see you later," he says, and I deliberately walk in the opposite direction from him just to refocus on Nordstrom.

Me: I'm in. Did you get Jon's approval yet?

I still can't believe I'm talking to him. I probably shouldn't have brought Jon into this, though.

Liam: Not yet. What are you doing right now?
Me: I just got out of class. I was thinking about getting a late lunch.
Liam: Will you be naked?
Me: Is there any other way to eat?
Liam: Wish I was there. Send pictures?
Me: Sure. What are you doing?
Liam: I'm at the studio, trying to firm up the cast for next season. I'll be here until seven and that's only if everything goes well. If it doesn't, I could be here all night. Can I call you when I get home?

We never really talked about his job. I have no idea what he does on a daily basis. If he actually calls me, maybe I'll get more insight into his life.

Me: I'll be up.
Liam: Gotta go.

I laugh as I stow my phone in my bag and make a mental note to send him a picture of a sandwich. I don't send nudes. I won't have time to go back to the house if I want to make the study session, so I head toward the sandwich shop in search of a sensual looking sandwich. It's amazing how a couple of texts can change my mood so dramatically. I need to tell someone about Liam, but Alli has a lab right now and Jessica will be in her nursing clinical all afternoon. I don't care. I type out a multimedia text to them. My words scream excitement and I probably look ridiculous smiling to myself.

Inside the shop, I stare at the menu board, trying to figure out which sandwich would look the sexiest and still be edible. When I finally figure out what to eat, the girl taking my order practically sneers at me showing her irritation to my good mood. She acts more like a barista than a sandwich artist—which is her actual title according to her nametag. Even she can't ruin my disposition, though. When my sandwich is ready, I find a table near the window that provides natural light for my photo and settle in. As I unwrap my lunch, I fluff the contents trying to bring out its carnal appeal. I've snapped four pictures when a shadow casts across my table.

"Damn, Billings. I wish I was that sandwich. You look like you're getting ready to blow it."

I look up about to tell Scott where to stick it, when I see Peterson standing behind him. Apprehension blares on his face, but he slides in across from me anyway.

"I have to get to class," Scott says, turning and bumping Dylan's shoulder with his fist.

Peterson nods and meets my eyes without a word. I haven't talked to him since the party, except for the text I sent informing him I was aware of his hookup. I take a bite of my sandwich trying to avoid his gaze. Dylan is still staring at me when I take a second bite.

"I guess we're even then."

I finish chewing and swallow. "What the hell are you talking about? We're not even," I say, glaring. "Chase is just a friend."

"I'm not talking about the guy you claimed was your brother. I'm talking about the B-list actor you hooked up with in Hollywood last weekend. I assume he's a friend of Sarah's fiancé?"

B actor? I want to smack him. Has he even seen Liam's show? I'm tired of men's pissing contests. "I don't know what you're talking about."

"There are pictures online of you leaving an L.A. club with some actor. Alli, Sarah, and Jessica are with you. And then someone posted a picture of him kissing a blonde inside the club. I can tell it's you. I say that makes us even."

"Just because I kissed him doesn't mean he carried me to his bed." I hope he gets the reference. "Besides you and I were over by the time I kissed him."

"I don't want us to be over," he says, his voice dripping with remorse.

"I guess you should have thought of that before you screwed the sophomore."

"Shit." He shakes his head. "I was drunk and hurt, and you wouldn't answer my texts. You disappeared at the same time the guy left. What was I supposed to think? You'd already lied to me about him."

"But, I didn't leave with him and I didn't sleep with him. And drinking is self-imposed stupidity, not an excuse."

"I'm sorry. Is that what you want to hear? I'm sorry." He glances out the window not meeting my eyes. I don't think he wants to see the finality in them.

"Yeah, me too," I say. We both know it's over. I've already moved on. He reminds me of a little kid and no matter how mad I am, I feel sorry for him. I get up and crumple the rest of my sandwich inside its wrapper. It's a waste, but I'm no longer hungry. I toss it in the trash and come back to the table for my stuff. I pull my backpack on and grasp his shoulder as I bend to kiss the side of his head. He leans gently against my lips and I hold them there longer than I should.

"I'll see you around campus, Peterson," I say pulling back. His whole body moves as he nods in acknowledgment. Peterson and I would have broken up even if he hadn't hooked up with the sophomore and I think he knows it. His stupidity just gave me the out.

I head to the study session knowing I will be early. I'm less excited about sending my sandwich picture now. Nothing will come of it. When I reach the empty room where the study group will meet, I sit down at a table and thumb through the pictures I took. None are sexy enough, but I pick the best one and send it with the tag *Hungry?*

It's after midnight and I've just checked my phone for the billionth time to make sure it hasn't mysteriously become sentient and turned off because it knew we had a nine o'clock class tomorrow. Nope, it's still on. I stare at the cracked plaster on the ceiling above my bed determined to just go to sleep because Liam has obviously changed his mind about me being worthy of his time. Or, maybe he just hooked up with some model he met on his way out of the studio after work. I don't know why I expected him to call at all.

I look around my room at the blank walls, wondering why I never bothered to make the room mine. It's been eight months since I moved in and I don't have any pictures up except the one of Alli, Jessica, Sarah, and me from high school, which Jessica framed for everyone when we graduated. Was Peterson right about me not letting anyone in because of Chase? Or, is it really because of my mother? I wonder how different I would be if my mother hadn't abandoned me. If someone had found her in time to save her, would I still avoid getting close to people or did her death take that from me?

Just after one the picture Liam took of him and me at the club lights up my cell's screen. Relief washes through me because I was starting to doubt I had a texting conversation with him at all. I push the button and take a deep breath. I need to get a grip if I'm going to be able to talk. When I hear his deep, sultry voice, a completely different feeling washes over my body.

"Meg?"

I guess I'd answered without speaking.

"Who else would answer my phone? Work didn't go well?"

"Yep. What time is it there? Did I wake you?"

"No, I was just finishing some homework." He didn't need to know I couldn't sleep because I kept thinking about his hands on me. No matter what I did, I couldn't push the lustful thoughts from my mind. His hands should have their own star on the Hollywood Walk of Fame.

"Don't talk about school. It just makes me think of you wearing a short skirt and me bending you over the teacher's desk."

I laugh. God, he's hot.

"You've got the most beautiful laugh."

Now I can't wait to go to sleep. I'm sure I will be laughing in my dream as he bends me over a desk.

"When are you coming to visit Sarah again? I'll save the date."

"Promises, promises. It's all empty promises from you. You'll never act on them."

"You didn't enjoy our night together?"

"You know my answer, you confident bastard. I wasn't the only one who enjoyed that night. Why did you call if you're just going to tease me?"

"Do you want me to hang up?"

"Tease."

Click. The phone goes dead. *Oh crap!* I'm not calling him back. *Crap!* I shouldn't have pushed him. I toss my phone on the bed. I'm pretty sure he'll call back. I can wait it out. Should I call him back? I pull the comforter over me as I try to convince myself to wait. I pick my phone back up and check my email. There is a notice from the University about parking restrictions, but that's it. Finally, my phone buzzes. I let it ring a second time before answering it so I don't seem eager.

"Stop teasing me," I say.

"What color bra are you wearing? Is it the purple one?"

"I'm not wearing a bra."

He's silent for several seconds, but I know the call hasn't disconnected because I can hear him breathing.

"And you call *me* a tease? Do you sleep naked?"

"No. I grew up with three brothers. What if there was a fire?"

He laughs. "How are your brothers? Hard at work at the marina?"

"Yeah. I just saw them the other day. I met my dad's girlfriend too." I can't believe he remembered the marina. He's so normal sometimes, as if he isn't on TV at all.

"You don't sound too enthused. Is she a crazy evangelical or a ho-ho-ho?"

I break out laughing. He said it so matter-of-factly, his words caught me off guard. "Neither. She was decent, maybe a bit leathery, but personable."

"Leathery?"

"Like she's been out in the sun too long—leathery skin."

"Other than being leathery—and I have to point out that is pretty superficial of you—what's wrong with her?"

I chuckle at his comment. "Nothing. She and my dad have been dating for almost two years and I just met her. And, it wasn't because my dad kept her hidden. It was because I've been avoiding my family. I realize I need to put more effort in them. I've been doing an awful job as a daughter."

"So you've been avoiding them because of your mom?"

How did he know that? "It's probably because of my mom." The reality of my words hit me and my breath catches. "I was the last to see her and my family blames me for her death."

"What happened to her?"

"You don't want to know my story. You'd rather think of me bent over the teacher's desk." I try to distract him.

"Come on, Meg. Give me some credit. I'm not that shallow. It seems to be bugging you. Why don't you just tell me? If you don't, I'll just blabber on about myself until you know my entire life's story"

I laugh again. He's not afraid to share, is he? "Are you sure you want to hear all my baggage?"

"What are friends for?"

"Is that what we are, Nordstrom, friends?"

"What's wrong with friends? I think it's respectable. I feel as if we made a connection. You don't consider me a friend?"

I can hear the challenge in his voice. "Since we used the politician's definition of hookup, I guess we're friends." I've been friend zoned. Great. I wonder if that will affect my midnight fantasy Liam.

"Friends talk. Share with me, Meg."

"Fine." It was just the one night anyway. Why am I hesitating? "It's not as if we will see each other again."

"Except at the wedding."

"Except at the wedding. Where do I start?"

He laughs, and I don't know if it is because he agrees with my comment or if it is because I am giving in.

"Why did you say the police didn't think your mom's death was an accident?"

"How do you remember that?"

"It's an odd thing to say, isn't it? Besides, I sort of have a photographic memory. It helps with acting. I convert words into pictures in my head to remember them better and when you said that, I envisioned her either being murdered or committing suicide. Neither a pleasant sight. It stuck with me."

I swallow the lump in my throat and try to form a coherent sentence, but can't. My silence tells him what my words don't.

"If it is too hard to talk about, we don't have to." He pauses as if waiting for me to jump in and start baring my soul. After a minute of silence he says, "I can tell you what's bothering me."

I nod, which he can't see, and then say, "That would be great."

"My little brother. My dumbass little brother is stealing from me. I had five hundred bucks sitting on my dresser yesterday when he stopped over and after he left, it was gone."

"What's he need the money for?" I ask, but I'm pretty sure I know the answer is either gambling or drugs.

"He's got a drug problem—designer stuff mostly. My parents cut off his money train hoping to curb his appetite, but he's still finding a way to meet his addiction. They blame me because of my prescription drug problem last year, though his problem is completely different."

"That sucks." I don't know what else to say. I've lived that. "Chase use to help himself to the cash in my purse, and then try to convince me this time he would pay me back. I guess I indirectly funded his habit." I doubt he remembers though. He doesn't seem to remember any of the bad stuff. "You should do an intervention," I say because it's obvious where this is leading.

"I know." He pauses and adds, "Did it really work for your ex?" His words are optimistic while his voice conveys hopelessness. "Did he stop for good? I stopped, but I'm the exception. I know a ton of people who just seem to use rehab as a vacation they take once a year. It's a joke, and most of the interventions I've heard about, didn't work long-term."

"Chase's didn't work, but he eventually came around. You'll never know unless you try."

"My brother is at the age where he thinks he knows everything and everyone else is an idiot."

"If he's eighteen, he either has to be a threat to himself or someone else in order to get him hospitalized against his will. And those are hard to prove unless he attacks someone or tries to off himself. He hasn't tried anything like that, has he?"

"No."

"Then the only way to get him help is to convince him to check himself in."

"Yeah, that's the tricky part. I told you he thinks he's smarter than the rest of the world, right? He probably thinks I'll blame Nak for the missing money or that I won't even notice. My roommate would never steal from me. My brother is such a little dipshit."

"Talk to a rehab center. I bet they would know how to approach him about getting help. I am sure they have a team of people who can put it together for you. When I did the one for Chase, it wasn't hard setting it up. The difficult part was figuring out what I was going to say to him."

"You must have really loved him to try to get him help and not just walk away."

"I thought I did. He obviously didn't love me more than the drugs."

"I don't do love."

"Yeah, you just have a bunch of friends you sleep with."

"I can't help who I've become. Besides, I don't get complaints."

"I bet you don't."

"Only that they want more." He slips into a girly falsetto voice. "Harder. Faster. Oh, right there. Oh. Oh god. Don't stop. Ohhh…" he trails off as if spent. I hope he's not mimicking me. Who knows what I said the night we were together? My brain was too absorbed in the moment to think beyond it.

"If you were in love, hundreds of women would go unsatisfied. What a tragedy."

"Finally, someone who understands. I can tell we're going to be great friends, Meg. You're really easy to talk to. Maybe I could call every night just to relieve the tension of the day."

"I'm not having phone sex with you." I hope he's joking. If not, he's more of a pig than I thought, being this is our first call and all.

"Phone sex? I just meant talk about the problems of the day to clear our heads. Sometimes, I have a hard time getting to sleep. I don't do phone sex. That's a video chat thing. I want to see your beautiful lips form that perfect little O. I'd miss that without the video. Picture guy, remember?"

Oh my god. What am I doing? I don't even know how to comment on that. Luckily, I don't have to come up with anything because he just keeps talking.

"Meg? Really? I shocked you again. You come off as this hard ass, but you're just a little innocent, aren't you? If talking about phone sex makes you blush then I know things that would turn you scarlet."

"Play on. I'm not shocked." I finally find my words, even though they're a lie.

"Maybe we should wait and build up to it. I always find anticipation makes the experience all the more enjoyable." Then his voice changes from sultry to boy next door in a beat. "What did you do today?"

I pause for a second, switching gears. "I ran into an ex at the sandwich shop. It was the first time I'd seen him since he cheated on me two weeks ago."

"Oh. I didn't realize you were on the rebound when we had our non-hookup or I may have given into your whining.

Was I whining?

"And I thought nothing I said would influence your bromance with Jonathan."

"Jon and I have a mutual respect for one another. We've been friends for a long time and he has helped me out of many situations. He's low maintenance and doesn't ask much of me, but when he does, I do all I can to accommodate."

"Even if it's not what you want?" I ask.

"Usually."

"So how long have you been in love with Jonathan Williams?" I ask.

He laughs. "And I was afraid you didn't understand."

"I get it. I do. Bros before hoes. I guess that makes me a ho."

"You're not a ho, Meg. You are far from a ho." He chuckles. "We could have done what we wanted, but I wanted to respect Jon's wishes."

"Oh. It was you who didn't want to hook up. What was wrong, performance anxiety?"

"Did I look as if I had performance anxiety?"

"No, but maybe it's only when you're on a real hookup and not a non-hookup."

"All right. Stop talking about my junk. You're giving me performance anxiety."

"The truth finally comes out," I say, and we both laugh.

We joke around for another hour and I don't believe I've ever laughed so much in my life. Then, when I realize that it's after three and I have to leave for class in less than five hours, we say our goodbyes. I could do this friends thing if it's what he wants. I'd like more, but if that's my only option, I could make it work, at least until Sarah's wedding. Who knows what will come when we're together on a tropical island for a week? Until then, I wouldn't mind getting to know him better. He's hilarious.

Liam

I pull up her contact on my phone and I can almost smell the sweet perfume of her shampoo. The picture of the two of us at the club messes with my head. I like hearing her voice. I never know what to expect with her, and not in the crazy girlfriend way. She's very realistic, but still unpredictable. My hackles don't go up with her like they do with some girls when I am in the "getting to know you" stage. No matter what I tell people, I do get to know a girl to a certain level before I bring her to my bed. I don't need to know her middle name or anything like that, but I do need to know my reputation won't be tarnished by a psycho smearing my name online. That's why waking up next to Tina bothered me so badly. I knew what she was capable of saying in social media. Maybe the fact I haven't claimed Meg the way I've claimed most girls I interact with gives us more to talk about. It isn't all about sex. She's different.

"Most guys hate talking on the phone. Don't you text?" she asks without a greeting.

"Meg," I say, relaxing into my pillow. "I text just fine. I prefer the phone because I've never had someone forward a phone call to someone else. But texts seem to go rogue on me all the time."

"Do you have girl trouble, Nordstrom?"

"Not now, but once two girls played me, sharing my texts between each other. I just prefer old school phone calls."

"You were sleeping with both of them, weren't you?" she says.

How does she know this stuff? It's like she reads me right through the phone line. "That was the biggest problem with them sharing notes. Transparency in that type of situation never works out."

"What do you regret more, the texts or sleeping with both of them."

"Both. What's *your* biggest regret?"

"Why do you always ask such personal questions?"

"Obviously, I want to get to know you better. Answer the question."

"Why do you want to know me better? Is it your thing? I mean, did you know the text sharers?"

"No." I laugh. "Why would I want to know them better?" They were completely plastic. "I was sleeping with them. You're different. So just answer the question."

"I try to live my life without regrets. I don't have any."

"Bull! Stop holding back. Just tell me. Everyone has regrets." She's obviously hiding something.

"I don't."

I wait silently for her to give me a real answer. She's clearly faking.

"This might not be my biggest regret…but my last breakup didn't go the way I wanted it to go."

"Break ups never go the way you want them to go. You have to be more specific."

"I'm starting at the beginning so I hope you have a couple of hours."

"We can talk all night. I have tomorrow off."

"I don't, but I'll survive. Okay. I ran into my ex from high school—the one with the drug problem."

"Failed intervention guy?"

"That's the one."

She explains all the details of her last break up with a frat boy—every mistake she made, every aspect she wished had been different. I listen silently even though it kills me she is telling me about sleeping with other guys.

"Okay. Yes, Peterson and I were sleeping together, but it was casual. I thought it was just casual. I didn't even realize he thought of it as a relationship until he went all caveman on me about Chase. Why do guys always act as if they don't care until you sleep with them and then all of a sudden they own you?"

"Meg, you sound like a guy. Guys say girls lure them in with sex and then act as if you're getting married."

She laughs. "That's what guys always say, but I think it's just the opposite. Do girls lure you in with sex and then act as if you're getting married?"

"No. I'm up front with them. I tell them straight up I don't do relationships. It's just sex and they know it from the start. Maybe you need to be up front with guys, tell them all you want is sex." She sounds like every guy's dream.

"I don't just want sex. You make me sound like a complete ho-bag. I've only slept with four guys, total. What's your number?"

"Only four guys, really? Am I in that four?"

"No. I mean all the way. Our non-hookup doesn't count."

"Girls always throw out numbers and in reality they mean that number times ten."

"It's my actual number. What's yours?"

I blow out a breath. "Honestly, I don't even know. A lot."

"And I let your tongue in my mouth. You make me want to wash my mouth out with bleach."

"Yeah, now that I think about it—me too." We both laugh and then I continue. "What about Chase? What's he want from you?"

"Chase thinks we should pick up where we left off four years ago as if nothing has changed. But I've changed."

"You're not going to get back with him?"

"I don't trust him, but we have chemistry. My mother always said finding a true spark with someone is rare and it's something to be cherished. I'm worried if I let him go, I'll never have it again."

"It can't be that hard to find. What are you twenty-one? Twenty-two?"

"I turned twenty-two in January."

"You have so many frogs to kiss before you bring one home." She's too young to worry about never finding a guy.

She laughs. "I'm not looking for someone to marry. I just want to find someone I have chemistry with. Because without chemistry, sex sucks."

I wish I could act on the chemistry we have. Our non-hookup was incredibly hot. "Are you still in love with Chase?"

"I don't know."

I expected her to say no and I hate that it bothers me she didn't. I don't mind competition. I enjoy it sometimes, but knowing she is still in love with him irks me, because I can't do anything about it. I can't get involved in the competition.

"What about the girl you used to live with, are you still in love with her?"

My relationship with Kelsey seems like a lifetime ago. "I didn't love Kelsey. Both parties have to be willing to share their worst before you can be sure of another's unconditional acceptance and that's what love is about, right? That's what the movies say. Love isn't real unless honesty exists. Chemistry and love are separate. You can have one without the other. Kelsey didn't even tell me she was married. Even though we lived together, I didn't know her at all. You can't really love a person unless you know them. I don't even know if real love exists. People use each other for what they want, what they need. Look at my parents. They coexist because they each benefit from being in a relationship. They don't even sleep in the same bedroom. They're not married. It's like a merger of two companies. My brother and I were just a way for them to expand their business."

"Wow. That's sad. Do you really believe that?"

"I've been in relationships. It's not as if I haven't tried to fall in love like in the movies. I just honestly don't think love is real. I think people fake it. They may think it's real, but it's not."

"In some ways, you could be right. I think love has different levels. People can fake anything, can't they? Maybe movie-level love doesn't exist in the real world. My parents had a shotgun wedding. I doubt they were in love when my brother Braden was born, but it seemed as if they loved each other when I was growing up. Maybe they were faking it. Their chemistry wasn't great. Maybe it was just my mom faking it." She pauses for a few seconds and I wonder what her clarification means.

"If love is based off of knowledge and trust, then I was never in love with Chase. We barely know each other," she says.

She gets it. How many people in the world would get my understanding of love? I like this girl.

Nak's words about getting into a girl's head burn in my ears. I've never met a girl I've wanted to know that well, until Meg. She's complex. There is so much I don't know about her, and if I could get inside her head, our first time together would be mind-blowing. Yes, I'm still thinking about being inside her. How could I not? The chemistry we have is scorching, and her dancing blew me away.

She's off-limits and I'm trying to respect that, so I'm also still hoping she will say something or do something that turns me off to help me erase her from my mind. I'm afraid the more I get to know her the less likely it's going to happen, though. I need to remember friends is all we can be. With her in Minnesota, it's not as if we can do more than talk anyway. At least she's starting to let me in and I enjoy our conversations.

"You don't trust Chase, right? Why? Other than lying and messing up your non-relationship with Peterson, what makes you hate him?" I ask because she's got to see the guy's a dick and if she doesn't see it now, she needs to.

"I don't know if I want to admit it to you."

"Just tell me."

"When we were dating, he cheated on me with six different girls and those are the ones I found out about."

"Did he wipe his feet on you after sex?"

"Shut it. I was not a doormat." She pauses. "Okay, I was kind of a doormat. But I was sixteen, stupid and in love."

Wow. I didn't even have to explain my comment to her. She got it right away. "You've grown up. But, you're still stupid if you're toying with giving him another chance."

"What do you know? You've never been in love. You just spend your nights hooking up with blond chicks. What kind of guy decides who to date based on the color of a girl's hair?"

I must have struck a chord with her because she sounds pissed. "How do you know I only date blondes?"

"I saw it on the internet."

"You've been checking me out, huh?" A smile spreads on my face because I like that she's checking up on me. That means she's thinking about me when we're not on the phone.

"No, Chase brought it to my attention."

Now I really don't like the guy. "I have my reasons for not dating brunettes."

"Like?"

"Every brunette I've dated has burned me. There was Val Marquez in sixth grade. She told everyone I drooled when I kissed. It was a whole year before I got my mojo back."

"You're basing it off a sixth grade crush?"

"There's more. The nanny."

"You orchestrated that. Did she get revenge?"

"Yep. The part I didn't tell you was we kept sleeping together—a quickie here or there in an upstairs bathroom, or if no one was home, the kitchen counter. We'd sneak into each other's rooms at night. I had sex anytime I wanted. I was living a sixteen-year-old's dream. On my seventeenth birthday, she told me she was pregnant. Happy birthday to me, right? She was Catholic and was going to keep it, so I needed to man-up and marry her." Meg's quiet and I wonder what she is thinking. I probably shouldn't have mentioned the kitchen counter or maybe she's wondering if I'm divorced with a kid.

"I denied it for a while. I was in shock. I never thought it would happen to me. After a month of her eating constantly, I noticed she was gaining weight, and I figured it wouldn't be long before she was showing. I didn't know what to do, so I confessed my problem to my dad. I didn't want to tell him, because he's kind of a force to be reckoned with, but I knew the longer I waited to tell him the angrier he and my mom would be.

"Right away, he wanted proof of the pregnancy. He made me go to the drugstore for a pregnancy test and then stay in the room while she peed on the stick. James Nordstrom, attorney for the stars, wasn't going to take the word of a nanny. I sat on the tub while she cried. She said she couldn't do it while I watched. We were in the bathroom for almost two hours before she wet the stick. It turned out she wasn't pregnant. She'd lied, and had been trying to get me to not wear a rubber since she told me about the pregnancy. I didn't understand why, but I always wore one and in that moment, I realized she was trying to get pregnant after the fact. The nanny was brunette."

"Two brunettes? That's all you've got? And I didn't really need to know about the quickie on the kitchen counter."

"All right. Last year, an underage brunette accused me of statutory rape, but I didn't even know her and definitely never slept with her. The police brought me in for questioning, but eventually dropped the case because of lack of evidence. Do I need to keep going?" I don't know what it is about her, but I want to tell her everything about me, even the bad crap.

"No need. I think I get it. What happened to the nanny?"

"She got sent home to her parents."

Meg gasps.

"What? I'm supposed to feel sorry for her? She lied to me. Technically, it was statutory rape. I was underage." I can picture Meg's eyes rolling and her head shaking.

"Or sexual harassment in the workplace," she adds. "How's the intervention planning going?"

"I'm meeting with the rehab people tomorrow to get Seth help before he becomes a statistic. The intervention is going to be on Tuesday. I have a couple more people to talk to, but it's coming together."

"Do you think he suspects?"

"I don't think so. Dad told him he had to be home to sign some papers for his trust fund. His eighteenth birthday is Sunday and he can't get into his trust fund if he doesn't sign the papers."

"If he signs the papers then he will have unlimited funds for his habit?" she asks.

"It's not that easy. He only gets a certain amount of money every month. If he goes to school, he gets more and it pays for his classes and room and board. It's complicated. With my dad, nothing is straightforward."

"Why didn't you do the intervention before his birthday? I was told it would have been easier to do Chase's if he was underage, but his birthday is in October so he was already eighteen before I figured out he needed one."

"He may be seventeen, but that doesn't mean he does anything he doesn't want to do. He knows my parents are on to his drug problem, but the lure of money is too great to ignore and he doesn't think they will do anything because they would be too embarrassed to have it come out in the press. My mom is sort of an activist against drugs and suicide. Her father had a coke problem and killed himself. So she's on the board of a bunch of foundations and it would be really embarrassing for not only her first son to go through rehab, but her second one too."

"Oh." She's quiet for a long minute and then adds, "I'm sorry about your grandfather."

"Thanks. From what I've heard of him, he was kind of a dick."

She's quiet again. She must be getting tired.

"I'm here if you need someone to practice your intervention speech on," she says softly.

"I still have to write it. I think I'll base it off what Jon told me when he confronted me about my prescription drug problem. It got me in. I should let you get some sleep now, though. You have class tomorrow."

"Yep."

"Call me after class. I should have my rough draft done by then."

"Goodnight, Nordstrom."

"Sweet dreams." I smile as the words leave my mouth. It sounds so corny and she doesn't even call me on it. She must be tired. We hang up and all I want to do is get her back on the line. I peel my ass off the bed and drop to the floor. I didn't make it to the gym today, meaning, I have three hundred crunches and twenty rotations of curls to do before I can go to bed.

I've finished my crunches and am halfway through my curls when thirst completely overtakes me. I set my barbells down, not bothering to push them under the bed. I'll have to finish before I can sleep.

After grabbing a giant glass of water, I head out onto the deck to rehydrate. The sun set hours ago and the air is starting to cool. I love spring nights on the coast. There's something about the salty air that's fresher in the spring. Nak looks up from his tablet when I close the door behind me. He's sitting at the table. We haven't talked much since he and Leslie got back together three weeks ago. She's been here every night.

"Who was that on the phone?"

I don't want to tell him because he'll tell Leslie and Leslie will tell Jonathan. I shake my head and shrug as I sit down next to him. I stretch out and take a deep, salty breath.

"You talked for a long time. Is there a new girl on the rotation?"

"Shut up about the rotation. There's no schedule, no organization, and no planning to my hookups. They just happen."

"Okay. How does a girl know you're looking for a hookup? Do you send out a multimedia text? A powerful hookup signal in the sky? Or, is it just a pheromone thing they can smell?"

"Again, shut it. The girls text me or find me at the club. It's not rocket science. It's organic," I say rolling my eyes.

"Here's the thing. You haven't been to any clubs in three weeks, no girls have spent the night, and you have been home every night talking on the phone. It makes me think you're either having phone sex because you're waiting for an STD to clear up, or you're in a relationship with a virgin. Which one is it?"

"Neither. You make me sound like a manwhore. I'm very selective. Girls are drugging me to ride on my dick. Remember?"

"Is that why you're not going out? Because Tina slipped you ecstasy?"

"I don't know. I just haven't felt it." I really haven't. The thought of going to the club and waking up next to some girl who only got with me because she wants to use me as a tool isn't that appealing. Honestly, I'm twenty-four years old and I've probably had sex in every position possible. Where do I go from here? Maybe Nak was right when he said it is worth getting to know a girl. Maybe that's what I'm lacking. The only person to intrigue me mentally is Meg. And maybe it's because I'm not supposed to like her that way, but it feels different with her. I don't feel the pressure to be someone I'm not with her. I can show her the real me and not worry she's going to expose me. If what Sarah says is true, she doesn't even use social media. I checked. It is strange though. It's almost as if Meg is hiding from someone or something.

Chapter 15

Liam

I spent the last three days writing my speech for Seth's intervention. Meg helped me hone parts of it so I didn't sound like a condescending big brother. "You're not his parent," she said, and I'm not. I need to deliver my words as if I'm talking to a peer, not a little kid, or he'll tune me out immediately.

She's really insightful and not shy about pointing out discrepancies in the world others avoid. Like two days ago, when I mentioned my grandfather's suicide for the second time, and she told me I needed to separate myself from him. "You never even met him so don't take on the guilt of his suicide. It had nothing to do with you," she said. And I guess it doesn't, but with the way my parents have looked at me since my motorcycle accident, I am starting to wonder if someday I won't be a coked-out junkie on the verge of suicide. It's common in my industry. Then Meg reminded me I was the one in charge of my own choices. I'm in the driver's seat and make the decisions, not my grandfather and not my parents. It's my life. I'm getting attached to this girl. And, I haven't hooked up with anyone since our non-hookup. I wonder what that says about her.

A text pings on my phone and I pull it out hoping it's from Meg—no such luck. It's my dad.

Jim: I know you're off today. We need to talk. Stop by the office this morning."

Crap. Now what did I do?

Me: I'll be there by 11.

I don't get a response. He's probably in a meeting and doesn't want to waste his time.

When I arrive at the firm at two minutes to eleven, I stop at the reception desk and hold out my parking ticket to be validated. Audrey takes the ticket, stamps it, and as she hands it back says, "He's waiting for you in his office."

"Should I be worried?" I ask, because her face gives no clues as to why my father called this impromptu meeting.

"I don't know, Liam. He didn't say anything to me."

"Thanks." I smile and head down the beige hallway to my dad's office. His large wooden door is cracked open and I can hear him on the phone. I peek my head in and he motions me to take a seat across from his immaculately clean desk. I sit, and as he continues his conversation, I take out my phone and send Meg a text. There is no indication Jim's phone call will end anytime soon.

Me: What are you wearing?

Megan: A white lace thong.

Me: Send a picture.

Megan: No.

She never disappoints. It's a game we've been playing this past week. I ask her what she's wearing and she tells me what kind of underwear she has on. Then I ask her to send a picture and she refuses. One of these days she's going to give in and completely shock the hell out of me. I am putting a mental picture book together of all the photos she's refused to send.

Me: I'm trapped in my dad's office waiting for him to ream me out about God knows what. I need a distraction. Please?

Megan: No. Chase is here.

Me: Why is he there?

Megan: He just asked me to get back together.

What? My dad picks this moment to end his call and address me. He slides a letter-sized piece of paper across his desk toward me and asks, "Do you know anything about this?"

The words "Fuck you," in my brother's handwriting, scrawled across the printed article catch my attention first. I skim the article and before I finish, he starts talking again. "Your mother and I haven't told a soul. I talked to the rehab place and they assure me the leak didn't come from them. That leaves you, Liam."

I ignore his glare and reread the short article.

> *Longtime drug and suicide prevention activist, Natalie Andrews, schedules another child for drug rehab on this coming Tuesday. Her first-born, actor Liam Nordstrom, checked into rehab last year with a prescription drug addiction and now Andrews' second child with prominent celebrity lawyer Jim Nordstrom is following his big brother down the addiction highway.*

The article goes on further to discuss the boards Mom resides on and my grandfather's suicide. It's short and I don't see the actual website it came from, but there's a shortened link. I grasp my chin in my hand as I look up to meet my dad's eyes.

"Well?"

"I've told a couple people, but they're not the type to do this." I tap the paper. The only people I've told are Jonathan and Meg. I haven't mentioned the intervention plans to Nak and I don't trust anyone but those three."

"Did the rehab place know about your stint in treatment?"

"No. I haven't even told the studio, why would I tell them?"

"You need to lock it down and figure out who's responsible for the leak. Your mother found this note on the dining room table this morning. Seth never came home last night and he didn't show up for school this morning."

"So what now? Do we cancel the intervention? It's not the first time he hasn't come home. He still has to sign the papers to get access to his trust."

"Your mother is worried he'll do something rash to harm himself."

"Do you think he'll harm himself or is it just Mom? Because Mom has issues. Seth seemed fine the last time I saw him." My mom is always acting as if Seth and I are going to follow in our grandfather's footsteps.

"Just help us find him. He won't answer his phone. Check with his friends and see what you can find out. And don't tell anyone our family problems. You know how embarrassing this is for your mother and me."

"Yeah. I'll see what I can find out." *Like I know his friends.* He's five and a half years younger than me. I knew who he hung out with in middle school, but not now. Damn! I'm going to have to call the studio and let them know this is out there, because I am sure they will get inquiries about my drug problem. I thought I had snuck my treatment past the press. It's been almost a year.

By the time I get to my car, I'm having second thoughts about contacting the studio. The studio's PR department could end up doing more damage than one article on a website. Sometimes they capitalize on any press just to bring attention to the show. The rehab stint fits with my character's image, so they wouldn't hesitate to exploit the article if I make them aware of it, and that would just embarrass my parents more.

I'm not worried about Seth showing up. He's always been a hothead. He'll cool off, realize he has no money, and return home to sign his trust papers. My parents have always coddled him. My bigger concern is who leaked the story to the press. I know my parents didn't tell a soul about the intervention and I know Jon didn't either. That leaves Meg. I wish it wasn't her because she's one of the few girls I've actually thought of as a friend, except maybe Ellie.

Ellie and Meg are similar in so many ways—both beautiful and smart—a combination so hot I couldn't help but want them. I stopped myself with Meg, but Ellie was a different story. We were friends for years before she changed the rules. She chased me long before I took what she offered, and she offered more than most men dream of. I tried to have a relationship with her. I did. She deserved that. We kept what we were doing from everyone we knew, especially her brother. But, I was young and stupid about girls. Our relationship was hidden. Nobody knew about it. There were so many girls around me all the time. With all the guys watching, I had to partake or they would find out about Ellie and me. Yes, I let it go too far and her brother told her about me and some girl at a concert. She blew up at me and I ended it. I know what motivated Ellie, she wanted revenge.

Ellie didn't sell me to the press. I had no career back then. I was just like a million other college freshmen. Instead, Ellie told her brother. She knew what would hurt me the most. She shared every lewd act we did and every place we did it. She told him things no brother should ever hear about his sister. When he confronted me, I didn't want him to think poorly of Ellie. It was my fault. I knew that. So, I admitted to using her for sex. Those words her brother would accept. No brother wants to think of his little sister as a sexual aggressor.

Ellie was no virgin when we hooked up. She surprised *me* with her knowledge. And even though I wasn't her first, she told her brother I was. I didn't share the truth with him though. It would have changed their relationship. Instead, I took a fist to the gut and let him hate me. He would have hated me anyway, but at least he wouldn't hate his sister.

The way I handled it pushed me out of favor with my friends. If it hadn't been for Jon, I don't know if I would have ever been welcomed back into the group. I told him the truth and he believed me. He convinced everyone except Ellie's brother to give me a pass. I don't think I could deal with losing my friends. With the family I have, the guys are more than just friends to me.

I don't know what motivated Meg to turn on me though. She doesn't seem to want a relationship. She has more guys than she can handle, and this morning she sounded as if she was getting back together with her ex. I can't imagine a story on some website would pay much, but there is no other reason to leak the intervention and it had to be her. No one else knew about it. I was looking for a reason to end what we were doing before I betrayed Jon, and I guess I found my reason to cut it off with Meg. I don't need any more proof. She knows what she did, and even though I like her, I don't need anyone who betrays my trust.

Megan

I sent Liam a text an hour ago and haven't heard back from him yet. He never answered the two calls yesterday, so I hope he sees this text. I'm tempted to send him a picture of the underwear I'm wearing just to get a response from him. He is supposed to let me know what happened at his brother's intervention. If it worked the way he wanted it to, he would have called me as soon as it was over. My only thought is that it didn't go well and Seth refused treatment. It wouldn't be Liam's fault, his speech was perfect. It almost made me want to check into rehab.

There's a quick knock on my door and then Chase walks in. "Jessica let me in." He sits on my bed and adds, "She was mumbling something about having to do an intervention on you. Is there something you're not telling me?"

"She's threatened to put me in treatment because of you."

His face crinkles with confusion. "What did I do?"

"Nothing, Chase. Just forget it." I hope he never understands my friends think I have an unhealthy addiction to him.

"Okay. Did you have time to think about what I proposed the other day?"

"Which proposal, the one where you offered to let me move in with you or the one where you offered to impregnate me? There were so many enticing choices, how was I supposed to choose?"

"The one where I asked if you wanted to get back together."

"Chase, we can't get back together, my roommates would kill me. Besides I don't trust you."

"What can I do to prove to you I am serious about us dating? Meg, I'm still in love with you. I want *us*. I want to build a life together. Yes, that means children. It doesn't have to be right away. You can finish your degree first. But you wouldn't have to work. We could travel. My app business can support us."

"All right, Chase, you can stop talking now. You are terrifying me. I'm not ready for any of that. We don't even know each other."

"We do," he says dismissively. "I know you better than anyone."

"No you don't."

"Just think about it. You will never have to work a day in your life. I'll take care of you." A text pings on his phone. "I have to go." His face changes from confidence to concern. "On second thought don't think about it, just go with the flow, Meg. We're going to happen." His eyes twinkle as he gives me that cocky smile. He licks his lips and grasps my chin as he presses his soft lips to mine. The muscle memory of us together floods my head. He pulls back. "Just a taste of what you're missing." He winks at me, then heads down stairs and out the door.

I'm stunned. We still have chemistry. It is obviously there. I suppose it will never completely disappear. I blow out a deep breath. It would be easy to take him up on what he's offering. I wouldn't have to worry about moving or grad school. I could just enjoy my life starting now, like Sarah. She doesn't seem to be worse for the wear being with Jon. Thinking of Sarah makes me think of Liam. He's not the type of guy who would settle down to one girl. But then again neither is Chase. Even Sarah has her doubts about Jonathan. Is that just the way men are? Peterson cheated and he was as vanilla as it gets. *Well that gives me my answer right there.*

I've changed. When Chase and I were in high school we used to talk about what we would do if we had all the money we wanted. Back then I may have joked about traveling the world and never holding a job, but I was a child. If he knew me, he would know I could never do that now. I need to work. I need to be able to support myself, because men are pigs and I will never give someone else the power to control me. I think that was part of my mom's problem—not that my dad would ever cheat, but she felt trapped, unable to fend for herself.

I wish Liam would call me back. I left a voice mail yesterday. He's got to have gotten it by now. He could tell me what to do, give me the guy's point of view. I pick up my phone debating whether I should call him when it lights with a call. It's Sarah.

Thank God.

She can give me real advice about Chase. I can't talk about the Liam factor, but she will set me straight on Chase.

"Oh, Sarah, I'm so glad you called. I need some advice. Chase was just here, and he wants to get back together. He told me that he never stopped loving me—that we could make it work now. What do I do with that?"

"You know you can't get back together with him, right? I mean, you know that or you wouldn't be asking me for advice. He's never treated you well. Even before he started using drugs, he treated you like you were a second-class citizen."

"I know," I admit slowly. Minutes ago I was telling Chase no and now I feel the need to defend him. Old habits are hard to break. "He just seems so different now though, like he's really trying. Did you know he bought me a new phone? It's totally loaded. It has everything. He just gave it to me as a gift—not to say he was sorry and he didn't expect anything in return. He never would have done something like that before. I really think he's sincere."

"He gave you a phone?" asked Sarah. "I bet it *was* totally loaded."

"Wasn't it sweet? So un-Chase. I priced it out, and he had to have paid close to eight hundred for it. I told you he's changed."

"When did he give it to you?"

"Right after we got back from your place. He just showed up with the new one. It had a red bow on it...a bow."

"You know…I talked to Liam today. He told me you two have been keeping in touch."

What? "He told you? He's really great. I wish he lived here. " Maybe she can tell me why he never called. "Is he mad at me?"

"Is there a reason why he should be mad at you?" Sarah asks.

"No, but I called him twice and he hasn't called me back. Did he say anything?"

"Megan, he thinks you leaked the story about his brother's intervention to the press. He only told you and Jon and it came out on Friday on Celebrity Daily. After the story broke, his brother disappeared."

"What? Did they find him?"

"No…He's still missing."

"Well…Jon's got a lot of explaining to do, because I didn't tell any vultures anything. You told Liam it wasn't me, right?"

"I tried, but…" Sarah stutters. "They can't figure out how else it could have leaked."

"They? Jon believes it too? I would never do that. You know I would never—"

"You wouldn't, but the Chase I used to know would. That perfect phone he gave you probably has a stalker app that gives him access to everything you say and text, and your e-mail."

What a fricking bastard. "Damn him…Always the user. Why do I let him do this to me over and over? I can't believe I trusted him again. I let him back in my life and he does this to me? I bet Liam will never talk to me again."

"So you didn't tell anyone about Liam's brother?"

"No…just Jessica and Alli…and they wouldn't tell anyone. I can't believe I fell for his BS. I am so going to tell him where to shove his phone. I should have done it as soon as I noticed him downloading my contact list. I'm going to kill him."

"Hey, Jon and I will replace it. Just tell us what you want and we'll send you a new one."

"That's okay. I still have my old phone. I'll just switch it back. It would be weird having you buy me a new one." I should have let Peterson pummel him. I collapse on the bed when the call ends. I'm going to kill Chase. I wonder why he would sell Liam's story to the press. Does he need the money so badly he would mess with another addict? Isn't there an addict's code? I want to text Liam to try to explain, but I don't want Chase seeing our conversation. Instead I shoot a text to Chase.

> Me: *Thinking about you. Can you stop over tomorrow so we can talk?*
> Chase: *11AM?*
> Me: *See you then.*

He sends a winky face emoji. *What a jerk.* He probably thinks he's going to get a green light on us. I just want to see his face. I can read him better in person.

I head down the warped wooden stairs to the kitchen, hoping to run into my roommates. Either of them could help me map out what I am going to say to Chase and I am sure they are both willing to share their opinions on the situation.

"Hey, did you talk to Sarah?" Jessica asks as soon as I step into the room. She's sitting at the kitchen table with her books spread out around her. Alli is standing next to the counter and it looks as if I've interrupted their conversation.

"Yeah. How did you know?"

"I talked to her before she called you. Did she mention her entire house was being swept for bugs?"

"No. You mean like hidden microphones?" I ask, Jessica.

"That's what she said. Apparently she and Jon have been having some of their personal information leaked, just like Liam, and they want to try to stop it before the wedding gets too close."

I'm quiet after hearing this. I wonder if Chase leaked that too. Now I feel really bad. I look up and Alli rolls her eyes as if Sarah is being paranoid.

"Hope it isn't my phone causing the problem. Or maybe I hope it is my phone. At least we could put an end to it," I say.

"Sarah said the paparazzi just show up wherever they are, as if someone is tipping them off," says Jessica. "That would drive me crazy."

"Isn't that part of the deal when you're engaged to a movie star? It can't be too surprising. They probably just follow her and Jon from the house," says Alli.

"It would still suck." I pull my water bottle from the fridge and turn before announcing, "Chase wants to get back together." I open the cover and take a sip.

"I thought you were already back with him. You mean there is still hope you won't?" asks Jessica. "I just assumed, because he's been over so often lately."

"We are not getting back together. Especially if he's stalking my phone."

"He was stalking your phone?" asks Alli.

"I guess. Liam only told Jon and me about his brother's intervention and it came out in the press. I only told you guys. How else could it have leaked? You know I didn't sell it, not with my history with the press," I say.

"I figured Chase talked you into it. He could always talk you into whatever suited him," says Alli.

I glare at her. *Seriously?* "You figured Chase talked me into selling secrets to the tabloids? What the hell is wrong with you?"

"That's not what she meant. We know you wouldn't," says Jessica. She always tries to smooth over Alli's blunt words.

I look between the two of them. "Whatever." I still can't believe Alli said that. "So what do I say to Chase tomorrow when I confront him?"

"Can I watch when you do it?" asks Jessica. "Because he has been so cocky lately when he comes over and he asked me if I would be interested in a naked sandwich. I smacked him. He's lucky I didn't remove his balls with my foot."

"I can't believe he asked you that." I totally believe it. "After tomorrow you won't ever have to see him again. So what should I say to him? I'm going to switch my phone back to my old one tomorrow morning, and I was thinking about throwing the one he gave me at his head. Or should I take out his baby maker? What do you think?"

"I'd go for the face. So he has to explain the black eyes and broken nose to everyone he sees. His junk, he can hide." Jessica smiles as if she can picture the encounter.

"Don't forget to tell him how good Liam was in bed," adds Alli.

"I never slept with Liam. I told you that."

Alli smiles and rolls her eyes again as if she doesn't believe me.

"I will admit if he offered I would have, but he promised Jon he wouldn't, and we didn't."

"Stop lying," says Alli with her sugary smile.

"I am not talking about this anymore. He and I are just friends. Accept it and move on." I take a large gulp of water and twist the cover back on. "Hopefully he'll forgive me for what Chase did because I really like him."

"Hold onto that. It will help you when you tell Chase off tomorrow." Jessica smiles. "I can help you kick him to the curb, if you want."

"No, I can handle it." And I think I can. He doesn't control me anymore. Ever since I met Liam, Chase's power over me has diminished. I just don't feel the same level of chemistry with him as I used to feel.

When eleven o'clock rolls around the next day, Chase is late. I rushed back from the cell phone store for nothing. He doesn't show until almost noon.

"Hey, babe." He kisses the side of my head. "I got hung up in a meeting with my business partners." I catch the hint of a girl's perfume and I am confident he overslept after spending the night with its wearer.

I give him an insincere smile and direct him upstairs. He sits on my bed, kicking his shoes off, and then leans back against my white headboard.

"You comfortable?"

He smiles a dirty smile and pats the bed next to him. I shake my head and his smile fades. "If you don't want to get back together, why did you ask me over?"

I hold up the phone he gave me and say, "I want you to explain how my personal conversations are being leaked to the media."

"What are you talking about, babe?"

I can't read him. He could be surprised I am confronting him or he could actually have no knowledge of it.

"I don't know what you're talking about." He looks at me, his blue puppy-dog-eyes wide.

"My private conversations are being leaked to the press. Did you put a stalker app on the phone you gave me?" I throw the phone at him and it hits him hard in the chest. *I missed.*

"Is there a stalker app on your phone?" He picks it up off the bed, where it bounced, and lights up the screen. "It was new when I bought it. I paid a premium price. It should be clean."

"Why did you give me the phone? Were you looking for a way to fund your new business?"

"My business funds itself." He shakes his head.

"How did the story about Liam's brother's intervention end up in the tabloids then?"

"How the hell should I know? Maybe he leaked it himself. Isn't that what narcissists do, leak crap and pretend to be surprised when it blows up the internet?"

"He's blaming me. I'm the only one he told." Let's face it, Jon didn't leak Liam's story. I get that. *I'd* blame me too, if I didn't know it was Chase. "He didn't leak it. You are such an ass. No one would do that to themselves."

"I don't know the guy, but it just sounds like something a cable actor would do to get his name out there. Look at all the reality stars who were nothing before leaking their sex tapes. Free publicity, it sells."

"Did you sell my phone conversations to the vultures?" I stare him down with my hands on my hips. "Tell me the truth." I know he did it. People don't change.

"It's me, Meg. What would my motivation be? Seriously, I have enough money to fund a small country. I don't need the microscopic dollars any story about him would bring. I'll show you. Do you want to see my bank accounts? My stock portfolio? What do I have to do to prove to you I didn't do it?"

"Show me."

He looks at me and rolls his eyes as if he can't believe I'm making him show me. Then he takes out his phone and pulls up a web page. It's a bank site. He's got hundreds of thousands of dollars just sitting there and more in stock. He couldn't just pull this out of his butt. It has to be real, but is it his, or his company's?

"All this is yours?"

He scrolls to the top of the page and points to his name. "That's my name."

"In your company's account, you mean? It's not just yours."

"It's all mine, babe. It's my personal account. See? Only my name."

"So you didn't put a stalker app on my phone and sell Liam's story?"

"Why would I waste my time? Honestly, your phone is clean. It's the best phone I could buy, I doubt anyone put anything on it. I think it probably has an app that notifies you of that."

Okay, now I feel stupid. "You promise you didn't leak anything to the press?"

"I promise, Meg."

Damn him. He has that cocky look which tells me not to believe him. I don't know what to do. "I can't tell if you're lying. I switched my number to my old phone this morning. You can have yours back."

He takes the phone and stuffs it into his back pocket. "If that's what you need to do to trust me, fine. I'll do whatever it takes. I will be here for you and I would never accuse you of selling my secrets. The guy's got to be a complete douchebag to believe you would do that kind of shit."

I don't know if he's being passive aggressive implying that I'm a douchebag for accusing him or if he is really talking about Nordstrom.

"I think I just need some space for a while until I get this all figured out. Can you respect that?"

"I can as long as you don't block me or change your number again. I won't bug you, just a text here and there. My company is releasing a new app in June, and I will be crazy busy getting ready for the launch. Then once it's out we'll probably be patching problems. It's been in beta for a year, but there are always glitches that don't show until the release."

"Wow. I didn't know you were working on anything."

"It's a big deal, bigger than Mad Moronic Monkeys, at least in bringing in the dollars. There are way more micro transactions and we're not selling the rights. We've got a huge following. Like I said, I'm going to be super busy, so you take all the time you need." He pats the phone in his back pocket and adds, "I love you, Meg. Don't let Sarah and some attention grabbing Hollywood actor make you doubt that." He kisses my cheek, and walks out the door, without looking back.

I don't know what it is, but I still don't trust him. He obviously didn't do it. He had no motivation. But he's not innocent—he did something.

Chapter 17

Liam

Desperate to find Seth, about a month ago, my parents lifted the gag order about sharing family problems and as the wall between our public and private lives became transparent, it transformed into a circus. In this ring, Seth's high school friends. It turns out Seth's secret drug habit wasn't news to them. The few I was able to get a hold of said his problem was worse than we thought. He wasn't just using designer shit, which is like Russian roulette as it is, but he hooked up with some harder core users as well. With him out of school, right before graduation, everyone at his school has heard the rumors of his disappearance.

In the other ring, my studio. I was right to think they would capitalize on my rehab stint. It's all over the tabloids bringing the show loads of exposure at my expense. I read an article this morning about how next season, my character would be going to treatment for his prescription drug habit. When they wrote my motorcycle accident into the mid-season finale last year I thought it was great. The accident happened while we were filming and I was just happy to still have a job after taking time off to heal. But, the article feeds the publicity to another level. Apparently, my Ashton Post character is a mirror image of me, and the show's writers don't ever struggle for content because they just copy my real life into the storyline. I know it's BS, but it still irritates me that the studio sanctions such garbage.

Finally, in the center ring, my mom's foundation friends blare insincere offers of help and prayers. Mom's colleagues may act the act, but we all know they are more concerned they will lose their top fundraiser before the fiscal deadlines are met. The positive in all the mess is Mom has found a friend in Blair Halbrook, the woman whose son overdosed two years ago and whose daughter first brought Seth's problem to Mom and Dad's attention. She's been giving Mom useful advice about not worrying about what other's think as long as we find my brother. She's right. Nothing is as important as finding Seth safe.

With that in mind, my parents and I have contacted all the hospitals and police departments in the area hoping for information that could lead us to Seth, but so far there hasn't even been a legitimate sighting of him. Of course, the missing person's report filed evoked more negative press for my parents and more exposure for me and the show.

It's been almost three months since Seth disappeared. I really thought the lure of his trust fund would bring him home as soon as his birthday passed, but either he can't find his way back or he's found a way to get by without the money. He probably got by for a while living off others. He could be living in his car, but if he's still burning through money like he was before he left, then he's probably hawked it by now or forgot where he parked it. I've seen enough movies to imagine what he would have to do to survive on the street. That thought rips a hole in me I can't patch.

This afternoon Nak and I are going to ask around at the homeless shelters. There is one that caters to youth between the ages of fifteen and twenty-one. We hope the people there may have seen him. The money for his car is most likely drying up. With the car's title still in my parents' names, the car wouldn't have brought its worth. For as much as I complain about my parents neglect in raising me, I realize not having a roof over my head and food to eat is a problem that never crossed my mind until now.

When Nak arrives, we head to the first shelter on the list. It's the youth shelter. A large guy, who resembles a bouncer who once threw me out of a bar, gives us a tour as if we are looking for a place to fund for the next year.

The thought occurs to me that if we find Seth here my mother will do just that.

"We don't really have anyone who fits your brother's description. The kids will be in the cafeteria for lunch any minute. If they want food, they have to eat with everyone else. You can walk around and talk to them, but don't ask too many questions. These kids spook easily. If they think you're cops, you'll clear out the shelter," the bouncer dude continues, guiding us through a long cement-block hallway and through a double door into the cafeteria.

"Do you get many drug users?" I ask, hoping to hone in on them right away.

"We get mostly runaways, some mental health problems, some prostitution. The kids have to be clean to stay here or clean enough to fake it. If they sell themselves or drugs on the property, they get banned from the facility."

I show him Seth's picture again. "Are you sure you haven't seen him?"

"Doesn't look familiar. You can ask Eddie over there. He's been volunteering here for three years. He knows everyone who comes through here." He points to a guy lining a garbage can with a bag, and Nak and I walk over toward the guy.

"Are you Eddie?" Nak asks and the guy nods.

"I'm looking for my brother and we were wondering if you'd seen him."

He takes the picture I hold up, flips up his glasses, and brings the photo closer to his eyes. "It's hard to say. How long has he been gone?"

"Three months. He was using when he left," I add. This guy gives off a vibe of someone who really cares for the kids.

"The druggies can't stay here. Have you tried the shelter on Stanford?" He hands back Seth's photo.

"We were there last week. We've also been to the ones on Celia and Renteria. We were going to check them again today just in case he came this week. He had a car when he left but we figure he probably sold it for drugs," I say.

"Have you tried the warehouse on Fourth? The white brick one—the fourth floor. It's bad down there. Think worst-case scenario and multiply it by ten."

"No, we haven't tried there yet. Is there anywhere else we should check out?" I ask.

"Helena Park. There's a lot of prostitution, but it's mostly drug-related. Oh, and there's a place in Little Korea I heard about, near Third, but I'm not sure exactly where it is."

"Thanks for your help," I say handing him the card Mom had printed with a picture of Seth, his name, and a contact number to call if he's seen.

He takes the card and puts it into his wallet.

Nak and I watch the kids file into the room. They are a mix of badass and beaten down. Seth isn't here. We wait until the tables are filled before we approach them. They don't even look at his picture before denying they've seen him. On our way out, a girl stops us, asking who we're looking for. Her hair is stringy brown, her eyes hollow, but she's willing to look at Seth's photo.

I may have seen this guy a week ago down near the bus station."

"Was he getting on a bus?" asks Nak.

"I don't know. I sat down next to him on the bench. We talked for a couple of minutes."

"What did he say?"

She shrugs. "The only reason I remember him is because I thought he was cute and he had expensive shoes."

"What was he wearing?" I ask. I know what he left the house in because Mom and Dad watched the security video of him leaving the house, but I want to know how disheveled he is after three months.

"I don't know. Jeans? All I remember is his shoes. They were like yours."

I look down at the green suede court shoes I'm wearing, remembering the server's remark about him having the same shoe. This is the first real lead we've gotten. Even the private detective Dad hired hadn't produced anything substantial. *Last week. That's good news.* "Can you tell us anything else you remember?"

"He was quiet. A lot of guys get all handsy with me, but he didn't. I wouldn't have minded with him."

"Thanks." I hand her the card with Seth's face and tell her to call the number if she sees him again.

"Is there a reward?" she asks.

Nak purses his lips, and I quickly answer. I know he's thinking she's just looking for money.

"If you call with a tip that leads to us finding him, you could get up to a couple thousand." I'll pay it out of my own pocket if I have to. My parents were told attaching a reward to our search would cause a flood of false sightings, but that was a month ago. We're more desperate now. I pull a fifty from my wallet and hand it to the girl. She stuffs it into her pocket and walks backward toward the dorm door as if I'm going to ask for it back. She smiles her first smile as she turns to walk through the door.

"That was a real lead?" Nak sounds surprised. "I figure you wouldn't give her money if you didn't believe her." He holds the door for me to exit. "To the bus station?"

"Yep."

We hit the bus station and the two other shelters we visited last week before showing up in front of the white brick building on Fourth that Eddie told us about. It's our last resort. I'm supposed to leave for Jon and Sarah's wedding next week. I need to find Seth before I leave. The building looks abandoned. I pull on the one door as Nak pulls on the other. Both are locked. I peer through the cracked glass of the door, cupping my hand over my eyes to cut the glare. "There's no one inside."

I start walking toward the narrow passage between the white brick building and the one next to it.

"You know, since Leslie and I are dating again, I'm like a sister to Jonathan Williams."

"I won't sleep with you then." I smile because I know he's implying Jon wouldn't be happy with me if he got killed today.

"We'll be fine." *I hope.*

Liam

Nak and I find a propped open fire door, hidden from the view of the alley, and peek inside.

"You brought your gun, right?" Nak's voice quivers, and it makes me wish I really had a gun.

"Of course. Did I tell you how much I appreciate…" I stop midsentence when the stench stabs my nostrils and swallows my head. My stomach heaves and I cover my mouth and nose with my T-shirt. It's not enough. I cup it tighter with my hand. We climb the stairs unsure what we will find on the fourth floor. When we reach the second-floor landing, we get a small taste of what's to come. A guy lies sprawled across the walkway as if lying face down on the cement is the most natural place to sleep. We don't speak as we step over him, but Nak points to his shoes.

Seth's shoes.

He's not the right build to be my brother and I cringe at the thought of why he's wearing them.

"Where'd you get these shoes?" I ask through my shirt while prodding him with my foot. A grunt is the only response I get and I'm pretty sure in his state, he doesn't know. We continue up the steps and figure out where the disgusting odor is coming from. The third-story landing is apparently a bathroom. A kiddy pool filled with human waste is pushed into the corner. Its contents nearly brimming the pool's edge. We move quickly to the fourth floor and when we step inside, the stench dissipates enough to uncover our mouths. Now the smell of both fresh and stale urine mixes with acrid, sweet smoke.

"Let's just hope we find him, because I'm not telling my mom some long-haired, balding guy was wearing his shoes."

"You're buying me a new pair of shoes," says Nak. He's joking, but I will. His comment helps me cope with this place.

We walk down a long, dark hallway with a single window lighting the far end. It looks like an office building stuck in the sixties. The transom above the first door we come to leaks smoke into the hallway and I try the handle. I recoil as my hand sticks to the knob, but I manage to unlatch the door enough to push it open with my shoulder. Nak walks through in front of me. We both silently survey the large room, trying not to bring attention to ourselves or maybe we are both in shock. This is ten times worse than the worst-case scenario I pictured in my head. I thought there would be a bunch of guys passed out on a couch with music blaring, but there is no furniture here except a couple of mattresses. A guy crouches on his knees ten feet from us giving another a blow job, and neither seems put off by us walking in the door. I scour each face to make sure it's not Seth. Who knows what he would do in his desperate state? I hope the money from his car has held out.

We continue deeper into the room examining the circles of two to three people huddling together. These humans are barely alive. The dark cave of the room sucks all life out of the atmosphere. I wonder how many here have family looking for them and how many will die without seeing their families again. I can't let Seth die here. We edge closer to one group, which has a guy who could be Seth, and they turn defensively toward us. I just need to see their faces. Nope, not Seth. On to the next clutch.

We make it most of the way around the room before the guy on the receiving end by the door approaches us.

"Sorry. I was taking care of business when you came in." He smiles as his eyes brush down my body and then up Nak's. *Worse than the third-floor landing.* "I only have one rule. First timers have to use a nickel in front of me before I'll sell you anymore. I've got kits if you need 'em."

I don't respond to the guy's words because I want to kick the shit out of him and we may need him to find Seth. That's when I spot a body slumped alone on a mattress next to the wall just past the dealer. It fits Seth's build. No shoes. I rush over, lifting the guy's head to see his face. My body begins shaking and I can't breathe. Not like this. I didn't want to find him like this. Tears leak from my eyes as I lay him flat on the mattress and pull out the syringe flapping in his arm. His eyes flutter, barely opening before they close again. I feel sick. I suck in a breath and I feel Nak's hand on my shoulder. I can't think. Tremors rake through me.

"Let's get him out of here," says Nak, helping me up.

I blow out the air in my lungs and we pull Seth up, draping his arms over our shoulders and clasping a hand at his waist. The dealer says something my mind doesn't process and I don't respond. I don't know how we get out of there, but somehow we make it past the poop pool and out the exit. When we get to the car, I support him while Nak opens the doors. We fumble getting him onto the back seat. The tops of his feet are bloody from dragging on the sidewalk but I can't do anything about it now. He's barely breathing. I punch "hospitals" into my phone and pull up the navigation to the closest one. I reach back and smack Seth in the stomach to keep him awake until we get there. I figure if he's uncomfortable, he won't stop breathing.

We pull up at the hospital emergency door and Nak runs inside to get help. I open the back door and push on Seth's shoulder.

"You stupid kid. What the hell were you thinking? You think we'd just let you die?" I hit him again in the chest. Tears are running down my face again by the time Nak returns with help.

Chapter 19

Megan

WTF? I end the call with Sarah midsentence, throwing my phone as hard as I can against the door and smashing it into pieces. I can't believe this. My whole life is out of control. I thought I was done being accused of leaking secrets three months ago when I gave Chase his phone back. I guess now I am leaking Sarah and Jon's secrets—not just Nordstrom's.

I pull the tabloid Chase bought yesterday, out of my desk. He and I were picking up ice cream to celebrate the success of his app launch when he spotted it in the checkout aisle. The second I saw it, I froze—a picture of Sarah's family's cabin on the front cover. I knew firsthand how it would destroy Sarah. I lived that sensationalized life before, maybe not to the level Sarah lives it, but in a smaller, local sense, and she completely discounts my experience when she accuses me of selling her out.

Does she not remember what happened when my mom died? I can't believe I'm the one being blamed.

I read through the article again. The details are shocking. I never talked on the phone about her and Jon meeting online or any of the particulars about their first sexual encounter, and I never mentioned any of the specifics in this article to Chase. It couldn't have been him leaking it. Yet, I can't imagine Sarah telling anyone but her three best friends those secrets. It has to be one of us.

But I'm the one being blamed.

And I am the one being uninvited to the wedding of the century.

I cram the magazine back into my desk drawer. All I need is for my roommates to see me with it. I have to get out of here.

I pick up the pieces of plastic that used to be my phone and shove them into my purse. First stop—buy a new phone. Second stop—pick up boxes so I can move home. I can't stay here if everyone thinks I betrayed Sarah and I can't stomach watching my roommates pack for the wedding.

The wedding was going to be my opportunity to prove to Nordstrom I wasn't the one who sold him out. *Now what is he going to think?* I'll never get a chance to talk to him ever again. That door is closed for me and locked with a billion dead bolts.

I slip into my running shoes, grab my purse, and walk down the narrow stairs and out the door as if my life isn't falling apart again. When I reach my car, tears threaten my composure and I pause for a moment to push them back inside. This isn't the worse thing to happen to me. I have to get some perspective. At least no one died. It just feels as if someone did. That's when I hear Chase call my name. Just what I need—more chaos. I lean my head against the hot metal of the car trying to gather strength before pinning on a fake smile and turning to face him.

"I thought we were doing lunch? Were you ditching our plans?"

"Sorry, I forgot. My phone broke. I was going to get a new one." I open my purse and show him the pieces to prove I'm not a liar. I wish I could prove I'm not a liar to Sarah.

"It looks like someone pissed you off. Hope it wasn't me," he says with a laugh.

"No, it wasn't you."

"You seem upset. Why don't we grab some lunch and then deal with the phone? Come on. I'm driving." He grasps my shoulders, pulls me away from my Beetle, and spins me toward his car."

His arm wraps around my shoulder and I lean into him. He's all I've got. He opens the passenger door of his sports car and I collapse into the bucket seat.

By the time our food arrives at our table in the café, I've told him about the call from Sarah and how I was no longer going to the wedding. I figure it wasn't him leaking it if he never knew the details in the tabloid.

"Two weeks before Sarah and Jon's wedding and I just got uninvited. We've been friends since we were fifteen and she believes I'd sell her private life to the press. She's nuts. I've heard of brides going crazy under the stress of their weddings but…really?"

"Well, that sucks. I guess you'll never see naked sandwich guy again." He smiles, and I want to slap him.

"You're such an ass."

"I'm the ass? I'm not the one accusing you of something you didn't do. Sarah's the one who crossed over. She and the actor are too narcissistic to see the truth. Their loss, my gain."

"What do you mean your gain?"

"It's the final straw. If I was you, I would never give the guy another thought. He's the ass, and Sarah's never been a fan of me. I figure she's been poisoning you about me. Now maybe you and I can finally move forward." He licks his lips like he does when he's planning to make his move.

I shake my head at his *me, me, me* attitude. I don't need his *two cents* right now, and I definitely don't need him making moves on me.

"Just chill. Sarah hasn't been poisoning my mind. She's been too busy planning the wedding of the decade, which I'm no longer going to be at, and I haven't heard from Nordstrom since April. That's three months. I doubt he even remembers my name." I'll never forget him, but he had no problem forgetting me.

"What are you going to do now?"

"I haven't talked to Jessica or Alli yet. I don't know what they believe. In reality, it could be one of them, or it could be the Pope. I can't care anymore. It's not my problem." It is my problem, but I'm trying to get through this the only way I can cope. "I think I'm going to move out of the rental and back home. My room is still there. Will you help me move?"

"Why don't you just move in with me? It's a big house. You could have your own room, rent-free, if that's what you need."

"My dad's house is rent-free, too. I was planning on moving home after the wedding anyway. Our lease is up at the end of July. That's just a few weeks away, and I'll be starting grad school a couple weeks after that. I need to spend some time with my family. You can understand that, right?"

"Why don't we head back to my house and get some boxes. You can take a look around and see what you think."

I haven't been to his house. I've been avoiding it, thinking it would be too easy for us to slip into our old ways on his territory. There is something stopping me from being with him. I don't know what it is, but right now, I am just too weak to fight.

We pull up at a huge estate, which looks way too intense to be owned by the Chase Maxwell I used to know. He parks the car on the drive just outside the open garage and looks to me. He opens the center console and pulls out the phone he gave me months ago.

"You may as well use this now that you know I didn't stalk the actor. It's just sitting here. No one's touched it since you gave it back to me."

"Thanks." I take it from him and put it in my purse. It will save me some money if I don't have to buy a new phone.

"I've been trying to get you into my lair for months and all you needed was for your friends to turn on you. They've been holding you back, babe."

His words spring my life's problems to front and center. I don't understand how Sarah could think I would ever talk to the press. She mentioned Alli said I was talking in private all the time. That's a lie. Yes, I've tried to keep my conversations with Chase private, but I've barely talked to him in the last three months. He's been busy with his app launch and I've been busy too. First finals, then graduation, and then I started working for Professor Dunlap. The research she was working on needed to be finished and written up so she could get published, again, and that is what I spent eight hours a day doing, sometimes ten, for the last month. We just finished yesterday. I've hardly been at the rental house. How would Alli know anything about what's going on in my life?

"You all right?" asks Chase as we reach the front door.

"Yeah. I'm just still a bit miffed about what happened with Sarah, but I'll get over it."

He opens the door and as we walk in, I realize his house is very much a bachelor pad. Black leather furniture with grey walls and white trim. The blinds are closed in the large room to the right of the entryway and even though it is the middle of the day, the room is black, except a small strip of light coming from the kitchen. Chase taps on his phone and the blinds slowly rise, revealing a large wall of windows.

"Why don't you have a seat?" He motions to the couch and walks into the kitchen. "I'm going to get us some drinks," he calls from the other room.

Now that the blinds are open, I see that the grey walls are covered in some sort of acoustical fabric, and four large screens hang on the wall in front of the sofa and chair arrangement. Tiny speakers circle the room at ear height. This must be where he plays video games. It makes sense— the room darkening blinds, the sound system, and the multiple screens. He returns with two large glasses of lemonade. I half expected mine to be spiked with alcohol—I could use it—but it is just plain, virgin lemonade. I guess it wouldn't make sense for him to have alcohol in the house when he's sober.

I sit back, crossing my legs, and when something scrapes against my shorts, I reach back to remove the source of the discomfort. It's a condom wrapper. I can tell by the size and shape. I pull it out of the crevice of the cushion. Yep, a used condom wrapper. At least it's not a used condom.

"Should I be worried about where I sit?" I hand it to Chase, and he smiles.

"I never said I would be celibate waiting for you," he says without apology as he shoves it into his pocket.

"Me neither," I say, though I've been nothing but celibate for the last three months. His eyebrows narrow and I can tell he didn't like my comment. *Too bad.* "Is this where you work?"

"No this is the playroom. I have a computer room downstairs. I'll show you around." He stands and offers me his hand. I take it and he doesn't let go. "Maybe you'll change your mind about moving in." We make it to the master bedroom and he playfully pulls me inside. "You have to see the bed. It's the best part. Well there's one part that's better, but you'll have to beg to see that." He scoops me up and tosses me on the bed. He starts tickling my knees like he used to do when we were in high school and I can't catch my breath. Finally he stops, but his hands linger on my thighs. He is so damn manipulative and charming, and I am at such a low right now. Part of me wonders why I don't just give in. It's not as if being with him again would add to my number count. Why am I resisting so much? I'm moving at the end of summer. I have a built-in out.

Just then, his phone buzzes. "I've got to take this. Don't move. It won't take long." He walks into the bathroom, closing the door behind him, but I can still hear every word he says. "Don't be mad. Don't. Something came up…work…I'll make it up to you on Sunday. I promise. Of course, you know me. See you then, babe." The door opens and he jumps back on the bed next to me as if the call never happened. I can hear both sides of his conversation in my mind. I've been in that conversation with him, how many times?

"Your partner in non-celibacy?" I ask. I expect him to try to lie, but he doesn't.

"She's just someone to fill my time until you see the light. I'd end it with her right now if you commit to us. Move in with me." He smiles that cocky smile and tries to melt me with the dirty look in his blue eyes.

I wish I could believe him. I get off the bed and smile back at him shaking my head. *Will he ever change?* At least he didn't try to lie about the call. "You promised me some boxes."

"I did." He stares at me a moment longer, as if analyzing my thoughts, then gets up and walks to the garage. I guess he must sense I'm not going to commit today.

I follow.

By the time Alli and Jessica appear in my doorway, Chase and I have most of my room boxed.

"You're moving today? I thought we were all staying until the lease was up?" asks Jessica. She looks pissed.

"Yep." I stuff my comforter from my bed into the box Chase just staged without looking up.

"She's moving in with me," says Chase nonchalantly as he tapes the bottom of another box.

I lift my head to meet Alli's eyes. "I'm not moving in with Chase. He's helping me move home. Apparently Sarah and Jon feel I am the person who leaked their love secrets to the press. I'm not. I figure if I move out of the house I can no longer be blamed for their problems. You two can draw straws on who gets blamed next." I know I sound bitter, but I don't care. I am bitter. I grab an empty box and push past them. "I've got to get my stuff from the kitchen."

"Don't let Jon's paranoia control you. You don't have to move out. It's their problem, not yours," says Alli as she trails behind me on the stairs.

"Well, Sarah called and uninvited me to the wedding, so it kind of is my problem. I'd rather not know about what is going on in their life, and frankly, I don't care anymore."

"Sarah will come around. She had to expect the paparazzi to up their game as the wedding nears."

I round the corner into the kitchen, setting the box on the counter. "Didn't you see the article that came out this week? It's pretty explicit. It wasn't just the paparazzi upping their game. It was personal, but it wasn't me. I'm just removing myself from the equation. Text me and I'll come back to help with the final cleaning." I open my cupboard and start loading my food into the box.

"What?"

"The tabloids know all the secrets about how Jon and Sarah met. I didn't do it. Yet, I'm being blamed." I can't say anymore without raging. I close the now empty food cupboard and move to the dish cupboard. I slide my plates just inside the edge of the cardboard box and then pull my glasses onto the counter. One by one, I shove the four glasses I own haphazardly amongst my cereal boxes and chip bags. I really should eat more healthily.

Alli still hasn't said anything. I don't care what she thinks. I stuff a few more items in the box and fold the corners in to close it. "The Wi-Fi router is mine, but you can use it until the end of summer. My dad has one and I won't need it until I move to California."

Just then, Chase appears in the doorway of the kitchen. "What are you moving to California for?" He sounds annoyed.

"Grad school," I say. Didn't I tell him where I was going to school? "I told you. I've got a full ride at UCLA. I'm pretty sure I told you."

"Nope." He draws out the word. "When are you leaving?" He's looking around the room, shaking his head like he used to when he was exasperated with my nagging.

"Five or six weeks. I thought I told you."

He shakes his head. "I thought you were going to the U."

"No. It was always between L.A. and New Jersey, never here."

"L.A. is where Naked Sandwich lives?"

Alli's expression turns to confusion. I'm not going to explain. "Haven't talked to him in three months. You're more obsessed with him than I ever was." *Total lie.*

"With you moving out there, I have less time than I thought. You and I are going on a date tonight."

Jessica chooses that moment to check on the commotion in the kitchen. *Great. Just great.*

"So you two are dating?" she asks.

"Maybe," I say. "I'm tired of people telling me what I can and can't do, and then falsely accusing me of selling their secrets. If I want to date Chase, I'm going to." I turn and lock eyes with him. "And, if I decide you're too much of a pain to date, I won't. My body. My brain. My choice." I scoop the box off the counter and carry it out of the room, setting it on the floor next to the front door. Then I head upstairs for another box and to escape the crowd following me.

Megan

Almost two weeks have passed since I moved back into Dad's house. Chase and I were too tired after the move to go on a proper date, so we ordered pizza. It felt a bit like high school, especially when my dad walked in on us. We were just eating so it wasn't as embarrassing as it was in high school. The scowl that appeared on Dad's face reminded me I had lied to him about Chase not being the ex I was going to get back with. It also reminded me about Dad's opinion of Chase.

Back in high school, my dad's opinion would have pushed me into Chase's arms just like my friend's opinion did this time, but not anymore. It makes me more cautious. I had a long talk with Chase about us not sleeping together until I get to know him better. I'm pretty sure he expected us to just jump back into bed. We're taking it slow. Saturday will be our first official date. He won't tell me where we are going, but he wants me to wear a dress. He's planning to take me out to a fancy restaurant and then we're meeting a couple of his friends at a club. I think it's good to get to know his friends. It will give me a better understanding of him than just believing what he shows me.

Chase is in Las Vegas at a software conference, right now, and he won't be back until late tonight. That's why he scheduled our date for tomorrow.

I'm glad I will have something to distract me tomorrow from the fact that I'm missing Sarah's wedding. I don't want to be sitting at home stewing over it.

Over the last week, Dad and I have talked a lot about Chase. As he stated before, he doesn't think I should give Chase another chance. His point is, I'm going to move anyway. And, to my defense, I'm going to be moving and if I don't check out whether Chase and I belong together, it may be one of those points in my life I wonder *what if*.

Surprisingly, Dad and Joann have dinner almost every night at the house. I guess I would have known that if I hadn't avoided the house. Joann usually makes the meal and asks me to join them. Even my brothers have showed up a couple of days. Tonight, it is just Dad and Joann, and I offered to cook. I haven't cooked for the family since the Thanksgiving from hell, but I figure I need to get over it.

I make a pasta and vegetable dish. My dad avoids anything green, so I thought I would show him how good vegetables can be if cooked right with a good, spicy sauce. It's a recipe I learned last summer, and even though I don't have a written recipe to follow, it turns out pretty tasty. Over dinner, I explain why I'm not going to Sarah and Jon's wedding. The words catch in my throat as I explain how Sarah called and uninvited me to the wedding. I still don't understand her logic—some picture got leaked from her graduation party and was supposedly taken by me because I was the only one not in the photo. I don't even remember taking the picture. If I was a revengeful person, I would open an account on Twitter and tweet the hell out of Sarah's wedding invitation, but I can't do that. I understand her frantic need to protect herself. I get it, but I'm not the one who betrayed her.

I regret not getting the opportunity to defend myself to Nordstrom. I was looking forward more than anything to being able to talk to him. It feels good to get all of the garbage with Sarah's wedding out in the open with Dad and Joann. I don't mention Liam, though. Dad doesn't need to know about him. Joann tells me Sarah will come to her senses someday and apologize. It won't matter by then—too little, too late.

After dinner, I change into a tank and my favorite workout shorts. Not because I plan to work out and erase the sadness that's clung to me for days by raising my endorphin levels, but because I want to wallow in self-pity in comfort. With the wedding tomorrow, everyone in the wedding party is celebrating. Alli and Jessica have been on the island for five days and if Nordstrom hasn't noticed before today, he is aware I am missing by now. My absence will just bolster his opinion that I sold his story to the tabloids.

The doorbell rings as I head downstairs and I hesitate to answer it because I am not only wearing the smallest pair of shorts I own, but I have no bra on under my tank. I wonder if Chase got back early from Vegas and came straight from the airport. I open the door and freeze at the sight.

Nordstrom stands on the porch holding a single pink rose and the most tentative smile I've ever seen. *God, he's gorgeous.*

My heart practically jumps out of my chest. I can't fight the smile spreading across my face and I try. I really try. I step outside and close the door behind me. His eyes rake over my body, lingering on my almost nonexistent shorts and my nonexistent bra. I cross my arms over my chest and attempt to find the appropriate words to get the answers I need, while simultaneously stopping my body from wrapping itself around him. I focus on his smile and try to forget I have almost no clothes on.

"Aren't you supposed to be on an island in the Caribbean?"

"I'm exactly where I'm supposed to be—groom's orders."

He hands me the flower and an envelope, which looks like hotel stationery.

"Why are you here?" I ask.

"Open it."

"No."

"Please," he says. "For me." His fingers comb through his hair and his dark eyes widen as they focus on mine.

I have no idea what to expect as I slide my finger to break the seal. I pull out the white paper with an embossed stamp from the island resort and unfold it to note the author first. It's not Liam.

> *Dear Megan,*
> *Please accept our deepest apology. We've been stricken*

*with the rare and sometimes fatal disease, Pre-wedding
Assholism. The symptoms include: falsely accusing best
friends of atrocious acts, stupidly uninviting them to your
wedding, and uncontrollably grieving when you realized
what you have done in your insane state. The only way to
recover and survive is to recognize you have contracted the
disease and rectify the situation before it is too late. I know
we have no right to ask anything of you, but if you could find
it in your heart to forgive us and come to our wedding, you
could save us from a debilitating end. Feel free to take your
anger out on Nordstrom. He is our new whipping boy and
at your disposal.*

Love always,

Jon and Sarah

I can't help but break out laughing as I smack Nordstrom in the
shoulder with an open fist. His jaw drops and he cocks his head in disbelief.
It feels good to hit him. He obviously hasn't read the letter.

"It says I can do that right here. You're lucky I didn't hit you harder." I
hand the paper to him and let him read it before smacking him harder on
the other side.

"Apparently I just have to take being beaten by you. That's what a
whipping boy does, right?"

I nod.

"Well, I'm not going to let you keep hitting me unless you agree to come
to the wedding with me." He looks down at me, his dark eyes sparkling with
anticipation.

"I'll have to think about it," I say. "Come back tomorrow." I reach
behind me, open the door and take a step back.

"The wedding is tomorrow. I have to come back with you before the
wedding or Jon doesn't want me back at all."

"Harsh. I guess the bromance is over." We fall into our banter easily.

"No. Because you are coming back with me tonight. Let's go pack your stuff. And get a bra on you. How the hell am I supposed to not touch these?" His hand hovers inches above my right nipple as it salutes him in complete obedience. Electricity shoots through my body, ricocheting off every extremity at the thought of him touching me. Somehow, I forgot how his presence awakens me.

"Come meet my dad," I say, turning and walking through the doorway. Though the last thing I want to do is to bring Dad into this, I need to let him know I am leaving for the wedding. I can't just disappear for days anymore without him noticing. We find him and Joann on the screened porch, off the kitchen.

"Dad. Joann. This is Liam Nordstrom. He's friends with Sarah and Jonathan, and has flown…" I turn to Liam and ask. "How long was your flight?"

"Six hours."

"Really? That long? Wow, they really owe you." I smile at Liam and then turn back to Dad. "He's flown six hours to apologize and ask me to go back with him for the wedding." I turn back to Liam. "Can I even say that with all the non-disclosure agreements?"

"Under the circumstances, I think you can," says Liam.

"So you are going to go to Sarah's wedding after all?" Dad asks.

I turn to Nordstrom and his eyebrows are raised as if he is asking the same question and he's nodding in encouragement. He mouths, *please*.

"I guess, I am." *He said please after all.* I smile at my dad and Joann. After our discussion at dinner, I think they understand.

"Have a good time," Joann says, returning a smile.

My dad takes out his wallet and then holds out a wad of cash to me. "Take it," he says. "You don't have time to stop at the bank. The wedding is tomorrow. When is the flight out?"

I take the cash and look to Liam.

"Whenever we get there. The plane is on standby, waiting for us. But we can't leave any later than two AM or we could be late for the wedding."

I head upstairs to pack, motioning for Liam to follow me. I don't know what to think about him being here. Does he finally believe I didn't talk to the vultures? We reach my room, which is a whole different issue. My room is a total disaster. But I can't care. There is nothing I can do about it. At least I have the excuse about still unpacking after the move. I hold the door open directing Liam inside. When we are both inside, I close the door and turn to face him.

"Why are you here? And what changed Sarah's mind?" I ask placing my hands on my hips and pursing my lips.

"Can I sit down?"

I nod.

He sits on the edge of my bed and admits, "I'm here because Jon asked me to come."

"So you don't want to be here?"

"I didn't say that. I'm not the type of guy who jumps off a cliff because his friend tells him to. But, I wouldn't be here if he hadn't asked. I'd be partying on the beach with my bros."

I guess I can accept that. "What changed Sarah's mind about me? I know what the letter said, but what really happened?"

"Sarah caught Red taking pictures of the reception area this morning. She never turned her phone in. There was a big blow up and she confessed she sold out to the press." He glances at me with raised eyebrows as if to say *can you believe that*?

I'm pissed. I glare at him. "Alli sold them out to the vultures and I got blamed. And the only reason they believe me is because they caught her red-handed." I walk over to him and smack him in the stomach with an open hand. "They sent you because they know I couldn't resist you. Damn it." I hold up my hand as if I'm going to hit him again but pause in midair.

He smirks, probably because of my lack of resistance. Then he reaches over his head and pulls his shirt off. "Does this help?"

Cocky bastard.

"Yes." I hit him again. "The skin on skin sound makes me feel better."

"I never knew that about you, Meg. It puts a whole new light on our non-hookup."

I chuckle at the mischievous look on his face.

"I can't believe Alli did that. Why would she just let me hang? Alli knew I wasn't guilty and she acted as if she believed I could be. What a bitch. I didn't sell you out either. You know that now, right?"

He looks at me as if analyzing my words and then says, "Yeah."

"And Sarah is not that much better than Alli. She should have known I would never sell anyone to the press. She just should have known that."

"She said she was sorry. She and Jon meant it. It was sincere."

"I know. I'm just…mad."

"Well, you can be mad on the plane. You have a six-hour flight to get over it, because it's Sarah's wedding and I think she needs your support more than ever after Alli betrayed her."

He's right. She apologized. I can make her grovel after the wedding. Tomorrow is not the day.

Two hours later, we board a gorgeous private jet at the Humphrey Terminal. It reminds me of our houseboat with its glossy wood accents and white walls.

"These are our best bet if we want to get any sleep," says Liam, pointing to two chairs that look as if they recline into beds. I plant myself in one and he sits next to me. The attendant gets us settled and runs through safety procedures just like on a normal flight, except she is talking only to us or rather me, since Liam already heard her presentation. She seems to have developed a camaraderie with Liam. I gather from their conversation that they played cards to pass time on the last flight.

The plane is taxiing and within minutes, we're in the air. When I look over at Liam, I see his mask going up and feel him distancing himself.

"Did Seth ever come home?" I ask, aching to talk to him.

"Yep. He did. He's in treatment." He has his unreadable face on.

"I'm glad everything worked out," I say. "I didn't sell you to the press, you know that, right? I told Alli about Seth. It must have been her. I'm sorry."

He nods. Then he reclines his chair. "We should get some sleep or we'll be zombies in the pictures tomorrow." He pulls up the dividing arm between our chairs and pushes my chair into a reclining position. He motions for me to flip on my side. I don't want to because I won't be able to see him, but I think he plans to snuggle and I can't pass on it. His arm curls around me and I can smell the hint of his cologne. *So good.* "We'll talk more tomorrow," he whispers.

I know he's a flirt and this is the way he treats all women. I'm not special to him, but it still feels good being in his arms. The heat radiating off his body sends tingles to my toes. Knowing he is so close, my body purrs. I've thought about his hands on me so many times. I've thought about his tongue dragging across my skin, and the way the heat of his body pressed against mine burns in the most delicious way. And now, that's all I can think about. His long fingers inch under the edge of my shirt and I start to fantasize about making up for the non-hookup we had three months ago. I'm wide awake, staring out the window at the black sky. I hear his breathing even out and I can tell by the weight of his arm he's fallen asleep.

I must have nodded off too at some point because now I am flush against Nordstrom's hot body and his morning wood is pressed between my butt cheeks. I'm not going to read into it. I know it is biological, but it makes me realize just how long it's been since I've gotten any. I probably should have slept with Chase just to curb my need. *Dammit!* I forgot to send Chase a text. He's going to come pick me up for our date and I won't be there. I don't have a phone to text him. I left it at home because it would just get confiscated when I arrive on the island, anyway.

"Liam," I whisper.

No response.

"Liam," I say again, louder.

His hips gyrate and he rubs against me with a sexy growl.

Screw Chase. I am not moving from this position.

He rubs against me again as his hand skims across my stomach and softly cups my breast. He squeezes my breast, pushing against me again, and then mumbling unintelligibly he falls back to sleep. Even unconscious he's good in bed.

Megan

I feel like such an idiot. The whole time he was at my house and with me on the plane, he was playing me. Liam acted sweet, but he was acting. And I believed him. I believed it was more than a favor to Jonathan. *Stupid me.*

I stretch out on a lounger, next to the pool. It's quieter than the beach and I'll end up with less sand in my privates. I'm a little hungover from last night's celebration, but nothing bad enough to stay inside and nurse. I haven't seen any of the other bridesmaids yet. They're all probably curled up with their significant others having morning sex. *Am I the only one not getting any?*

The real reason I chose the pool is that the groomsmen seem to be using this area to meet up and I want to run into Liam. I want some answers. I figure, I'm more visible here. I really thought when I got on the plane to fly to this paradise the day before yesterday, I may still have a chance with him. After all, I wasn't the one who leaked his brother's story to the press, and he flew all the way to Minnesota to ask me to come to the wedding. I thought Jon gave us his blessing to be together when he sent him with the apology letter. But now, I know I was wrong. Liam lied about talking after we got sleep. He ignored me yesterday.

It was as if he was avoiding me even as we walked arm in arm through the crowd at the end of the wedding ceremony. I kept thinking, why isn't he looking at me? He wouldn't look at me. The custom gown formed to my every curve and he never acknowledged it. I felt radiant in it and he never made the effort to see it. We shared one dance, the one required of a bridesmaid and groomsman who are paired, but that's it. His solemn mask was up the entire dance. He didn't even smile. As the night progressed, I thought I felt his eyes on me a couple of times, but when I turned to catch him, he was always looking the other direction. It was just wishful thinking on my part. I guess now that the wedding is over, he's no longer obligated to talk to me.

It doesn't take long before the guys notice me. As I'm pulling my sunscreen from my bag, Hayden Nappo plops down on the chair next to me and immediately offers to help apply it to my back. He's probably the least noticeable of Jonathan's groomsmen. He's good-looking by anyone's standards with spiked, bleach-blond hair and a well-groomed beard, but next to the other guys in the group, he fades into the background. I had a good conversation with him last night at the reception, though, and danced with him a couple of times. He's really funny, and I take him up on his offer for the sunscreen. There's no sign of Nordstrom and a girl's got to prevent burning—especially in this equator sun.

He taps out a beat on the sunscreen bottle as he squeezes it out into his hand and it reminds me that he's the drummer in a band. I'm sure he's had his share of women.

"I'm going to undo these strings." He pulls on my bikini strings, laying them gently by my sides. "You don't want to get tan lines."

I'm positive I'm showing some serious side boob, but I don't care. I know these guys see way more than I'm showing, all the time. He smooths the lotion onto my back and even gets the back of my legs and arms, which I am grateful for, because now that my suit is untied, I can't reach back to do it myself. He's gentle and respectful of my body, not trying to cop a feel like I'm sure Nordstrom would and before I know it, he's done.

"How's that?" he asks, setting the sunscreen on the cement near my chair.

"Great. Thank you."

He lies on the chair next to me and asks, "Are you staying the whole week?"

"I had planned to, but now I don't know. Are you?"

"No. We've got to leave tomorrow. We're still touring and people get suspicious when one of your best friends is Jonathan Williams and you reschedule a week's worth of shows. It's a dead giveaway that it's for his wedding. We have to play Plano, Texas tomorrow night. There are only so many days we can take off without inciting riots."

"At least you got to come."

"I'd never miss Jon's wedding. Hell, I wouldn't miss any of the guys' weddings. When we were in high school, the guys—Jonathan, Chris, Liam, Nick, and I made a bet. We each put a thousand bucks in and we had Nick's dad invest it in his record label. The last one of us boys to get married gets the pot. The profits are valued around a million right now. Since Chris and Jonathan are already out, by the time I wait out Nick and Liam, the investment should be double that. If any of us miss another's wedding, we forfeit our winnings."

"Do you have to get married to win?"

"Yep." He nods with a big smile.

"Do you really think you can wait out Nick?" I ask, because of all the groomsmen, he seems the least likely to settle down.

"Nick will be the next one to jump. He's been engaged three times already. Liam is going to be the tough one to wait out. He doesn't have a committing bone in his body." He pauses and adds, "If you're not doing anything in ten years, want to get hitched?"

"Sure, if you split the winnings with me." I smile. He's easy to talk to, and we chat, soaking in the sun and recovering from last night's partying, until some obnoxious asshole I'm pretty sure I'm falling for plops himself in my personal space—not just any personal space either. *What the hell?* He collapses on top of me with his head resting on my booty without saying a word.

Hayden flips onto his side facing me and asks, "Is he bothering you,

Megan? I'm pretty sure I can get security over here and have him banned from this area if he's a problem."

"I'd like to see you try," Liam announces as his hands fluff my butt like a pillow.

"Do you mind, Nordstrom," I say, looking over to Hayden and rolling my eyes.

"I don't mind. For as amazingly tight as your ass looks, it is actually quite comfortable."

I reach back, flicking his cheek with my finger, and he pinches my butt in retaliation.

"Megan, don't you see? He's just marking you as his property, so the rest of us will leave you alone. I can smell the urine from here. He just peed all over you," Hayden says as if it is completely obvious.

"I'm not marking her. Besides, she's not your type."

"You have no idea what my *type* is, Nordstrom." Hayden stands, glaring at him, before walking off. Hayden's a nice guy, but in a contest against Liam Nordstrom, he would lose. And, I am sure he knows that or he wouldn't have left.

"So, it wouldn't bother you if I hooked up with Hayden?" I ask, pulling at the fabric that covers my behind before it ends up looking like a thong.

"Why would it bother me? You and I are just friends and barely that after you blabbed to the world about my brother's intervention. We're not dating. Besides, I'm pretty sure he's gay."

I want to buck him off me and scream I'm sorry for telling anyone, for trusting the wrong person with his secret, but I can't because my bikini top is untied and my words wouldn't be enough anyway. Instead, I focus on the last part of his statement, just to keep the knife he stabbed me with from doing any more damage. "You've been friends for years and you don't know for sure if he's gay or not?"

"I've never been close to Hayden and it's not something us guys discuss."

"Seriously? You discuss girls, right?"

"He never does. I don't care if he's gay. Statistically, one of us guys should be. That's not the issue. I'm an actor—I have hundreds of gay friends. I just want my friends to keep it real."

"So you think he's lying?" In my head, all I can focus on is that the leak about his brother's intervention ended my chances with the only guy in the world to excite me since Chase.

"I don't know. It's probably more of a personality conflict than anything. Let's just say, if I played for the other team, we still wouldn't get along." He wraps his hands around my ankles and smooths his thumbs across the arches of my feet. Every single thought in my head is gone. I can't even remember what we were talking about. Then his strong hands trail up my calves and I'm pretty sure he can hear me panting, but seems to ignore it.

"Hayden's a storyteller. He tends to share more than I would about everyone else around him, but he keeps himself private. I don't like that."

I'm done talking about Hayden. Nordstrom's hands have rendered my brain mush. His thumbs are now brushing the tender skin behind my knees and I need to change something before I start moaning.

"Will you tie my suit string, so I can flip over?" I reach up and tie the top string, but with him laying the way he is I can't reach the bottom without completely exposing myself.

"Why would I want to do that?" he asks, flipping over and resting his chin on my behind.

"Because you're my friend and that's the kind of thing *friends* do for each other."

He huffs a hot breath through the thin fabric covering my backside and I close my eyes trying to stifle a whimper. Why did I have to talk to Alli about his brother? WHY?

"Fine." He sits up, straddling one of my legs as he leans his hard body unnecessarily against me to refasten the string. I have to remind myself he treats all women like this. He uses his body as a weapon, like men are always accusing women of doing. It's not personal, that's just how he is. It's probably why I'm so attracted to him. He climbs off of me and lies on Hayden's vacated seat.

After flipping onto my back, I adjust my chair into a sitting position and turn toward him. Oh! Now that I can see him, I'm in actual physical pain. He's wearing Caribbean Ocean blue swim trunks and nothing else. He looks even sexier than he did last night. And last night, in his tux, he looked better than any man I've seen in my whole damn life. I can't help but imagine him waist-high in the water with nothing between us. *Friends. We're friends.* I have to divert my eyes, looking instead toward the poolside bar, where Hayden is talking to one of the other groomsmen.

"So when are you heading home?" Liam asks.

"I was originally going to stay the whole week, but I don't know if I want to now. How about you?"

"I'm flexible. Do you want to go for a walk? I feel like everyone's staring at us here."

I look around and the only people I spot are the other groomsmen at the bar. *Oh.* And the impeccably dressed, middle-aged guy, who is staring right at me. "Who's that guy in the Polo and deck shoes?" I ask.

Liam sits up and says, "That's Jim, my dad. He's not really happy with you right now." He stands up and waits for me to join him.

I lean over and pull my cover-up from my bag, slipping it over my head as I stand. "What did I do to Ji…?" I don't finish my sentence because I know exactly what I did.

"Come on." He motions toward the gate with the path to the beach and I gladly step in front of him. I can feel his dad's eyes on us and it makes my stomach churn. As the gate closes behind us, and we head for the beach, I say, "So your dad hates me because of the leak about Seth's intervention. Did you tell him it wasn't me?"

"He knows the story. He's Jonathan's lawyer and was in the thick of it when it all went down with your friend Alli."

"She's not my friend. If he was there, then why does he still hate me?"

"He asked Alli about it and she denied leaking the intervention."

"And he believed her? I'll never believe anything she says again," This has been a nightmare.

"She convinced Jim she wasn't involved. He usually can read people pretty well."

"Great. So what you told me on the plane was a lie?"

He shakes his head and shrugs. "I don't know what to believe. I told Jon I'd get you to the wedding and I did."

Well, that explains him ignoring me yesterday. We walk in silence until the beach ends at a rock cliff, which goes straight up with no way to pass. There's nothing more to say. I don't know why I continue to walk with him. He plops down on the sand with his feet almost to the water's edge and takes a deep breath.

I sit down next to him. I want to say F-you, but I also want him to know it wasn't me who sold his brother's information. I dig my toes into the wet sand as I think about how to put it into words. "I'm sorry that I told Alli and Jessica about your brother's intervention. I was just really freaked out at the time. I didn't tell anyone but those two and I would never tell the vultures."

He scoops moist sand into his hand, holds it up slightly and lets it drop, sifting it between his fingers. I can't tell whether he believes me. He's not even looking at me. When his hand is empty, he asks, "What had you so freaked out that you had to share what I confided in you." He looks toward me, finally meeting my eyes.

Will it matter what I say? Will he ever believe me? I don't really want to tell him the whole truth, but I know I should. My head shakes as I try to force my thoughts into words. "I told you my ex tried to kill himself after I did the intervention on him, right?" He looks away to the waves breaking about thirty feet out, but I continue anyway. "It was a bad time in my life. Sarah, Jessica, and the lying bitch were all there. They understood how messed up I was then. When you told me about your brother's problem, I was brought back to that time. I trusted them or I would have never shared anything you said."

I could have said more. More about my mom's death, about how my world turned upside down inside a month of the failed intervention, but I don't. I'm not going to delude myself into thinking anything with Liam Nordstrom could be more than a hookup. I may as well not torture myself.

"Seth is in rehab now, but who knows if he will make it through? He disappeared for three months. No one knew where he was. Nak and I found him in a heroin den two weeks ago. It was the scariest place I'd ever seen. But what scared me more was the thought of losing my brother. He stopped breathing. He almost died, so excuse me if I'm a bit pissed at you."

I gasp. "I'm really sorry. I had no idea." I close my eyes because I can feel them welling up. My carelessness almost killed his brother. "You have to know I never thought me sharing my problems would hurt him." I suck in a shaky breath. I know I need to share Mom's story with him. He needs to know why I had to talk to my friends about his brother, no matter how much it hurts me.

"Within a few weeks' time every hope and dream I had, shattered. First, I find out I meant less to Chase than a bag of pills. Every thought about he and I having a future together, every dream of us going to school together, sharing an apartment—gone. Then, when my mom disappeared, I was devastated even more. I wanted so much for it to be a hoax, for her to have faked her death to escape her boring unfulfilling life. But I knew when the words '*they found the body*' came out of Braden's mouth, there would be no happy reunion." I avoid looking at Liam. I can't watch his expression change as I mutter the words—*she killed herself.* The pity in his eyes will harden, turning to indifference as if her death no longer holds pain. All empathy vanishing because she chose to die and therefore doesn't deserve his compassion. I've seen it for years. Every single time it comes up.

"Why weren't my brothers and I enough to live for? Why couldn't she see she could tell me anything? I told her everything about me. Hell, if she needed to escape so badly, we could have gone somewhere together. I would have left with her. I thought she loved me, us, my whole family. But it was fake. If she loved me, she never would have left." I shake my head, trying to change the words I know are true.

"Mom had drugs in her system when they found her body." I suck in another shaky breath. "The coroner said she took something that could have reacted with her antidepressants. She had to have gotten them from my purse. My ex was always stashing pills in there and I found an empty bag at the bottom after she disappeared. It was one of his. I'd completely ended it with him, stopped taking his calls, and changed my number. I was so messed up, I didn't even realize it was there. And, I was so wrapped up in Chase's problem, I didn't see what was happening with my mom. If I'd only paid attention, maybe she wouldn't have died. If I had just flushed the damn pills, she wouldn't have gone out on the thin ice and maybe I would have had more time to get her help. If I had stayed with her or insisted I take her home, I could have saved her."

My cheeks are soaked with tears. I hate that I'm crying. He sits up and moves closer to me, wrapping an arm around me. His touch feels so good. I've told him bits and pieces about my mom, but I've never told him about her demise.

"My entire family blames me for her death. And they're right. They just don't know how right they are. I've never told anyone about the pill bag in my purse. Not even Sarah, so please don't tell her." I look to meet his eyes, dark but sympathetic, and he nods. "My friends had begged me to break it off with Chase long before the failed intervention. They pleaded with me. But no one could tell me anything. And it killed my mom."

His thumb softly strokes my cheek, but he's silent.

"She was working late at the marina, trying to get invoices out. I told my brothers I would stop and check on her on my way home. I was texting a friend when she asked me for some ibuprofen. I told her there was some in my purse, and to help herself. She must have found Chase's bag." The numbness is back. I can feel my brain trying to erase the memories. The feeling of guilt is overwhelming. Liam pulls me in closer and I rest my head on his chest. He smooths his thumb gently under each one of my eyes, and I start bawling. I've held it in for so long. I've never admitted to anyone her death was my fault. It's like a muddy hole I can't claw my way out of. The more I think about it, the deeper the hole gets.

"Meg, she chose to take the pills. You didn't force them down her throat. You didn't kill her. She did it to herself. Just like Seth—no one forced him to put a needle in his arm."

There is something different about him, as if he believes me for the first time. His fingers comb through my hair as his eyes search mine. He looks relieved that I'm spilling my dark secrets. He always bugged me on the phone saying I was holding back. Just like Peterson had said. But I never felt comfortable telling anyone until now. I never wanted to tell anyone until now. It all comes rushing out and I can't stop it.

"The night she disappeared I hadn't noticed anything out of the ordinary. She seemed normal for her. Her medication kept her even, never too down and never too up. When I left, she seemed okay. But when my dad knocked on my bedroom door wondering if I knew where she was, I felt in my bones something was terribly wrong. I knew. She wasn't home and wouldn't answer her phone, so we drove down to the marina. Her car was still parked in the lot, but the office door was locked. My dad was convinced someone had abducted her in the parking lot. It had started snowing and thick heavy flakes erased any evidence of her existence. For weeks, her disappearance was all the news talked about. Her face was everywhere. It was my face. I looked like her and everyone thought it was me. Strangers would stop me in the check-out line to tell me my family was looking for me. Eventually, I just stayed home. I couldn't leave the house and face them.

"We cooperated with the police the best we could for the first week, until some nationally-known, celebrity journalist started making accusations and inferring my dad was somehow involved in her disappearance. My dad was a successful businessman, ethical and well-liked, a pillar in the community, but he had enemies. He'd doubled the size of the marina the year before by out-bidding a developer who just happened to be on the city council. Then a guy Dad fired, a disgruntled employee, said he saw Mom out with another guy the day before her disappearance and my dad became the police's number one suspect. It was a lie. The guy just wanted revenge and may have been paid by the city council member. The media became vultures. They didn't want the truth. They spread speculation after speculation as if they were facts. The police stopped looking for my mom and started looking for evidence to support the lies in the media. That's when my dad lawyered up and stopped helping the police build their case against him."

Liam wipes his thumb under my eyes again and kisses the top of my head. I didn't realize I was still crying.

"By that point, it seemed everyone was convinced of my dad's guilt. But I knew he could never hurt her. He worshiped her. The police knew my mom had depression, but conveniently it never made it into the news. The whole investigation focused on the sensationalized story. Divers were sent in to search the icy waters of the river and within hours, they found her purse. It had her phone and keys still in it. I was the one who identified it—confirmed it was hers. When I saw the black leather with white piping bag being handed out of the open water, I started vomiting. I had stood on the shore watching from the beginning, hoping and praying they wouldn't find anything. Luckily, Sarah, Jessica, and Alli were with me and they helped me to keep going. Mom had always been the one I confided in. She was more like a sister than a mom."

"Did they find her body right away?"

"They didn't find her for another two weeks, miles downstream. Her body bloated and battered, so I was told. I never saw her body. It was a closed-casket funeral."

His fingers comb through my hair again as his thumb strokes my ear. "You wouldn't want that picture in your head. It's probably for the best."

"I know." I swallow hard, trying to gain control of my emotions. "The coroner determined she drowned, but couldn't determine for sure whether it was foul play or not. The body was too beaten up. There was no sign of sexual assault, so they decided it was most likely suicide. They didn't have any evidence against my dad. And the drugs were in her blood, meaning she took them long enough for her body to digest them before she entered the water. Which brings us back to her death being my fault."

"No one can say the drugs are what made her go into the river." His dark eyes penetrate my gaze. He looks as if he's serious, but I know he is just trying to make me feel better.

"Don't you see? She was sick. She didn't know what she was doing. It's as if she was a child who took the gun out of my purse and shot herself. If she hadn't found the pills, she wouldn't have died."

His arms wrap tightly around me and he holds me for several minutes in silence. He knows I'm right. My sobbing stops by the time he kisses the side of my head again, and says, "You carry a gun in your purse?"

His tone of surprise makes me laugh. "No, it's a metaphor. I don't have a gun in my purse. That's crazy."

"I'm glad you're not crazy," he says, and I realize he's playing me.

"Me too," I say, trying not to reveal how true the statement is.

"Thanks for trusting me with your story, Meg." His hand cradles my chin and he turns my head to meet his lips. He kisses me so tenderly that more tears form in my eyes. I feel closer to him than I have felt with anyone before him. How does he know exactly what I need?

He stands and extends his hand. "We're going in the water. I'll show you how to body surf." An absolutely dirty grin appears on his face as I give him my hand. He pulls me to my feet, waits for me to slip my cover-up off, and then we run straight into the ocean. He doesn't stop until the water is up to my chest. I'm having a hard time staying upright as waves crash into me. He smiles, watching me struggle through several hits, and then moves behind me, wrapping his arms around my waist to steady me. His body is like a fortress. He blocks wave after wave as he just holds me. I feel so strong in his arms as if a heavy load has finally been lifted from my shoulders and with him, I could withstand anything. As the waves bump his body into mine, I start to feel something more than invincible. His hands begin to smooth softly over my body, and I decide I'm not moving from this position to learn how to body surf. *I'm good here.*

"In a couple of minutes, we're going to move over to that ridge line." He points to a spot not more than twenty feet from us where the waves seem to be breaking a little more harshly. "Close your eyes," he says, splaying one hand across my bare stomach and pulling me tightly against him. I do what he says and then he asks, "Do you feel the pull and push of the water?"

I definitely feel it. I let the wave hit and retract before I answer, "Yes."

"When we go over there, I want you to recognize the pull of the ocean wanting to drag you out farther. Feel it." Just then, the current pulls us both back and slightly apart. "Four. Three. Two. One. Now the push." His lips press against my neck, sucking in a way that almost makes my ovaries burst.

The wave pushes his body against mine. "It's all about anticipation. The pull is always followed by the push. It's much like sex, only the pull leads." His lips attach to my neck again.

"I am so horny right now." The words spill from my mouth and I wonder what happened to my filter. I've completely lost it. Liam opened the spigot of truth and now I can't shut it off.

"I know," he says, as his fingers dip below the waistband of my swimsuit.

Does that mean he's horny too or that he knows I am? I shouldn't have said that out loud. It's such a rollercoaster with him. I never know where the "just friends" line is drawn. The bond of truth I feel with him right now feels like so much more than friends.

Oh. His hand dips lower and I no longer care about the friends tag. With just the touch of his hand, my body is clinching, and I'm already panting. I know from experience that it is not instinct to do what he is doing with his hand to pleasure me. It has to be taught. My mind fogs as I no longer care.

"Do you feel the pushhhh…and the…pulllllll?" His words correspond with the wave motion and his body pushes against me and pulls away. "Push," he says as he pushes a long finger into me.

It's too much. I go off unexpectedly like a chain of firecrackers—hard and fast. He ratchets the intensity with his finger until my vision starts to blur. Liam stills without removing his hand, practically holding me up. His breathing is as loud as mine. He embraces me for several minutes, letting us sway in the waves. I could stay in this position all day.

"That explosion almost took me out, too." He laughs as his hand slides up to my stomach. "Should we get back to the lesson?" he says as if nothing had passed between us. He reaches down and adjusts the front of his swim trunks. "Where were we? That's right—the push and pull of the waves. After you've felt the pull, you can anticipate the push. At the last second of the pull, you need to jump up, flattening your body on top of the push wave, and then let it ride you in."

"Seriously? You're teaching me how to ride a wave. I thought it was going to be some complicated actual surfing move. I used to do this as a little kid."

"So you're experienced. I bet it's never been this fun. Or satisfying."

The smile in his voice makes me turn around to see his gorgeous face. His hands naturally move to my rear end. "No. You're definitely good at satisfying. It makes me wonder, how many girls you've taught to *ride* a wave."

"Not many. And you are by far my favorite. Should we go try it?"

I nod. His "by far my favorite" comment makes me smile as I follow him to the break ridge. The water is deeper, the waves hit harder, and it is tougher to stand without Liam behind me.

"Ready?" he asks. "Feel the pull."

The pull almost pulls me under.

"Wait for it. Three, two, now."

We both jump and I do my best to flatten on top of the wave. Liam grabs my hand and we ride the wave together for about thirty feet, like two hulls of a catamaran. It's remarkable. I didn't know you could ride a wave so long without a board.

I clamor to my feet, not at all gracefully, and Liam hooks an arm around my waist, pulling me to him. He clasps my chin with his long fingers and tilts my head up to meet his lips. He presses into me with his tongue and bubbles fizzle from my stomach to the tips of my toes. My whole body relaxes to the point where if he weren't there holding me up, I'd flop like a rag doll to the sand. He pulls back and says, "We should grab some lunch before we miss it."

He stuffs his hands in the pockets of his swim trunks and tips his head toward the resort house. I'm not sure what to think. We walk down the beach in silence, not touching. Is he still acting? Do I dare let my brain think it's more?

We sit at a table with all the other groomsmen in the outdoor restaurant. Now that we're seated, Nordstrom's hand is on the back of my chair and his fingers are tickling my shoulder. I'm wide awake, nervous, not knowing what to expect from him.

Some of the stories being shared by the guys are completely BS or maybe I *am* a naïve little girl from the Midwest. I just don't think it's likely a guy could run into a complete stranger on his way to get ice in a hotel, have sex with the girl against the ice machine, and then go back to have sex with two girls he left in his suite. Hayden is telling the story, but it's about his bandmate Nick, and it kind of epitomizes what Liam had said about Hayden sharing other people's stories. I look over at Nick and he's nodding with a smile, pushing my skepticism away. I lean over to Nordstrom and ask, "Do you think that really happened?"

He shrugs and whispers, "Obviously Hayden is obsessed with Nick's sex life." He raises his eyebrow as if he told me so, then caresses my cheek with a swipe of his thumb. "Do you have plans the rest of the night?"

His question wipes all thoughts from my head. It takes a good thirty seconds for me to respond. "I was thinking about asking Hayden up to my room just to check out your theory."

He pulls back, his face menacing, and he looks from Hayden to me. "Go for it. But he won't give you what I gave you an hour ago."

"Yeah, what was that all about? One minute you're despising me and the next you're giving me an orgasm. I can't keep track of your moods." I must have said the O-word too loud because a couple of people at the table turn and smile at me.

"I didn't want you to be sad anymore."

"So you just dole those out to girls to cheer them up?"

"When I like them."

"Good to know." At least he admits he likes me. I glance up and Hayden is scowling at Nordstrom, and then he makes eye contact with me. His eyes say *be careful*. I smile back. Liam and I are just friends. I know sex means nothing to him. I'm not one to let a man hurt me—not since high school.

I look back to Nordstrom. He's so damn hot. I am probably going to hate myself, but I don't see what choice I have. The chemistry with him is off the charts. And, if I'm being truthful with myself, the chemistry with Chase has completely dwindled since I met Liam. I need to take advantage of whatever he offers. I do feel as if we are friends. He's the only person I have ever told about the drugs in my purse. He didn't judge me. He didn't turn me away. Instead, he just wanted to make me feel better.

We chat with the groomsmen for another hour, finishing our meal, and make plans to meet as a group on the beach for the scheduled clam bake at eight. As we're leaving, Nordstrom says, "I'm supposed to meet up with Jim and Nat before they head off the island. Can I hook up with you after I get done with my parents?"

"What time?"

"An hour and a half tops? I'll stop by your room."

"Yeah, that's fine. Say hi to your parents for me." I smile snidely, knowing he won't mention me to them.

He laughs and says, "I will," before walking into the building.

I need to get a grip on what I'm doing. Maybe some time away from him will help me clear my head. I climb the big staircase to the second floor and start for my room. About halfway down the hall, Hayden stops me. He looks as though he's been waiting for me.

"Are you feeling all right?" he asks in the most casual tone.

"I'm great. I was just going to grab a shower."

He purses his lips, hesitating and then says, "If you're looking for a relationship with him, it will never happen. He doesn't do them. Never has."

"I'm not," I say. "We're just friends."

He nods. "You mean fuck buddies?"

I shrug. "We haven't slept together," I say as I wrap my arms tightly across my front, having no idea why I'm explaining myself to him.

"I just assumed when you were talking about orgasms you had."

"Nope. Haven't." *Damn*. I wonder what else he heard.

"Don't sleep with him. For years, I've watched him use women. He gives them just enough for them to believe they have a chance of being more than a plaything, and then cuts them off when someone better comes along or the weather changes. I don't want to see you get hurt."

"What's going on between the two of you? I didn't think guys stabbed each other in the back like girls do, but you two seem to have a venomous hate for each other. Or, is it just a cock-blocking thing? He told me you were gay."

To my surprise, he laughs.

"I'm not gay and he knows it. Just because I treat women with respect? He's such an ass." His expression turns serious. "Did he tell you he slept with my baby sister? Eighteen years old and he used her like a whore."

The real grit comes out.

"I'll be careful," I say because there's not much else I can say to that. I guess it explains the issues they have with each other.

"See you tonight," he says, touching my arm before heading off toward his room.

I know if it had been Nordstrom touching my arm, I would have opened the door and dragged him inside. Part of me wonders why I'm always choosing the wrong guy. Too focused on finding chemistry, I miss the ones who would treat me right. How did I get to this point? Hayden is good-looking and in a band. He's got to have a dark side. All artists do. Yet, he's not an ass, so I'm not attracted to him. Is this all because of my mom's mistakes? If she waited for the right guy instead of settling with my dad because she was pregnant, would she have ended up killing herself? If I settled for anything less than who excites me the most, will I end up doing the same? I'm never going to get Nordstrom. Not for keeps, anyway. I tap the keycard against the sensor and open the door.

Liam

I stop in my room to string together a couple of strands of brain cells before meeting with Jim and Natalie. The door opens a minute after I arrive and I look up from my facedown position on the bed. Nak and I are sharing a room to keep up appearances while Leslie's parents are on the island. It's a hassle to keep his clothes here and her parents know they're sharing a bed, but it helps keep it on the up and up with Jonathan's relatives. Jon doesn't only think of Leslie as a sister, she's his cousin.

"You doing all right?" Nak asks

I massage the back of my neck with my hand before flipping over onto my back to talk. "Um…I don't know. I'll be better after my parents leave."

"Are you worried about Seth?"

"I'm scared as hell he's not going to make it through treatment. He's barely an adult."

"Have you talked to anyone about what happened last week?"

I shake my head. I brushed over it with my parents, but it's too soon. I can't even process it."

"No poop pool stories at the clam bake tonight?"

"No."

"I saw you with Megan. You get everything worked out?"

199

"I am supposed to meet with Nat and Jim before they leave. Dad is going to tell me what an idiot I am. He saw us together at the pool." I slip into the mocking voice of my father. "You never make the right choices, Liam. When are you going to grow up?"

Nak smiles. "If he was there with us at the drug den, he'd never talk to you like that again. Just tell him what happened."

"He'd probably blame me for not getting Seth into treatment sooner."

"Seth is an adult. You're not his nanny."

"I know. It's probably because he and Mom are worried about Seth and then they see Meg here. Dad thinks she sold the story outright to the press, but that's not true." I sit up and push my back against the headboard, pulling a pillow onto my lap. "Did you know Meg's mom killed herself? When Meg was in high school. And, with everything she told me about what happened, there is no way she would have talked to the press." I look up from the pillow on my lap, meeting Nak's eyes.

"When Meg wasn't here when I arrived on the island, part of me was relieved and the other part was frustrated. I wanted to see her. I wanted her to clear her name. Then Jon asks me to fetch her and beg her to come to the wedding and I was relieved again. But what she did triggered Seth to run away and you saw what that led to. All day yesterday I ignored her. I'd done my part. I'd got her here." My fingers fidget with the corner of the pillow.

"And then today, I walk out by the pool where we were all supposed to meet and Hayden is rubbing sunscreen all over her. His hands were everywhere. I almost lost it. I don't know what my problem is. For three months, I've been trying to get her out of my mind and I can't. Even with what happened to Seth, I still can't stop thinking about her."

"Sounds like you need to get laid. If that doesn't take care of it, then maybe there is more between you to explore."

"Daniel Nackerson, you are a genius. That must be it. I haven't slept with her yet. That's the power she holds over me. All I have to do is fuck her out of my system. What I was doing wasn't working so try the opposite. Jon basically gave me his blessing, right? I wouldn't be going against any man code." I stand with renewed hope and start digging through my clothes for a shirt and shorts.

When I get to my parents' room, I hesitate by the door, inhaling a deep breath, and letting it out before knocking. Mom opens the door.

"Oh, good, Liam, you're here. Are you all packed?"

"I'm not leaving today. I'm taking the flight on Saturday." I make the decision right then to spend as much time as I can with Meg. I may as well do it right.

"But your brother needs you," Mom says, stuffing a makeup bottle into one of her bags.

"He can't have visitors for two more weeks. How is me coming home today going to affect him in any way?"

"We need to have a united front to show him how much we care. He can't do this alone," she says, looking over at Dad.

"Well, I'm staying because he's not going to know whether we have a united front or not for two more weeks. I know how strict the rehab places are about their no contact policies."

"You know, don't you? You've been through it yourself. Maybe you need to come home to help your mother deal with what we are going through with Seth in treatment. Your mouth and that girl put us in this situation. Take some responsibility."

Take some responsibility? I want to deck my father. "I am the only responsible person in this family. I'm the one who found Seth and rescued him from the hell he was existing in. If I hadn't found him, there is no doubt in my mind that he would be dead. You may have hired some guy, but I went out and did it. One thing rehab stresses is taking responsibility for your own actions. I am not responsible for Seth putting a needle in his arm. He's eighteen. He's an adult."

"Liam, we are all grateful you found your brother, but if you are staying because of that girl, you need to rethink it. When it comes to women you are not a good judge of character."

"I'm staying because I need the vacation. I've spent the last month tracking my brother down. I start back to work next week. I'm going to spend the week relaxing. And you're wrong about her. She comes to the table with her own tabloid baggage. She'd never sell anyone to the press. It had to be the redhead."

My dad looks at me with his famous furrowed eyebrows. He's not happy with my decision to stand my ground, I can tell. I stare at him unwavering.

"I've made mistakes in my life and I am sure I will make more, but I'm not mistaken about her."

Megan

Not long after I return to my room, there's a knock on my door. I'm dripping wet, fresh out of the shower. It's too early for Nordstrom so it doesn't matter what I look like. Jessica probably wants the nail polish I borrowed from her yesterday. I stretch a towel around me, tucking it together between my breasts and answer the door as I blot my hair with a second towel.

"Damn," Liam says as his eyes slowly inspect my entire body, starting at my damp hair and working his way down. "Damn. Just damn," he says.

I back away as he stalks toward me. His eyes spear me as fear permeates my body. I don't know where it comes from—I'm not scared of him. I've never felt so vulnerable, though. He grasps my arm without a word and pulls me against him. One hand slides to my ass and the other pulls the towel from my hand, drops it and curls into my hair. His lips are on mine, burning and claiming. His tongue pushes into my mouth and the fear dissipates, spreading in a wave of heat to the tips of my fingers and toes. He tugs on the towel covering me and it falls to the floor with a soft thud.

"The couch or the window?" his gruff voice asks as he pulls away from my mouth.

I look around trying to figure out what his words mean.

"Make a decision or I will."

"The window," I say, and he backs me up against the window.

"Good choice." His mouth covers one of my nipples.

Holy… It's painful, but the sensation drives right to my core. I moan and Liam pulls back, determination spreading on his face.

"I feel as if I've waited long enough. It's been long enough, right?" he asks before he sucks my other breast into his mouth.

"Yes," I breathe as my body arches against him. He reaches behind his back and pulls his T-shirt over his head like the slow motion of a TV ad. His shirtless skin singes me where we connect.

He groans as he nips me and then pulls off.

"Turn around," he says.

I do it, and he presses his body against mine again. He wraps his arms around me and asks, "What do you see?"

I ignore his words because his hand has found its way to the place that doesn't allow me to think and all I can do is whimper.

"Meg, open your eyes and tell me what you see. I want to know what you see."

I open my eyes and try not to focus on where his hand touches me. "The ocean."

"What else?"

"The beach." I grind back against him, frustrated by his complete control. I reach my hands into his hair and pull.

He groans.

"What else?" He bites my ear and pulls me closer, locking me in place with his stance, like he did in the water. My eyes focus to give him what he wants.

"A tree with white flowers."

"Good. What do. The flowers. Smell like?" his sultry voice demands as his mouth sucks wet kisses across my back.

"I don't know," I pant. "I can't think."

"Concentrate, Meg. Tell me what they smell like."

"Skittles and saltwater taffy." I say the first thing that comes to mind.

He half chuckles and half groans. "Flowers that smell sweet and salty like you."

His tongue swipes up my neck and I almost 'gasm right then. His hands move to caress my butt cheeks for a couple of seconds, and as his lips devour my neck I hear the rip of a condom. Finally. I am so ready. I look down to see only his bare, toned legs. "I didn't think when you said we would hook up later you meant this."

"If you don't want this, tell me now."

"I want this, Liam. There's nothing in the world I want more."

"That's what I wanted to hear. Grab the sill," he says, grasping my hips and pulling me back. His fingers graze the place where the mere thought of being with him has drenched. "This is going to be hard and fast. We'll savor next time."

I don't have time to process his words because his knee spreads my legs, and he slams into me, thrusting so hard and deep my hand flies to the window to brace me before my face smacks against the glass. It's never felt like this. I can't even wrap my head around it. I am completely consumed by the buzz in every inch of my body.

"Sweet mother of…" he grunts, before letting out a breath. "You feel like heaven. Why didn't I take you the first night we met?"

One of his hands moves to my breast and as he pinches and tugs, he starts moving again. This *is* going to be fast. I'm going to lose it soon. No one has ever hit the place where he's hitting and I think the half scream, half moan that keeps escaping me tells him just that. Both hands move to my hips again, the pace picking up. My mind has already surrendered to him and my body can't hang on any longer.

He grasps my shoulder, his body curving around mine with each thrust. His other hand smooths across my hip and down, pressing at just the right spot, releasing every bit of the built-up tension at once. "Ohhhh…" My whole body shudders and I literally see stars. He drives hard one last time and stills.

"Christ," he grunts. I can feel his heart beating against my shoulder, his body wrapped around me. He's holding me up as we both pant, trying to catch our breaths.

Oh, my, god. That was… Wow. If that was sex, it is the first time I've ever had it. I rest my head against the cool, air-conditioned glass.

"Did I hurt you?" he asks sweetly, still panting in my ear. His cheek rubs softly against mine. For as raw and animalistic as the last few minutes have been, he is equally sweet and tender now.

"If by hurting, you mean ruined me for all other men, then, yeah, you hurt me."

"Good," he says, kissing the side of my head. I can hear the smile in his voice. His arms unwrap from around my waist as he slowly peels his hot skin off me. He retreats to the bathroom and I get a glorious view of his backside.

How can anyone be that beautiful? I know he's disposing of the evidence of what we just did. I don't regret this and I will never forget it. I realize I haven't moved off the window, so I stand and walk to the drawer where I had stashed my entire unpacked suitcase. I find a white lace thong and pull it on.

"You won't need those." Liam stands in the doorway, his hands grasping the top of the jam. He's completely naked without an ounce of modesty. Not that a man of his blessings needs modesty. *Definitely not.*

"I only brought the one condom, but I'm not leaving. You shouldn't have answered the door in just a towel." He walks to the bed, pulling the blankets back before sitting on the sheet. He watches me as he calls the front desk and asks the concierge to send up the largest box of condoms available. Or is it a box of the largest condoms available? I'm still trying to get my thoughts straight as I process what just happened. *Probably the latter.* That thought makes me blush inside.

"Am I going to get charged for that?" I ask, faking a scowl.

"I'm pretty sure it's on Jon and Sarah. It's an all-inclusive week, right?" He pats the bed next to him

"Let's hope their statement isn't itemized." I climb onto the bed.

"I say we order another ten boxes. Jon's got the money."

I laugh. "It's great to see you're so open to spending Jon's money."

"It's okay. He'll never know it was me using them. He can't get mad at me."

I punch his shoulder, not hard, but hard enough to change his smug face. He's still my whipping boy after all. I guess that means he's not telling him about our hookup. What happens in paradise, stays in paradise.

"Lay down and flip over," he says. "I'm going to give you that backrub you wanted the last time we were together."

"Bossy, aren't you." I can't believe he remembers. A backrub was what I bet against his naked sandwich. I turn over, and he kneels next to me.

"Oh hell. Those condoms better come soon. You have the most amazing ass." He caresses my behind and then leans down to kiss its left cheek. His hands smooth down my thighs and my muscles stiffen. I don't know why. This just feels so personal and after what Hayden said the last thing I want is to think of this as anything but sex.

"Relax." His thumbs, oh so slowly, brush up my inner thighs.

I mumble an obscenity into my pillow, and he laughs.

"You've got to slow it down, Meg. We're just getting started." He's teasing me now.

There's a knock on the door and his hands leave me. He quickly picks up the towel I had dropped on the floor earlier, wraps it around his gorgeous torso and a minute later he returns, pulling a box of condoms out of a brown paper bag.

He drops the towel back on the floor, straddles my hips, sets the box on the bed, and then starts massaging my back. His hands are like magic, tensing my core while releasing my muscles. I know I'm falling for him—him and his magic hands. This feels so intimate, it scares me, but even my brain welcomes the connection.

"This feels right," he says as his fingers graze the side of my breasts. "I wasn't sure you would ever open up to me. I'm glad you did because this is so much better than a non-hookup." He leans closer to my ear and I can feel him hard against my back. His hands slip under me, cupping my breasts as his lips singe my shoulder and neck.

Was he waiting for me to break down and spill my secrets? "Was it a test?" I ask.

"Well...I couldn't be with you if you weren't going to be honest with me."

"It's not natural for me to open up, but you're easy to talk to. You're the only guy I've ever told about my mom."

"I understand why you talked to your friends, and I can see that after all you went through, you wouldn't leak anything to the press." We're skin to skin and his lips have moved up to my ear. He moves his hands from my breasts and uses my butt to push himself up into a standing position with his hands still on me. I glance over my shoulder at him. He just walked up my butt from the downward dog yoga position. He is so flexible. Liam stands, posturing over me.

"You need to flip over again. I want to feel your gorgeous legs wrap around me and after hours of foreplay, I want to see that perfect O form on your lips. We're going to savor this, remember?" His eyebrows raise, a smile brewing under his skin as he stares down at me.

Hours?

"You're beautiful when you sleep, and I could watch you all night, but we're going to miss the clam bake if we don't leave this bed." I open my eyes, and Liam is lying next to me, his finger drawing a figure eight on my stomach. "I guess we have left the bed. So I should say this room."

"Can't we just stay here?" I pull the sheet up to cover me and turn onto my side away from him. His hand moves to my hip.

"No way, Meg. If neither of us shows up they'll all assume we're doing exactly what we're doing."

"Does it matter what they think?"

"No. But the guys and I only get together a couple of times a year. I want to go."

"You go. Just send Hayden back up to fill your spot while you're gone. He's not gay by the way."

Liam breaks out laughing. "Did he ask you out? Hell, Meg, I only left you for a half hour and he hit on you?"

"No. I asked him if he was, and he said you were cock blocking. You're a jerk for lying to me." I turn over to see his face and his eyes light with amusement.

"He does it to me all the time. He's always telling girls I don't play for their team. I wasn't the one who started this war."

"I suppose he doesn't even have a baby sister?"

"He told you about Ellie? That was not completely my fault." He collapses into his pillow as if he wishes I didn't know about her. "It's his twin sister. She's only a few minutes younger than him. We were friends and then she changed the rules. She pursued me. She threw herself at me over and over again. I was only eighteen. I messed up, but it didn't happen the way Hayden thinks." His expression turns heavy. "I've atoned for my mistakes."

I laugh. "You've atoned? What does that mean?"

"She wasn't innocent and I let him think she was. I let everyone think I was the bastard and I almost lost all my friends."

"It's kind of a douche move to sleep with his sister."

He shakes his head as if I'm not understanding.

"So was all this just a ploy to see who could get in my pants?"

"No. I tried not to want you this way, mostly because of Ellie. Sarah thinks of you as her sister and that makes you Jon's sister. I didn't want a repeat of what happened between Hayden and me. But I can't help the chemistry I have with you." He trails a single finger from my navel to the tip of my breast. "The part about him sharing everybody's secrets and not his, is the truth. Besides, we're friends and you barely know him. Admit it, you'd rather be with me and I waited long enough."

His lips cover mine, not letting me answer. He's right, of course. When he pulls back, he jumps off the bed. *Where does he get the energy?*

Even though I didn't get another shower before throwing clothes on, we head to the clam bake. Everyone is already eating by the time we arrive. Liam and I squeeze onto the bench between Jessica and Nak. I'm starving. The food smells great with garlic, spicy sausage, and roasted vegetables.

Liam rises, and leaning into my ear, he says, "I'll get us some plates." Then his lips touch mine. It's chaste, but any more at the dinner table would be gross.

Jessica grabs my knee and whispers out the side of her mouth, "Are you and Liam hooking up?" Her eyes are wide, but there's a huge smile on her face.

I bite my lip and nod. "He's incredible." Jessica and I haven't seen each other since yesterday. The last she knew Liam was ignoring me.

"He's even better looking in person," she adds. "So hot."

"I heard that, Jess," says Jeff, putting his arm around the back of her chair.

"I know," she says with a giggle, and then we both break out laughing.

I can feel Liam approach. My skin buzzes with excitement—probably a remnant of the incredible orgasms he doles out. He sets a plate in front of me. It's heaping, not the skimpy plate most guys would fill for a woman.

"I bet you're starved. I am." He leans in my ear again as he sets his plate down, he whispers, "You are the best work out."

He doesn't eat off my plate, which impresses me. Most guys act as if my plate is their back up. Instead, he refills his plate and returns with an extra crab cake for me. As he pushes it into my mouth, his fingers linger on my lips and I suck them in. That's when my gaze bumps into Hayden's. He's watching me intently, shaking his head. *I don't care.* I can only control myself for so long. If Nordstrom uses me, I'm going to enjoy it.

Chapter 24

Liam

That little dick. He's talking to Meg again, filling her head with all kinds of half truths about me. He acts all high and mighty, as if he's never made any bad choices in his life. I've seen groupies funnel in and out of his band's buses, and Nick is not the only guy to take part in that candy. Hayden is so full of it if he thinks he's more virtuous than me. I've heard the stories. Hell, I've seen it for myself. I can't wait for him to leave tomorrow. Then, I'll quickly make his words a distant memory in Meg's mind.

I walk up behind them, winding my arms around her. Her body melts into me, and as a victorious smirk forms on my face, I glance at Hayden. "Here you are," I say, my voice sweet as saltwater taffy. "Nick and some of the other guys are getting ready to do karaoke over at the pavilion. Should we head over?"

"I'll sing with you, Megan. Nordstrom peels paint when he sings," Hayden says smugly. *Woo, nice one.*

"Okay, I'm not the best singer, but I can lip-sync while dancing to Timberlake and you'd be convinced he flew to the island just for the night." I nuzzle into her neck. "Come dance with me. You know you've been dying to ever since our first time." Her head curls toward me. "Is that a yes?"

211

"Let's go, before I change my mind," she says, grabbing my hand and pulling me toward the pavilion.

I look back at Hayden and he flips me the bird. I silently laugh and then give Meg my full attention, hanging my arm across her shoulder. "I thought we settled this competition between Hayden and me." I'm not going to say I claimed her because she complained on the phone about guys who sleep with a girl and then act as if they own her. I need to act indifferent.

"We were just talking."

I wish I could crawl into her head and have a look around, just to see what she's thinking.

When we reach the pavilion, Nick has just started cooing a Sheeran song. I cover Meg's ears. I don't need any more competition. Nick uses his haughty British accent like a snake charmer uses a pipe, except he hypnotizes girls to fall on his dick.

"Don't listen," I say.

"But, it's so good." She smiles as if she's joking, but I can see her eyes glaze over as she spots Nick on stage.

I have to work fast to pull her back to me. My hands slide to her jawline and I lift her chin covering her mouth with mine. My tongue pushes into her mouth and I envision pushing into her hours ago. Damn it. I'm hard just thinking about it. Her responsive moans tell me I'm the one she's thinking about now. I continue to kiss her until Nick signs off. I can't dance with a hard-on so I move her toward the table where Nak and Leslie are already seated. Immediately, Gorboni joins us with two girls I don't know and we listen as some old guy sings a country song that sounds a lot like a dog slowly drowning. I guess not everyone here has talent. Nick joins us at the table alone and we all shoot the bull until the server comes for our drink orders. I slip her our requested song for karaoke.

Three songs later, Meg and I are up on the raised platform, freestyling through the hip-hop song in perfect sync. God, I love the way she dances. It's as if she's making love to me right on stage and no one else exists. It's not a show, either. It really feels as if no one else exists. My theory about a girl's dancing holds true with her. On the dance floor, our bodies move in perfect harmony without needing instruction. It's instinct. In bed, it's the same. No thought required. No awkward pauses. Every movement synced as if choreographed by a higher being. It's the best sex I've ever had. Even now, as we gyrate tandemly in classic boy-band-esque style, I can't help but think about being inside her again.

As we catch our breaths, exiting the stage to whoops and claps, I pull her to the side, not wanting to return to the crowded table before tasting her sweet lips. My hand slips to the back of her head and I feel a shiver quake over her body. I press my lips to her soft, luscious ones and claim her mouth. Even though she hates that word, it's the best description. Her mouth is mine. She's mine. *Shit*. What's wrong with me?

My tongue makes a final call, before I pull back. She's amazingly beautiful in the moonlight—a soft sheen on her face. She smells floral and sweet and salty. A growl churns in my throat and I have to kiss her again. *She is mine*. I push into her mouth again and one of her hands presses against my chest as her other grasps my bicep, pulling me closer. I could stand here kissing her all night. I'd ask if she wants to go back to her room, but I refuse to give up an opportunity to dance with her, and we *are* going to dance again tonight. We kiss through another song and then head back to the table, the sexual tension between us so thick I swear it glows like an aura.

Two hours later, I slide my hands down the silken skin of Meg's perfect ass as I peel her out of her panties. We danced two more times on stage and I'm so tired, I thought about just going to sleep when we got back to the room. But, as I watched Meg lift her dress over her head, I realized that wasn't going to happen. I'm rock hard and it is not going to go away on its own.

"I thought we were going to sleep," Meg says meeting my eyes.

"Yeah, about that…if you actually want sleep I'm going to have to go back to my room, because the big guy downstairs doesn't want to sleep when you're in the same bed."

She smiles as she presses her lips to mine and pulls me in to deepen the kiss.

The next morning, I order room service breakfast as we linger in bed. I don't make it out of the room to say goodbye to Nick and the guys and I'm okay with it. With everyone trapped in their own separate lives, the time we get together is scarce and almost sacred. Normally, it would have bothered me giving up my bro-time, but I'd much rather lie in bed with Meg. We've spent most of the morning talking. It's so different for me. I don't usually reveal myself to girls. Sure, I give them enough so they think they know me, but I usually hold back. The mysterious brooding persona has always worked for me in the past. It doesn't work with Meg. I feel as if I am baring my soul, and she hasn't lost interest yet.

I've given her an overview of Nak and my adventure in the heroin den.

"You know, when we made it to the fourth floor and I saw the guy on his knees in front of the other guy, I didn't think anything could be worse than that. I mean selling your body for a high, you can't get lower than that. But then when I found Seth, part of me wished he had been the guy by the door on his knees instead of the zombie with the needle in his arm. At least the guy by the door was breathing. The whole ride to the hospital I kept thinking he was going to die. I kept hitting him, trying to keep him awake and the whole time, I couldn't get rid of the feeling of impending doom."

"That must have been awful. I'm sorry he ended up that way." She lays her cheek against my chest and I feel a tear against my skin.

"He's all right, Meg. They got him breathing at the hospital right away." I stroke my hand through her hair. "He was sitting up by the time my parents arrived. I never told them how bad he looked when we found him, but I think they know somehow. He's got a long road ahead of him in recovery and I'm going to do everything I can to make sure he pulls out of this."

"I think you are wrong, Mr. Nordstrom," she says lifting her head and looking me in the eyes.

"What am I wrong about now?"

"I think you're wrong about love not existing. It's obvious you love your brother or you never would have gone through all that to keep him safe."

I smile at that thought. "You may be right," I say, before kissing her forehead. "You may be right." I push the emotions her words spark to keep tears from forming in my eyes. "I *do* love my brother."

She snuggles her head into the crook of my arm as her arm stretches across my stomach. It doesn't feel sexual. It just feels natural as if she's always been there next to me. I have never felt closer to a person in my life. She calms me.

"Why did you wait so long to tell me what happened to your mother?" I ask. I want to fall deeper into her. I want to know how she thinks.

She lifts her head and rests her chin on my chest, meeting my eyes. "You really do know how to ask the tough questions, don't you?"

"You have a problem with that?"

"No. Not with you. I don't tell people about my mom's suicide because I don't like to disappoint them."

"Explain."

"You tell people your mom died and they look at you as if you've suffered a loss, which you have. You tell the same people your mom committed suicide, and they're disappointed. Disappointed in her for taking her life, disappointed in you for not stopping her, disappointed they couldn't stop it themselves. I don't like disappointing people. Besides, they look at you differently as if her suicide rubbed off on you. Once they know, you are now infected with their worry that you will follow in her footsteps. It's hard to make people forget once they know."

"It's like being an addict. Once people know you're an addict, they don't ever look at you the same way again, except in your case, it wasn't anything you could control."

"You can control being an addict?" she asks with a smile in her voice. I know she's right. Addicts don't have control.

"I can now," I say. "For the most part anyway. I can choose to stay away from drugs. I just meant they look at you differently for something that didn't involve you."

"Yeah, and they act as if you no longer suffered a loss because she chose it. I didn't choose for her to kill herself."

Everything she says makes sense. Everything about her makes sense. Our talk is not helping me get her out of my system. If anything, it makes me want her more.

Chapter 25

Megan

I'm sitting at a table near the pool with Jessica, Jeff, Leslie, and Nak. We are the last of the bridal party left on the island, besides Nordstrom, and he insisted I go ahead to meet up with everyone while he stopped at the gift shop. He's probably picking up more condoms for our last night together. I'm trying not to worry about what's going to happen after we leave the island. Nordstrom and I have talked a bit about being together. After all, I will be living in Los Angeles by the end of next month. But it's one thing to be together in paradise and a completely different story to be dating in the real world. I'm afraid Liam will realize how messed up I am and decide he's better off without me.

"Sarah says you start at UCLA this fall. That's where I went for my undergrad. It's a great school. You're going to love it," says Leslie. She glances at Nak and some unspoken words pass between them.

Jessica pushes out her bottom lip as if she's pouting and says, "I'm so sad you're moving. I'll be stuck with Alli, while you and Sarah get to hang out all the time." She touches my shoulder and adds, "At least you'll get away from Chase." She smiles.

Chase has completely slipped my mind. He is the least of my concerns right now.

"Who's Chase?" asks Leslie.

"Her kryptonite," answers Jessica. I can't believe she said that. Doesn't she know Nak is Liam's roommate? I glare at her, but she doesn't even look at me.

"He's just an ex-boyfriend," I say trying to downplay her words.

"A toxic ex-boy toy she can't seem to stay away from," Jessica adds.

"Really, Jess? He's just an ex. I'm excited to move. L.A. has so much to offer. Please tell me you are never going to talk to Alli again. I don't even know how you could consider it," I say changing the subject.

"I don't know. I just feel sorry for her. There has to be a reason why she felt so cornered she would sell Sarah's secrets," says Jessica.

"Yeah, there's a reason. She was born without a soul and has no conscience," I say, and the more I think about it the more I believe she's always been too self-focused to care about anyone else.

"Did I miss anything?" Liam asks as he pulls up a chair next to me.

"Just talking about Chase," says Nak, raising his eyebrows and glancing toward Liam. He's going to tell Liam what Jessica said about Chase, I just know it.

"A distant memory," says Liam. He dumps the contents of his purchase on the table and I expect a box of condoms to come tumbling out, but it's not condoms.

Skittles and saltwater taffy.

"I brought snacks. Meg's favorites." He opens the bags and scoops some Skittles into his mouth before turning to me with a smile. "You want some?" he asks still chewing, a devilish grin brewing on his face. "These two candies will always remind me of paradise. What do you think, Meg?"

Oh god. He's doing it again. He's trying to shock me, to make me so flustered I'm speechless, and it's working. He bought the candies I told him the flowers on the tree smelled like outside the window. I stare at his gorgeous grin for several seconds before I reach over, grab a pink saltwater taffy, hoping it's cherry or at least strawberry, and start to unwrap it.

"Are you sure you don't want vanilla?" Liam asks, his grin growing bigger.

"I'm sure," I say. Last night we talked about vanilla verses spicy sex, and then discussed the places on the island we wanted to explore. My top pick was the top of the bar by the beach. He couldn't decide between the beach, the pool, the public bathroom on the first floor of the resort, or the rock wall that goes straight up at the end of the beach. "I was thinking about taking a run down to the end of the beach later. I'm going to need the energy." I pick up a couple of the flavored taffies.

"Let me know. I'll go with you," says Liam with a smile. His dark eyes meet mine as he pops the vanilla taffy into his mouth and swirls it around on his tongue.

"If you two are done candy humping on the table, then we need to figure out what we are doing this afternoon," says Leslie.

Liam wraps his arm around me and kisses my forehead as the group starts to discuss our entertainment options. I enjoy the public display of affection. It makes me think his comment a few days ago about Jon never knowing it was him using the condoms sent to my room is no longer true. If Leslie knows we're together, Jon will know we're together. I am not a secret anymore. Somehow, that makes this more real, more of a big deal.

We spend the afternoon on the beach, taking turns on the water jetpacks. There are two, each one with its own instructor, manning the controls and showing us how to move around. Liam and I go first. It feels a bit like strapping on a rocket that you can only partially control. It is crazy exhilarating and the experience makes me want to drag Liam down to the rock ridge at the end of the beach for twenty minutes of alone time.

Instead, he goes up for a second time with Nak because Leslie is afraid of heights or maybe she's just too smart to strap herself to a water explosive. I watch as the female instructor flirts with Nordstrom while he gets suited up for his second flight. He smiles but doesn't respond the way she wants him to and that puts a smile on my face.

After a couple of hours pass with the group, Liam and I decide we need some private time. It's our last night together before we go our separate ways. Sure, we've made plans to see each other in a month, but that feels like forever after the week we've spent together. We don't speak as we walk down the beach. His hand rests on my hip and his finger teases under the waistband of my shorts. My hand is under his shirt and I can feel every tightening and release of his muscles as we walk.

We are about three quarters of the way down the beach when he turns, wrapping his hands around mine and pulling me close to him. The buzz that hums across my skin from his touch sparks a nervousness inside me I've never felt before. The closeness I feel with him is foreign. I've never let a guy inside my walls like I have with him. I've never let another human being inside my fortress before. It's as if I've given him a key to unlock every vulnerability I have. With his past, I know the probability of us lasting is nonexistent. I will have my heart ripped out. It's too late to change, too late to stop how I feel about him. I guess I should just accept my fate. I lean into him and one of his hands moves to the back of my neck. His touch triggers a burning in my core I can't douse. I need to enjoy it while I can. I doubt I will sleep tonight, knowing what's to come.

"This isn't going to end tomorrow." He definitely can read minds.

"I know," I say, questioning my words as I say them.

"I live in Malibu. We can walk the beach every night if you want."

I smile at the thought. I can picture it in my mind. I want to believe him. I do. He takes my hands and pulls them behind me, moving his hands to my behind. His mouth presses feather light against mine. I breathe him in. Even when he's not trying, he smells delicious. He pulls back when I smile.

"Have I told you how much I love your smile?" he whispers inches from my face.

"No, you haven't," I say with an even bigger smile. "You always know how to melt away my worries."

"Don't worry about tomorrow. We've got this." His lips touch mine again. "What we have will still be there when we see each other in a month."

I believe him. He's right. What we have will overcome the distance.

Megan

"It doesn't matter," I mutter. "I don't care." I cover my face with my pillow. "I can't believe I let this happen." I roll over onto my stomach and start banging my face into the pillow. I crawl off the bed and check my phone for the hundredth time before typing out a text.

A week.

A whole week has passed without a word from Nordstrom. The last thing he said to me was, I'll call you when I get home, then he kissed me with the most tender lips, his fingers tugging gently on the hair at the back of my head. We discovered that simple act drove straight to my core. I never knew such an innocent action could affect me that way. Liam seemed to enjoy nonchalantly doing it in the most public places and then watching me squirm wantonly.

I should have listened to Hayden. Instead, I let Nordstrom suck me into his sex web. And the minute I am out of sight, he forgets about me, abandons me just like Mom did. What is it about me that makes people walk away from me? Am I unlovable? Chase chose the drugs over me. My mom chose death. Even Peterson chose another girl. I thought Liam was different. I thought maybe my luck had changed, but it wasn't real. I've sent him exactly twenty-one texts. They started out sweet and flirty, telling him

I could still feel his hands on me, and how I'd been ruined for other men. As each one went unanswered, they disintegrated from there. Today's text is full of sarcasm and frustration.

> Me: *Friends? Whatever. If you've been in a coma, call me when you get out, otherwise, don't bother.*

I don't expect to get a response. It's more about making me feel better. I know it will be awhile before I can move on from him and I hate being so pathetic.

Sharing my secrets with him was my first mistake, falling for him my second. I gave him a piece of me I've never allowed anyone else to glimpse. He took it and tossed it in the ocean. I'm never sharing that part of me with anyone ever again. It's gone never to be recovered. Just like Mom.

All I know is either he never made it home or he's the biggest liar I've ever met, even bigger than Chase. I really thought we had gone to the next level—we'd moved beyond friendship in the days we lived together as a couple—slept together as a couple. He must have thought differently. I don't want to be that girl who assumes she's more important to a guy than she really is…but what the hell? How could he not call? It shouldn't surprise me. He cut me off before without any regret. Fuck him.

I stash my phone in my back pocket and sit on the bed when I hear the knock on my bedroom door. I hope it's not Chase. With the mood I'm in, I may just sleep with him to validate I'm not a total loser. The door opens and it's my brother Wes. He plops his butt on the desk chair and looks around the room.

"So you're almost packed?"

I don't have the energy to tell him I never unpacked when I moved home, so I just agree.

"Yep, getting ready for the big move."

He nods. "Are you doing all right?"

"I'm all right."

"Why have you been crying so much? Are you pregnant?

I want to say, *do I look stupid?* But I don't because that would be calling Mom stupid and everyone knows she wasn't. "No. Why would you think that?"

"You left for Sarah's wedding with some guy after you told Dad you weren't going, and then when you came back you were all sunshine and rainbows. Now you're barricaded in your room, just like before the guy showed up. I worry about you."

Translation: You seem depressed. Do you need to get on medication?

"I'm not Mom, Wes. I'm fine. I spent a week with a guy in paradise and I thought we had more than we did. He turned out to be a big dick. I'll get over it."

"If you say so. It just seems more than that. Guys don't usually mess you up like this."

"I'm entitled to be a bit off." I explain to him all that happened with Sarah's wedding and Alli. I even tell him all about Liam, giving him the watered-down version a brother can stomach. It feels good to tell someone. "Now, in a couple of weeks, I'm expected to drive across the country, move into an apartment with a girl I've barely talked to, and start all over with school. I'm stressed, yes, but I'm not going to end up in the psych ward."

Wes's skeptical expression is not new to me. Statistically, my brothers and I are at a higher risk of getting mental illness because Mom had depression. We're at a higher risk for suicide because Mom killed herself. We're always looking for signs in each other, hoping to catch the illness before it resorts to Mom's level. They all think I'm more susceptible because I look like her.

"If I didn't let Chase kill me, why would I let some guy I've known for only a few months get to me? No guy is worth killing myself. I'm stronger than that." I need to start listening to myself. "No guy is going to have that kind of control over me."

He smiles at me. "Chase stopped by the marina looking for you while you were out of town. I didn't even know you were talking to him again. He must not know you very well anymore if he was looking for you at the marina."

"Thanks for the heads up."

"Are you coming to Joann's house for the birthday party tonight?"

"Of course." *Damn.* I forgot about Dad's birthday. "What are you getting him?"

"Tyler and I are getting him an ice fishing camera. You know, the kind you feed into the ice hole so you can see the fish biting on the line. Do you want to go in on it with us? It's kind of pricy."

"Yes. How much?" He tells me the price, and after I gasp, I silently wish I had another option. Dad is worth it, though. Wes says I can owe him. My brothers definitely make more money than I do and honestly I don't know if getting an advanced degree will change that. Someday, they will each have their own share of the marina—while I do God knows what. I wish Mom hadn't ruined that part of my life for me.

The next day, I'm feeling pretty good about showing my family I'm not on the verge of suicide. At least I got out of the house and didn't think about Liam for a couple of hours. I wonder what happened with him. Did I suck in bed? Was it too good? Was it just the idea of a relationship? I never pushed wanting more than friends. He's the one who kept talking about being together when I got out to L.A. He sounded as if he was going to keep in touch. Why didn't he?

My phone buzzes with a text and I still want it to be him, but it's not. It's Chase.

Chase sent me a nasty text the day after I got home from the island and I've been avoiding him ever since. I had called him from Sarah's phone to explain why I couldn't make our date. I didn't just blow him off. I imagine if the tables had been turned and I was the one kicked to the curb, I wouldn't have even gotten a text from him. I would have showed up at his house without any warning. I get that he's mad about me ditching our date, but… really? I wanted to go to the wedding and he knew it. When Liam showed up with the apology letter, I couldn't say no. It is probably time for me to talk to him, though.

Chase: I'm leaving my mom's house. Are you at your dad's?
Me: I'm here.
Chase: I'm coming over.

I barely have time to dress before he's at my door. I should have told him not to come because I still wouldn't put it past me to sleep with him just to prove I'm desirable. And that's the last thing I need. He leans in and kisses my cheek as he closes the door behind him.

"So how's your mom?"

"Great. Tell me about your trip. You went to Sarah's wedding, right? The last I knew you weren't going. Did Sarah apologize?"

"She did. It was Alli who leaked the information to the press and she got proof. I'm sorry I accused you."

"It's about time you came to your senses." He sits down on my bed and stretches out as if he owns it. "I have some great memories from this room. And this bed. We really should make more." He smiles the dirty smile that always made me melt, but I don't melt. All I can think about is how much I would like to make memories with Liam, not only on my bed, but on the phone, or just talking.

I laugh to cover what I'm really thinking. "I'm not in the mood, Chase."

He turns to me his blue eyes pinning me. "You slept with him, didn't you?"

"With who?"

"The naked sandwich guy. I thought we were getting back together and then you spend the week fucking him."

"What?" How would he know that?

"The guy falsely accuses you of selling him to the tabloids, calls you a liar and you spread your legs for him?"

What the hell? "What I did and didn't do on my trip is none of your business."

He runs his hand through his hair, taking a deep breath. "I'm sorry. It just frustrates me. You know I'm still in love with you."

"I'm still trying to figure us out, Chase."

"But now that you know it was Alli who leaked that crap, you can't blame me anymore, and we could get back together. I mean, you're not with the actor, either. I warned you he was a bastard."

"How do you know we're not together?"

"I can tell. If you were with him you would be all giddy and defending him. But you're not. I know you better than anyone, Meg. That's why we belong together."

I sit down on the bed next to him, and he places his hand on my knee.

"You are right about him. He is a bastard. He never really wanted more than sex." It hurts to say it out loud. I really thought Liam and I had moved into a relationship. And then he just walked away.

"What an ass. You deserve better. You deserve me."

He wraps his arm around me, and I rest my head on his shoulder. *I'm just so tired.*

"So are you ready to give me a second chance?"

I glance up to meet his eyes. I don't know what to say. And he doesn't give me time to think. He tilts my head and presses his lips to mine. Before I can suck in a breath, he pushes me onto my back and pins me with the weight of his body. I kiss him back, but it doesn't feel right. There's no effervescence. I don't know if I have the energy to stop him until his hand slips under my tank. *I have to stop this.* I push against his chest, but Chase takes it as a positive reaction from me. His lips move down my neck and I can finally breathe.

"Stop. I can't do this."

"Your lips say no, but your body says, *ravage me.*"

"No, Chase. My body says no." I pull myself up on my elbows. "I'm not ready for this." It's going to take a while before I can move on from Nordstrom. He *did* ruin me for other men, even Chase. "I don't know. I think I just need some time for myself," I say, closing my eyes.

"It's our time, babe. Don't squash it. I've waited for you to see the error of your ways and now that you figured it out…"

I crawl out from under him. The error of *my* ways? What did I do? There is no way I am to blame for what went wrong with us. "I'm moving in two weeks. What's the point?" It's not worth it for me to argue because he always wins our arguments.

"What's the point?" His fingers brush across my cheek. "You don't have to go to school, babe. We can start living our life together. If you feel you have to work, you can do books at the marina. I'm sure your dad could find a job for you. Or we can travel like I said.

My head is going to explode. I can't believe he just said that. He doesn't know me at all. "I need time for me to be me. I don't want that kind of commitment. We don't even know each other. I'm going to finish school. And that's the most important thing to me right now."

"Let's beta it for the next two weeks then, and see how it goes. We can figure out the rest later. I'm flexible." He completely ignores my words. And I am too weak to push him away.

Liam

As I struggle to repair the complete evisceration of my heart, I bury myself in work at the studio. Production for season four of *Impassioned* started, and since I'm the actor who brings in the most publicity for the show, my character is now the focal point of the ensemble cast and, of course, is addicted to painkillers. Some of my cast mates act as if I'm sleeping with one of the writers to up my screen time, while others are looking at me to bring them along on my rise to stardom.

My character has a new love interest this season, and since I can't control my real love life, I pour everything I have into Ashton Post's relationship on screen. Somehow, it is easier to touch another woman and kiss another woman when I'm not me. I think of it as therapy, a way to heal my soul, but I know it is not real. The director seems pleased with my performances, but the newbie actress who takes the brunt of my acting must think I'm a total jerk. On set, our relationship is real, palatable, but I don't exist off set for her. She's made several attempts to change that, but up until today I never considered it.

Last night, I stopped to see Seth at the rehab facility after getting home from work. I remember what a big deal it was when he visited me, so anytime I get out of the studio before visiting hours end, I make the effort

to stop. I want to be there for him and let him know that even though I'm busy at the studio, I will make time for him. Instead, Dad hijacked my one-on-one time with Seth and spent two hours talking about the wedding. He rehashed everything that went down with Red and kept asking me about Meg. I guess I made an impression on him and Mom when I stood up for her and he figured we were still together. I couldn't tell him otherwise.

"Hey, Liam. Is there any way you could give me a ride home?" my work girlfriend, Kat asks as I round the corner heading for the exit from my dressing room.

I stare at her with Ashton Post's brooding face, wondering if it is just a ploy to get me to talk to her outside of work.

"I wouldn't ask, except I rode in with Vera, but with the change in schedule, she left after lunch. If you can't, I can call an Uber, but then I have to walk all the way to the gate."

"It's no problem," I say trying to shut down Ashton's persona and revive Liam Nordstrom. Our characters have chemistry and maybe it's time to see if we have it too. "Do you mind if we stop for some food? I'm starved."

"PLEASE. All I have in my apartment to eat is a bag of kale, a bottle of wine, and some Chinese noodles. With the hours we've been keeping, I've had to choose between working out and getting to the store. And, since I was in my underwear for most of the scenes we've filmed this week, I chose the gym. I figure I can eat at the studio."

"I guess we shouldn't hit the drive thru then." I coax a smile onto my face. I've got to get out of this funk. We reach my car and I open the door for her to get in. When I'm settled in my seat, I start the engine and put the car in drive, not sure where I'm going because I never bothered to ask her where she lives.

"Can we go somewhere with real food?" she pleads. "We're done with the underwear scenes. Aren't we?"

"Unless Chris wants to reshoot them. It wouldn't be the first time. He's kind of a perfectionist when it comes to the bedroom scenes."

"I thought it was just me. He does this all the time?"

I nod. "I think he directs porn in the off-season."

She laughs. "He seems the type. I mean, did we really have to shoot that scene nineteen times? It wasn't us. We were perfect. I bet your hand was cramped from fondling my breast. My lips were ready to fall off. I'm not complaining, but shouldn't he figure out where the cameras need to go before we start making out?"

I laugh. It feels foreign to me.

"Can we eat at Pascal's? I don't care if I have a pasta bump tomorrow. Chris should have gotten the camera angle right the first nineteen times if he wanted my belly flat. I am. So. Hungry." She dramatically stretches out the last four words.

This girl is actually funny.

At the restaurant, I stare at Katya from across the table. Her dark hair should be a flag for me, but I'm so numb I don't care. Work girlfriend. Brunette. Broken rules may be just what I need. Her hazel-colored eyes catch me watching her, but it doesn't slow down her talking. I'm grateful I don't need to talk. Our meal is reminiscent of a date and it reminds me Meg and I never went on a proper date. We went from almost hooking up, to talking on the phone, to vacationing together. There was nothing normal about our relationship. No wonder she got scared and bolted. The buildup was too quick.

"Why haven't we ever done this before? Vera says you just got out of a relationship."

"Yep."

"Do you want to talk about it?"

"Nope."

"I don't really know many people in L.A. I just moved here before production started. I'd really like it if I could get to know you outside of work. You don't break character on set and no matter what the tabloids say, I don't think you and Ashton Post are the same person." Her nose crinkles and it reminds me of Meg. "I mean, we did spend the day groping each other. We should at least be friends."

She's right. I swallow a bite of my food and take a drink of water as I figure out how to play this.

"All right, what's your most embarrassing moment?"

"You start with the hard questions, don't you?"

"Nothing worthwhile is ever easy."

We talk for another hour and by the time we make it back to her apartment, I feel a bit more relaxed. I walk her to the door because honestly her neighborhood doesn't give off a safe vibe.

"Do you want to come up?" she asks, her eyes wide and pleading.

I nod, slipping my hand around hers, and Ashton Post follows her inside.

Chapter 28

Megan

I thought the drive to California would be therapeutic, a way for me to put my past behind me and pull myself together before starting grad school. Instead, the four days alone in my car just confused my feelings. I talked to my friends. I listened to my entire music library three times, and I even wrote a letter in my head to my mom. I had plenty of time to second-guess my life choices.

Jessica says in the month since the wedding, Alli pulled out of medical school and is talking about starting a clothing line. I bet her parents are livid. That thought makes me smile just a little. I don't care if she had a complete breakdown, I am never talking to Alli again. Her parents were overbearing, so what? They weren't serial killers. Bad stuff happens to everyone. My mother, most likely, committed suicide. She took pills she found in my purse and walked out on thin ice. I don't know why she did it and I probably never will. But you don't see me selling Sarah to the tabloids and framing Alli. I have no empathy for her.

I pretty much broke it off with Chase before I left. I agreed not to block his calls and cut him off completely, but I don't see a future with him. He says he loves me. I don't think he is capable of loving anyone but himself. When I told him I was leaving for California and nothing he said or did would change my mind, he looked at me as if I was insane. He didn't offer to follow my dream. He wanted me to fit into his life. Chase believes I will come to my senses and move back home by Thanksgiving, but that's not going to happen. I am more determined than ever to make my life, mine.

I understand why people change their plans when they fall in love. I look at Sarah and Jon and know Sarah made the right decision to quit school and move away from home to be with him. But with my past, with the history with my mom, I can't even think about quitting school. If my mom hadn't gotten pregnant and left school, would she have ended her life? I know I will never get the answer to that question, but until I graduate, it will always be my motivation to finish my degree. I want to be the best person I can be.

My new roommate stands next to the building's entrance. She's shorter than I pictured. Her blondish hair falls just below her shoulders, and she's not wearing stilettoes with her shorts, which is what I expected after talking to Sarah about fashion differences between the Twin Cities and L.A. Maybe that's only in Sarah's world though, not the average person's. Arianna and I have talked on the phone a couple of times, but mostly texted each other. I think it's hard to get to know someone in a text thread. That thought makes me think of Nordstrom and his aversion to texting. My brain needs to be rewired.

I introduce myself to Arianna as she holds the door for me.

"I've got your key upstairs. Like I said, the apartment is really small, but the bedroom closet is decent-sized, unless you're a clotheshorse." She takes one of my bags and adds, "It's faster if we take the stairs. The elevator is super slow."

"It feels good to use my legs after four days of driving, but I have a lot to carry up."

"I'll help you. We can use the luggage cart in the hall on the first floor for the rest of your stuff. I think the guys in 113 stole it from one of the hotels down the street. It just appeared one day and it still has the hotel nameplate. No one says anything because it's great for carrying crap to your car and they let everyone use it. The guys are complete horn-dogs, though, so don't let them touch you."

"Thanks for the warning." I smile at her. "I'm not looking for anything right now. I just want to concentrate on school."

"So you don't have a boyfriend?" She stops on the steps waiting for my answer.

"Nope."

"Good. My last roommate's boyfriend slept over every night. After a month of sleeping on the couch, I decided to take back the bedroom and started going to bed early to reclaim my space. It didn't stop them though." She starts climbing the stairs again. "They'd go at it when they thought I was sleeping. I'd wake up to grunting and her headboard smacking into the wall. It was so gross because the beds are only a few feet apart and I could smell them. I can deal with a scattered hookup every once in a while, but not every night and not while I'm in the room."

I laugh. "Don't worry. I'm pretty private. I won't do that to you." We make it to the second floor and start walking down the long corridor. "I've got a roommate horror story that tops yours. I'll tell you about it sometime after I have a couple hundred drinks in me." This is a new beginning I don't need to tarnish it right away with tales from my past.

"Great. We're going out Saturday night. I hope you don't have plans. Nikki and Trina, across the hall, know the DJ at one of the big clubs and he's promised to get us in. I've never been there, but it's a big deal to just get entrance into it."

"Sounds great. I don't have much to unpack anyway."

"I'm not one of those club hoes out partying every weekend, but you have to let loose once in a while and classes don't start until Wednesday," she says with a smile as she opens the apartment door.

The monochromatic white coloring of the apartment gives it a sleek, modern feel. There's a breakfast bar with three white stools. The kitchen cabinets and countertops are white and even the leather sofa is white. It's bigger than I expected, and really clean. I hope Arianna isn't a clean freak.

My thoughts must show on my face because she says, "It's not usually this clean. I just wanted to give us a starting point."

She shows me the bedroom that we will share, and it does seem small.

"I see what you mean about being on top of each other in here, but it's doable."

She helps me get the rest of my stuff and we talk for the next couple of hours while I unpack. I check the time to make sure it isn't too late and then call my dad to let him know I arrived safely. I think I'm already feeling at home in this new place, and relief washes through me as I realize, *I can do this.*

Chapter 29

Megan

Our group settles onto the tall stools that surround the fluorescent-pink glass table, and as the conversation picks up, I feel completely removed from it. The girls don't even seem to realize I'm here. They're talking about some guy they all know and the skank girl he is now hooking up with. I look around the club remembering the last time I was here. Sitting in the VIP section was such a different experience than this. It's as if it is a completely different club. This section is crowded and there is barely enough room to walk between the tall tables. My stool has been bumped three times already as clubbers pass by our table.

My thoughts are on Liam as I listen to the girls drawl on and on about the slut sleeping with the guy who is so obviously one of their exes. I remember our dance and how perfectly our bodies moved in unison, his hands on my hips pulling me against him and me trying to catch my breath. I think about all the times on the island when he held me, not for sex, but just to be close. It felt so good to be in his arms.

"Arianna says you're fresh off the boat from Minnesota. I suppose you've never been in a club like this before?" the blonde named Trina announces. I didn't have the energy to explain Minneapolis is a big city and I've been to many clubs. It isn't even the first time I've been to *this* club.

"You're not in Kansas anymore," Nikki adds, *as if* she has any clue where Minnesota falls on the U.S. map.

I hate that saying. People think Minnesotans either live on a farm or in a fishing shack in the woods. Almost four million people in the metro area does not qualify as small town in my book. I smile and roll my eyes at Arianna. At least my roommate is smart enough to know Minnesota is about as different from Kansas as Texas is from Alaska.

I glance up at the VIP area half wishing I would miraculously spot Liam coming down the stairs to rescue me from this conversation. I miss him. I'll probably never know what happened with him.

"Don't bother," Nikki says looking up to the second floor. "They never associate with us little people. Theo was supposed to get us bottle service tonight. I don't understand what happened. He is *so* on my shit list." She glances over to the DJ booth and scowls at the guy who met us at the entrance and got us into the club. I guess we're lucky we got in at all.

"My cousin did shots with Tom Fallston once. She let him, you know, under the table right in front of everyone," admits Nikki. "With his hand," she clarifies.

Oh my god. At least I didn't let it go that far with Nordstrom at the club. My thoughts go to the push and pull lesson in the ocean. I thought I meant something to him, but all he wanted was an easy lay. He obviously didn't feel the mind-blowing chemistry I felt.

"I would totally do Fallston, even if he is a douchebag," says Arianna, breaking through my self-loathing. She is the opposite of Alli. Arianna puts it all out for everyone to see. I think we'll get along just fine for the next few years as roommates.

"My cousin didn't care either," says Nikki before taking a sip of her martini. "She gave him her number, but he never called." *Typical.*

"A guy I used to date, my freshman year, just got a role on that new show on *AMC*. He was a waiter when I knew him. Who knew," adds Trina. "This is probably your first experience being anywhere near them. You don't run into many celebrities in Minnesota, do you, Megan?"

"Shhh," says Arianna, shaking her head. She probably doesn't want to make me feel bad. She knows I have a close friend who lives out here, but I haven't told her anything about Sarah.

"I bet she doesn't," says Trina. Her eyes are tracking a guy behind me and I turn, but don't see anything exceptional. I must have just missed him.

"No. We're pretty isolated up there. The snow keeps us inside most of the year," I say, hoping they all realize I'm being sarcastic. I don't need to impress these girls. I'm not going to tell them one of my best friends is married to Jonathan Williams, I've played strip poker with Jake Gorboni, I've done shots with the lead singer and drummer of EXpireD, and I've been felt up by Liam Nordstrom in this very club. Let them think what they want.

Just then I feel large hands grasp my shoulders. It doesn't surprise me some drunk has decided to introduce himself to the group and has picked me to be his liaison. Nikki's jaw is practically on the table. He must be hot. I tilt my head back to see what everyone is staring at.

"Were you going to tell me you were in town, Meg?" Liam squeezes my shoulders, staring off across the club and not meeting my eyes. He is completely serious and sounds mad, as if I'm the one who didn't answer *his* texts.

Nikki's jaw drops to the floor. I can see her out of the corner of my eye. Trina starts making whimpering noises as if she has to pee. I look to Arianna as I respond to him. "Well, maybe you should have called me. Or did your phone break?" I need to stay calm.

"Yeah," his voice sounds indifferent, cold even. *He's good.* "Did yours?" He squeezes my shoulder again as his gorgeous dark eyes find mine. "How long have you been in town?"

My heart is hammering and I am sure he can hear it above the pounding of the music. "A few days," I say. "You could have at least sent me a text."

"I did. I even called." His expression lightens, turning mischievous. "I'll forgive you if you dance with me."

"Forgive me?" I want to smack him upside the head. "Who are you here with?"

"Nak, Gorboni, and a few other guys. I came down for some air, but I would rather dance with you. Come," he says again, letting go of my shoulders and reaching for my hand.

As much as I crave his body, I don't know if I can survive another round of Liam Nordstrom. Round three would definitely damage me beyond recovery. I decide he can wait a bit longer.

"Liam, this is my roommate, Arianna. Arianna, this is my *friend* Liam." He glances at me, his dark eyes burning me, and I wish I knew what he was thinking. Maybe we're not friends anymore. He reaches a hand out and shakes her hand. I'm not sure if she knows who he is or not. I can't read her face in the shadows of the dim light, but Trina and Nikki definitely recognize him. Their eyes are wide with disbelief as I stand up and add, "Trina and Nikki live across the hall from us. This is Liam Nordstrom."

Liam nods and grasps my hips pulling me against him instead of shaking their hands. My heart starts racing uncontrollably. His touch is like a shot of adrenaline, one I haven't felt in what feels like forever. I don't know what he wants from me. He is such a bastard. I'm being stupid. He made his intentions clear weeks ago.

I need less inhibition if I'm going to dance on stage. I don't know if I've made the decision or it is just inevitable, but it is going to happen. I slam my drink, smile at Arianna, and say, "I'll be back," trying to reinforce that fact in my mind. I know that even if Arianna doesn't know who Liam is she will by the time I return, and I will have a lot of explaining to do. I don't really want all this to come out so soon, but I can't stop it now. I wanted to get to know my roommate better before my friends influenced how people saw me. I guess that's out.

With his hand on the small of my back, Liam guides me across the club to the dance floor where we danced the last time I was here. As we hit the edge of the crowded floor, he reaches for my hands, covering them with his and securing them to my hips.

Just like before, we dance through the throng of bodies until we reach the raised stage.

"You're not nervous, are you?" Liam asks so close to my ear his hot breath sends a hum down my body. I shake my head even though it's a lie, and he motions for me to climb onto the stage. I'm pretty sure there is no graceful way for me to clamor onto the platform in the dress I'm wearing, and I shake my head again. I don't remember how I did it last time. It seems so much taller today. Maybe it is a different stage.

Liam almost smiles as he sits on the edge and pulls himself up. Then he turns and offers me his hands. The next thing I know he's lifting me into the air with just my hands and I'm on the stage. He spins me around, locking me in a hug, and I swear that he sucks in as if he's smelling me. I hope he likes my perfume. I can't ponder that long before he's grinding against me. *Oh god, I should never have agreed to this.* It's going to mess me up so badly. I need to put up a wall with a poster that screams "just friends" in fluorescent-orange or I am likely to press my lips to his face and devour his gorgeous almost smile.

I roll my head back and forth across my shoulders, trying to relax and Liam pecks my cheek. That didn't help. I need to loosen up or I will look too stiff.

A new song comes on and he spins me around to face him. He consumes me as if I'm prey with his analytical expression. Then, before I have a chance to wonder what he sees, his lips are on mine. My body melts at his touch and as he pulls back, he says, "See I knew you could relax."

I try to scowl but he touches my cheek and I smile instead. Then, he grabs my hips and lifts me into the air. I arch back and his nose skims my stomach as I drop back to my feet. The tempo picks up and we're dancing sped-up swing with a hip-hop twist, just like the last time. Soon, we've burned through two songs and I'm feeling comfortable anticipating his moves. As long as I don't think too much about being naked with him or being visible to the entire club via the giant Jumbotron, I will survive this.

"Over my back and through my legs," says Liam, and I don't have time to protest before he's bending over, I'm rolling across his back with my legs straight out and he's pulling me through his legs. As he turns to face me, he's actually smiling—a real smile that penetrates his eyes—and I think I just impressed him. He spins me around and is grinding against me. I feel him. He definitely liked the flip. We're both moving slower now, trying to catch our breaths. He's kissing my neck as his hands run up and down my sides. My hips are moving slowly as I push back against him. I can't resist. I don't get to feel this good very often, I might as well enjoy it. Suddenly he spins me.

"So that's how you're going to play it," he says into my ear. "You fight dirty, Miss Billings."

I smirk because I know I've affected him. I make him as uncomfortable as he makes me. We dance through one more song, before he jumps off the stage and tells me to trust-fall backwards into his arms. I don't trust him. Not after the silent treatment. But somehow, his sultry voice convinces me to do it anyway. When his arms close around me, my adrenaline level is so high I'm shaking. He holds me tight and tucks his head so his lips are at my ear.

"You're shaking."

"I know. I was nervous." I don't tell him it's not the dancing. It's him and our whole situation. I want him to be mine and it scares me to death.

"I've got you, Meg. I've got you." He rubs my arms as if he's trying to warm me up. "It's funny you didn't seem nervous at the end."

His eyes buzz with excitement and he mumbles under his breath as he rights me on my feet.

"I just don't know what you want from me," I admit, looking around the club to get my bearings. We start walking and I don't think we are going in the right direction. This club is so big. Finally, I recognize the grand staircase that leads to the VIP section. The bouncer unlatches the rope for us to pass as he fishes a golden wristband out of his back pocket. He holds it up as if asking Liam whether I was worthy of having access or if I would just be in the section as long as I was useful.

"Come on upstairs with me. There's a private room up there where we can talk." He nods and the bouncer affixes the band around my wrist without even talking to me.

"No." I pull my banded hand away seconds too late. I can't go to a private room with him. "I'm going back to my friends. Thanks for the dance."

Chapter 30

Megan

L iam rolls his eyes as I turn toward the direction I think my roommate is seated. He grabs my hand, following me through the crowded club. I know I'm just a prop, someone to V-block the other girls, but his grasp still feels unbelievable, firm and hot, making my insides raw and vulnerable.

We get back to the table and I can tell the girls have filled Arianna in on Liam's identity. All three of them have their phones out. Arianna pulls her purse off my chair and I climb onto the high stool. Liam stands next to me, his hand on my sweaty back and his face heavy in thought. It's funny that just minutes ago, he had the brightest smile I've ever seen.

"So how do you know each other?" asks Arianna, with an amazed look on her face.

I look to Liam to see if I should show all my cards or not. He raises an eyebrow as his thumb creeps under the V on the back of my dress and slowly strokes my bare skin. *That isn't helpful.* "We met through friends," I say.

The server interrupts, setting drinks down for the rest of the table. "Liam, I'll have someone bring you a chair in a minute. Can I get you your usual?" she says.

"No. A Jameson on ice for me. Meg?"

"The same for me only with Coke and ice," I say.

"Thanks, Rosie," Liam says and as soon as she leaves, the guy who met us at the door approaches.

"So this is the girl?" the shorter, dark-haired man says doing a fist bump/handshake combination with Liam.

Liam smiles. *What girl? I'm not the girl. I can't be the girl.*

"Where's our bottle service, Theo?" asks Nikki. "You promised us bottle service."

Theo smiles with an unapologetic shrug and turns back to Liam. "You were right about her." He glances at me. "Perfect."

"Definitely one for the next," says Liam, and then winks at me.

I wish I understood what they were talking about.

"Got that track you promised to listen to," Theo says taking a step back.

"Right behind you," says Liam, then leans in and speaks only to me, "Don't go anywhere. I'll be right back." His thumb caresses my back with one final stroke and my body clinches where no one else can see. *Holy stilettos* that hit deep.

The second he leaves, the girls are all over me.

"How do you know Liam Nordstrom? And don't give us this crap about you met through friends. Who are your friends?" asks Nikki.

"One of his best friends is married to one of my best friends. I met him at this very club in the spring. It's not a big deal."

"You've slept with him, haven't you?" asks Arianna, though it is more of a statement.

"We're friends."

"You either have or you're going to. His hands were all over you. He either expects to get some or he's already had it," says Trina.

"Or both," adds Nikki. "Is he as good as they say?" She must be friends with the girls I met in the club bathroom the first time I was here.

A smile spreads across my face.

"Okay. Is it a friends with benefits?" asks Nikki.

I shrug because, honestly, I don't know what it is. I need to change the subject with something that will distract the conversation. "Did you see anything when I did that flip across his back? It wasn't a full frontal was it?"

"No, the camera angle was off. No lady parts," says Trina. "You still haven't told us about you and Nordstrom. It's like we don't even know you."

Seriously? I met her yesterday. She *doesn't* know me. "There's not much to tell. We hooked up a couple of times. But we're friends." *Did I say too much?* I can't tell them he's devastated me and I cried for weeks when he never called.

"Oh my god. Is that a gold wristband?" asks Nikki, grabbing my arm and examining the band the bouncer attached. "Did you go up there? What's it like?"

"I didn't go up. Liam wanted to, but I told him I needed to come back here."

"So we could go up with you, right? You *are* my new best friend, Megan. Did he say he was with Jake Gorboni?" asks Nikki.

We talk for another fifteen minutes about celebrities until a group of guys approaches the table. A couple of them know Nikki. She begins introductions and I start to wonder if Liam will ever return. What am I going to do if he does return?

"And this is Megan. She arrived a couple of days ago from Minnesota."

"Let me guess, you want to be an actress?" says tall, dark, and adorable.

"Nope. Grad school."

He introduces himself in more detail, and we talk about the club and the music, and he reveals he's a native of Los Angeles but has been out of the country traveling for the last six months. He doesn't look the blond, surfer stereotype with his dark hair and skin, and light-colored eyes. He's a bit of a flirt and a good distraction from Nordstrom, who I'm sure has completely forgotten about me with the gorgeous blonde standing next to him at the DJ booth. I struggle to stop watching as her long fingers touch him. His arm. His back. His lips. *Arg.* I need to stop obsessing over him. I turn to Neo Lund, a.k.a. tall, dark, and handsome as he leans down closer to my ear.

"What are you studying in school?"

I gloss over my education plans and he smiles as if he doesn't believe me.

"You are such a liar. There is no way you're an applied mathematics major. I have a degree in applied mathematics and chem."

"I am." I laugh. "I like the theoretical part, the way numbers sort out."

"You are way too beautiful to be a math major." His eyes peruse my legs and then meet my eyes. I could easily say the same thing about him.

"What color are your eyes? I can't tell in this light," I ask, and he smiles.

"You tell me," he says, leaning in to give me a closer look. He is inches from my face.

His eyes are the most interesting color—sage-green brimmed with whiskey-brown. His whole look is gorgeous. His dark hair makes his light eyes pop. "Green, right?"

He shrugs, standing back up. "It depends on what I wear." His hand grasps my shoulder. "So you live next to Nikki?" His face crinkles as if he feels sorry for me.

"Don't hold it against me."

He laughs and looks over to her. "So you know her well?" he asks. Our voices are soft enough and the music is too loud for her to hear our conversation.

"Just met yesterday. But I am a pretty good judge of character." I am a good judge of character. I just make poor choices and ignore common sense. I don't add my commentary though.

"So now that you're done traveling, what are you going to do?"

"Probably go work for my dad. He runs a plastic extruding business." He takes his hand off my shoulder to pull a business card out of his wallet, and hands it to me. It looks generic with a company logo, an email address, and a phone number. "That's my cell. Keep it." He smiles.

I'm not sure if it is supposed to impress me or if it is just a ploy to give me his number. I stuff the card into the small purse slung across my body.

"What are you doing with your degree?" he asks.

"I was thinking I would discover an algorithm that cures cancer. Or one that protects people's identities. I don't know. I shouldn't have to have it all figured out by the age of twenty-two. Maybe I'll teach," I say and that's when I feel Nordstrom's lips on my neck. I know it's him because I can smell his clean, expensive cologne and my whole body purrs to his touch.

"Did you miss me?" he mumbles against my neck.

I realize in this moment no other man exists in a world with Liam Nordstrom, no matter how good-looking. His breath heats me to the core. I visualize him behind me, grasping my hips. *My brain is mush.*

"No," I say, and he pulls back, staring into my eyes. He can tell I'm lying.

"I missed *you*," Liam whispers. Somehow I doubt that. Out of sight, out of mind, seems more his style. Then he turns and fist bumps tall, dark and handsome. "How've you been, man?"

Lund looks between Liam and me, shaking his head. I imagine my body's response to Nordstrom is more visible than I want.

"I thought you said you just moved here a couple of days ago. How do you know this player?"

I open my mouth to answer when Nordstrom interrupts.

"I take offense to that," he says with a not quite serious face. "She's best friends with Jonathan William's wife. We were paired at the wedding ceremony and shared a blissful week on a Caribbean island." *Claimed.* Damn him. Of course, the music quiets just as Liam opens his mouth and the whole table hears his explanation.

"Oh," Lund says. He half smiles, then another look I can't interpret crosses his face.

I glance to Arianna, and she's scowling at me. I guess I should have told her about Sarah right away. That's not my personality though. I mouth, *I'm sorry* to her, and she shakes her head. I don't know her well enough to figure out if she is mad or not. A bouncer brings a stool for Nordstrom and he sits down between me and Arianna.

"So, Arianna, where exactly is this apartment you share with Meg?" Nordstrom asks, placing his arm across the back of her chair. I'm distracted by his arm and don't realize what he's asking until it's too late.

Trina answers quickly. "The Plaza. And Nikki and I live right across the hall in 211. You should come hang with us."

"What's Meg's number?"

"Cut it out, Nordstrom. I don't want you to know where I live."

Trina looks at me as if I just threw her phone into the toilet. Then she smiles at Liam, flips her hand as if dismissing me, and says, "She's just joking. They're in 212. We should meet up with your buddies upstairs and head over to the apartment later. I make a mean apple shooter." She crosses her legs using the seductive move I patented.

"No," I say, without any further explanation. I wasn't prepared to see Nordstrom tonight and why is he being so inquisitive. I know we talked about dating after I got to L.A., but that was before he gave me the silent treatment. This isn't right. He can't have it both ways. I turn and ask, "Lund, do you want to dance?"

He takes my hand and we make it about five steps before Nordstrom spins me around and asks, "What are you doing, Meg?" His dark eyes penetrate me, his chest puffed out.

His expression reminds me of when I answered my hotel suite door wearing just a towel. My heart races. I swallow hard and say, "I'm dancing with my new friend." I stress the word *friend*. "That's what clubs are for, meeting new people and dancing."

"You're not leaving until we talk," he whispers in my ear before turning back to the table.

I smile at Lund and say, "Actors. They're so dramatic."

He laughs and we start dancing. Lund can dance, but our rhythm seems off from the very start.

"So what's with you and Nordstrom? He made it sound as if you two were dating, but here you are dancing with me."

"We may have dated for a week, but I haven't talked to him or seen him for a month."

"You're not the reason he took himself off the market? He's seems a bit pissed about us dancing together. He's glaring at me."

"Definitely not. That's a weird comment. Why would *you* know if he's taken himself off the market?"

"I just got back into town. I had lunch with a bunch of friends today, and one of them used to hook up with him every once in a while. She was all bent out of shape because he's off the market."

"It's not me. We're not together."

He grasps my hips and grinds against me as he speaks into my ear. "I think it is. He looks as if he's going to vomit."

"Good," I say, reaching up behind me and combing my fingers through his dark hair. The chemistry between us is nowhere near what I have with Nordstrom, but I don't care. Liam doesn't get to call all the shots.

On the way back to the table, he says, "I'm here if you are interested in revenge sex."

"I'll keep that in mind," I say with a laugh. I'm glad he understands. I look up and Nordstrom's brooding eyes are tracking us, but by the time we make it back to the table, Liam seems to have regained his composure and is talking to Arianna.

Nordstrom leans into me and says, "You're not leaving with anybody, but me," then turns back to Arianna without another word. I have to remind my body he has no claim on me. I step closer to Lund. I can see on his face I'm not fooling him with my false interest.

"You like him, don't you?"

I shake my head. "I wish I didn't. But I've never been good at controlling chemistry."

"My friend Tara acts lost around him, too. Does he have a magical dick or something?"

"That must be it," I say with a laugh, but I'm serious.

He smiles and tucks a strand of my hair behind my ear. "You should probably sort that out before we go out." His light eyes are intense.

Nordstrom nudges me and asks, "Are you ready to go, Meg?"

It throws me off because in reality that is all I want to do. Leave with him. Be alone with him. Give myself to him over and over again. But I recover quickly. "You can go. I came with the girls. It's our night to get to know each other before classes start."

An absolutely cocky smile ghosts on his face as he says, "Girls, Daniel Nackerson, Jake Gorboni, Tom Fallston, and I have a great table in the VIP section with much better service. What do you say we take this party up there?"

They betray me quickly by standing and downing their drinks. Then, they glare at me as if I'm slowing them down. I turn to Lund and he's already backing away. He points a finger at me and says, "You've got my number. Give me a call when you sort it out." Then, he sits in Trina's chair as his friends take over the other vacated seats. I follow the group to the guard at the VIP section. The girls each get their own gold band and Nikki acts as if she is gaining entrance to the pearly gates of heaven. She doesn't realize the VIP area is a cornucopia filled with temptations that damn you to hell.

Chapter 31

Liam

The smile on Nak's face when he sees Meg is priceless. He knows how much finding her means to me. It's even better than finding out what Sarah knows. The only reason I was able to force myself to the club tonight was because I knew tomorrow I would get more clues into the complex mind of Megan Billings from one of her best friends. Sarah invited me over for dinner tomorrow, but seeing Meg tonight is definitely better, more telling. She is still attracted to me. It is so obvious. The way her pulse on her neck speeds when I touch her, how her breath hitches when I look into her eyes, and the way her body melts into mine—all prove I own her. I hate that she has the power to make me doubt myself. It has never happened before in my life. I've never been so hung up on a girl.

"Megan. How have you been, babe?" Gorboni booms as we reach the table. He turns to Fallston and says, "Don't ever play strip poker with this girl. She is the luckiest S.O.B. We were at Williams' once and I was doing all I could to cheat and she still beat me."

"I count cards, Jake," Meg says as if it should be obvious. "And I didn't win. I went to bed before I lost my shirt."

"My shirt," I correct. She was wearing my shirt. The thought makes me smile.

"You count cards?" asks Fallston. "You should come to Vegas on Wednesday with Jake and me."

I don't like the way his eyes sweep over her body. I wrap my arm around her, splaying my hand across her stomach to claim her, and motion for the girls to file in onto the couch next to Fallston. They look completely lost for words. I hope this wasn't a mistake. It won't be if I get some alone time with Meg. I lead her to the other end of the couch by Nak. I trust him.

"My classes start on Wednesday, but maybe some other time," says Meg.

What the hell is her problem? "Don't encourage him," I whisper. I need to get her alone. It's too easy for her to deny us with all these people here.

Our server appears and I lean into her asking her if the private room is available.

She nods, then disappears to the bar for a minute and returns, discreetly handing me the key card. I've never used it before. I know guys who have and I know it will cost me. I don't even know how much, but I am desperate and this might be my only chance.

"We have to talk, Meg. Alone." I stand up and offer her my hand. She looks at me questioningly. "Meg and I need to talk. We won't be long," I say to the group to force her hand.

She stands, looks to her friends, and then back to me. Her eyebrows are knit in concern, but she follows me anyway. I tap the card against the plate on the wall and the door pops open. I open it wide and it is just as Fallston described it. A floor-to-ceiling window into the club covers one wall. The window vibrates to the beat of the music. The room smells of lemon and smoked wood, and the lighting is soft and romantic. A dark, wooden, just-the-right-height-for-fucking bar sits to the right of the window. It seems out of place with all the glass and metal of the club, but somehow makes the room feel warmer and more comfortable. What I wouldn't give to use this room to its full potential with Meg.

She stops a couple of feet inside the door.

"I can't be in here with you. I have to go," she whispers. I don't believe that's what she wants, but something is stopping her with me. I'm not going to force her into something she doesn't want.

"We will just talk. I promise." I take her hand and lead her toward the bar. When we reach it, I grasp her hips and lift her onto it. I don't want her bolting out of the room until we've talked. Jumping down with those heels would be a challenge and should slow her down just a little. Her breath catches as I set her down. My hand automatically slides to the back of her neck because I know it makes her vulnerable and right now, I need all the leverage I can get. She holds all the cards. I stare into her eyes hoping to read some unspoken message. Her bottom lip pulls in and it takes everything I have not to suck it back out with my mouth on hers.

We stay silent for several minutes, just staring at each other. Then Meg speaks. "What do you want from me, Nordstrom?"

"Everything," I say and I am not lying. I want everything with her. I don't know how I could have made it clearer.

"I don't know what that means."

"It means all we talked about on the island. It means we'll date only each other. It means we'll be together and not block each other's calls."

"It's a little too late for that, don't you think?"

"I'm still open for it. I can get past what happened in the last month, if you can," I say hoping maybe she will share why she stopped taking my calls after the island.

"Well, I'm not. You think I'm just here for you to play with, a toy. I'm not your toy. You have no claim on me. I can't do this with you, Liam. If you want to be friends, we can be friends, but I can't let us be more than that. I'm not going to sleep with you again," Meg says. She looks down at her sandals, avoiding eye contact.

I step back and crouch down, imposing my face in her view. "I am not toying with you."

"You are if you think I can forget about what happened after we left the island."

"What?" I pause gaping at her. "Did you get back together with Chase?"

Is he the reason you're throwing us away?" Nak said, Jessica called him her kryptonite.

She turns her head toward the glass wall and says in a snarky tone, "Yep. I got back together with Chase."

I don't know if her goal is to hurt me or if she's being sarcastic. It would explain why she stopped taking my calls and cut off all communication with me, though. I grasp her chin and turn her face until our lips are almost touching. I can see the pulse on her luscious neck pump. She can't fight it either. I press my lips to hers and her mouth opens. My tongue pushes into her and I'm in heaven. *I could devour her.* My hand slides to her ass and as I pull her closer, she responds fully to my kiss, pushing her fingers into my hair and moaning as the kiss deepens. I'm standing between her knees and as her legs wrap around me, I kiss down her neck. When my lips reach one of her breasts, I take the tip into my mouth. I don't care that I'm leaving wet marks on her dress. I need this. And she's not fighting me. Her eyes close and the sweet little mewling noises she's making tells me she wants it too.

I want to take her right here on the bar to prove our chemistry is worth more than anything she could possibly have with her ex, but we still haven't talked. I pull back slowly. It's hard, very hard to do. We're both panting, trying to catch our breaths as I lean my forehead to rest on hers. "Be with *me*, Meg," I say, hoping to pull her back into my world.

"You're a liar, Nordstrom."

"I never lied to you. I meant every word I said on the island."

"You said we would just talk and now you're using sex to trap me in your web. I can't do this again."

I shake my head and put my hands up in surrender as I step back. I don't know what to say because, yes, I want to show her what she would be giving up, but I also just want her. "I don't want to lose you."

"We can be friends, like I said, but we can't sleep together." She's still panting, and I don't believe what she is telling me.

"So you choose him over me."

She opens her mouth, but nothing comes out. Then she takes a deep breath and shakes her head. "I just can't be more than friends, okay? That's all I want."

Now, I take a deep breath. I can't believe this. Doesn't she feel the electricity between us? *What the hell?* I can't even look at her. My breathing hitches in a bad way, and I have to turn my head because I'm afraid she'll see how pathetic I am.

I swallow hard and say, "If we're friends, you can't block my calls. Otherwise, you're an ex." I still picture all the unanswered texts I had sent her. She could have just told me all we talked about on the island was a lie. She could have answered one of the twenty-three calls I made to her and told me not to plan our future together because she found someone better.

She rolls her eyes and I know she's never going to take my calls. I gulp down my emotions and try to sell the most difficult acting job I've ever done. I harden my face and help her off the bar. "I hope he realizes how lucky he is to have you."

She doesn't say anything, just nods. I don't believe he does.

"Can you find your way back to the table?" I ask. I need a drink or ten before I can head back there. Nak is going to wonder what happened, and Fallston will give us shit about using the private room so quickly. I caught the smirk on his face when the server handed me the keycard. No one needs to know she gutted me in here. I need a few minutes to compose my face to show indifference. I lead her to the door and watch it close behind her, knowing I may never see her again.

Chapter 32

Liam

By the time I stumbled back to the table last night, I had finished off half a bottle of whiskey. I usually don't drink to excess especially since the studio sent out the press release talking about my stint in rehab. Ever since then, anytime someone snaps a picture of me with a drink, the rumors fly saying I'm spiraling into an abyss. Even the wait staff at the club seems to think it is their job to keep me sober. The look of worry that crosses their faces when I don't want my usual tonic with lime tells me they discuss my well-being amongst themselves. Alcohol was not my problem though…well, at least not until last night.

Nak said I made an ass of myself when I got back to the table. Apparently, I asked Meg detailed questions about her ex-boyfriend's anatomy. Who, I guess in reality, is her current boyfriend. I'm not the kind of guy who gets jealous. I'm the king of indifference. *Why does she affect me when no other woman does?* I've never gotten drunk because of a woman before, and I don't like the control she has on me.

After I dragged my butt out of bed this afternoon, Nak and I discussed all the mistakes I made last night. By the sounds of it, he played his role of wingman valiantly, smoothing over the conversation at the table and dragging me out of the club before I could make the situation worse. I would be surprised if Meg ever talked to me again. I should just move on, but I can't. She captured my attention from the first night we danced. Our bodies fed off each other with no effort at all, anticipating exactly what the other wanted. Sex with her was the best I've ever had. No one else even comes close in comparison. But that's not all I miss.

The truth is, I just miss her. I miss her laugh. I miss her smart comebacks. I miss talking to her. I miss the taste of her. My biggest regret is not taking her on the bar last night. If I could go back in time I would have fucked her until she didn't know her own name and definitely didn't remember *his* name. Hell, if I could go back in time I would have flown to Minnesota with her from the island and she never would have gotten back with that asshat.

Before last night, it had been a month since I'd heard Meg's voice. I don't know how many unanswered texts I sent her. That's a lie—forty-three. I'd called at least half that many times, hoping to catch her off guard, but it just rang and rang, not even going to her voicemail. It's as if she'd completely blocked me.

I open the one-sided text thread on my phone and think back to the island, trying to figure out where it went wrong. The week with her was like high definition. My life until then hazy in comparison. It was as if my world finally came into focus—so clear and vibrant that it was impossible to look away. She turned my old fuzzy sitcom reruns into a clearly-defined realm. I saw all the flawed pock marks of my past for the first time.

I thought we were on the same page when she got on the plane to leave. We had talked about our week as being more than a vacation hookup. We talked about being a couple. I assumed we were exclusive. I don't know what happened. When I saw her last night, I was pissed. I fully intended to bitch her out, but when I touched her silken skin and felt the energy coming off her, the fact she blocked me didn't matter anymore. All that mattered was being with her.

I down a large glass of water, trying to rehydrate my body to recover from the worst hangover in recent memory. I am supposed to be at Jon and Sarah's by seven. That's only two hours from now, which means with Sunday traffic on the One, I need to hit the shower and get ready. I'd skip it all together except I need some answers from Sarah. Like, why the hell would Meg flirt with Lund to make me jealous, and make out with me when she has a boyfriend? Was she with him while we were on the island? Was I just a distraction? It felt like so much more. *Shit*. I was just a distraction for her.

The second I walk into the courtyard at Jon's house, I spot her. She's sitting next to Sarah. Her eyes widen as if she didn't expect to see me either. I take in a deep breath, trying to cleanse away all my thoughts about being with her. I turn on brooding mode and hope, for once, she won't see through the disillusionment mist I'm projecting. I kiss Sarah's cheek and thank her for inviting me, and clap-shake Jon's hand, before sitting next to Meg at the table. I don't kiss her cheek. It would hurt too much.

"Hey, Meg," I say with a nod, trying to display apathy.

"Hi."

"Was that so hard?" asks Sarah. Then she offers us both drinks.

"Whatever you're having," says Meg to Sarah.

"I'm just having lime water. I caught some bug down in South America. My stomach is still a bit iffy. I don't want to throw up tonight's dinner."

They've been back for two weeks. How could she still be sick? I look to Jon and he's smiling from ear to ear. He wouldn't be smiling if that was the real reason she's given up alcohol. I want what they have. I want it all with Meg. Is that wrong?

"Then a Whiskey Coke for me. Nordstrom will just take the rest of the whiskey bottle, no glass," Meg says with a spiteful expression.

Sarah looks at me for an explanation of Meg's comment.

"I am sorry I lost control last night. You blindsided me when you told me you got back together with your ex."

Sarah turns to Meg, her lips hardened into a straight line and her jaw clinched. I guess this is news to her. "No, Megan. You are not back together with Chase. You can't get back with him."

Now this is getting interesting. Sarah obviously hates the guy.

"She's already back with him," I say.

Meg twists in her seat and faces Sarah with an apologetic, yet defensive expression. "I'm…"

"He's the reason she blocked my calls and didn't respond to my texts for the last month. She couldn't even break up with me in a text? *Stop calling me. I'm back with my ex.* How hard is that? "

Now Meg turns to me, anger burning in her eyes. "I didn't block you. You never called. You're just trying to make it look like it's my fault. I never blocked your calls."

"Didn't answer my texts or calls, how is that different from blocking?"

"You are the one who didn't answer my texts and calls. Stop trying to turn it around."

"I haven't been with anyone since we were together on the island. Hell, I haven't been with anyone else since the night I met you. I'm not the one who got together with my ex."

Jon chuckles, and I turn to scowl at him. I know I'm being a whiny-ass little girl, but I don't need hecklers from the audience. He smiles with his eyebrows raised, and I can tell what he's thinking. Karma is a bitch. I've completely fallen for this girl and she doesn't want me. I've lost my mind. And he's right.

"You're not back with Chase." Sarah looks to me as if asking me to clarify. "She can't be back with him. You better not be back with him." Each time Sarah opens her mouth, she sounds less confident.

I find satisfaction in Sarah's reaction. Somehow, I feel as if I just tattled on Meg.

"What are you smirking about, Nordstrom? You are such a jerk sometimes," says Meg. "I'm not back with Chase. I just don't…I can't…I can't be with you."

"Why?" I don't care Sarah and Jon are listening. I don't care she lied to me. I want to know why.

"I just want to be friends, okay? That's all we can be.

"Why? Why can't we be together? You just admitted you lied about being with your ex. What is stopping us? After the wedding, you seemed willing. What's changed?" I watch as Sarah and Jon make eye contact, then both rise and head into the house without a word.

I get up, make Meg a whiskey and Coke at the bar and hand it to her, hoping to relax her enough to get an honest answer.

"I'm waiting," I say without looking up as I pour myself a club soda and squeeze a sliced lime into it. When I sit down next to her, I take out my phone. She still hasn't answered. I type out a text.

Me: I want you, Meg, always and forever.

It's the truth. I don't know how else to say it. I expect her phone to ping or at least vibrate. It is sitting right there on the table, face up. It doesn't even light up.

"You totally block me." *She blocked me.* "I just sent you a text. It didn't even register on your phone. You blocked my number."

"I didn't block your number. I don't even know how to block a number." She picks up her phone and lights the screen, then hands me her phone. "See? You never sent a text."

"Well…I sent it." I hand her my phone to prove my point.

I watch as her eyes get as big as an anime character's. Big and blue and gorgeous, they glance up to meet mine. I think she's reacting to the always and forever in the text I just sent, but she's not. "Whoa. You know what this means?" A smile blazes onto her face. "You're not the ass I thought you were."

I scowl at her. I'm not an ass. I'm not going to let her dismiss the words I wrote.

She looks back down at my phone and begins reading through my texts. "I can't believe you actually sent these. Why didn't I get them?"

"You didn't block me?" I don't really need to ask because I can tell by her expression she is completely surprised by my texts.

She glances at the phone in my hand and lets out a breath. Her lips purse as she shakes her head. "This has to be Chase's fault. I don't know how to prove it, but he did this. I'm sure of it. He gave me that phone and he somehow blocked you. I can't believe I never realized he was manipulating my phone. I mean with all the crap that happened with Seth's intervention, I should have thought of this. He's just…so good at lying."

"Wait a minute. You let him mess with your phone? Why would you let him have access to your phone?" After all that happened on the island, why would she even hang out with him?

"I didn't give him direct access, but he bought me the phone and set it up. He downloaded all my information from my old phone when he switched over the number to the new phone. He must have gotten all my passwords. Liam, I'm so sorry. I blamed you, but it was him."

I shake my head. "Why would you let him buy you a phone?"

"I thought he'd changed. He brought it over as a gift—no strings attached. I didn't think he was capable of doing this. I'm sorry." Her face is full of remorse.

I watch her for a couple of minutes as she reads the texts I sent her. She seems to have disregarded my "forever and always" comment. I thought it would have a bigger impact on her. Chase ruined that too. I watch her for a while trying to guess which one she is reading when her eyes pop up and meet mine.

"Stop watching me, Nordstrom. Find the texts I sent you."

I find her contacts, but can't find my name. "He deleted me."

"Look under Naked Sandwich." She smiles and continues reading.

I pull up Naked Sandwich and start thumbing through her texts. Wow she sounds pissed in the last one she sent.

Friends? Whatever. If you've been in a coma, call me when you get out, otherwise don't bother.

I scroll up.

I bought a bag of Skittles today and ate the whole thing myself. Didn't think of you once.

Her text is really funny and I can't help but laugh. I look over to Meg. Her expression is unclear. I take several minutes to read through the thread before I glance up at the picture of us at the club. She still has it as the contact photo.

"Who is this naked sandwich dude? This isn't even my number."

She looks up again, "What? That's the number you put in. I never changed your number."

I tap to call the number. "It's not what I put in your phone. Who have you been sending my texts to?" The call rings and rings without going to voicemail. "I just called the number you were texting. There was no voicemail."

"I know," she says. "Your voicemail never picks up." Her eyes are still glued to my phone.

"I'm going to delete this one and put my real number in your contacts." She jumps up and grabs her phone. "No. Don't."

"What the hell, Meg? Don't you want the right number?"

"Not on this phone. I have to get a new phone. Chase probably has an app tracking every keystroke I make. I don't want him to know I'm on to him."

"Oka...ay." I take the phone back from her and she sits down. "I'm going to check to see if my number is blocked." I go into the phone's settings to find the list of blocked numbers. "Mine's the only number blocked." A text buzzes on my phone. Whoever it is can wait. I'll check it later. She's still reading the texts I had sent her. Her eyebrows knit for a second and her reaction makes me wonder which text she's reading. It's probably the one where I laid out my plans for our first official date. It's not the reaction I wanted. I was hoping it would make her smile.

"I think we need to get revenge on your asshole ex," I say and she looks up to meet my gaze for a second before returning her attention back to my phone. I can't tell what she is thinking, but I want to kiss her so badly.

The click of Sarah's heels on the cement breaks our connection and at that moment I realize this was a set up. We are sitting in the courtyard of Jon and Sarah's house because they knew we were fighting and wanted us to put our problems behind us.

I'd talked to Jon when they got back from their honeymoon. I tried to be vague about what had happened between Meg and me, still unclear if the whole "you're the only person who could bring her to the wedding" was an open invitation for us to hook up or not. I hoped it was. I figured if I was the only person who could do the job, he knew about our connection. Sarah probably heard the whole story from Meg. What Sarah and Jon hadn't planned on was the club fiasco last night.

"So...Did you work it out?" asks Jon, setting a pile of plates and silverware on the table in front of us.

Sarah sets a tray of appetizers down, and I look to Meg to confirm we are good, but she doesn't look up. She is still staring at my phone.

"We're good," I say, but as I watch Meg, I can tell something is still wrong. She finally glances up and sets the phone down.

Sarah smiles and doesn't say a word, but I can see the satisfaction smeared all over her face, and I know she and Jon schemed to get us together.

Over dinner, Meg and I explain our theory on how Chase successfully kept us apart by sabotaging Meg's phone. Meg thinks he's been stalking her phone since he gave it to her. She says he knew all about us hooking up on the island and he told her before she left, he could tell she was no longer in contact with me because of her mood. She's either really gullible or he's a really smooth liar for her not to know he was stalking her before today.

We spend a good portion of the night talking about ways to get revenge on Meg's ex. I want to film a sex tape on the stalked phone because he'll watch it, giving us the ultimate revenge. I plan out the filming in my head as Jon quickly shoots down my idea. His point being Chase would post it online. And he's right, but that doesn't stop me from wanting to make one.

We all joke around as we explore our revenge angle. Sarah wants to use a baseball bat to break his knees. She sounds as if she wants to do it personally. I guess this past year dealing with the paparazzi has jaded her a bit toward violence.

"I still think the sex tape is the best option. It wouldn't have to be that graphic. We could angle the camera tastefully so nothing vital is showing," I say. "He's going to know what we're doing even if it's a black screen. As long as he can hear the moaning, he'll know."

"I'm not doing a sex tape with you, Liam," says Meg. Her eyes meet mine and I sense a sadness in her.

"You want revenge on him, right?" I ask, reaching out and covering her hand with mine. She closes her eyes and nods. We settle on a text from Meg to Sarah on the stalked phone to start the revenge on Chase. Meg asks me to write it. I would have rather seen it in her words, but I know the points to hit home that will trigger a man's rage.

"You're not going to punch me for hooking up with Meg, are you?" I ask Jon before I start reading the text I wrote. He shakes his head and I continue. "I met up with Liam last night. I don't care he never called. When I saw him, I had to have him. He's like a drug my body can't live without. We went back to his house and barely made it inside, before he was inside me. He took me hard against the door, not even taking time to undress. It was the best sex of my life and when I collapsed into his arms, exhausted, he carried me to his bed, ripped off my clothes and started all over again. He was inside me more than not the rest of the night. I'm so sore this morning I can barely walk." I finish reading the text and look up. Meg looks intrigued, but still unhappy.

"Okay. Anyone with half a brain could tell a man wrote this text," says Sarah, reaching for the phone. "This part where you say 'he was inside me,' a girl would never say that. She might say he took me against the door, she might think about a guy being inside her, but she would never talk about logistics of the act in a text—at least Megan wouldn't."

"She's a writer." Jon reminds me. "She knows this crap."

We hone the text to make it sound more like Meg, and Sarah adds a few details which make *me* blush. I hope it eviscerates Chase. I feel a sense of great satisfaction when Meg hits the send button and I hear it ping on Sarah's phone. The two send a couple more texts back and forth to make the revenge text more convincing. We joke around about Chase's reaction as we eat dinner but Meg seems more distant by the minute. By the time we leave, I am convinced something Meg read in my texts upset her. I walk her to her car because I still don't have a way to contact her.

"So when do you think you'll get your new phone?" I ask, leaning against her car.

"Classes don't start until Wednesday so I should be able to get one by Tuesday."

I expect the light bulb to turn on and remind her she doesn't have my number. I figure if she doesn't know how to block a number she doesn't know how to access the auto reject list on her phone. "So you'll call me with your new number?"

"Yeah. I'll call you."

"Do you need my real number?"

Her eyebrows furrow and she looks up at me for the first time since we came outside. Her eyes examine me as if she's analyzing every imperfection of my soul. Then, she opens her purse and pulls out a pen and a business card. "Just write it on the back of this. I'll add it to the new phone."

I flip the card over. Neo Lund. *Bastard.* I turn to the back and scratch out my number, handing it to her without a word. We stand there for a long minute before she speaks.

"Well. I have to go, Nordstrom. I still have unpacking to do."

I know it's an excuse and I walk away without even kissing her. I start my bike and pull on my helmet. I don't know what's going on with her. Even though she knows I didn't abandon her, it doesn't seem as if she wants us to be together.

Megan

Damn smiley face. It's still burned on my retina. Someone should outlaw emoji's. The picture with Liam's hand covering some girl's hand as she leans into him mocks me even more. I couldn't help but see it. When the text attached to it flashed at the top of his phone tonight, I had to click on it. He said he hasn't been with anyone else since he met me. He's such a liar.

> Kat: *The paps caught us Thursday night. Guess our secret's out.*

The texts above it in the thread tell me all I need to know.

> Kat: *Six more times today? That's probably a world's record. I think*
> *you left a permanent handprint on my left breast.*

> Liam: *Stop complaining. You loved it.*

I don't want to start back with him if he is lying to me. I've been through that before. I know what I am about to do is wrong, but it's not any worse than him lying. I hate I've resorted to the tabloids to get information. I told myself I never would. I don't need another liar in my life, though. I type his name into the search engine and up pops the picture from the text.

> *Costars Liam Nordstrom and Katya Avery caught together*
> *after dark: The two were spotted leaving West Break*
> *Studios together on Thursday night for dinner and some*

off-screen action. Sources tell us we can expect to see some hot and steamy scenes between the actors in season four of Impassioned.

So she's his costar and a brunette. He told me he wouldn't date brunettes and after his experience with the makeup artist, he wasn't going to date people from work, either. I flip through the pictures of them together: in the car, walking into a restaurant, in front of an apartment building, going inside hand in hand. *What a liar.*

Even if he didn't abandon me like my mother, I can't let him back into my life.

The morning after my awakening, I rise early determined to cut all ties with my past. I should say, all testosterone-filled ties. I hit the phone store first thing. I not only get a new phone and number but a new carrier as well. I don't want there to be any chance Chase could tap into my new phone. If I could easily change my name, I'd consider it.

I could trade in the phone Chase gave me and get the latest release, but I opt for a cheaper phone instead. I'm not done with Chase's, because I haven't figured out the best revenge yet, and I'm going to transfer my contacts manually, just in case the phone has a virus that would infect my new phone with a stalking app. I'm not sure what he is capable of doing, and I won't let him manipulate me anymore.

On my way back to the apartment, I stop at the local coffee shop for my caffeine fix. With latte in hand, I lay both phones out on the table and start entering my contacts into the new phone. I even got a new email account. I don't want any cross-contamination between the accounts in case Chase has access to the old one.

I've made it to the R's when a text pops up on my old phone.

Arianna: I thought you said you didn't have a boyfriend.
Me: I don't.
Arianna: The guy sitting on the couch claims he's your boyfriend.
  Anyway you could come get him out of our apartment?
Me: Fine. I'll be right there.

I thought Nordstrom had to work today. He couldn't wait for me to call him? I'd entered his number into my phone, but that doesn't mean I was going to call him after seeing the text last night from Kat. *Six more times?* By the time I get back to the apartment, I have an outline in my head of what I'm going to tell Nordstrom. If he thinks I'm going to believe a word he says from now on, he's crazy.

When I open the door, I've already pulled up the tabloid article on my new phone to have it ready, but when I see him on the couch, I quickly stuff the phone into my bag.

"Why are you here, Chase?"

"So you do know him?" asks Arianna as she rolls her eyes and walks into the bedroom, closing the door behind her.

"It's good to see you too, babe. He stands and starts walking toward me, stopping a foot in front of me. A cocky smile fills his face as if he just made the biggest grand gesture ever. "I thought you would be happier to see me."

"I'm not. What do you want?"

"Well, I'm here." He sits back on the couch. "I got to thinking I could move out here. If you feel so strongly about finishing school, then I can meet you halfway. Most of my work is on the computer. I can live anywhere."

"I don't want you here." I sit in the chair putting as much room as I can between my body and his. Not because I'm attracted to him, but because I have a strong urge to bludgeon him to death on the white couch. "If that's what you took away from our last conversation, then you don't know me at all. I don't trust you, Chase."

"I know you better than anyone. Just give me a chance to prove myself to you. I came all the way here."

He obviously thinks he deserves more appreciation than I'm showing. He doesn't know me. "Nordstrom knows me better than you." It's true, even if Nordstrom is a liar. I know why I say it. I want to hurt Chase for all the manure he's dumped on me. I want to add to the knife wound inflicted by the text Liam sent from my phone to Sarah last night.

"He's cheating on you. He's shagging his costar. It's all over the tabloids."

"The tabloids are just PR. I've met her. They're not together. It's just for the show," I lie.

He stands and starts pacing back and forth, running his fingers through his hair as if he's making the toughest decision of his life. I hope he doesn't propose. I will definitely bludgeon him. My eyes sweep the room for a good object for his demise. The large stone bowl by the front door where we put our keys is my best bet. It wouldn't break if struck against his skull, and if I use both hands to swing it, it wouldn't be that heavy. He huffs out a breath on his third pass in front of me.

"I'm not the person I was when we dated. A ton has happened since high school. It changed me."

"I know what happened to your mother, Meg."

"What? Did you read it in the tabloids?" I ask because everyone thinks they know what happened to her. Only Liam and I know the truth about the pill bag in my purse.

He sits on the ottoman in front of me and looks me in the eyes before speaking. "She committed suicide."

"That seems to be the consensus."

"She had my drugs in her," he says with a very somber face as he tracks my reaction.

"The drugs you left in my purse?" I ask, hoping to finally get clarification on the theory that's plagued me for more than four years. He remembers the drugs.

"You have to understand, Meg. I went to the marina looking for you. It's your fault I was there. You cut me off. I didn't know how else to get a hold of you."

My head explodes with possible scenarios. "I don't understand. You were at the marina the night my mom died?"

"We were just talking when she asked me for something to get her through to the weekend. I don't remember what I gave her, but it was enough to get her to the weekend. I felt as if we were finally connecting. I always felt as if your family was judging me and here your mom was asking me for a pick-me-up."

I stare at him, shaking my head. It can't be. He couldn't have just handed pills to her. I don't even know what to say. His eyes lift to mine.

"I thought you would be happy to finally know the truth. I thought she was going to space them out over the week, so it blew me away when she downed them all at once right in front of me."

"You just let her?"

"I couldn't get a hold of you. I didn't have your new number."

"Why didn't you call my dad?"

"I wasn't going to let your dad judge me for giving her pills."

"So you just left and let her die."

"She was fine when I left. I don't know why you're so mad at me. There is nothing I can do to change it. You're always telling me you don't trust me and now that I'm telling you the truth, you get mad. What is it you want? I'm here. I'm telling you the truth. And we're supposed to move forward."

"Forward into what, Chase?"

"Forward in our relationship. You don't need the actor because I'm here."

"You are such an ass. You think just because you tell me one truth in the last seven years, I trust you."

"You blocked Nordstrom from my phone. You changed his number in the phone so I couldn't text him. Who was getting my texts?"

He looks to the door and then back at me with a coy smile. Now he knows I know. I can see the cogs turning in his head. He's smart and he'll come up with a lie quickly. I'm not going to give him a chance to work through all the possible scenarios.

"It was a cock-blocking thing, right? He was making an impression on me and you didn't like it. I get it. But what I don't understand is how you can be so heartless. You are the most soulless person I have ever met. You don't care about anyone but Chase Maxwell. You may act as if you care, but it's just an act. You don't care about me. The only reason you want me is because you can't have me. You need to leave."

"Just give me a chance to explain. You don't understand," he pleads, but I'm not giving him another chance.

"It doesn't matter what you say. Everything that comes out of your mouth is a lie. I'm done listening."

"If you shut me out again, you'll end up all alone and full of regret, just like your mom."

He uses the words I am most afraid of—full of regret—and then compares me to Mom. I squish my eyes together, trying to stay composed.

"I would rather die alone than be with you. Get out." I open the door. How dare he mention my mom? He grasps the back of my head and smashes his lips on mine. I feel nothing. Nothing, but rage. I smack my fist as hard as I can into the back of his ribcage and he pulls back.

"I should have leaked all his lame-ass texts he sent you when I gave his brother's story to the tabloids. Even after all these years, you believe every word out of my mouth. You are so gullible. You know what?" He looks me straight in the eye. "I'm the one who connected Alli with the press. She didn't want to do it at first, but I convinced her it was the only way to get the money she needed to break the financial umbilical cord with her parents. It wasn't hard to persuade her. I used the same tactics I used to use on you. Remember the condom wrapper you found on my couch? Guess who I took right there where you sat? And it wasn't our first time, either. We used to go at it all the time in high school. You almost caught us a couple of times, but you were too naïve to suspect your best friend." He seems to catch himself as if there's a drop of remorse in him and he looks away shaking his head. His hands clinch in fists at his side as if he's fighting some sort of inner turmoil.

"Get out," I scream. I can't believe he just admitted it.

"Regret, Meg, that's all your future holds without me," he whispers as he walks past me, his voice so cold my body shivers.

I slam the door the second he's out and the large stone bowl clatters across the table with the force of the thud. I collapse against the back of the door and explode into tears. I'm numb.

Wow.

I focus on the most important parts of his confession. I can't believe he gave Mom pills. As I am wiping my eyes, trying to come to grips with the fact Chase could have saved my mother and didn't, Arianna comes out of the bedroom. The thing I hate most about living in a one-bedroom apartment with a roommate is there is no such thing as privacy.

"I've got to get to work. I get off at eleven if you want to talk," says Arianna, approaching the door.

I stay on the floor and slide over to get out of her way. "Thanks," I say. "Sorry about the yelling."

She gives me a sympathetic smile and walks out the door. I reach up and deadbolt it, afraid Chase may come back. Then, I pull my purse off the table above me, take out my new phone, and type out a text.

Liam

I'm stopped on my motorcycle outside Kat's apartment building when I feel my phone vibrate in my jacket pocket.

"Thanks for the ride, Liam," Kat says into my ear as she climbs off my bike. She removes my spare helmet and hands it to me. "Remember, I have a six-fifteen call time tomorrow, so I'm catching a ride with Vera. Enjoy your morning off."

"I will. See you around noon." I don't have to be to the studio until later and I am looking forward to sleeping in for once. I pull my phone out of my pocket and pull up the text.

> Meg: Chase is here. I just had a big blow up with him. Can you
> come pick me up at my apartment? I don't want to be alone.
> Me: Be there in 15.
> Meg: He's outside the door, harassing my roommate. She has to get
> to work. I'd better go talk to him.
> Me: Be there in 10.

I bungie my extra helmet to the seat behind me and restart my bike. Kat is already to the door. Her building isn't far from Meg's if I take back streets. I wave to Kat and speed off. I can't believe that douchebag flew out here. The text I sent to Sarah last night from the stalked phone must have hit its mark. I just wish I had been there when he showed up.

When I arrive at Meg's, she's standing just inside the building's door, arguing with a preppy-looking blond guy. I turn off my bike and pull it back on its stand before climbing off. By the time I get my helmet off, her body slams into mine. My arms wrap around her and her body softens in my grasp. I tilt her head up to look into her eyes, my brow questioning. Then she buries her head in my chest without a word.

The guy follows her to the curb. Big mistake. I straighten, standing tall and step in front of Meg to protect her, my hand reaching back to hold her close behind me.

"You must be Chase," I say, sizing him up. He's a couple of inches shorter than I am and definitely doesn't follow a workout regimen. "You need to step back because you are done talking to Meg."

"This doesn't involve you, asshole."

Could he possibly be that stupid? "That's where you're wrong. Anything you say to Megan involves me. She obviously doesn't want you here. You need to leave." I step closer to him, nudging him with my arm. And as he steps back, he glares at me as if his expression is supposed to scare me.

I take another two steps closer to intimidate him, leaving Meg back by my bike. I can see his body stiffening. I know he's sizing me up, getting ready to fight. *Bring it on.*

"In your mind, you're trying to figure out whether you could get a good punch in before I flatten you, aren't you? You are going to have to start it. You've figured that out already. I'm not stupid enough to punch first. But don't get me wrong, once you start I will finish it and you won't be standing."

His jaw ticks and I can tell he's come to a decision. I hold my hands down and out to the sides, trying to encourage him to take a shot. I really want a chance to pound this guy. I take another step forward. His eyes flip between me and Meg several times. Maybe he hadn't made his decision yet.

"Meg…"

My fist slams into his soft gut and he topples over, dropping to the ground. God, that felt good. I guess I was wrong, I am that stupid when Meg is involved. "I told you, you were done talking to her. Were you not listening?"

He looks up at me, not a trace of cockiness left on his face, as he tries to suck in the breath that's been forced from his lungs.

"Do you want more? Get up. There's plenty more where that came from."

He shakes his head as he stares at the ground.

"Meg and I are leaving, now. If you ever contact her again I'm going to mess up that pretty little face of yours."

I can feel his eyes track me as I walk back to my bike. I wish he would come at me for another round. My swagger invites him. Then I hear it—the rustle of his jeans scraping, the sound of his shoes on the pavement—all tell me he's changed his mind. I turn with my fists poised to fight. This is going to be fun.

Meg runs in front of me and for a second, I can't tell why. Is she defending him? Then I watch amazed and amused as Meg spins around in some fancy combination of dance and kick boxing, nailing Chase right in the groin with her foot.

"Pay attention! We're done talking!" she screams at him as he crumples to the ground again. She reaches for my hand and practically pulls me to my bike. "I didn't know who else to call," Meg says as if she didn't just take out her ex's junk.

"I have to be honest. I am more than a little afraid of you," I say as I unbuckle the spare helmet.

"You should be," she says, and I fit it to her head, ignoring the douche on the ground behind me.

She closes her eyes stopping me from reading them. I can't help that my thumb lingers on the soft skin of her neck as I fasten the strap under her chin. Everything she does surprises me.

It feels like forever since I was inside her. I want to taste her neck, her lips. Instead, I pull on my helmet and climb onto my bike. The sooner we leave, the better. I rock it off its perch and motion for her to climb on. She sits on the seat behind me and, one by one, I position her feet on the back rests, pulling her knees up against my hips. Then, I reach back with both hands, grasping her hips, and pull her flush against me. She wraps her arms around me and the heat of her body burns in all the right places.

"Have you ever ridden before?" I ask.

"No," she says all breathy, and I hope it is because she is touching me, and not that she's scared to ride a motorcycle.

"Hang on tight, and when my body leans, just give in to it. Follow, don't fight the movement. I won't let us wipeout."

She nods against my back and we speed off down the street. I won't hold back next time we run into Chase and I hope he realizes it. The ride to Malibu takes longer than usual. I drive slower because every time I kick it up, she tenses, and even though I savor her clinching me between her legs, I figure she's been through enough having to see her ex.

She still hasn't said anything by the time we get into the house. I understand her not talking during the ride, but it's been five minutes since I shut the bike off. I look at her questioningly. I wonder if she's changed her mind about Chase.

"It still smells like her," she says as she hands me the helmet she was wearing.

Not what I expected her to say. I take it from her and sniff it. "It smells like you, Meg. It may smell a little bit like my work girlfriend because I dropped her off after work today, but mostly I smell your vanilla saltwater taffy." I smile, licking my lips. She knows the reference.

"Your work girlfriend. What does that mean?"

"The actor who plays my girlfriend on the show, nothing more. She's just my costar." I set the helmets on the bench next to the door and she doesn't ask any more questions.

"Are you going to tell me what happened with Chase?" I say as I take two wine glasses off the rack and pull a bottle of Riesling out of the refrigerator. I remember she likes sweet wine. I open the wine, pour it, and hand her a glass before she speaks. He must have really messed her up for her to be so quiet.

"Can I finish this before I tell you?" She holds up her wine glass.

"Sure." I grab the bottle and lead her to the deck. We may as well enjoy the breeze off the water. By the time we are seated in the lounge pit on the lower deck, I'm refilling her glass. She downs the second glass and scoots closer to me. I fill her glass again and wrap my arm around her. Her body molds into mine.

"Chase admitted to leaking Seth's intervention. I'm really sorry. I should have killed him when I had the chance." I feel her breath hitch. She can't possibly feel responsible.

"Meg, Seth was headed down the path he took long before the intervention leak. We just didn't know it. He would have ended up at the drug den at some point." In my heart I know it's true. I don't know why I wasted so much time blaming her. "I even told my dad that on the island before he left. No one blames you. And what Chase did doesn't matter anymore."

"It matters to me."

I lean my head against hers. "I didn't mean it that way. I just mean, the leak didn't doom Seth, and we've found each other again. We should just forget about Chase. I'll get my dad's firm to write up a restraining order against him. I don't even want revenge anymore. He's too toxic to mess with. Sometimes, it's just better to cut your losses."

"He was sleeping with Alli. He convinced her to sell Jon and Sarah's secrets to the press. My friends always said he was toxic. I wish I had listened. He said something else too." She closes her eyes and a shudder rakes her body.

I squeeze her tighter and say, "Just tell me." I hate that she is holding back with me again. "I thought we were past keeping secrets from each other."

She looks at me with knit eyebrows.

"I'm serious."

She knows I'm right and blows out a breath as if exasperated. "He was there the night my mom died. He gave her a handful of drugs and watched her take them all. Then he just left her. He didn't call anyone. He didn't drive her home. He just left her. He could have saved her." Her eyes fill with tears, and my heart sinks.

"Aw, Meg." I wipe my thumb under her eyes as her tears start to fall. "Now I'm going to have to kill him." I close my eyes, trying to calm my rage. She didn't need to know this. Why would he tell her? "What else did he say?"

"I don't remember. He thought telling me would make me fall into his arms. I can't believe he just left her. He could have saved her. He has no remorse whatsoever. How could I have dated him for so long?"

"I won't let him hurt you again." I pull her onto my lap and hold her. She tucks her body into mine. I don't say anymore. We sit melded together with just the sound of the seagulls for almost fifteen minutes. Her breathing has calmed and she's no longer crying.

"What do you want me to do, Meg? Do you know where he's staying? I can go mess him up."

She shakes her head. "He's a sociopath. I don't want anything to happen to you."

"I'm still open to sending him a sex tape." I say it to make her laugh, but instead she sits up and turns to me with a scowl.

"What do you want from me, Nordstrom?"

What is that supposed to mean? I unwrap my arms from around her as she climbs off my lap. She sits next to me on the lounge pit. "What kind of question is that?" I thought she knew where I stood.

"I want you to spell it out because I'm confused. You're sleeping with your work girlfriend. Don't you think it would upset her if we made a sex tape?"

"I'm not sleeping with Kat." I laugh because she must have googled me. "That's just the tabloids. I thought you didn't read the tabloids."

"I saw her text. It came in on your phone when I was reading the texts you sent me. You must have seen it. The one where you set world records in the number of times you did it and your hand made permanent imprints on her breast."

"That was just for work. We had to do take after take of the same sex scene because the director is obsessive about camera angles. We didn't really have sex."

"What about the picture of the two of you walking into her apartment hand in hand?"

Her words wipe the smile off my face. I lick my lips trying to find some moisture in the air. She's not going to like what I have to say.

"When that picture was snapped I fully intended to have sex with Kat. You'd completely ignored me. I was looking for a way to erase you from my memory. I'm going to be completely honest with you just so you know my state of mind. We made out for a while, but when it came down to taking our clothes off, I couldn't do it. She's a gorgeous woman, Meg, but she's not you. I realized I was playing a role. It was Ashton Post in her apartment, not me, and I stopped it. *Liam* stopped." I stare Meg down. "I told Kat how much I love you, how much I missed you and then we just talked. We never slept together. We're just friends. And not the kind of friends you and I were."

"Back up," she says, glaring at me.

"What? I missed you so much. I couldn't figure out what happened with us. I didn't know why you were being such a bitch."

"You know what I'm talking about." She narrows her eyes at me.

I knew what she was talking about. I grasp her chin in my hands, tilting her head up, and locking in on her beautiful blue eyes. "I love you, Megan Billings. I've known since we were on the island. You were right. Love does exist. Real movie love. You and I are proof."

She shakes her head slowly as if she doesn't believe me.

"Stop fighting us. You know you love me. You wouldn't have called me if you didn't. I'm not going anywhere. You may as well admit it."

"You're my best friend, Liam. I needed to tell you."

"Because you love me." I smile, raising my eyebrows. She knows I'm right. "Let me show you how good life can be. You already know how good we are together."

"Okay," she says, barely audible.

"What was that?" I ask, cocking my head as if I didn't hear her.

"I love you. Okay?" she says louder.

"What? I didn't hear you."

"I love you. Don't push it."

I bend to press my lips to hers and her hand threads into my hair. As I pull her back onto my lap, she turns to straddle me, not breaking the kiss, and I pull her closer, my hand firmly planted on her ass. She pulls back and it almost physically hurts me. "What's wrong?" I watch her for unspoken messages.

"What now? I don't want to be just friends with benefits." She picks up her wine glass again, taking a sip as her eyes watch me.

"I'm going to tell you what I want." I turn the dangle of her earring between my thumb and finger. "For starters, exclusivity. We see only each other." Her lips twist as if she has a question. I want to know all her concerns.

"What about Kat?"

"Ashton Post will still have to kiss her on set, but I won't be there and Post can't come off set anymore." Her nose crinkles, but she seems to reconcile herself with my answer. It's my job. She's mature enough to understand that.

"I also want to be present for all the little moments of your life, like breakfast and basketball games." I kiss her nose, and she smiles. "And all the big moments like when you walk across the stage to get your diploma. I want to go to your dad's for Thanksgiving to meet your brothers. And, you're meeting my parents this weekend after we visit Seth in rehab."

Her hand slips and the wine in her glass spills down the front of her shirt. "I'm not meeting your parents this weekend," she says.

"Yes, you are." That means she agrees with everything else. I help her off my lap and lace my fingers with hers as I pull her back toward the house. "And, we have to post selfies of us together. Come on we're taking a bath." I lead her upstairs to my bathroom as she argues about meeting my parents.

When I start filling the tub she asks, "Why are we taking a bath?"

"It's the perfect backdrop for our selfie and unless you want me to suck the wine out of your clothes, you need to take them off to wash them."

"I'm not doing a selfie with you in the tub," she says, her eyes wide as if to say, *you've got to be kidding.* She didn't even react to me sucking the wine out of her clothes.

I grab the bottle of vanilla-scented bubble bath from the linen closet. The one I bought because it reminded me of her. As I dump some under the running water, I say, "You're right. We need lots of bubbles."

"We're not doing a selfie in the tub," she says again.

"It will be very discreet. I promise. Lots of bubbles. The only people who will know it is you are Sarah, Jon, Kat, Nak, Leslie, Jessica, Jeff...my parents, and of course, Chase." I tick them off on my fingers. "Ten people tops."

Her eyes bulge. "Your parents?"

"They'll know after you meet them on Sunday. Don't worry, I've already told them about you." I pause as I reach around her and pull two towels off the shelf.

"What did you tell them?" Her voice cracks.

"That I'm in love with you."

She gasps. "I'm the last to know?"

"There was that whole problem with our phones. I first suspected I had an issue with you after the night I met you." I step in front of Meg and skim my hands up her sides under her top. I slide her shirt over her head and toss it on the chair in the corner of the bathroom. I hear her breath catch as my hands move to cup her breasts. "I told myself I just needed to sleep with you. That if I slept with you, I could get you out of my system." I pull my shirt over my head and throw it on the chair as well. "I couldn't sleep with you because you're Jon's sister, but then Jon gave me the okay. And that was what I tried to do." I watch as Meg unbuttons her jeans. "I wanted to do that," I say pointing to the button on her jeans.

She cocks her head. "Fine," she says and re-buttons them before reaching for my button.

"Once I slept with you, I knew—there was no escaping Meg Billings. I probably should have told you on the island. I guess I was in denial."

Until Meg, sex was always like eating Chinese food. It was good. It satisfied me for a short time, but in an hour or so, I was always hungry again, always still wanting. With Meg, I'm not wanton—I want her. It's different. She satisfies me in a way I've never been fulfilled before. It's like other girls are vegan Chinese takeout and Meg is Thanksgiving dinner with apple pie à la mode. Maybe that's not a good enough analogy, but being with her is unlike anything I've ever experienced—so much more filling, so much better.

I kick off my jeans as I pull open Meg's fly. I slide my hands in, peeling her out of her tight jeans. As she steps out of them, I'm overwhelmed with the need to take her against the tile wall. Or in front of the mirror? I could make her decide. No... I shake that thought from my head. We need the picture.

Megan

I stand naked in front of Liam. Bubbles foam from the running water, clumping in snowbanks along the edges of the large, soaker tub and even though he stares at me as if he wants to take me where we stand, he doesn't touch me. He made me remove my own panties and bra implying we wouldn't make it into the tub if he helped. Now I'm not sure what I'm supposed to do.

I feel as if the second I step into the tub my life will be changed. There will be no going back. I've known for a while he was different than all the other guys. He and I connect on so many levels and that scares me to death. Not because I think he will do something to hurt me—he won't—but because I want everything with him and I don't know if that is in our future.

"How does this work? Do we get in at the same time? Face each other? I've never really done this taking a bath together thing before."

"You've never?"

"No." I scowl at his doubtful expression. "In high school, you don't really have leisurely sex—not when you live at home with your parents—and who has access to a bathtub in college?"

"You're a bath virgin?" His smile reaches his eyes and I swear his already blessedly large appendage grows another inch. Not that I'm staring at it or anything. "Don't worry, I'll teach you," he says. "Step in over here and put your back against this edge."

I step into the steaming water and lean against the tub's wall as he instructed. The heat of the water embraces me, calming me. *I can do this.* No matter what happens in the future, I'm in.

"Now, slide forward and let me climb in behind you."

I scoot forward and he steps in, positioning himself with his knees on either side of me.

"We need to get the picture first." He scoops the bubbles, pulling them in to cover my breasts. "Wouldn't want any nip-slips."

"I never agreed to the selfie."

"I'll let you have final approval."

"Fine," I say. I wish he knew what the word really means in female language. But it doesn't look as though he does because he has his phone in his hand poised to take a picture.

He brushes the hair from my neck and tilts my head to the side. His lips whisper kisses up my neck as I glance up at his phone. Click. Then his fingers brush the side of my breast and as the kisses become more urgent my eyes close. Click. He takes two more pictures, but without even looking at them I know he will be posting the second shot. It felt the most genuine, the most uninhibited.

"I've got my pick already, but you get to make the final decision," he says, swiping through to allow me to view them.

The second one is perfect. Raw sensuality spills from the photo. With my eyes closed and the camera angled the way it is, I still have plausible deniability. "I still need to get a job after I graduate. So it can't be the first one. It should be the second one. It's the best."

"Yes. My pick, too."

"You know the internet is forever, right?" I say as he types one handed on his phone and posts the picture.

"I do." He smiles. "I never post selfies. This is a big deal for me to post."

He shows me the post. The tag reads, *#LoveIsReal.* Then he drops the phone onto the rug with a soft clunk and wraps both arms around me.

"Are you declaring your love publicly? Is that why it's such a big deal?" I ask.

"Our love. And yes."

"Is it for Chase?" I'm not really sure why he had to post a selfie of us in the tub.

"It's for me, Meg. I want my friends and fans to know how happy I am. And, if he sees it, all the better." His hands smooth across my skin to cup my breasts. "Does it bother you that I want to tell people about us? I've never wanted to inform the world before you."

I think about it for a minute before answering. "You posting makes it feel real."

"It is real. Love is real." He quotes the post. "How do you feel about a Christmas wedding?"

I almost choke on my tongue. "Uh…what?"

"Christmas. I was thinking if we tell your family at Thanksgiving we could pull a small wedding together by Christmas. Did you want a big wedding?" He leans to the side to see my face.

"Uh…"

"I am serious. If you want to," he says, his voice sweet and tender.

"I thought we were just going to date exclusively."

"We can live together, but not without something official in the works. I need a bigger commitment than my parents have. I want to get hitched." His dark eyes consume me.

"Why? I'm never going to be some carefree plastic blonde who can pin a smile on her face to go to yoga class. I'll never fit into your world."

"You already know I don't want plastic." He pauses and I feel his breath catch. "Let me tell you what I see when I look at you. I see a girl who makes decisions for herself." He brushes a strand of hair away from my cheek. "I see a girl who's honest, who isn't afraid to say no. She doesn't care whether I pay attention to her or not. Sometimes, I think she wishes I wouldn't, that I would just leave her alone. She doesn't need me. And in a world where everyone is stroking each other to get ahead, it's refreshing not to be used. Look at social media. It's all about connecting with the right person who will connect you to an even bigger, more important person. Hollywood's the same, only worse. It's all about who you know, who you're sleeping with or worse yet, who they think you're sleeping with. It's all for show. *You* don't do anything for show, not that I can see. You just are. And to me, that's super special. So don't run from me. I know I don't deserve you. But I'm not going anywhere. And all I want is a lifetime of the commitment we deserve. Is that asking too much?"

His words give me strength. He understands me. "Okay, let's get hitched," I say. "But I have to finish school first."

"That's my girl." His face lights with the most brilliant smile before he glazes my neck with a million kisses.

THANK YOU for reading *Between Friends*. I hope you enjoyed Megan and Liam's story. If you did, please consider posting a review on Amazon, Goodreads or the bookstore where you purchased the book. Reviews are one of the few ways readers can let an author know what they loved or hated about the story.

After Megan's story, the celebrity/college romance continues in *Between Scenes*.

Between Scenes (Book 4)

(A Stand-alone Between the Raindrops Novel)

Katya Avery is out of options. She's going to have to smile and sell this acting job to make the fans believe she's still with Jake, the guy who just days ago publically humiliated her. It's an act—a means to an end—but the distain in Micah's eyes every time Jake touches her slays her and all she wants to do is tell him the truth.

Other Books by Susan Schussler

Between the Raindrops (Book 1)

Hollywood hottie, Jonathan Williams can have any woman he wants as long as he is willing to be used for his celebrity status. But when he falls for a girl he anonymously connected with online, he finally sees hope for a normal relationship. That is until he reveals his true identity to her on stage at a rock concert and the press begins to pursue *her* relentlessly. Now he has to decide whether to protect her from his tabloid ridden life by ending their relationship, or to selfishly drag her into his world.

Between the Lies (Book 2)

Now that Jonathan and Sarah are engaged, the media is even more determined to pull them apart. It doesn't help that a stalker is sending threatening notes, that someone close to them is selling their intimate secrets to the tabloids, or that Jonathan's gorgeous ex-girlfriend would do anything to get him back. When Jonathan starts keeping secrets from her, Sarah has to decide whether to live with the lies or walk away from him forever.

Acknowledgements

To my readers—thank you for devouring every book I put out. Your comments and messages keep me motivated and, of course, your reviews are always appreciated. I love to hear your ideas, thoughts and passions. You make this all worthwhile.

Thank you to the writers of Women on Writing. You are an author's dream support team. You re-energize me, always holding me accountable and pushing me to be better.

Thank you to the amazing women of Midwest Fiction Writers. You inspire me with your talent and willingness to share your knowledge.

To my brilliant editor, Michelle Garner—thank you for making my vision complete. Your understanding of the English language and your patience with my comma dyslexia are true gifts and I couldn't have put this book out without you. You are amazing at what you do.

Thank you to my fabulous beta readers, Gloria and Ann. Your insights made Megan's story purr. Thank you for your honesty and for reminding me "revenge is sweet."

To my critique partners Crystal and Mary Jane, you saved Megan from enduring another life altering tragedy. Thank you for your encouragement to make bold moves. I appreciate your intuition and so does Megan.

Lastly, to my family—thank you for your un-ending support and encouragement. Even though romance is "not your thing," you let me bounce ideas off you with minimal complaining. I, also, appreciate your patience and understanding when it comes to meals and a clean house. Thank you to my husband for being my HEA inspiration and for always believing in me. I love you.